The SYNDICAT
Part II

by Mark Cunnington

Trio Publishing

Also by Trio Publishing

The Syndicate
The Syndicate 2nd Edition
Return of The Syndicate Part III
Running The Syndicate Part IV
Revenge of The Syndicate Part V

First published 2000
Reprinted 2002
Reprinted 2007

Published by Trio Publishing
50 Gillsman's Park
St. Leonards on Sea
East Sussex
TN38 0SW

ISBN 0 9537951 1 X

Printed and bound by Chandlers Printers Ltd
Bexhill-on-Sea, East Sussex

INTRODUCTION

This is a carp fishing story in which fortune plays a starring role and in many ways this is not unlike the sport itself. Luck has always been an integral part of angling, although the fortunate are ever in denial and talk of skill, forethought and other such attributes. Chance, by its very nature, is a random thing. It can bring good or bad onto the heads of the good and bad and there is seemingly no justice as to how the two pairs line up. This tale has a strong element of chance, or fate, if you prefer to call it that. All our lives are governed to some extent or another by the making of apparently innocuous choices that create wave-like effects and end up as major events. The theory is that a butterfly can flap its wings in south-east England and through a random connection of little nicks and nudges a tornado may form in California as a direct consequence. In this instance it's not a butterfly flapping its wings but a carp wafting its fins that creates all the fun.

Our story starts where we left it, only with the teller of this tale now out of prison.

Chapter 1

Eighteen months. Eighteen months and no time off for good behaviour. The one good thing about it was it gave me time to finish my previous tale, to dish out the dirt and the truth hoping that the shit stuck and the truth hurt. That eighteen month loss of freedom taught me a lot. How to nick any car for a start and wipe out a burglar alarm system come to that. It taught me that life is a strange thing, what it didn't teach me was how much stranger it was going to get once I got out!

I won't bore you with the myriad of mixed up emotions I felt as I finally walked clear of that prison into the arms of the woman who had waited for me, or of the surreal feeling of being home again. I won't bore you with the details of the gushing body fluids or the rubbing of body parts that occurred that first night either. Nor will I use up your valuable time with me rambling on about how utterly weird it was to be back with Sophie in my own home, as repaid for, over the last eighteen months, by my old mucker, Rambo.

Those first few weeks were in their own way just as difficult to deal with as my first ones in the slammer. I had to totally re-adjust to a normal life, to start to consider how I was going to function and to survive now I was free. Free to live, free to spend money provided I could earn it. Free to go where I wanted, free to have sex. Free to watch television when I wanted and to watch what I wanted and free to go fishing. Now there was a subject that wracked my whole body with conflicting emotions. I was also free to go into shops, free to go into pubs . . . free to break the law again, I suppose. The list of things I could do and that were at my disposal were endless.

Paradoxically I was free to consider all the shackles that would soon be imposed on me by the necessity to earn a wage and do all the things in life that constituted living. Free to be at such and such a place at a certain time and free to have to work there for 'x' amount of hours. Free to do all the jobs that I didn't like doing. Free to have to do all the things that stopped me from being really free, if you see what I mean. In prison I had lost my liberty, in fact a great many things had been taken away from me. In amongst those things that I had lost were all the day to day worries that are attached to modern society and if I am honest those were the things that were freaking me most.

In prison, I ate, slept, washed, shit, daydreamed and wrote 'The Syndicate'. Apart from a little social interaction that was virtually it. Now life wasn't like that. Would I cope with going back to work? Would anyone want me to work for them? What about all the people who knew me and knew what I had done? How would they treat me? How would the world treat me? The pressures built upon me and knotted my guts. An eight turn grinner, I reckoned.

After a couple of weeks of living in limbo, milling around doing nothing, 'trying to get my head together' as we rock stars say, I finally got around to going down to the garage to have a look at my fishing gear. It was still exactly as I had left it after I had returned from the session to end all sessions. Then it had been but a short trial before my enforced session at Her Majesty's Pleasure.

The sight of all my gear brought the memories flooding back. I picked over it with an almost squeamish air, like looking through the belongings of a recently deceased relative. With a slightly disgusted expression I ran a piece of paper through one of my Delkim alarms, holding it as if it were a dog turd. The blue l.e.d, for which Rambo had undoubtedly been suckered for an extra fiver, stared back at me as before. It was dull, the alarm was lifeless, the battery flat, all of them euphemisms for my state of mind and the state of my life. I must have been on a bio-rhythm low for fleetingly I considered suicide.

I pictured the headlines in something like 'The Angler's Mail' - "Carp angling jailbird found dead in garage. Police confirm suicide."

Or in 'The Sun' - "Convicted carper catches conclusive cold. Terminal tackle tightens into tourniquet. Mr Matt Williams, a convicted carp angler, was found dead today in his garage after he was found garrotted with a length of 30lb Amnesia hooklength. A police spokesman said that Mr Williams had used the centre pole of an aluminium buzz bar to tighten, propeller like, a loop of Amnesia hooklength around his neck until he had died of strangulation and blood loss. He said that there were no suspicious circumstances and the police were treating it as a bit of a laugh really! He added that Mr William's partner was in negotiations with the company that produced the line to make a series of television adverts applauding the lines' robustness, abrasive qualities and wet knot strength. Apparently the knot used had been a blood knot, literally and figuratively as Mr Williams' jugular had been cut."

Or 'The Sunday Sport' – "Naked angler murdered by Fishmen from Mars. Exclusive pictures on pages 3, 4, 5, 6, 7, 8, 9 & 10."

I put the alarm down and gave a twisted smile as I snorted some air down my nose. The thought of my own suicide and the repercussions of it had cheered me slightly. Was I mixed up or what?

Looking at all the gear strewn all over the garage everything looked a complete mess. Yes, my gear really was reflecting my life. How could I feel like this? All the time I was in the nick I prayed for the day that I would be back home. Now that time had come and I just couldn't seem to deal with it in any shape or form.

I fumbled through my rucksack and found the diary which I had used to keep a record of the weights and numbers of all the fish that Rambo and I had caught. Sophie had brought this to me as a reference to help me write my story accurately while I was in prison. When I had completed 'The Syndicate' I had given it back to her and she had put it back from where she had found it. I briefly flicked through the pages, which were mainly just catch statistics for any given day. There was the odd weather observation but no references to any of the shenanigans and stroke-pulling that had been happening at the time. I had been that paranoid about it getting stolen.

How sad were we?

For some reason I put it in my pocket and then went to the back of the garage to the bait freezer. I opened it up and the hint of that smell came to my nose and even more memories came hurtling into my head. There was just one bag of red boilies left in the freezer. I picked them out, rubbed the white frost away from the bag and gazed at them.

"You boys caused some aggro," I whispered to the bag, "and it still goes on." I wondered how deep the other members of the syndicate had been cut by all the happenings. "Not as deep as me," I mumbled, "not as deep as me."

I put the bag back and shut the freezer door and walked out of the garage without so much as a glance at my tackle.

That night I had a terrible nightmare. I'd had a few bad dreams while I was in the jug but nothing so vivid or so surreal and horrific. I can only assume that part of its content was brought about by looking at my fishing gear and the recollections that were inherently linked to that tackle.

Some dreams are hard to recall, but not this one, it was gruesome. I still shudder involuntarily as I recall it now. For some reason I was walking through this old, dilapidated house and couldn't find my way out. After what seemed an eternity of walking blindly down dark, damp corridors that seemed to weave a maze of intricate, interlocking confusion I finally opened a door. The sudden shock of what appeared before me scared me shitless and every other door that I opened after that one seemed to pursue the same bizarre theme. Every time I opened a door one of the old syndicate members would be behind it, either screaming in agony, screaming for my head or just plain old screaming. Each one to a man was in the realms of purgatory and all were damaged - in the most sickening of manners I might add - by having been impaled on, sliced up by, gouged and gutted by various fishing implements.

Behind the first door there was Watt, covered in blood from what appeared to be the bottom half of an umbrella pole that had gone clean through his head and out through the other side by at least two foot. On seeing me he started to curse and tried to attack me. As he charged at me the pole caught on the door linings and jarred his head backwards. Apparently unperturbed he tried repeatedly to get out the narrow opening but the pole kept catching and kept on jarring his head back. Every time his head was jarred back time and time again, more snot and gore would bleed from the massive entry and exit wounds. It was clear he hadn't the brains to think about turning sideways, probably because most of them were on the floor. The shock of his rage and gross appearance made me turn and run, only to end up barging blindly into another room.

In there Dave and Tony, whose backs faced me, were sitting watching an old Richworth bait video (true horror indeed). They slowly turned to see who had disturbed them . . . but no . . . they couldn't turn. I could see the muscles and tendons straining in their necks, guttural screams emanated from them as they voiced their frustration at their incapacity to move. My curiosity briefly conquered my terror and

3

I walked to the front of them to see that they were hideously staked out with stormside poles to hold them rigidly facing the telly. Each of them had Fox series 3, size two hooks, put through their eyebrows and into their eyelids to make immobility complete. They could not so much as blink despite the slow trickle of blood that ran into their eyes. I dragged my unbelieving eyes away from the gruesome scene and suddenly noticed that the telly appeared to have no 'on/off' button. Neither did the video.

Dave gasped the words, "looped video tape . . . never ending. Want to die now!"

"Die!" screamed Tony.

"Die!" screamed Dave even louder.

"NOW!" Together and louder still.

Reeling with sickness and fear, all curiosity now totally evaporated, I stumbled from the room and blundered into another door directly opposite the one I had just vacated. The door gave way at the first merest touch and I fell through it and landed on it. From all fours I looked up to see Mike, whose head was like Pinhead in the film 'Hellraiser', only it was covered with a multitude of stringer baiting needles that had been plunged into his flesh. He saw me and started to laugh, I got up onto my feet to see that it was Mike's head all right and that was all. His body lay crumpled on and old Argos sunlounger, the severed neck pumping a rivulet of blood all over the floral print cover. I knew that soon the black elastic bands underneath would perish and break, momentarily giving the corpse a hint of life as it jolted down a few inches under gravity's endless pull.

I fled, my brain asking the patently absurd question:- Who had the comfy bedchair if Mike was on the floral print lounger? Seconds later I had the answer as one came winging its way down the corridor, about six foot off the ground powered by an invisible propulsion unit and anti-gravity pack. Kipper was flat out on it. It semi-victory rolled 180 degrees and amazingly Kipper stayed attached as if glued to the bedchair as I'd always suspected he was in real life. He was dead of course, or on second considerations perhaps he was just sleeping and with that vision I promptly woke up.

Soaked in cold sweat I sat bolt upright and turned to Sophie and wobbled the lump under the duvet with my left hand so as to wake her and tell her of my nightmare. To my incredulity Harry shot from beneath the covers and jammed a carbon fibre throwing stick straight down my throat by virtue of my shock-horror, gaping mouth. I felt the cold end of it tear deep into my oesophagus. I tried desperately to gag it out but he had me in a vice-like grip. It was then that I noticed the handle end had been hacksawed off. Laughing hysterically he started to trickle boilies down the stick from the bottom of a clenched fist. They were mini-boilies and one quickly lodged in my windpipe. Insanely I wondered what flavour they were. I grappled the air with flailing arms frantically trying to grab the very thing that could no longer get into my lungs. The effort made my body require even more of the life-giving oxygen it lacked and soon I was a spent force. I had nothing left to give.

Nothing except my life that is. I was going to die.

Soaked in cold sweat I sat bolt upright and turned to Sophie and wobbled the lump under the duvet with my left hand so as to wake her and tell her of my nightmare. She turned over slowly, scraped her long straight hair back off her face and peered at me in the early morning daybreak gloom.

"What's up, Matt?"

"Ohh! I have had the most awful nightmare," I said to her weakly, gingerly rubbing my Adam's apple and praying that reality was finally with me. "It started off blood and brains and ended up with me deep throating a throwing stick."

"A what?" she asked, still not really awake and certainly in no shape to hear the rubbish I was spouting.

"A throwing stick. It's a . . . it was being shoved right down my throat," I gabbled, trying to paint a picture of the implement and how it had been used on me with my pathetically inadequate words.

She looked at me quizzically. Struggling to carry the message across I fell rather lamely on sexual allusion. "Well, imagine giving oral sex to a carbon fibre horse who's vital girth statistic wasn't as impressive as the length and you'd somehow managed to swallow the lot."

She looked at me bemused. "What are you on about?" She held my stare and a flirtatious smile came across her mouth as if understanding had just come to her. "Are you trying to turn me on or something?" And with that she turned over and snuggled under the duvet.

After a minute she asked, "Matt?"

"Yes," I said croakily. It might have been psychosomatic but my throat did feel kind of sore.

"Or should I call you, Dobbin?" And with that she turned on me with animal passion and my dream went on the back burner as I went on my back. Perhaps now I could imagine slightly better how this particular type of fun felt for her.

After a while, ok, after a short while, I lay there and realised that I had, in more than one way, come to my senses at last. Similar to how I had seen the light about Watt's egotism and in a weird way how I hadn't seen the light of my obsession with the Tom Watt Twenty Trophy, I felt that it was all starting to make sense.

Once again Sophie was the heroine. My admiration and love for her had never felt more earnest. She had stood by me then, in the midst of the TWTT, while I had abused our relationship. She had waited while I was still abusing it because of my loss of liberty and was now helping me through my difficult stage of re-associating myself with life. What a woman she was.

As she lay snuggled up to me, her head nestling on my chest, I felt that things were going to work out. That morning we talked. Probably for the first time since I had been out, we talked as a real couple. We talked of our future, of our desires and how to achieve those desires. Maybe my dream was the unconscious pus that had laid festering in my brain and now it had been lanced, so to speak, and come oozing out, it could finally heal. Whatever it was I felt much better.

As we talked about various things the conversation eventually came around to fishing. Although I felt happier about all things I was still touched with ambivalence over this one subject. It had given me so much and yet had taken so much away, over two years of my sodding life for a start and that didn't include any time before the TWTT. Yet in a way, although I had paid big time, I was still thrilled by the way that me and Rambo had, on the fishing front at least, sorted Watt out. What wasn't so thrilling was how I would react if I started going again. Having been through something as titanic as the TWTT what would a 12-hour session on a club water feel like? Would I merely be going through the motions? Did I even want to go through the motions?

"If you still want to go I really don't mind," said Sophie. "I know how much you like fishing, I knew that when I first went out with you. I don't think something like before would ever happen again and that was the only reason our relationship went through the mangle. When you were just fishing like any normal carp angler would do, there was no problem."

I smiled inwardly at those last few words wondering how many relationships had been holed and sunk on the jagged rocks of carp fishing. But I knew what she meant. Kept in moderation carp fishing was not to be a bone of contention between us. It was up to me and I honestly didn't have an answer to the question of whether I was up for it or not.

Over the next few days my brain untangled itself as did the knot in my stomach. I'm hard pressed to explain how I pulled myself around, perhaps it wasn't me, perhaps it was Sophie who had achieved it all. To think that suicide had actually crossed my mind, albeit fleetingly and surely with no real intent? Who knows? I was just glad to be on the road to recovery and through the worst of it. I realised that I still had an awful long way to go to get back to living an ordinary life but the big difference now was that I felt as if I could face it.

One morning I started reading the actual manuscript of 'The Syndicate' that I had written inside. It was really hard to read my crappy handwriting but I read it all in one sitting staying way up into the middle of the night to do so. What made it even more poignant, from a personal point of view, was that I could remember at what stage I was gulag-wise in relation to what stage I was at in the book. When I finally finished the last page, my head aching from the effort of reading so much in one lump, I was proud to have managed to have set the record straight while under such personal duress. I was convinced that without attempting to write it, my time inside would have been even harder. I decided there and then to ask Sophie if we could get it typed up into a legible format and to post it off to a publisher at sometime in the future.

Reading it again had bought back memories much like the time I had sifted through my tackle in the garage. But this time there were to be no nightmares to follow after I finally hit the pillow and fell instantly to sleep. When I awoke, Sophie had already gone to work. She had obviously decided not to wake me and crept out of bed so that I could have a lie-in undisturbed. I felt terrible guilt and knew that pretty soon I was going to have to get a job. The bank statement that had arrived a couple of days ago showed another cash credit for the mortgage from Rambo. I knew that he would be aware that I was out but perhaps his continuation of the mortgage payment meant that he realised that my acclimatisation would take a bit of time. I wondered when, if ever, I would meet him again.

After showering I hunted out some clothes and thought about breakfast. Inside the pair of clean jogging bottoms I had put on I found, of all things, a nicely washed but not ironed fiver. Things were looking up, I told myself and went downstairs and made some breakfast, although I could just have easily had dinner seeing what the time was.

The newspaper was on the kitchen table and I flicked through it starting at the back page. After reading a few articles about football I turned towards the front of the paper only to drop half a teaspoonful of yoghurt onto the racing page. I wiped it off with an index finger and then sucked the offending bit of yoghurt into my mouth. Right underneath where the blob had gone was a horse's name. 'Free fisherman'. I kid you not.

Not exactly conspiring to identify with the occult (I was definitely not going to read my horoscope either) I felt a strange inkling that something was afoot. A found fiver. The veritable truth, spin dried but certainly not spin doctored. The divine intervention of gravity inspired, bacterially fermented milk landing on a name so personally linked to myself that it had to be. Had to be. A coincidence bet that was surely anything but.

I got my coat and rushed straight down to the nearest bookies only to find that no such horse was running but had done on Tuesday, today was Wednesday. I had read yesterday's paper.

"So it ran yesterday?" I asked, wanting to make absolutely sure.

"Yeah, and it's still probably running now seeing as I backed the fucking thing," said a rather upset punter unashamed of his rather cliched joke.

"If it's any consolation, I was going to back it as well."

"None whatsoever, mate," said the upset punter.

I left. It was all ridiculous, what was I thinking of? I went and blew a couple of quid of the fiver on a coffee. As I sat there drinking it I noticed that I had the diary from my fishing tackle in my coat pocket. I took it out and started to peruse the pages. The heaviest amount of catch details were around the September and October months. I looked at the entries and let out a low whistle of approval. We had caught some fish all right. On one day I had taken six fish a 24, a 21, a 12, an 18, a 22 and a 20 (I never bothered with the ounces as long as it was 20+ that was all that mattered) and I nodded my approval.

"Got your lottery numbers sorted then?" said the waiter smiling as he passed by.

"No. These are a list of fish weights that I caught about two years ago," I said.

7

The waiter's smile disappeared from his face and he gave me a cold look. I wanted to say: 'No, it's true. Look at all these pages, they're all fish weights, you see we had this group of us and we all wanted to catch more than each other and . . . and we all ended up hating each other and I went to prison for something I did to one of them.' He'd only think I was winding him up even more.

I drank up and left. Walking home I pondered if in fact this last incident was the something that was a foot. As I took each step it came more and more to the fore of my mind. Yes! This was it! By the time I got to the newsagent I was shaking with apprehension and excitement. Three quid. That was all I had on me. With quivering hands I grabbed a lottery form and meticulously copied the fish weight list onto the lottery grid. 12, 18, 20, 21, 22 and 24. I checked them. I checked them again and finally I checked them again. I whizzed down another couple of lines to use the three quid up. I ticked the 'Wednesday' box and handed in the form.

The woman who had entered it into the machine gave me a look that said 'moron'. "You've done seven numbers on the third line, love."

Feeling stupid I snatched the form from her and scrubbed a number out not even thinking about which one to eradicate. I had my winning line.

That night I sat with Sophie and watched the draw. I had not told her of what had happened but had just given her the lottery form. I knew my numbers, they were indelibly etched in my head. Just before the draw started the phone rang and she went to answer it. While she was out the room the numbers 12, 14, 6, 44, 35, 36 and a bonus ball of 28 came out. I was gutted. I had been so convinced. So fucking stupid.

Sophie rushed into the room still on the phone squealing with delight shaking my lottery form. "We've won! We've won!" she screamed.

My mind raced. The second line. It had been the second line, one of the two I'd just banged down. No wait! The third line. It had been the third line! The one that I had scrubbed a number from. That had been the one. Amazing. A feeling of immense excitement welled up inside me. I'd only cracked it that was all.

Actually I hadn't cracked it, in fact it hadn't been any of my lines. I hadn't even won a derogatory tenner. It had been Sophie's mum's line, the one she had been doing from day one. It had been her mum's winning line while she had been on the line to her mum. She had won nearly two million quid and she gave Sophie and myself £250,000.

I was so shocked and dazed I can't really describe it but exhilarating, ecstatic, elated euphoric exaltation comes close. After it had all happened and she had got the cheque and given us our share and we had banked it and then it had cleared, did I really let it all sink in. Then and only then, Sophie and I sat down and thought. And after much thinking we gave ourselves five thousand each to blow on an indulgence.

Five thou. I searched my soul and deep inside I knew, I just knew. This would be my way back. A chance to rekindle my love affair in idyllic surroundings. Although Sophie had decided to spend her money on a shallow, superficial, materialistic yearning for an entire new wardrobe of clothes, I was on higher much more altruistic ground. I decided to blow my share of the money on the carp fishing holiday of a lifetime. But not alone, I wanted to take somebody else with me. Guess who that somebody was going to be, provided I could find him?

Chapter 2

As the penny dropped, or rather pennies, all 25 million of them, I felt somewhat at sea. Since coming out, my mind had been in a constant whirl and just when I thought it had settled down fate had sliced the top of my head off, shoved an electric mixer inside it and given it a good old spin round again. Apart from actually winning myself, which naively I thought I would, I was living out the fantasy of millions of people throughout the land. I was living proof of that most amazing of fantasies, that of winning the lottery, or to be more precise about it, winning a lot on the lottery. No, let's get it right, a relative winning lots and lots on the lottery and donating lots of that lottery lolly to my partner, who bless her cotton knickers, was going to share it with me. However tenuous the line of financial inheritance it still meant I was quids in.

It was 'ours' and although I could imagine lesser relationships going down the pan as the winning half suddenly saw a chance to better themselves, I knew that Sophie and I wouldn't disappear around the 'P' trap. The lure of the ticket holder to go onto a much more exciting lifestyle and perhaps, even more pertinently, a much more exciting partner, must be very strong. Not my Sophie, she was a wonderful woman and yes, I would have said that before her Mum came up trumps. Honestly you cynics.

Two hundred and fifty thousand quid. It was a tantalising amount of money. We couldn't just think that was it, no more work and live an extravagant lifestyle. No, it wasn't enough to do that (I bet you're thinking 'poor old sod') but it was enough to make us think that as long as we didn't go berserk we were effectively sorted for life. We decided not to buy a large house, or a flash car for that matter but to just spend our five thousand as either of us wanted, store the rest and feel our way along. A few wise investments and we could have a great life. I just couldn't take it all in, it was fantastic.

Weight and worry vanished from my shoulders and it was a marvellous feeling. I had often heard rich celebrities plugging their latest book, film, CD etc on a crap chat show say – 'Of course, I don't worry about money.' Or - 'Money isn't an issue with me.' Or - 'I don't do it for the money.' Well, what I had concluded then had proved itself by how I felt now. No they didn't worry about money because the stupid bastards didn't have to, they had plenty of it. How crass to say such a thing, how condescending, how pathetic. I wasn't worried about money, I had no need to be, I was worried about finding Rambo and picking the ultimate place to go carp fishing. I had been worried about telling Sophie of how I intended to spend my part of the money but I needn't have concerned myself. She had told me that fishing wasn't to be a bone of contention and true to her word it wasn't.

When I finally summoned up the gumption to tell her what I was going to blow my self indulgent wad on she was unfazed.

"That's great, Matt," she had said. "I bet you'll have a brilliant time. It'll help exorcise all the demons from the thing you most like doing. It'll put it all back into perspective, all that animosity and competitiveness will be gone. You can pick somewhere lovely to go and fish and do it in the most perfect of circumstances rather than in the worst."

Her words washed over me. Was I the luckiest git whoever lived, or what?

"I want to take Rambo with me," I told her. "It's the absolute minimum I can do after all the strings he's pulled for me."

"Yes, and you can offer to pay back all the mortgage repayments as well."

"You sure," I said frowning.

"Matthew!" She said sharply.

"I was only mucking about."

She looked at me knowingly. "No you weren't."

I laughed. "I wonder what he's up to. I'm surprised he hasn't come to see me yet. He must know that I'm out . . ."

At that precise moment the doorbell rang. I rushed downstairs to be confronted by none other than a double glazing salesman who I gave very short shrift. Ok, I had considered that it was going to be him, Mr Camouflage, but the incident over the winning lottery line hadn't totally been forgotten, just pushed to the back of my mind for a few minutes.

A week later I was in the garage enthusiastically sorting out my fishing tackle. How different my frame of mind was compared to the last time I had looked at the mass of discarded, muddy gear. This time I was up for it, it was like it used to be with the close season. I had been denied access but it was time for it all to start up again and there were a million things to do and to sort out before the big day finally came and I, along with many others, were back at our favourite sport. There was one major difference though, I had money to spend and my sorting out was to be on a different plane from normal, this time things wouldn't be cleaned or tidied up or repaired. No! If I wasn't too keen on it, it was out on its ear and I'd buy myself brand new. It was a much more appetising situation altogether.

I banished the bivvy. A 50" overwrap for a Nubrolli was certainly not spacious enough for me anymore, I needed to get something much more trendy. Three new Shimano baitrunners were another must and some new scales. I couldn't see my old 32lb Avons coping with the size of fish I was likely to be catching. Following that theme I would need a new extra-large unhooking mat and weigh sling, something with enough material to be able to act as a spinnaker for a small dinghy. I'd need new leads, hooks, line, hooklength material and anything else that took my fancy. I would need all the gear that I didn't realise I needed until I saw it. All the clobber that you can't possibly have enough of when you've got money in your pocket. I felt great!

It was heady stuff and by the end of that morning I had spent over a grand, or at least I would do when I next visited the local tackle shop. At about one, I went back inside to make myself a bite to eat. It was to be a solitary meal because Sophie was still working and was not about. It hadn't taken her long to decide that she wasn't quite ready to chuck her job in, she wanted to evaluate things in a few months time when she felt that she would make a more reasoned decision about her career.

I rustled up a light snack and sat munching toast, casually reading the trash in a tabloid newspaper when the doorbell rang. I went and opened the door but there was nobody there. Blaming kids, I slammed it shut and walked back into the kitchen, I had only got back to my chair, hadn't even sat down, when it rang again. With a mild expletive I turned and retraced my steps back to the front door, I was about three strides away from opening it when a ball-like object plopped through the letter box. I immediately knew what it was, I had used its kind before, it was a hand grenade!

"KABOOM!!" said a familiar voice via the letterbox. "You're dead, boy. Let me in and I'll scrape you off the walls and give you a decent military burial."

"Rambo!" I screamed and rushed to open the door.

"Er . . . mind the grenade," said the letterbox, "it's a live one."

"You've got to be joking," I said as I opened the door to my camouflaged clad, fishing buddy.

Jesus, he was a big son-of-a-bitch. He was larger than life in real life. I had an image of him in my head, you have to remember I hadn't seen him for over a year and a half, which was somewhat over powered by seeing him again in the flesh. Or I should say, in the camouflage. There was a point, maybe his skin had been tattooed in that pattern as well. Not many people can aspire to being even more intimidating and threatening in the flesh rather than in the imagination but Rambo was one such person. And a friend, which was relieving.

"No, I'm not joking," he said rather indignantly as he picked up the offending item and popped it inside his camouflage jacket.

"You mean it's not a dud one?"

"Where would I get a dud one from?"

"You're the bloody arms dealer aren't you?" I said laughing.

"Not a lot of call for dud hand grenades," he explained earnestly, "people tend to want one's that work. I mean what would have happened if the two you pinched off of me had been duds? You'd have looked a right fool. And what about my situation? My status as a creditable arms supplier would have been seriously eroded." His facial expression changed and a look of mock concern came over it. "Talking of credit, have I invoiced you for them yet?"

I laughed again and went to shake his hand. It was like putting it in a vice and having a boisterous five year old swinging on the tightening bar.

"Good to see you, mate. I have got some amazing news, you are just not going to believe it, but first things first. Come and sit down, let me make you a cuppa, Sophie's not in at the moment but she'll be pleased to see you when she gets back from work."

"She will?" said Rambo not seeming too sure. "I decided to come when she wasn't around just in case there was any shit from all what happened. I wondered whether I would be the last person she wanted to see."

I assured him he wasn't and after I had made the tea the pair of us sat down for a long chat. Naturally we went over much old ground and eventually some new ground as well but I kept my big secret under wraps for the moment. It seemed that I was forever thanking him for all the help he had given me, especially while I was in clink, but he would hear nothing of it. Every now and then we were reduced to tears of mirth as we recollected some bizarre incident or more often than not some piece of hideous misfortune that had happened during the TWTT race. It is a strange human trait but the expression 'one day you'll look back on this and laugh' seems forever true. Even as I told him of my darkest hours I found humour in each situation. Perhaps it was because of my newly acquired good fortune that I could be this way but I'm sure that most people, once they are the other side of blackness, can react this way. Perhaps the only thing we never get over is the death of a person close to us or losing a forty at the net.

"Is Watt dead?" I asked. I could get over that and be laughing about it in about two seconds.

Rambo said that he wasn't, in fact nobody from the syndicate had pegged out that he was aware of. Quite a few of the people who were on the receiving end of the goods that constituted his latest arms deal were probably dead but that, he suggested, was their own fault. Basically business was good. Although the world seemed to be managing to avoid the big full-scale global conflicts that had been popular a couple of times before there was seemingly no end to the parochial war market. In fact this was very useful to the more individualistic arms dealer, the smaller merchant, the one who supplied the nuts and bolts of armed conflict. Supplying 20 million pound fighter planes wasn't really Rambo's bag.

"Cash flow. That's the trouble with being in that sort of league, getting hold of enough dosh to buy up front before you can sell," he explained.

"Haven't you got a 60 day account with whoever makes them," I asked with a big grin.

Rambo rolled his eyes and continued. "Now a crate of AK 47's, that's different. You'd be amazed at what bargains there are to be had from the old Soviet block countries. As long as you avoid their Mafia, you're laughing."

And he was. I shook my head in amazement. I really didn't have a clue what Rambo got up to or how he went about his business and to be honest I didn't really want to be partial to the ins and outs of it. On the other hand there was something that I wanted him to know about and after I had spent a good half an hour telling him about my weird feelings on release, my strange dream and then the odd compulsive belief that I was going to win the lottery, I told him. I told him that Sophie and I were up to the tune of 250K. More importantly I told him about the five thousand that was at this moment smouldering in my personal bank account and I told him how I wanted him to help me spend it.

He was genuinely pleased for me and for about five minutes he just kept on laughing and generally slapping me on the back, picking me off the floor and then slapping me on the back again.

"You jammy bastard!" he snorted, enthusiastically. "You jammy, fucking bastard! Talk about jumping out of the frying pan into an extremely well upholstered comfy chair. What a result!" Again he smiled and looked at the floor shaking his head. "So. You want to take me on the fishing trip of a lifetime and foot the bill for it, eh?" he said beaming.

"Yep. It's by way of a thank you for looking after me. Sophie said that she wants to pay back all the mortgage repayments as well."

"Does she indeed. You don't though?" he added craftily, picking up on how I had phrased the statement.

I felt flushed with embarrassment as he had hit a nerve. He seemed not to notice or not to care and waved a magnanimous hand.

"No, that's all water under the bridge. I'll stop the repayments after this month and you can take me on holiday and that will be great."

"So it's a deal," I said.

"It is." And rather ridiculously I shook his hand on it. My eyes watered but they weren't tears.

That afternoon we went down to the local newsagent and bought every carp fishing magazine they had, carried them back and perused them for carp fishing holiday ads.

"I don't want to fly anywhere," I told Rambo. "I want to drive, take all my stuff and my own bait."

"And what bait would that happen to be?" he asked laughing.

"Your bait," I conceded. "The best bait I've ever fished with. But this time, can we get someone to roll it for us? I don't think I could stand doing it like we did last time. In any case it'll remind me of all the shit that happened before. This is a once in a lifetime trip and I want it to be special, you know red carpet stuff and that means no unnecessary graft. We're going Club class, man. Club class."

Rambo nodded. "Yeah. Why not. I'll just tell the geezer who we get to roll it that if he ever divulges it to a living soul, I'll break his fucking legs."

I nodded with a sneer to show my approval. I couldn't see any sane person not getting the gist of that sort of a threat. Then again how many sane boilie rollers were there? I tried to imagine doing it for a living day in and day out. Sure most jobs have an element of monotony but that one would take some beating. I suppose it all boiled down to, if you can excuse the pun, how much trick machinery you could afford to make life easier. Stupidly I imagined the coyote character from the Roadrunner cartoons with an 'Acme boilie-maker' being delivered to him in a large box and then him getting run over by the train after it came out of the tunnel he had just painted on a solid wall of rock.

Rambo was not entertaining such thoughts but as always was on to practicalities. "The recipe will need to be changed slightly I guess, to make the baits harder and we'll probably need a larger size but that shouldn't be a problem. Going back to what you said about not flying, which country do you fancy?"

I had already given this some prior consideration. "I don't want to go somewhere where we're taking a chance. I want to go somewhere prolific with some real big, lunking carp but on a reasonable sized water. I don't know about fishing on an inland sea, something as big as say, Cassien. I'd prefer it to be a little more intimate than that, somewhere where they had a limit of ten or twenty anglers and an acreage of single figures. Owned by a Brit would be nice. Good facilities, showers, Sky TV piped to every bivvy, room service, sherpa service should you wish to move onto fish and adult entertainment every Friday."

"Oh look," said Rambo, "here's one that's just right. Oh no! The owner's mother is half French."

Ignoring Rambo's pee take I added, now warming to my pre-conceived notions. "And I don't want to go to anywhere that has an ad proclaiming that 'it's run by carp anglers for carp anglers'. Or, come to that, if it says anything remotely relating to 'doing the business'. So there."

"And they say money doesn't change people," remarked Rambo, dryly.

"Do they?" I asked. "They'd be mad if they said that."

So we looked and continued looking. We, or rather I, dismissed the Fishabil and Dream Lake type of venue because of their size and number of anglers that were likely to be there. I wanted something smaller and perhaps more exclusive, if it existed.

Most of the waters we looked at were French but that was fine by me, I think that I had more or less accepted that France would be our country of destination. Pretty predictable but so long as the water was right it didn't matter. In the very last magazine that we looked at I thought we might have found what we were looking for. It was called 'Le Lac Fumant' – 'The Smoking Lake'. What an odd coincidence. Images of my final dastardly deed on the old syndicate water danced across my eyes. Maybe, with a twist of ironic fate, this was to be the venue. I carefully checked the details. It was eight acres apparently, ten anglers maximum and was an old water in terms of its original construction. There was the normal allowance of night fishing with no permits required and fish 'up to 40lb+' with a good smattering of 30's. Adjacent to the lake was a converted 19th century stone cottage which was inhabited by the owner but was available for meals, showers, satellite TV and other such niceties should the inside of a bivvy become oppressive. The blurb claimed that this was the first time that the water had been advertised in the angling press but had been running purely on recommendation for over a year.

"What do you think?" I asked Rambo.

"No fifties, then?" he exclaimed.

"There will be when we get there," I assured him. "There's this high forty that is feeding it's fat face just so that I can catch it when it reaches fifty pounds."

Rambo cut to the chase. "Just phone them up and suss the owner out. If he's Mr Bullshit, forget it."

I nodded. The eruption of commercial carp waters had bred its own type of manager/owner, whatever you like to call him. There's the one who claims there is a forty swimming in his puddle but that's never been caught or the 'you should have been here yesterday, mate', individual, who assures you as you sit there runless without a carp movement to your name, that a bloke had eighteen fish out just the other day. From your swim as well. He then asks what bait you're on, where you're casting to and what rig you're using. When you tell him he just screws his nose up and gives you an encouraging smile that tells you in no uncertain manner that the reason you're blanking is because you're shit at carp fishing. If our man in France was one of those we'd blow him out.

I phoned the number. "Le Lac Fumant," said a very English voice. "How can I help you, chief?"

Straight away I got the impression that I was talking to some sort of eccentric. A nutter, in short. "I'm just phoning about your lake, to get a bit more information." I said.

"What can I say, chief. Quality. The lake is quality," said the English voice underlining and bolding in red ink my previous assessment.

"Quantify 'quality,'" I challenged him. And he did. An hour later I put the phone down.

"Well?" Asked Rambo.

"If it's as good as he says it'll be brilliant," I assured Rambo and then attempted to regurgitate all that the owner had told me.

The lake was as described in the ad, just over eight acres and with all the facilities. It was very much like an English estate lake, full of features such as three islands, rushes, weedbeds and tree-lined margins. With ten anglers allowed on the water at any given time there was loads of room. In fact he told me that there were twenty swims to chose from, each positioned so that there was little chance of encroachment from another. The owner had discovered the place a few years earlier when he, his wife and daughter had taken a holiday in a nearby gite. A simple walk had lead them to the lake and he had fallen in love with it. Unfortunately his wife had subsequently fallen out of love with him and a messy divorce had ensued.

With the home in England sold to sort out the financial implications of the divorce he had returned to France, with his daughter, to attempt to buy the property that had so captivated him. A new life in a new country was the thing that he desired. and had been the motivation for him to make the journey. As luck would have it the old woman who lived in the cottage had just about stiffened on the mortuary slab when he arrived to make his enquiry about purchasing the property. He had spoken to the first person he had seen who happened to be the only surviving relative of the old woman and things had gone well from there. The purchase had been completed and as his mother had indeed been half French, living there and the language were not a problem.

The problem was how to make some revenue, not much as his needs were simple, but something none the less. The large black shapes cruising just below the surface of the lake had been of little consequence to him and were certainly not viewed with any commercial aspect. A holiday cottage offering B&B seemed the most logical course of action until one day a chance encounter with a pair of Dutch brothers had altered the tack of his thinking. On hearing his English accent whilst talking to his daughter in the local shop the Dutch lads had asked him if he knew of any lakes or reservoirs in the vicinity which might hold carp. The pair of them had just finished fishing another lake about a hundred miles away. They had packed up a few days early because the fishing had been so bad and rather than return home were using the spare time to try to unearth a new venue. He had cordially invited them back to look to his lake and after a lengthy investigation the Dutch boys declared themselves to be absolutely besotted. Over an evening drink the pair of them told him of the hidden gold mine, in carp fishing terms, that he now owned. They showed him magazines and books that astonished him. He had no inclination as to the huge amount of money that was involved in the game of catching carp. By now it was clear which way his path lay.

He read up about carp, had the cottage converted and let the Dutch lads fish the lake while this took place. They brought friends and their friends brought friends and all of them paid for the privilege. By May of this year everything was ready for a proper commercial start to business and the advertisements had gone into the relative magazines. The fish that had been caught so far were the ones mentioned in the ad and there were still plenty that hadn't.

"Do you think that fish of that size and number could be naturally produced without any interference and stocking?" I asked Rambo.

It was the one thing that had me worried, the amazing string of coincidences that had occurred in him getting the water and discovering it's worth didn't bother me at all. I was the beneficiary of a long shot, why shouldn't he be one as well?

"Possible, if highly unlikely. Perhaps this place has been stocked by an unknown person with a good strain of carp years ago. I mean Redmire was originally stocked with a good strain of fish and then the natural quality . . ."

"Don't you start saying that bloody word. He," I nodded towards the phone, "kept saying it every other sentence."

". . . of the water," continued Rambo, "produced sensational fish. Maybe this bloke stumbled upon a water that is the French version of Redmire."

"What a Rougemire?"

"If you weren't paying for me to go on this trip, I might just slit your throat," Rambo warned me.

"Where's your knife?" I taunted him. "You haven't got your knife."

Like lightning Rambo pulled out a huge knife from the bottom of his trouser leg and thrust it within an inch of my nose.

"Look, here it is," he said, his eyes glinting with devilment.

"Oh yeah. I can see it now," I said, my eyes going cross-eyed as I tried to focus on the point which was too close to my face for comfort. In a flash the dagger was re-trousered.

"So, what do you think then?" said Rambo as he slumped back in his chair.

"I'm impressed to be honest. The guy does seem to be a bit of a dork but in a nice kind of way. He's not an ex-carper trying to jump on the 'make a living from my hobby' bandwagon and I think that he's genuine. Nobody would make up a story like that, it's too far fetched, too much luck involved. The actual lake sounds lovely. The longest cast is about 90 yards, although he did say that from some of the swims a cast to the island is a big one fifty but if you want to fish to it you just pick a different swim. There's no need for boats, rowing out baits and huge great big reels and rods. It'll be like fishing something a bit bigger than the old syndicate lake with the same amount of people with much more and bigger fish."

"Whereabouts is it?"

"Apparently it's between Tours and Poitiers at a place called Manthelan, just over the river Loire. We'll have to look it up on a map. He reckons that if we go on the motorway it's about 7-8 hours motoring from Calais. What d'you think?"

Rambo shrugged his shoulders, "I always tend to go with my gut feelings in situations like this so if it feels good I would say go for it."

To be honest I was convinced in my own mind but to make sure I phoned the bloke back and told him how important it was to me that I got this trip right. He said that he couldn't agree more and realised how hard it was for me being where I was to make a decision by what someone was saying down a phone. In the end I just did what Rambo suggested and went with what I felt and booked us in for the first two weeks of September. The owner, Bob, had given me a list of dates that I had checked off with Rambo to make sure that he was clear. Those two weeks already had eight anglers booked in, all of whom had fished the water before and therefore we made up the full compliment. I told him that we would book an evening meal for ourselves as and when we wanted it once we were there. This could be eaten either in the cottage or delivered to our bivvies. This gave us a nice degree of flexibility, I mean you wouldn't want to have to go away from the lake to eat if the fish were really having it.

Bob had told me that those two weeks had always fished well and this seemed to be backed up by the other lads who already knew the water being there at that time.

"It'll be just like the opening couple of weeks at the old syndicate," said Rambo.

"No it bloody won't," I told him. "It'll be quality. Bob said it would be quality."

"Good," said Rambo, "that sounds right up my street."

Chapter 3

We're all going on a fishing holiday, no more worries for a week or two. Sun and laughter on a fishing holiday, we'll make our dreams come true, for me and you. We are going where the fish are bigger, we are going where the fish are huge. We've seen it in the advert now, let's see if it's true.

And if it wasn't the shit was going to hit the fan big time. I'd seen Rambo erupt before and just because he was on a freebie wouldn't make him any the less violent. I was worrying over nothing, I told myself, it was going to be great and there were other far more pressing things to concern myself over. I had three weeks to organise everything and the first thing was to get down to the tackle shop and unload some of that hot, steaming money on the goodies that I had promised myself.

I waltzed into my local tackle shop, which fortunately enough was a good one and started to ask to look at this, that and the other. The shop had recently changed hands while I was 'away' and the owner never knew me from Adam. I could sense his air of melancholy as he went through the motions of showing a host of tackle items to a person who he considered to be a time waster. I had convinced myself that I badly needed a new bivvy and after getting out about three different types I plumped for the Hutchy Apotheosis Big Boy and told him that I would take it. The effect was like a dose of Prozac and it perked him up no end. Once he knew that I was serious he was all over me like the proverbial rash. To be honest I loved it. Although Sophie and I had never been hard up I could never have gone out and splashed out the amount of money that I was going to in one lump. I felt good about spending the money and he felt good about me spending it in his shop. In the end the pair of us worked each other up into such a state of euphoria that it was hard to say who was going to have to go out the back to have a lie down first.

As well as the bivvy I also purchased my three new Shimano 8010's with standard handle, they had ample line capacity seeing as we were not going to have to cast to the horizon. To put on the reels I chose my old favourite, 15lb Big Game line in white. I took a chance on Reuben Heaton 60lb scales being adequate rather than the Weighmate 110lb electronics on the grounds of the possibility of gizmo failure. 50" Fox folding landing net, 46" Nash monster sling, Hutchy 48" big kipper sack and Nash 42" monster mat. I know that I could have got some products that did two jobs but I was on a spending roll and it felt too good to stop and start worrying about saving a few quid here and there. I bought masses of sundry items like hooks, bombs, swivels, rig bits and bobs and on a whim I treated myself to an Angling Technics bait boat with chargers. Just to show that I still had my feet firmly planted in reality I passed on the remote echo sounder that was available to compliment the boat but not the custom bag or the spotlight. It seemed churlish not to get the xenon beacon, stern light and the solar charger come to that, so I bought them as well.

Just when I thought that I had finished I grabbed three of the Delkim TX2000 micro transmitters and the RX2004 receiver to compliment the Delkims Rambo had got me during the TWTT race. With the receiver I was working on the theory that you never can tell when you might be on a four rod water and although Le Lac Fumant was a three rod venue it seemed short-sighted to buy the three rod receiver, besides the four rod one was much flasher. While saying that I would plump for the RX2004 my mind made the obvious tiny association, although for me it was probably a quantum leap. Spare buzzer! I could really do with a spare buzzer for cover and now that I had the RX2004 receiver having only three heads was utter madness, so I bought another buzzer with another micro transmitter. For some reason Rambo had bought me Delkims with blue, red and green l.e.d's originally so I naturally plumped for the newer, classy, more expensive white l.e.d rather than the yellow. To be on the safe side I bought another Shimano reel so that I had four of everything. I then bought some colour coded hangers of various weights and sizes. My set up was going to look so cool.

I did wonder if I should have bought four new rods there and then but I liked the three I had so I made a mental note to phone up when I got back home and order another one. I knew that the blank was still in production and I was confident that a little extra cash incentive would let me jump the list so that I could have it made up in time.

After the shop owner had totted up the damage and given me a descent discount (I wasn't that stupid) I asked if he could deliver it all seeing as I had decided to walk down to the shop for a bit of fresh air and exercise. He glanced at his watch.

"Let's see, it's 4:20 now. I'll tell you what, I'll shut the shop, put it all in the van and give you a lift home with it now if you like."

He'd sold his quota for the day. "Lovely, mate. That'll be fine," I said.

By the time Sophie had got home from work I'd set the bivvy up in the back garden, fitted the transmitters to the alarms and put batteries in everything. She actually caught me pulling line from the one rod I'd got set up right round the side of the house. I kept giving the line a little tug and then started to grin, another little tug and another grin.

"What on earth are you up to?" she asked

"Watch this." I said.

I held up the receiver box, tugged the line and the channel one l.e.d flickered into life. I cranked up the volume from zero to nine and tugged again. Decibel city.

"No wires!" I exclaimed. "The modern miracle of FM radio transmission encompassing unique individual transmitter codes."

She looked at me with pity. "What else have you bought?" she said resignedly.

"Come and see," I said enthusiastically.

I was twenty-eight going on six. I dragged her up the garden to look at the Hutchy Apotheosis Big Boy. Sophie very kindly said that poor old Mr Hutchinson could be sued under the trade description act when I was inside it. I explained to the giggling schoolgirl that it still only referred to the bivvy regardless of who was inside it and double regardless of the size of their tackle, wedding or fishing. She was so immature sometimes.

I pulled her coat. "Look at my boat! Look at my boat!" I said as I jumped up and down on the spot, pointing.

"Ohh! That's a nice one," she exclaimed with false interest, "and what does that do?"

"You see you have this radio controller," I waved it in her face, "and you steer the boat wherever you want, usually somewhere difficult to cast and you can drop off all your boilies exactly where you want them. You can get loads of them on the boat. Then you can bring it back, put your terminal tackle in it and put that out there as well." I was aware that I was starting to get spittle on my lips and was talking far too quickly. "Look! Look! It's got a little light at the front and a red one at the back and this one is a flashing beacon for on the top. It's also got this little utility light you can plug into it so that you can see where to put the boilies in the dark and you can charge it up with this," I showed her the solar charging panel, " by putting this in the sun and plugging the lead into the boat."

"Do those new reels wind themselves in?" she asked nodding at the Shimano's.

"Don't be ridiculous," I said.

She raised her eyebrows and kissed me. "Mummy's going to make the dinner."

When I had finally calmed down, put all my gear back into to my garage and made sure that I had all that I needed, mostly in duplicate, sometimes on vital components in triplicate, I turned my thoughts towards the extra rod. A quick phone call and some pleading to a busy rod-builder ensured the promise of me getting my fourth rod in two weeks time. All I had to pay extra for was a guaranteed overnight delivery. Sorted.

My next acquisition was to be transport. I wanted to travel in a bit of comfort and style so hiring out a Ford Transit van was a no-no. What I needed was something a bit up market. Over dinner I told Sophie my thinking about the car.

"Why don't you have a look at one of those MPV type cars. My friend Danielle, you remember Danielle don't you? Danielle and John? The couple who can't have children?" I nodded. "They've been having IVF treatment and now she's expecting triplets. They're going to get one, it's got seven seats but you can take out or leave in as many as you like. There's loads of room inside if you just have the front two."

I nodded and grunted my approval of her thinking through a mouthful of chips. Quite unexpectedly Sophie's eyes glazed over and she let out a simpering sort of sigh.

"Imagine having three babies all at once. Imagine just having one. Just one tiny little human being that relied on you to love and look after it. I suppose it must be the most wonderful thing in the world to make a baby."

By now I had frozen. My mouth was wide open, gaping, ready to accept three

21

oven chips impaled on a fork that was being held by a hand, arm and body that was paralysed. Underneath the surface of this apparent physical calmness was a raging torrent of cerebration. She was suggesting a world of extra commitment, erosion of leisure time, stinky nappies and sleepless nights. And not from belting runs at three o'clock in the morning either.

"What d'you mean?" I asked attempting to keep the strain and tension out of my voice.

"Well," she continued wistfully, "haven't you ever contemplated the idea of being a parent? We're not getting younger are we and seeing as how we've got this bit of financial security it's . . . well, it's just made me start thinking, that's all."

I tried to think clearly and come up with logical, constructive opinions. "Kids! You must be bloody joking!" Was all I could blurt before some semblance of rationality kicked in. " We've got plenty of time for children. This money can give us the chance to live an enviable lifestyle for a couple of years. We can do all the things we've always wanted to do while we're young and there's just the two of us. We can start a family later." 'Much later' I added but only to myself.

"Yes. You're right," she said her eyes clearing back to normal. "That car I was talking about though, it'd be well worth looking at."

"I'll get on it tomorrow," I said pleased that the subject of children had been finished with.

The next day I was as good as my word and was up at the crack of just gone eight. After an unhurried breakfast I went into town and finally found a car dealer who had the franchise to sell and hire a good selection of people carriers. They specialised in the Peugeot 806, the Citröen Synergie and the Fiat Ulysse which were actually all the same vehicle apart from a few aesthetic details. Apparently the three companies had developed the car between them to save costs. It looked as if the vehicle would be ideal and the costs fell within my budget, to be truthful I'd have hired it even if they hadn't been, but there we are. As we were going to France and with a perverse logic I chose the Fiat, a nice blue one and arranged to pick the car up the day before we left.

"Can you make sure that you take all the seats out apart from the front two?" I told the salesman. A quizzical frown crossed his brow but he nodded in the affirmative. Transport all done and dusted.

A couple of days later I had a letter from Bob confirming Rambo and myself's booking along with a detailed map of how to get to Le Lac Fumant and some colour photos. The pictures of the lake looked fantastic, every bit as good as Bob had related during our telephone conversation. The letter asked us to try and to be at the venue by Saturday 2nd September at about 2pm. There was going to be a reception for the anglers who were fishing the two weeks with some food and drinks. It was a sort of get to know you thing and the concept of it seemed a good idea. Bob had enclosed two little blank name badges for me to fill in so that everyone would know the name of the person they were boring to death with their fishing anecdotes. After the little get together it was off to the lake to set up and start fishing, hopefully two cracking weeks of carp fishing heaven, pack up on the Saturday morning ready to be back to work on Monday. Except I wouldn't be going back to work. Life's tough.

The next thing to get sorted was bait. We had heard of bloke who, by all accounts, was very good and would roll up whatever you wanted. He rolled his own stuff, he rolled the big bait companies stuff and he would roll your own personal stuff. Popular rumour had it that if you turned up with a ground pet mongrel or grandmother and had made sure they weren't too gritty, he would roll that as well. He was into rolling bait. Bait rolling was his bag and the baits that he rolled and put into bags were Rolls-Royce baits. He was rolling Rollers. He lived about an hour from where I lived so I phoned him up and told him that I would like him to roll my own mix for me, told him the time scale and told him how much.

"It'll be 75kg worth of dry ingredients" I said matter of factly.

There was no way I was going to run out and besides we had decided to have them air dried and they would last if we had any left over. I was hoping for some sort of exclamation over the size of the order but it never came. It was not a problem, I just had to bring everything along and I could pick it all up a week later.

With military precision Rambo arrived at my house with all the required ingredients in the back of his car at the appointed time. I jumped in the front and we were off. An all too familiar smell filled the car and the associated memories of the time that Rambo and I had grafted our nuts off to mix 50kg of it re-run in my head. I have to admit that I had a sort of Pavlov's dog response to the smell of the bait. Whereas with Mr Pavlov's mutts it had been a simple salivation at the sound of a bell, mine seemed to be a smell induced starting of my memory video tape. It was never the same bit of tape but most definitely it was always from the same tape, the syndicate TWTT tape.

During the course of the journey I bragged to Rambo about my newly acquired fishing tackle and our mode of transport to get us to Le Lac Fumant. He nodded enthusiastically and only started to laugh when I told him about all the extras I had bought for the bait boat.

"Did you get any decals for the boat?" he asked chuckling. "You know a go-faster stripe or something?"

I told him that I hadn't.

"How about a little man to water ski behind it? Of course there's this company up in London that do engine upgrades to make your bait boat the quickest. They rewind the engine and alter the gear ratio giving it better torque and a wider power band. They also replace various bits of the boat with carbon fibre to make it lighter and they give the keel a polish up with a machine similar to the one they used to polish the Hubble telescope observation mirror. They then coat it with a PVA lacquer to make it cut through the water faster due to an improved drag factor. The only trouble is you can't actually pick the boat up because it's too fucking slippery so you have to wear special tacky gloves or use tweezers. Actually years ago during the cold war the SAS had some converted to carry a small nuclear depth charge payload."

"Why on earth would they do that?" I asked playing up to his piss take.

"To kill the KGB trained dolphins."

"Why," I asked again, "were the KGB training dolphins."

"To take out the nuclear payload bait boats, stupid," Rambo explained as if I was the most idiotic bloke in the world.

Rambo's little gem of a joke was the perfect encapsulation of the madness that was the arms race. On a more realistic theme, but only just, I wondered if the boat was going to be a bit of a white elephant. No, I was sure that it would have its uses, there was bound to be some situation where it could justify the money I'd spent on it but maybe Rambo was onto something, a go faster stripe, now that would be cool.

The pair of us jabbered on during the trip. I really enjoyed Rambo's company and I felt that he enjoyed mine. The time of the old syndicate had truly bonded us, at the start of it I was a bit frightened of him but now I considered him to be my best friend despite knowing little of what he did or what he was outside of the carp fishing scene. It mattered little to me, we were a carp fishing team.

The journey time flashed by and after a couple of wrong turns we eventually found the address we were looking for. I went up to the front door while Rambo started getting all the mix bags out of the boot. The door knocker was a brass moulding of three boilies on a hook each the size of a golf ball. The hook was welded to a hooklength of wire with a similar diameter to that of a coat hanger, from the end of which the whole contraption pivoted. I rapped the three giant boilies against the hard wood door, thinking more along the lines of goof ball than golf ball in terms of the occupier's mental state. I heard footsteps from inside the house and then the door opened.

Rather disappointingly an ordinary looking bloke smiled at me and asked. "Matt Williams?"

"Yeah, that's right," I said and held out my hand to shake. It was taken by a hand sheathed in a surgeon's disposable rubber glove.

Just as my hand realised that it wasn't touching flesh but rubber and my mind was asking why, the smell of a hundred flavours charged up my nose with the infectious enthusiasm of a plague of rats sewer storming.

"Come in. I'm just labelling up an order."

"Right thanks, I'll just help my mate in with all the stuff," I explained and went back down the path to meet Rambo half-way carrying all 75kg of the mix in one go.

"Well?" he asked.

"Head case. The house absolutely stinks of flavour."

"Good. That means he's busy, which means he knows what's what," said Rambo.

I quickly grabbed the case of bottles that were our flavours, enhancers and amino blends, shut the boot down and scampered back into the house. By then Rambo and the mix were in the lounge, the lounge mind you, where our new acquaintance was indeed labelling up an order.

The room was just choker with bait making stuff. There were two huge rolling tables and the walls were wallpapered with photos of fish, literally. Even around the window reveals there were photos of fish. It was the most bizarre room I had ever had the chance to look at. It was totally bereft of any furniture, no telly, no chairs, no tables, nothing. Ok there were the two rolling tables but seeing as I had never spotted them in either MFI or Ikea I was happy to exclude them from being described as furniture. It looked as if he must have knocked all the mixes up in another room as there were no provisions to do that in the lounge. There was a small compressor sitting right in the centre of the room and one of those metal, bazooka-looking compressed air guns. This must have meant that the mixes were sausagefied and rolled in this room but that was all. Given the fact that they would have to be boiled somewhere else, the mix knocked up somewhere else and the baits dried somewhere else it seemed safe to presume that the whole house was devoted to making boilies. The owner of the house of boilies could see that we were gawping and offered an explanation.

"This," he swept his arm around the room expansively, "is the 18-22mm room. All the photos are of fish caught on my bait or on bait rolled by me. I've just started on the ceiling. See? The Sistine chapel will be nothing compared to this."

He nodded to the far corner where about fifteen photos were on the ceiling. For a second he stopped putting labels on the bags of boilies and checked one of the baits with a micrometer he had in his back pocket.

"22.32mm. Within my permitted tolerance."

He then took the boilie to a small picnic table and spun it on the table with a thumb and forefinger. The boilie whizzed round and after an initial movement in the direction of the way the thumb had spun it, it rotated on the same spot.

"Look. No travel. This means it's perfectly round and will catapult very accurately. Actually I'm toying with the idea of a rolling table that puts dimples on the boilies as they are rolled, much like a golf ball. This means that you could put spin on them and they would bite into the air and you could either draw or fade them, if you were skilful enough with a throwing stick, that is. It could be a real edge in terms of baiting up accurately."

The pair of us stood in silence as all of this washed over us. To be truthful it was more like a huge breaker smashing us into the shingle. Rambo came up for air first.

"The 18-22mm room?" he asked slowly.

"That's right. There's the 8-12mm room, the 13-17mm room and the 25mm plus room. Then there's the knocking up room, the boiling room and the drying room."

I glanced over at Rambo who glanced back. I was a bit like one of my new Delkim transmitter alarms and Rambo was the receiver box. My look sent the message – 'this bloke is a total loony isn't he.' We role reversed and Rambo's look told me – 'you bet he is.' Some might call it rudimentary telepathy but if you took our batteries out we couldn't do it.

"Where do you sleep?" asked Rambo.

"Up in the loft. I've had it converted so that I can get a bed and a few other bits of furniture up there. It's all heated and quite comfy."

"The gloves?" asked Rambo frowning even more.

"They stop my hands smelling. When you're constantly making bait you need these disposables or the smell just gets into your hands and lingers for days."

A bit lost for words but feeling the need to say something, I said. "You're certainly all geared up for this boilie lark,"

It was a vacuous remark and not received at all well.

"It's not a lark," he instantly reprimanded me, "it's a science and a business."

"Absolutely," I flustered. "Er . . . sorry I can't remember your name."

He had told me on the phone but I was unsure of what he had said and didn't want to offend the guy any more than I already had. In any case he was patently barking mad and I didn't fancy him freaking out while I was around. God alone knows what might happen.

"Pup. People call me Pup."

Rambo and I looked bemused.

Pup explained. "It's an acronym. It stands for Pop-up Pete. My pop-ups are pretty legendary."

I suddenly felt an overwhelming desire to laugh and had to fight it with all my might. It was like I was back in school assembly with the headmaster ranting at us over some petty outrage and then somebody farts. As soon as I thought about that I wanted to laugh at that as well. My lips were pursed tight and I was starting to snort down my nose and my shoulders were just starting to bounce. I was gone. My eyes started watering and I desperately choked out some words that meant that I needed the toilet and staggered out of the room.

After a phantom slash and having calmed down I went back into the lounge to find Rambo finishing off giving Pup the secret of the century, the details of our boilie. Rambo never mentioned anything about breaking Pup's legs and the pair of them seemed happy enough.

Our baits were destined to be made in the second bedroom, or the 25mm plus room and to spend some considerable time in the drying room. We wanted pretty hard baits and ones that wouldn't go off or mould. Rambo didn't fancy putting any type of preservative in them because he reckoned that it was hard to get hold of a preservative which hadn't gone past its sell by date. I'm still not sure if he was serious or not about that little paradox but we weren't having any potassium sorbate and that was that. What we were having was air dried baits plus a pop-up version of the bait as well.

Pup assured us that all would be ready in a week's time. I asked him if he ever went fishing.

"No. I haven't got the time what with the business. To be honest I'm not really that interested. I'm just into bait. Making bait, rolling bait and experimenting with bait. I suppose anything to do with bait is what I'm most interested in. Come and look at these." He beckoned us over to the corner of another room.

And with that he subjected us to a half-hour showing of his collection of old ready-made boilie bags, old base mix bags and his anthology of rare flavour bottles. He collected hand written recipes by famous anglers like others collected lyrics of celebrated songs. He had original bait making implements and had managed to acquire virtually every article ever written about bait. This large collection was getting a bit out of hand and had already made inroads into the 8-12mm room.

"I get a lot of pleasure from these articles," explained Pup "especially now that my girlfriend has left me. They give me something to read before I finally go to sleep."

In the light of Pup's preoccupation with bait (maybe he had been a carp in a previous life, if he had he would have been a bloody great fat one that got caught a lot) I balked at the idea of thumbing through any of the magazines in case some of the pages were stuck together. I couldn't begin to be anything other than amazed that he had managed to get a girlfriend in the first place let alone lose her.

I didn't know about his hands not smelling because of the gloves but every other bit of him must. The whole house stank. A host of different smells would get up your nose, sometimes singularly when you would fleetingly think that you could identify it and then it would be gone to be replaced by a group of others. It was a sort of aromatic blitzkrieg and the place that took the pounding was the nasal passage. Nothing that stayed in that house stood a chance of remaining impervious to the odious odour onslaught and that included loft dwelling humans, gloved or ungloved. I imagined that the very fabric of the house smelt of carp baits, certainly a small patch of the curtains could be hair-rigged with a good degree of confidence in catching. It was amazing, the whole house was a shrine to carp bait and its production. Perhaps the house was a parallel to the small over-fished day ticket water that got peppered with thousands and thousands of different boilies. Perhaps as I swam around the house going from one different smell to another that was as close as I would ever get to living out the human equivalent of a carp in one of those sort of venues. Or perhaps I'm just talking bollocks.

We said our goodbyes to Pup but it was just au revoir. I would be back in a week to get our bait. On the threshold I asked Pup what he thought the best ever flavour was. He answered with no hesitation and was adamant in his answer, there was no ambiguity. It was definitely . . . but that's just one person's opinion and it would be unfair to voice it.

When we were back in the car I looked solemnly at Rambo.

"Not so funny now?" he asked.

"A bit sad, I suppose," I replied earnestly. "I guess we were there, in that deep, only it was fishing rather than bait making. Incidentally, what about confidentiality over our bait? Did you threaten to break his legs?"

"Nah," said Rambo, "we won't have any trouble with him. That boy is good, touched, but very good."

Rambo put the car in gear and drove off. On the way back I had a rising feeling of excitement. Had my life taken a fluky turn for the best or what? As I sat in the gloom of the car I just couldn't really believe how things had turned around since the initial despondency of my release. It was all coming together so perfectly. The money, the new gear, the place we'd picked, the car, the bait, the bloke making the bait, it all seemed top notch. I hadn't cast a rod in over a year and a half but I was up for it. I just couldn't wait. It was going to be so different from last time, it was going to be so great.

Chapter 4

Can you remember what it used to be like waiting for the close season to end and to start fishing again after that lifelong three-month break? No scrap that, can you remember what it used to be like waiting for Christmas to come when you were a kid of about five or six years old? At that age the prospect of waiting the final two weeks until Santa delivered, was a mind-numbingly ridiculous amount of time to be kept hanging about. Minutes stretched to hours, hours to days and days to weeks, weeks to . . . you get the idea. Waiting to go to Lac Fumant, my sack of presents, I was transported back into being that child.

To stretch the analogy even further I constantly wondered what I was going to get in my sack of goodies once it was full to the brim. It wasn't football boots, Scalextrics or a new bike that were my desires this time around, it was huge, great big carp. As before I did live in slight trepidation of the joy-killer gift, namely the much feared and loathed garment present. Whether it turned out to be socks or a jumper, a scarf, anything along those sort of lines, those boring presents were my today's euphemism for a two-week blank. However, true to my childhood beliefs in the inherent goodness and let's not be bashful about it, the very existence of the fat, bearded, red-robed one, I pushed it hard to the back of my mind. Santa would deliver the goods and so would Lac Fumant I kept telling myself.

Despite all my efforts to convince myself the problem still loitered in the back of mind, even though the little man who lived there was frantically trying to bury the notion by shovelling a pile of dead brain cells over the top of it. Perhaps the fact that I wanted it to be so perfect, more for Rambo than for myself, made me apprehensive of any failure. I think that whenever you take a mate fishing to a place that you recommend or chose you want them to do well. I suppose it's so that you can bask in some sort of reflected glory and the desire for things to go well is likely to be directly proportional to the amount of time, effort and money devoted to the session. This was going to be the carp fishing holiday of a lifetime and so it would be in terms of planning and luxuries but the thorny subject of catching to complete the equation still existed. Deep inside I felt that my luck had changed and that I was on a fortunate lucky streak. It was going to be great I was sure, besides, I told myself, who had drunk the glass of milk and scoffed the biscuit if not Santa himself? Adults and children have to believe in something.

Not having to go to work meant that I had everything sorted out in the tackle department two days after the visit to Pup. I had gone over my gear, both the old and the new with the proverbial fine tooth comb. Nothing had been missed. Everything had been checked, cleaned, checked again and neatly packed away and realistically it was all over bar the waiting and loading of the tackle into our vehicle.

I had enough of everything for the worst case of worst case scenarios. The first day I had spent entirely on tying up rigs, the second putting line on my reels, cleaning and getting everything packed away in its rightful place. I also had bought some French currency for motorway tolls and other incidentals although all petrol and major purchases would be on my credit card. The only things left for me to do were pick up the bait, pick up the car and find a spare pair of pants and a toothbrush to take with me. Joking aside I did have my clothing sorted out as well as a fair bit of additional food and cooking equipment even though we had the option of getting at least one prepared meal a day.

I did give the bait boat a quick run out in the park boating lake but after half an hour I felt pretty confident with it. It was simple enough, the boat had a fast and slow movement forward and you could steer it left and right via the two jets that pushed the boat forward. The boat could be reversed up, by using the single, forward facing jet and while in this mode the left and right steering levers operated the appropriate loading doors. As a further facility there was a cut-out either side for the main line to go through if you wanted to dump a terminal rig as well as bait. It was an impressive bit of kit, but like most anglers I suppose that I needed to get over the slight feeling of guilt about having such a tool. If Tradders saw me with it I'm sure that he'd have hated me for life but on reflection he probably did already so it made no odds. At least I didn't need a bait boat to get out seventy yards like he would if he tried to cast it with his glass fibre rods and Mitchell 300's.

On the third day after the visit to the house of boilies the ferry tickets came in the post. We were going to go on the Dover-Calais boat. I had considered the hovercraft or even the Seacat but the boat nearly always ran whereas the other two could be disrupted by weather and you'd still end up on the boat. The tunnel was the other option but a nice crossing up on the deck of a ship seemed more appealing somehow. The fact that I'd chosen the boat because of hassle with the other options if the weather was bad and yet was thinking of a perfect crossing might seem a bit confused. Not so! Idealism based on a certain pragmatism. Whatever it was it didn't stop me having very little to do and loads of time to do it.

If I'd have been fishing, even if I had been sitting by my rods blanking out, the time would have passed quickly. How often have you got to a venue for ten, sixteen, twenty-four, forty-eight hours or whatever it was and clicked your fingers and it's time to go. As you pack up you think to yourself - was I really here for that time? How could all that time just go so quickly? But it has and it did, but not for me, not in this instance. It dragged on and I re-lived a bit of my childhood waiting for the very exciting, special day to come. All of this reminded me a bit of how the time had froze when the old syndicate lake had iced up and the four of us had to just sit it out. That had been pure boredom but this time it was the expectation of future events that had applied the chronological brakes. Eventually a couple of centuries passed and it was time to go and see Pup and get the bait.

It was all ready as he had promised and the site of all those bags of large red boilies made my heart pound. Try explaining that to someone who wasn't a carp angler. – 'Ooh! My heart just went into palpitations when I saw all those big red balls, darling. What a carpet of baits they would make, I tell you.' You'd either get banged in the teeth or get an indecent proposition.

Pup had experienced it all before, handing over vast quantities of boilies was the sign of a successful business and had become second nature to him. He must have rolled over a million boilies and knowing him he may even have kept a record of every single one. They were his children, even if this particular mix wasn't made from his own genes but from a donor, a type of in vitro fertilisation courtesy of Rambo's boilie recipe.

"That is a very interesting mix and attractor combination you've got there," he told me as we loaded about eighteen, five kilo bags into the back of my car. "I'm very impressed, I'm sure that you will do well. I have a sort of sixth sense when it comes to bait that other people have asked me to make up. You don't roll as much bait as I have without knowing, just knowing what mix will be a good one."

"It's a very successful bait. Quite a lot of people have gone to some considerable trouble to try and find out what was in it," I told him thinking of all the strokes the old syndicate members had pulled in trying to find out what it consisted of.

Pup nodded. "I can imagine."

"No, you can't," I told him. The depths plumbed during that time were not easy to conjure up from a healthy mind.

Pup seemed untroubled by my non concurrence. "Do you know that when I first started making up my own bait I used to try it out on my cat? If the cat liked it I proceeded with that particular bait, if it didn't, I didn't. How embarrassing to work as unscientifically as that, still I was only an apprentice in those days, not a mastercraftsman as I am now. Mind you, I suppose it did help me on my way, especially with one of my earliest mixes. As usual I gave the cat some of the mix, I never gave it finished boilies only the mix in paste form, for obvious reasons, and in the morning the cat had died."

"Christ! What on earth had you put in it to do that?" I asked.

Pup held up a hold-on-a-minute hand. "You misunderstand. It wasn't a poisonous bait but a very good one. The poor old cat liked it so much that it jumped up onto the table where I had foolishly left the rest of a kilo mix in a plastic bag and ate the lot. It was so stuffed that it fell asleep and died in the night through choking on its own vomit. I've still got the plastic bag in my collection, complete with claw ripping and teeth marks where it had attacked the bag to get at the mix inside it."

"What was the cat's name, Hendrix?" I asked.

"No, Tiddles," said Pup frowning, my joke flying about 36,000 ft above his head.

After we had put all the bags in the boot I straightened up and eyed Pup gravely. "There's just one thing I want to tell you, Pup, it's not a threat just a fact of life. Between me and you, don't ever think about making up our bait for anyone else. Rambo is a real hard case and he'd be down on you like a ton of bricks if he found out."

"That's just what he said about you," replied Pup, "and I'll say the same to you as I said to him. Confidentiality is assured. I destroy all recipes like yours once the order is complete."

I immediately imagined Rambo's recipe bursting into flames after it had said 'Your mission, should you chose to accept it, is to roll 75 kilos of the following mix.' I then jumped to a mental picture of Pup bolting down a sheet of A4, masticating for all he was worth, literally eating Rambo's words, having rolled God knows how many thousands of our 25mm aired dried specials.

"Oh . . . Right, that's fine, then," I said meekly.

I handed Pup his money in a small wad. He put it straight in his pocket not bothering to count it. Suddenly and quite unexpectedly Pup grabbed my arm. He was still wearing the gloves, or more likely a different identical pair.

"Do you think I'm a sad bastard?" he asked intently.

I mean what do you say to a person who has collected an old Bait 78 mix bag and kept it in another plastic bag to stop it getting dirty? And now the cat bag story.

"Believe me, mate, I've dealt with carp anglers who make you look . . ." I faltered thinking of Watt, Kipper, Rambo, even myself during the syndicate time. I was groping for a reasonably honest comparison. ". . . Virtually normal," I said, not giving one.

I had first hand knowledge of obsession in carp angling. The only difference between Pup and myself was that I had managed to pull out of it while he was still ensnared in it, albeit in the bait making slice of the carp cake. An Englishman's home is his castle, or in Pup's case, his boilie making factory.

He seemed pleased. "Really? Good. Well, all that's left to say is - have a great trip. Let me know how you get on. One other thing, I've put you about 100 of my own pop-ups in one of the bags just as an alternative to your ones. My pop-ups are legendary."

A legend in his own microwave I thought and thanked him and promised him that I would let him know how we got on provided time got it's act together and let me get to the departure date. I told him that if I caught a fifty I wanted the photo of it somewhere prominent in the 25mm plus room.

"Right by the light switch is a very nice spot," he gushed. "What say I reserve a 7x5 plot for you?"

"Sounds good to me," I said laughing. "I'll be in touch. Take care. Bye."

I got into the car and pulled out of Pup's drive. During the journey home I hoped I wouldn't have an horrendous accident where I got killed because I wanted to go on my fishing holiday and I didn't want the boilies ruined.

My excitement gradually increased over the next few days. I had considered a trip to a local water to get back into the swing of things but I decided that my rejoining of the fishing world would be at Lac Fumant. It would be a symbolic re-birth of my favourite pastime and a new chapter in my life. My life would be richer, more interesting and far more auspicious than it had before. The word 'richer' being the operative word. Was all this true? With all the dosh I was set for life. Sternly I told myself that the money would never change me but who was I kidding? It already had. If I wasn't careful I might turn into something undesirable. I had read about women who were shopaholics, usually married to a high income hubby and invariably with time on their hands. I filled both sets of criteria only from a male point of view as regards the partner details.

I certainly couldn't deny the thrill of buying all my new gear and with still a week to go I asked Sophie how she felt about me spending a bit more of my five thousand. I needed the buzz, man. I needed my plastic swiping kick and with a neat 250k behind me there would be no credit card bill downer on the small fix I required. I knew it was wrong but I was touched by the hand of decadence.

When I asked her, Sophie smiled at me and shook her head and started to laugh. "What on? You can't need any more fishing tackle, surely?"

This, although not true, was not what I was after. A new SLR and a video camera were the items I had suddenly decided that I simply couldn't function without. Both of which, as I succinctly pointed out, were useful implements in themselves as well as an excellent duo for recording the holiday in heaven.

Sophie shrugged her shoulders and said why not. Why not indeed? I spent a whole day going round to different retailers, picking their brains and haggling for a good deal. I wasn't up for spending more than a grand and in the end I bought a Canon Eos and a Sharp Viewcam with spare battery for about eight hundred including loads of 35mm print film and ten 8mm video cassettes. I congratulated myself on my frugality and knew there and then that any hope I ever had of being exactly the same as I had been before the Gods had smiled on me were dead and buried.

At last the night before Christmas came. Early in the day I walked the four miles to go and pick up the MPV just to give myself something to do and to try and tire myself out a bit. We were leaving at 2 am and I planned to try and get some sleep from early evening until our departure time. I thought the walk might help me get to kip at the early time that I had decided to go to bed. I hadn't been sleeping properly for about a week because I was too excited and that was at a normal bedtime, let alone a seven o'clock touch.

Walking to get the car on a perfect end of summer morning I contemplated the situation that was my life. I was Mr Simultaneous-four-runs-on-four-rods-Smith. I walked leisurely down the bright street and in and out of the dappled, leafy shade. Even at this early hour the sun was already warming my back. It was a beautiful morning, one that would have given pleasure to simply be out walking, but my feelings were even more powerful than anything nature itself could bestow upon an individual. I was healthy and rich. Life's two great attributes, in their rightful order and I was about to partake on an adventure appertaining to something I loved doing. I found myself, for about the thousandth time, unable to believe my luck. I was Mr Simultaneous-four-runs-on-four-rods-land-the-lot-and-they-were-all-thirties-Smith.

Only a while ago I had speculated on how people might treat me if they knew I had done time. Now, especially when I was spending money with them, they seemed to fall over themselves in an effort to be nice. I could have casually dropped into the conversation that I was a mass murderer. 'Really, Sir. Is that cash or credit card?' They wouldn't have cared. Money was a God or if not that, then plainly a religion. A religion so magnanimous that it forgave virtually all indiscretion. The one proviso was you had enough of it and were spending some of it with the person who was passing judgement. Of the rest you could still persuade them to be benevolent in their assessment towards you without directly spending money on them or on their goods. This was done not by yourself but by the natural predisposition towards greed by the people involved. They were simply hoping that you might spend some of it on them at some unestablished point in the future. Business people were tarts. A sweeping generalisation but one that was hard to argue against.

I could see why Sophie's Mum had decided on no publicity and likewise the only person Sophie and I had told was Rambo. It would only be a matter of time before it was twigged and then the fun would really start. The pair of us wouldn't be in the direct firing line but we'd have to dodge the odd bit of shrapnel. Whatever, I was all for it. I was convinced that money shortage problems were worse than money surfeit problems. Besides if we played our cards right we could always be away on holiday or at the very least out to lunch.

Within the hour I had the keys to the Fiat in my hand. The garage had taken all but the driver and passenger seats out as requested. There was an awful lot of room behind those two seats, which was good because we had an awful lot of gear. Having completed the formalities I got in the car and drove back home. It felt a bit strange driving what at first felt like a small bus, with its high driving position, no real bonnet length in front but I soon got used to it. The Ulysse had 1.9 petrol engine, power steering and air conditioning. It was more of a drive than I expected it to be and I could tell it was going to be ideal but having said that I sure wouldn't want to own one. It cried out 'family man' and 'sprog city' or 'taxi driver' and I had other ideas about what hot number Sophie and I were going to get to pose in.

The name of the car I thought was rather apt, it's the Roman name for Odysseus, give or take one letter. Now he was the main man in the Greek epic the Odyssey which tells of his wanderings and fascinating adventures. It was written by a bloke called Homer who later appeared as a yellow-skinned, dysfunctional father in a cartoon by some American called Matt something-or-other, which as you know is my name. Would our journey be as enthralling and as littered with action? Would the captain of our ferry boat smash us to pieces on Calais harbour wall because the sirens were giving him the come on? Maybe I'd have to tie him to the mast and give the rest of the crew wax earplugs. I was after carp not bloody sea nymphs.

I drove the car home via a thirty mile detour to familiarise myself with all its switchgear. It would be dark when we left and I didn't want to be groping for the indicator stalk and after finding it see the windscreen wipers start to move. When I returned home Rambo was there waiting. He had unloaded all of his tackle out of his vehicle and onto my front drive. I carefully backed down the drive and jumped out of the Fiat.

"What d'you think, then," I said as I let the rear door up to reveal the huge loading space.

"Very nice, boy. Very nice. Let's have a sit in the front."

I ushered him to the driving seat and opened the driver's door. He leapt in with his usual liquid athleticism and surveyed the layout.

He was impressed. "Spot on. Air conditioning and the personal bonus of a car which I can actually sit up straight in without smacking my head on the ceiling."

"Glad you approve," I said smiling. "Shall we get loaded up and then have a bite to eat?"

"Sounds good to me," he said.

With that we started to put Rambo's stuff into the back. It seemed strange me taking the lead and suggesting that we do something or other but I realised that it would be a temporary thing. Once we got to Lac Fumant I knew Rambo's superior fishing ability would come to the fore and I would be relegated to my number two position. I hadn't touched a rod for a long time but Rambo had been fishing a number of waters and had caught well. If anything the situation would be even more reinforced than when we had last fished together. I was thinking of writing 'bale arm open' on the back of my hand before my first cast. A stuffed churner into the margins followed by a bird's nest was something I was keen to avoid. Maybe I'd use the bait boat all the time.

After all Rambo's tackle was loaded I opened up the garage where my gear was kept and we loaded it all in plus the boilies. It didn't take us all that long to have everything in the back of the Fiat. Once it was all in the car I had the natural desire, well natural to me anyway, to want to hook everything out and check that item 'A' was safely in place. Then item 'B' and so on. When you go back and check a locked door as many times as I do this sort of thing is accepted. You know that you have done it but it wouldn't hurt just to check and make doubly sure.

"Jesus Christ!" howled Rambo. "I saw you put the bloody bait boat in."

"And the rod bag?"

"You know you put the rod bag in," Rambo replied somewhat exasperated. "You've put it all in. I saw it with my own two eyes and so did you."

"So that's the lot then?"

Rambo nodded. "That's the lot, boy. Believe me, that's the lot."

"So we're ready to roll? Nothing else to do?"

Rambo looked at me and gave me a twisted grin. So that was it, we were ready at last. The moment I had been waiting for had almost arrived. We went in for some food and frittered the afternoon away talking about bygone days. I showed Rambo the camcorder and told him I wanted to make a video diary of the whole two weeks.

"I hope you've got plenty of 8mm tapes," he said.

"You know what I mean. It'll be great to look at in years to come what with all the stills as well. The new camera should take excellent photos."

"They'll look good on Pup's ceiling," said Rambo sarcastically.

"If I get a fifty it'll be right by the light switch, old son. Not just stuck up on the ceiling. Do you know that he asked me if I thought he was a sad bastard or not? And he told me that you told him that I would deck him if he revealed our recipe to a living soul."

Rambo shrugged. "I felt sorry for him. I must be getting old or going soft or mellowing out or doing something. I don't know."

"You couldn't have felt that sorry for him or you wouldn't have threatened him at all, via me or yourself."

"That's true," said Rambo, the perky inflection in his voice hinting that something good had just been pointed out to him. Maybe he was a bit embarrassed at his perceived compassion.

"Did you tell him the truth?" asked Rambo.

"No. He's me two years ago. Bait division though."

"Ha!" said Rambo, pleased. "You're even worse than what I am."

"Do you know what my ambition is with that camcorder?" I asked, changing tacks.

"I dread to think. Does it involve Sophie?"

I'd be lying if I hadn't considered that. "No," I said indignantly. "My ambition on the holiday?"

"Come on, try me," said Rambo with false weariness.

"To video a real take. To actually have the video running on the hangers as they whop up to the top. No editing and no false runs, as it happens, for real. Video the whole fight and land the fish, the weighing, the photographing and release. The whole nine yards all in one take. One take of one take." I added, feeling pleased with myself.

"And the fish is a forty," said Rambo.

"And the fish is a forty," I agreed.

"Knowing your luck at the moment it'll probably be a fifty. I bet you never dreamt the pair of us would be here about to set off on a two week, wacker track. Plus the little bonus of 250k in the bank."

"It's down to 246k now," I informed him.

"Poor sod."

I laughed. "I know. It's amazing. Six poxy numbers and your whole life is turned around. Think how much effort you would have to put in to get the sort of money we got and we got it because we knew someone who picked out six poxy numbers. Didn't even have to pick them out ourselves. It's weird and in a way it's wrong but I'm happy and fatalistic about it. It was my destiny to become stinking rich and to contribute absolutely nothing to the process of making it happen."

"You're not alone on that one," said Rambo sincerely and then with his tongue firmly in his cheek he continued. "Come the day of the revolution all hereditary wealth will be distributed amongst the masses and the disenfranchised heirs put against the wall and shot. I'm just hoping to get the contract to supply the guns and bullets, that's all."

The pair of us rattled on. Sophie came home from work and we had a fish and chip supper. Rambo produced a bottle of champagne and toasted our new found wealth. Sophie and I kissed. We were happier than we had ever been. Our relationship had stood some testing moments, all brought about by my crazy behaviour, but we had turned the corner and found a pile of money around it. The future was bright, in fact it was so bright we were wearing welding goggles rather than shades. It was a terrific meal to depart on.

Later that evening Sophie and I made love while Rambo watched telly downstairs. It was a deep and moving experience, the best since I had been out of prison. I loved her intensely and I was sure that she loved me the same. We told each other to be careful and in our emotionally charged state the pair of us had a few tears as it finally dawned that we would be apart again, if only briefly. I realised that I had always been lucky. Lucky to have her.

That night I couldn't sleep, it was impossible. I dozed fitfully and was awake to turn the alarm off before it sounded. I kissed Sophie while she slept and she roused from her slumbers to say goodbye, we had another round of 'I love you' and 'take care' before I dragged myself from her. I wanted to go and stay all at the same time.

Eventually I went downstairs to find Rambo all ready to go in his camouflage trousers and jacket. We had a quick cuppa and a slice of toast and went outside. The stars shone down from a breathless and clear night, I stood and admired the spectacle and felt my whole body tingle. The weather was mild and muggy, it was a perfect night for travel. We smiled at each other like Cheshire cats that had gone to bed with coat hangers in their mouths.

The Fiat started up first time. I pulled slowly out of the drive, my heart pounding with excitement and expectation when all at once, I suddenly remembered. I stopped, reversed the car back into the drive to its original position and made Rambo get out. He stood on my front lawn and took a video of me pulling out of the drive and a little way down the road until I was out of shot. I stopped again, he ran to the car, hopped back in and we were off!

CHAPTER 5

The journey from where I live in the county of Sussex to the port of Dover is only a short one and with little or no traffic on the roads we made good time. In just over an hour and a quarter we approached passport control where we showed our passports and ferry tickets. A rather sombre official gave us a lane number and we followed the sign for cars going to the ferries. Shortly we came to a huge area of marked off lanes and we went into the lane that was headed by our number. There were few cars in the lane and we drove virtually to the front where we parked. As is often typical in these sort of situations we had time to spare, time which had been allowed as a safety buffer just in case something unforeseen had arisen. The pair of us sat in the car and I had a last look at the directions that Bob had sent me. We were going to use the motorways all the way so it looked as if it was going to be pretty straightforward.

The pair of us talked quietly, mainly about the prospects of catching well at Lac Fumant. We also wondered what the other eight blokes who were going to be there would be like. How good they were likely to be and how we would get on with them. I hoped that they would all be likeable types, I didn't want anything to remind me of how bitter we had all become in the old syndicate. Being a smallish water there was a good chance that we would have to get to know them pretty well and there was the added factor of the introduction party. Bob liked the idea of everyone getting to know everyone else and had said that it worked a treat. My thinking was that it had gone well (if indeed it had) because he had really only had word of mouth references from friends and acquaintances. Now that he was advertising to all and sundry with all and sundries' prejudices and chips on their shoulders it might not be so hunky dory. Still, wait and see on that one, at least he had said that the other eight were all anglers who had been there before.

The meeting party was the main reason why we were leaving so early. We wouldn't be fishing until much later in the evening but the introductions commenced at around two in the afternoon. We were due to sail at 4.15am and should be off the boat and onto French soil by six. That gave us eight hours to hammer down the motorway in the fast lane to cover the 350 or so miles Bob reckoned it was from Calais. I had it worked out that we would make it in six hours if we didn't stop for anything other than petrol and a piddle, provided the Paris ring road wasn't an eight lane parking lot. It would have been hopeless to have attempted such a distance on the UK's pathetic roads in that time but whatever you felt about the French they had a descent transport policy. The Mickey Mouse road along the Sussex coast was laughable but once on the French side we'd be virtually on the motorway before the back wheels were off the boat.

Apparently, to underline our lack of infrastructure a friend of Sophie's had taken the Eurostar from Ashford and although the station was impressive enough the train poodled along on clapped-out track until it resurfaced in France. Once in a country that knew how to put down a railway the thing hammered her down to Paris at 180 mph. Both our road and rail networks never managed to equal that of the French. It was a small mercy that I didn't live in somewhere like Manchester or even further afield, it would have made the journey much more of a slog.

Although it was a good half an hour after I had turned off the Fiat's engine it didn't seem that long before we were told to board the boat. The queue of cars that made up our fellow passengers slowly moved onto the ship and we were soon technically afloat. Once parked up Rambo and I climbed the metal steps out of the bowels of the ship and up onto the passenger decks. I had with me a carrier bag full of odds and ends of food which I suggested we could eat up on the top deck. I also took the camcorder for an update of the video diary. The two of us made our way up to the ship's stern open deck and sat on one of the benches there. The sky was still perfectly clear and the temperature was warm, there was just the gentlest of breezes. It was a smashing night to be crossing the channel.

As the ship left her moorings I looked out across the resplendently lit port of Dover through the liquid crystal display of the camcorder. Whilst videoing our departure from England I was fleetingly filled with the fascination of travel. Normally I would have been fast asleep but here I was on board a large ship off to carp fish in a foreign country. Where were all the other people on board her going? What were they up to? What did they do with their lives? And this was just one ship! All over the world there were thousands of ships, thousands of aeroplanes, thousands of trains and millions of people all getting on something that was going to take them to somewhere else. To support the people who were actually going somewhere there were countless employees who ran the travel industry. From the person who sold you the tickets to the pilot or driver who ultimately took you. Then there were all the ancillary firms from catering to the company making the nuts and bolts to go into the aeroplanes. It made my head hurt to try and think of even a small percentage of the multifarious links and connections that made up the entire travel industry chain. And it went on day and night, 24hrs a day, every day of the year.

I was still videoing as the ship pulled out of Dover harbour and headed into the open sea. Once the harbour was of little visual interest I focused the camcorder onto Rambo who was eating my food as if it would be his last meal in two weeks. I panned across the rest of the deck, it was empty and with that I stopped the camcorder and went and sat next to Rambo. I took out a sandwich and started to munch on it. Sitting there with Rambo as if we were on a ghost ship that was moving under its own will, it all seemed quite the opposite to my previous mental meandering. Paradoxically it felt as if we were the only two people in the world travelling as we sat on the deserted deck eating tuna sandwiches, gazing at the stars and occasionally getting up to look at the wash of the engines coming from the back of the boat. We were in a world of our own, a carp fishing adventure world. It wasn't some cruddy virtual reality computer game but a real adventure in the real world. The breeze, much stronger now that we were up to cruising speed and out to sea, invigorated me and I breathed the salty air deep into my lungs. This was what life was all about. The fact that it was night time and there was no-one about seemed to turbo-charge the whole atmosphere. The hairs on the back of my neck tingled like they had when I had looked up at the stars earlier. I felt so alive, so animated, so excited with the whole experience.

I told Rambo what I was thinking about and he listened to my musings in silence except for when he wanted something else to eat. He nodded and smiled but I could tell that this part of the journey didn't hold him like it did me. Perhaps it was mundane to him. Perhaps he needed to be under mortar attack or at the very least to have some murderous terrorist handing him a large cheque to get his blood bumping. On second thoughts that was ridiculous, it would have to be cash, he'd never accept a cheque. Now there was an idea, maybe being offered a cheque instead of cash would get him stoked up. Whatever, I was feeling high even if he wasn't. This was true freedom, not the false freedom that I had been handed when I walked out of those prison gates. How could I have ever imagined that this would be happening to me? If I'd have jumped over the side I'd have bounced back up onto the deck. All that remained in the short term was my luck to hold out and turn into the form of great big, lunking carp. May the fates be with me and bless my boilies with the seductive charm of . . . the thing carp find most seductive.

"Are you excited?" I asked Rambo, unable to resist the possibility of disappointment. I wanted him to feel like me.

"Only about the prospect of you having some chocolate in that bag of yours," he said nodding at the Tesco carrier.

I dug out a couple of chocolate bars and passed him a Kit-Kat but put the Mars bar back in the bag. "Aren't you excited about going, about being here, you know, on this boat." I said slightly peeved by his flippancy.

"Yeah, too right I am. I'm not that old or cynical that I don't get excited about going carp fishing. Especially something like this. I guess I tend to keep it a bit more under wraps than most. A bit like you and the chocolate," he said nodding and smiling at my goody bag yet again. "But don't you worry, boy I'm up for it all right."

I laughed. "I bet there've been hundreds of carpers like us going out, full of exuberance and yet totally pissed off when they come back after suffering the dreaded. Imagine how we'd feel coming back after a two week blank."

"We'll never know because we are going to slaughter them," said Rambo positively

He was right. We were going to slaughter them. We had the gear, the bait, the venue and the know-how. Well, I hoped we did. Images of large carp swam across my stream of consciousness and when my guard was down Rambo swiped the bag from my grasp.

"Yes! The Mars bar!" he said triumphantly holding it aloft.

"We are going to get fed at the lake you know. You haven't got to eat for a fortnight now," I said a bit annoyed. I had a soft spot for Mars bars.

"It's this fresh air and early start, I'm starving. What else have you got in this bag?"

The crossing was uneventful, there were no sirens, no icebergs and nobody pulled the plug to let all the water out of the channel. Or, on looking at the watch, Le Manche, we were over halfway. By now there were a few people up on the deck with us. They'd had their breakfast, purchased their duty-frees or whatever it was that had detained them in the ship and now they were up with us as the dawn light started to leak in from the east. I supposed that many of them were off to some French hypermarket for just the day. Only a country as dumb as the UK could make goods so expensive that it was actually cheaper to make the journey abroad to go and buy them.

My mental illusions of there being thousands of people connected to what we were doing and us somehow being alone on a ghost ship were now fully vanquished. Little pockets of passengers stood by the railings down the side of the ship or sat on the benches or stood in circles talking. One poor sod was actually throwing up over the side, God knows what he'd have been like if it was rough because the sea was the proverbial mill pond. At one stage I was convinced I saw a carp top out to starboard but Rambo said it was just a coot, I expect he was right.

The camcorder came out again as we pulled into Calais harbour and once we had come alongside the pair of us made our way down to the car. Driving off the boat and into France I clocked the odometer back to zero because I'm a bit of an anorak about things like that. I like to know how far it is from one place to another, to the mile. We went straight through customs, followed the appropriate sign and within ten minutes we were on the A26 heading for Paris at a steady 80mph.

At first it seemed unreal, there were no other cars for the first fifteen minutes once we had burnt up the few ferry cars that had gone the same way as us. It was short lived and a BMW hammered passed and I felt a bit happier than I had before. I don't know why particularly, maybe it sort of confirmed the fact that we were on the right road or something stupid like that. Motorway driving can be an odd experience but in a watery dawn light with virtually no traffic it was even odder. So often in the UK you are dictated to by other external forces in terms of how you drive and how fast. Not this time, the application of a little extra pounds per square inch pressure to the gas pedal could make a considerable time difference to our overall journey. Going 80 instead of 60 would shave an hour and half off a 350 mile journey and how much harder was it to go 80 instead of 60? After much deliberation I reckoned it was about the same effort as pinning down a snail for the duration but not as much as squashing it. In the time it took me to think about this and work it out in my head we had covered three miles.

We ate up the miles with ease, on the signposts everything seemed even more digestible. The smaller kilometres got gulped down at an even faster rate, true there were more of them, but it seemed to enhance our road burning capabilities. In less than an hour we had shunned the opportunity of two weeks in the south of France and had turned off the A26. We had ignored the turning to Reims, Troyes, Dijon and the eventual lure of Lyons and the AutoRoute du Soleil and gone A1, AutoRoute du Nord. True we could chose again at the Paris ring road, in fact we had to take the exit to both Lyon and Le Mans but our jaws were firmly set. There'd be no pouncing about on the beaches of Nice, Cannes and St. Tropez with the bronzed, physically perfect, topless, thonged, jet-set, it was two weeks at Lac Fumant in a bivvy after carp. No contest!

As we neared Paris the traffic increased, in fact it had being doing so rather surreptitiously since the completion of the first hour and it had dawned on me, my second dawning of the day, that it was actually rather busy now. It was still a great morning for driving and everyone was going for it, perhaps they all had average mileage rates to hit as well.

Tiny, old 1000cc cars came struggling past us at about two mph quicker than the speed we were doing, the guts being absolutely thrashed out of them. Their drivers were all inclined slightly towards the wheel, which was gripped tightly by two hands at the classic ten to two position. It was as if they were trying desperately to encourage the car to go faster by sheer will power and body posture. With their grim expressions on their faces, eyes staring intently ahead, right foot absolutely nailed to the floor, they cut what we considered to be figures of ridicule. The most embarrassing bit, for them, was the seemingly everlasting time it took for their poxy little car to inch level with and finally overtake ours. Their eyes never once flickered towards us during this process of crawling down Rambo's side of the car. Rambo himself took great pleasure in eyeballing them with his sternest expression. It was a good job they didn't rubberneck or the shock of him giving them the look might have made them crash.

Rambo had his own pet theory for the unusual body position and air of discomfort. He was sure that they were peddling to help get the extra speed.

"Look out. Here comes another fucking one of those Flintstones," he would say, angling his head to look in the wing mirror at the slowly emerging slugmobile. "Wait till he comes alongside and put your foot down a bit."

There were some cars that you couldn't muck about. The BMW's, Porsche's and other similar pacey automobiles came by at about a hundred and one bloke on a Yamaha R1 must have been doing a ton-fifty, which was about his decibel rating, seeing as he had a race can on the bike.

"Jet coming!" Rambo had said and it had certainly sounded like it.

You had lorries stuffing other lorries, cars pulling out here and nipping back in there, the odd offensive gesticulation and plenty of horn and flashing lights. Yes, we were driving in France all right, the country of car carnage. I wasn't scratching my head to work out what mental kink made the French so aggressive behind a wheel,

I was just happy to keep out of their way. In fact my knuckles were a tad on the white side so I was obviously in full motorway, avoid the mad French, concentration mode. It was just a total crank up of the heat compared to driving at home.

Eventually we hit the dreaded Paris ring road and it was pretty packed. Eight lanes at times and not the place to get tucked into the wrong lane before your exit junction appears with little chance of getting over. By now there seemed to be even more motor bikes chopping in and out of lanes, especially when the traffic slowed right down. The riders put both legs down dabbing the bike through the gaps in the cars, sometimes even cutting across at ninety degrees. Some had helmets others didn't. It was totally mad. We made much slower progress but thanks to Rambo's eagle eye as befitted his Chief Navigator appointment coupled with Overtaking Traffic Analyser (first class) we found our exit ok. Again we blew out Lyon and hit the A10 and started to mile crunch again.

We had covered about two hundred miles plus in just over four hours. It was ten in the morning and we decided to pull into one of the many huge lay-by's and have a drink. It felt good to get out, have a stretch and feel the sun. It felt good to have a pee as well. The lay-by was very attractive with lots of wooden benches and seats set under trees. It seemed another definitive moment for the video diary so I shot Rambo coifing his soft drink and making rude gestures to camera. What a star, so natural.

"You'll be in the loo making a video of me having a piss next," he said to camera and then added. "I should have got one of those camcorders then I could have taken a video of you videoing me. Don't start laughing you'll get camera shake. We must have a bankstick with a camera adapter in amongst all that sodding lot in there that you can use."

With that I ran, still filming, up to the car and zoomed in and out on the tackle through all the windows of the car. I was trying to do something similar to those type of documentaries where the camera jerks along seemingly in the thick of the action rather than just recording it as a dispassionate bystander.

"That bit should be quite good," I beamed, pleased with my artistic input into the scene.

"Maybe we should have gone to Cannes for the film festival after all," said Rambo, sarcastically.

I tried to counter. "I think you ought to stop wearing camouflage clothing. You're not going to stand out very well on this video."

"That's the whole idea, boy. That's the whole idea."

Refreshed from the short break we were back on the road. Rambo was a real hot shot when it came to chucking the correct money into the bucket at the motorway toll booth, which was a good job. He wouldn't have looked too cool picking a load of change off the deck. After the re-start 80mph felt like it was 80mph but after less than fifteen minutes it was back to feeling about fifty and slowing to under fifty felt like we'd broken down and Rambo had got out and started to push. We passed

Orleans, topped up with gas and were heading virtually south-west, still on the A10 AutoRoute l'Aquitaine. One little extra bonus to casually drop into conversation to impress dinner guests was that the gas stations in France sell porno videos. I'd have to write to my Euro MP about it, signed – 'Disgusted,' Sussex. Disgusted our petrol stations didn't.

As we skirted Tours we crossed the Loire. Any large river looks appealing and this was no different, she looked lovely glittering in the sun as we hammered over her at eighty. Yeah, don't forget to smell the roses. Shortly after the crossing we came off the motorway and real time and speed had to be obeyed. It was then that I had to concentrate on driving on the right for the first time. The directions Bob had given us were precise and clear, once in Manthelan we turned off by the small Elf garage and bumbled happily down the small lane. A slight air of tension gripped the two of us as we were about to find out if it was better to travel than to arrive.

"There's the sign," said Rambo and he pointed to an arrow shaped board which had emblazoned across it - Le Lac Fumant.

I signalled left, cut across the other side of the road and we headed down an appealing leafy lane. At the bottom there was a car park and away to the right, down a footpath, we could see the converted cottage. I parked the car and turned off the engine and looked over at Rambo and gave him a broad grin.

"We're here, mate. We've made it in one piece and it's only twelve-thirty. Not bad going at all. Come on, let's go and have a quick look shall we?"

"Too right," said Rambo. "It looks like the previous lot of anglers have already gone and our bunch yet to arrive, we might be able to go round the place on our own and suss it out a bit."

I could sense that Rambo was champing at the bit and had his carp fishing head well and truly screwed on. Carp fishing's deadly duo, as I sometimes liked to imagine ourselves but only to myself and when in moments of self-delusion, leapt from the car and headed to the lake via the footpath. No-one was around the cottage so we just followed the path which slightly descended once it had passed the cottage. As we walked down the path it felt pretty warm, much warmer than it had been at home, a fact underlined by a lack of any sort of wind. Being a coastal living resident it is usually one of the first things I notice about being inland, there would be no south-westerlies ripping in off the sea that was for certain. I felt my tee-shirt start to stick to my back and perspiration beading on my forehead, whether this was solely down to the heat or the certain amount of tension I was feeling was unclear. In a matter of moments I would be casting my eyes on what we had travelled all this way to cast into. Would it live up to my sky high expectations?

The path entered a small cluster of trees that tantalisingly hid everything ahead of it and then, as we came through them, Lac Fumant opened up before us. Our eyes filled with a vision of heaven. It was majestic. It was everything that Bob had said and more, it was everything I had hoped for times two, maybe even three and believe me I had hoped for a lot, I was that greedy kid at Christmas. Come to think of it, Lac

Fumant was your best ever Christmas present, your most amazing night out, your most phenomenal sexual experienced all rolled up into one great big, mind-blowing package. Above all else it really did look to be the ultimate carp fishing venue. As we stood dumbstruck by the exquisite vision that lay in front of us a big carp, a possible thirty by Rambo's reckoning, topped out no more that twenty five yards from the bank.

We started walking around gabbling with excitement to each other and pointing and gesticulating to features, fish signs and actual fish. The place was packed with some very big carp some of which showed themselves as they topped out or nudged through the pads. The pads, and there were quite a few sets, gave the lake that special look. Perhaps it was their spread of greenness that contributed more than any one single thing to the overview of splendour. Monet would have wet his pants. The lake had a nice array of other features, there were areas of tree-lined margins, weedbeds and three islands which themselves had features around their margins. All the islands were within easy casting reach, no more than seventy yards tops from the closest bank. They were big enough for ten people to have a couple of baits on them without posing any hassle to anyone else. The water was awesome and its colour, a muddy chocolate, although in itself not especially lovely, hinted at the amount of fish that were grubbing up the bottom.

The lake was similar to a figure of eight with two large circles intersecting but narrowing at the waste to make the shape. One of the islands was in the middle of that narrowing and could be hit from either bank whereas the other two could be cast to from the closest bank but were a good one-fifty plus from the other bank. I immediately thought that my bait boat could be used to come in from a side that would be less likely to have been fished. Bob had indicated that there was no provision for a rowing boat so that augured well for my fiendish carp catching concept. Apart from that single idea the whole lake was so perfect from a fishing point of view it seemed difficult to see one swim as being more advantageous than the other. It was impossible to pick a swim that didn't look 'carpy' for want of a better expression and in keeping with this the fish did seem to be spread right across the lake. What one swim might not have in terms of easy island access it made up for in the perceived quality of its margins, pads and weedbeds. The weedbeds seemed to just be that, large black areas of dense weed with the rest of the water apparently clear. It was the most complete water I had ever set eyes on and one that I felt, despite my abstinence from the rods, I could fish well. This was no sprawling, barren, pit with hidden underwater features, this was a classic carp water, the type of which has been written about time and time again. I just hoped that the carp had read the book and would do what it said they should.

The banks were covered in lush green grass and although you could see where anglers had fished you could tell that the place had only been subjected to light pressure. If I could have picked my spot there and then I would have been struggling. Even Rambo admitted that he would have been spoilt for choice and concluded that a word with Bob could be most enlightening.

"Perhaps there'll be a draw for swims," said Rambo, teasing me.

I physically and mentally winced but it did make me wonder how Bob would decide where the ten of us would fish. Rambo and I would be at a distinct disadvantage seeing as all the others had previous knowledge of the lake. Still we would no doubt find out fairly soon.

We carried on walking around the lake's edge like two Adam's in the Garden of Eden. If ever there was a place that would start to convince me of the benevolent hand of an Almighty Being then the splendour of Lac Fumant was that place. But then on the other hand why allow any disease, hook pulls and snap-offs? Appeasement by human sacrifice could be the answer to pacify our malevolent God and I knew several carp anglers who I'd be more than happy to offer up. Luckily none of them would be spoiling this holiday.

We completed the journey around the lake's perimeter and started back up the path. I had never felt so hyped up about the idea of fishing a specific water but walking up that path a fire was raging inside me. I wanted to run back down with all my gear and start fishing that instant. The excitement, my enforced break and what I had just witnessed with my own two, bulging eyes had left me aching to cast a rod. It was going to be a tremendous holiday but I wanted it to start now. The introduction party was going cause excruciating delay to the whole thing, I felt as if I needed to commence tout de suite.

The feeling of frustration mounted inside me but I managed to contain it. I had waited long enough and when I reflected on the wave of luck that had swept me like some serendipitous surfer on an unbreakable board of bedazzling betterment, I couldn't grumble at my few extra hours of delay. Well I could but it would be a bit pathetic.

As we reached the cottage a voice shouted out. "All right, chiefs!"

It was Bob waving from the door, beckoning us over to him. He was wearing an old tee shirt that had the words, 'O Lord help me to keep my big mouth shut until I know what I'm talking about.' It looked ancient, all faded and slightly threadbare around the collar. He also sported a back to front baseball cap, cut down denim shorts and a pair of black plimsolls that young children wear in PE. You know the type? The ones that they wouldn't be seen dead in once they're old enough to understand adverts and the absolutely vital concept of the £50 training shoe.

We walked over to him. Bob came out from the doorway and held a hand up to the sky. "Quality weather, eh?"

As we nodded our agreement another figure appeared from the door, and what a figure it was. You could tell it was a good figure because it didn't have much on to hide it up, just a tight, white crop top and short skirt. The young girl was drop-dead gorgeous and she moved in a lithesome manner that convinced you that she knew that you knew that she was drop-dead gorgeous. She was young, nineteen maybe twenty, but I felt reduced to an incoherent, spotty adolescent under the onslaught of her voluptuous beauty. My eyes drank in her amazing body as she came and stood alongside Bob. Just when I was convinced that I'd had my fill of beauty, that my desire for visual stimulation had been sated, I realised I was wrong. I wanted more and had to let my eyes run over her again and again. She had lovely, square white teeth that were enhanced by her golden tan and her long, bra-strap length blonde hair shimmered with vitality. Just to the side of her belly button she had a small black tattoo that looked like oriental writing and on her perfectly manicured fingers she had several rings including one on her right thumb. She was something else.

"This is Rebecca, my daughter," said Bob proudly. "Rebecca this is Matt and Rambo, if I remember correctly."

Rambo and I nodded.

"Hi, boys," said Rebecca smiling. "Nice to meet you, Rambo and you too, Matt."

Her manner was easy and confident. We made eye contact as she said my name and my heart skipped along a bit faster. Her eyes were a deep brown and had burnt through me like a laser through butter. Whatever swam in Lac Fumant couldn't possibly be as big a catch as her.

CHAPTER 6

Bob ushered Rambo and I inside the cottage and into a spacious dinning room. There was a large table that was heaving under the weight of a pile of food, a cold buffet that would grace any occasion, let alone a carp fishing introduction party. We had put on our name badges, rather self consciously I might add, and helped ourselves to sandwiches, some quiche, crisps, chicken drumsticks, cocktail sausages and a soft drink. Rebecca had floated off to the kitchen and I sneakily spun a glance at Rambo to see if he was looking at her arse as she walked off. He then looked across to check out if I was checking out her arse but of course I was already checking out him, checking out me, checking out him, checking out her arse having previously checked out her arse myself. I pulled one of those faces that indicates supreme sexual allurement and Rambo nodded.

"There's a mile of food. Are you sure there's only ten anglers coming?" I said to Bob trying to start up small-talk. I wondered whether he was aware of the ogling that his daughter must get from all the anglers who fished his water.

"You haven't met Luke and Greg. If you left them they'd eat that lot on their own . . . Oh look! It's Ian. All right, chief!" and Bob walked over to greet the newcomer who clearly wasn't.

I looked over casually to see a bloke in his mid-thirties sided by the largest rottweiler I had ever clapped eyes on. It was enormous, its head was the size of a basketball and what was more it was coming towards me. Bob was plainly going to introduce Ian to myself and Rambo and the mutt was coming as well. Unsure what to do and if the truth was known, slightly paralysed by fear, I stood my ground as the dog reached me and then bent its head down to start nuzzling around my groin area.

"Who's found a friend then?" said Ian. "He likes you, Matt, does my Spunker."

At least Ian could read name badges. I'd met a few dog-on-a-string-types who couldn't even do that. Mind you this was a case for dog-on-a-hawser and as for the name. What was all that about?

Still somewhat confused by what Ian had said my mind was soon whisked off the subject because my feet were whisked off the ground and I was more concerned about what the bloody hell was going on. The dog had pushed his nose between my legs and lifted me clear of the ground by raising his huge head and I was now balancing in mid-air, legs spread-eagled, the fulcrum of which, was my scrotum. The dog was now a seal and I was the ball on the end of his nose, or rather my balls were on the end of his nose with my full weight on them. It was not a position for bargaining or for radiating dignity.

"It's his party trick," explained Ian to Rambo. "Spunker loves lifting people up."

Rambo looked at me in bewilderment as I tottered tantalisingly on my testicular tackle. I saw Rambo's face harden and his eyes narrow. A look of cold aggression came over him, it was how I used to remember him before we became friends and how he was during much of the syndicate time.

"Does he like being lifted up?" asked Rambo.

"Hmmm. Nobody's ever tried it," admitted Ian.

With that Rambo got hold of the dog's stumpy tail with one hand, yanked him backwards causing me to crash to the ground and then grabbed his collar with the other hand. He then clean and jerked the dog right above his head. The expression on the dog's face was a picture, it had never been treated like a rag doll before but Rambo had chucked his huge bulk up in the air with consummate ease. Here was the true Rambo uncloaked, like a weightlifter holding a bar he held Spunker upside down, legs up to the ceiling, way above his head until he got three green lights and then he put him down. Fairly gently it must be said and the right way up. The dog recovered part of its pride, recalled its image and turned and glowered at Rambo who held his stare. It growled menacingly but then backed down and went and sat at Ian's side. Great start I thought. My best mate was involved in a personality clash with a large dog about who was the toughest, meanest son-of-a-bitch.

Ian seemed unconcerned about the whole incident and enthusiastically explained why he brought Spunker on all his carping trips.

"I owe that dog," he told me. "He saved my life you know."

Ian went on to tell me how one morning Spunker had chewed through the electric cable of his alarm clock radio and had not been woken because of it. Consequently he had not caught the train to work as usual and had been spared the horrific rail crash that had happened. Over forty people had lost their lives.

"I think he'd had a premonition you know and that was his way of saving me."

"What about him gnawing on 240 volts?" I asked.

"Yes. His coat stood up on end for about a week after and his eyes have never really lined-up properly since then but apart from that he's as right as rain. He doesn't chew cable anymore, either. Mind you he chews everything else, he chewed through the water main last week, the house got flooded. I've had to buy stainless steel buzz bars because he can get through aluminium and mild steel. Funnily enough he never chews anything in his own bivvy."

"His own bivvy?" I asked slowly.

"He's a big dog and he needs his own personal space," Ian explained matter of factly.

I marked Ian and Spunker, I couldn't face asking why he'd called him that, down as a pair of nutters but once off the subject of his life-saving hound he did provide me with info about the rest of the lads that were coming. He said that they were a great bunch and that we'd have a real good time with them and definitely have some laughs. They were all 'characters' and not just boringly normal like him. I nearly choked on my drink at that one. The two guys Luke and Greg, who Bob said would eat all the food, were a real couple of lardies. Forever having fry-ups and forever breaking bedchairs they were affectionately known (supposedly) as the Fatboys. Then there was the Cowboy who was not only besotted with carp fishing but also with the wild west. He came from St Austell in Cornwall which was west all right, if not wild. Or perhaps it was? There was Japp and Vim, the two Dutch brothers who had met Bob purely by chance and told him of the potential of his newly acquired fishery, and Alistair and Paul. Seemingly these last two were at opposite ends of the mental acumen rainbow and whereas Alistair had the pot of gold, Paul had the crock of shit being as thick as it. Alistair, Ian told me in hushed tones of great reverence, was the most lucid, intelligent carp angler he had ever met. He was known as a 'thinker', Paul on the other hand was more likely to apply warmth to heat-shrink tubing via a blowtorch. Paul had been caught sitting in a fully zipped up bivvy with his butane/propane gas stove on full blast and once during a terrible storm had tried to pull some downed electric cables away from his rods with a carbon fibre landing net handle. He was known as a 'thanker' because that was what he was forever doing after someone else had got him out of his self-constructed, shark infested, pool of high danger. Paul was twenty-one which was tantamount to a miracle by the sounds of it.

While deep in conversation with Ian, the room had filled with some of the people he had talked about. The Fatboys were very well named and the two lads in the Ajax football shirts could safely be assumed to be Japp and Vim. Rebecca was back in the room and greeting the four lads with kisses to cheeks and hugs. For some insane reason a pang of jealousy shot through my soul.

Ian started to ramble on. "That Rebecca, she's a cracker isn't she? She's always flirting and flaunting it about as well."

'Not with me she isn't,' was the pathetic notion in my head.

"Of course those two Dutch lads keep on at her all the time. They want her to go and do some work for them, well their dad really. Actually they wanted Spunker as well but no way. No way."

I had no idea what Ian was on about but then another figure arrived, a slim chap with greying hair in his early forties. He had a concerned look on his face, the thinker, perhaps?

"Here's Alistair. Look, I'll catch up with you later, er... Matt. By the way, nice car that Fiat of yours, bet it made a change using it without the baby seats and all the kids."

"I haven't got any kids . . ." I began but he was gone.

Gone to pray at the temple of carp fishing knowledge that was Alistair by the looks of it. Along with all the others. Everyone except Rambo and myself had moved, iron filing to magnet, next to Alistair. Rambo came over to stand next to me.

"There's going to be trouble," he said.

"Who with?" I asked with a voiced tinge with disappointment, my heart starting to sink.

"That dog," said Rambo.

I gave Rambo an old fashioned look but I could tell he wasn't joking although the relief of him saying that it was Spunker and not one of the carpers made me want to laugh.

"There can only be one physically supreme person in a group. Ordinarily in a group like this everyone would know that it was me and that would be the end of it, it's a sort of dominant male thing. Now with that dog entering into the equation, it wants to be the dominant male and sees me as a challenger."

"Come off it. That type of thing doesn't work inter-species," I said, feeling that Rambo had flipped.

Unperturbed he carried on. "That dog thinks it's human. Something has happened to that dog to seriously jangle it's brain. Believe me, I know about animals, I've shot enough of them and most of them were human. War brings out base instincts. I know about base instincts."

Why Rambo was theorising, I could see Rebecca was coming away from the crowd and walking towards us over the top of his shoulder. It was another base instinct that was forming in my mind as my eyes feasted upon her boobs, no bra underneath the crop top and her long, tanned legs.

"The mutt did get two-forty volts through its chomping tackle a few years back," I said quickly as Rebecca flowed magnificently across the floor as yet unnoticed by Rambo who had his back to her.

"Case proved," said Rambo triumphantly.

Rebecca pulled up alongside Rambo and squeezed his right bicep with a saucy sort of smile on her gorgeous face.

"You're very powerful aren't you," she said in a voice laced with seduction.

I time travelled back to being fourteen as Rambo turned to see who had dared laid a hand on him. My God she had one amazing body.

"I saw what you did to that dog. Very impressive," she cooed.

Rambo looked a bit lost for words under the onslaught of such laudation from one so lovely.

"He's a big, strong boy," I blurted and wished I'd kept my stupid gob firmly shut.

Maybe my year and a half locked up with a load of men had stripped me of what little skill I had in fraternising with the female sex. Whatever the reasons I was sounding like Mr Superklutz.

Rebecca gave me a weak smile. God knows what she was thinking of me.

"Look, I'm just about to get the alcoholic drinks. Would you prefer wine or lager?"

I was about to ask for a coke, a bag of crisps and to go outside and sit in the car until mum and dad had finished drinking but I managed to tell myself that I was twenty-eight not fourteen. What was the matter with me? One cracking bit of stuff in my presence and I fell apart at the seams. Eventually I managed to ask for a lager like Rambo had. Rebecca departed, the pair of us watching her go.

"Ever seen anything much nicer than that?" I asked Rambo.

Rambo pushed out a bottom lip as he considered my question. "Nah," he agreed.

Rebecca bought back our drinks, gave us both a radiant smile and went off to mingle with the others. Within the half hour a stetson-hatted individual and gormless looking youth had arrived to make up our full company. The ten of us were all present and correct.

During the party all the other lads went out of their way to talk to Rambo and myself. It would have been easy for them to clique-up and ignore us as they were all old friends who hadn't met for a while but they made the effort. Apart from Ian telling me his dog's life story we were soon talking about our common interest. Rebecca. No, no. Carp fishing! Everyone to a man was expecting to catch some good fish and everyone said that Lac Fumant was the best fishery they had ever visited. For most of them it had been virtually a year since their last visit apart from Japp and Vim who had fished the water in early April. There was much speculation as to whether someone would catch the water's first fifty.

Japp and Vim spoke excellent English with a slight American accent and with a 'sh' for 's' and 'v' for 'w' but apart from that they were nearly always word perfect. They said that they had seen a couple of fish that would be candidates for the spot by the light switch on Pup's wall. I told them that Rambo and myself had taken a quick look at the lake and had spotted loads of fish. We thought the water was magical and looked amazingly prolific.

"You see, Matt we have fished the water many times," said Japp. "But we have caught or seen caught maybe only twenty-five percent of the fish. While we are not at the water maybe another fifty percent have been caught. Bob has told us of the catches while we are not here, most of them are by people here today or their friends but that still leaves a large number of fish that haven't been hooked. And amongst those fish are some of the bigger ones. Alistair thinks that there is a lot of natural food and that is why it isn't so easy. You see, the fish don't really need our bait and that is why the water is harder than you might think it would be with so many uncaught or lightly caught fish. If you are a reasonable angler you will catch but don't think it will be a fish every hour. You will have fun as well when the fish aren't biting. There are some very funny people here, especially the Cowboy. He will . . . Crack you up as you say."

"You see, Matt," said Vim taking off from where his brother had stopped. "We are all good friends. We may make fun of each other but it is not nasty. Poor Paul, he gets the worst of it because he is young and not very clever, and even Alistair, who is as good a carp fisherman as you would ever meet, can be made fun of. We hope you and Rambo will join in our fun and catch many fish. Having a good time and catching carp is what our two weeks at Lac Fumant is to be about."

I reminded myself what had happened during my last carp fishing exploits but this seemed to be turning out totally different. These blokes really did seem genuine. Was it a charade? To good to be true? Or was my luck just rolling on.

"How will we decide who fishes where?" I asked Japp and Vim.

"Bob decides. There is a tradition which I think he will continue," said Japp. "But we will know shortly. Come and meet Alistair."

Japp and Vim introduced Rambo and myself to Alistair and we shook hands. He did have the look of someone who gave life a lot of consideration, he had dark eyes that seemed to flit from one thing to another very quickly. Intense was the word that sprang to mind. He had deep vertical creases in the skin between his eyebrows. Here was a man who could concentrate.

"Ah! You're our new guests," he said pumping mine and then Rambo's hand enthusiastically. "I have something for the pair of you that you may find helpful. I'll tell you what it is first and then you can decide whether you would like it or not."

With that he reached into a small rucksack and pulled out some A4 sized sheets of paper. I looked quizzically at Rambo who raised his eyebrows up and the corners of his mouth down.

"If you would like them, these bits of paper have on them a detailed map of Lac Fumant. They show depths, features, known spots where takes have been had and at what times those takes have happened. Also marked are my surmised carp patrol routes as I have established them during my visits here and conversations with others who have fished here. On the back there are a list of baits that have been successful. Now I know some lads like to work out that type of thing for themselves but if you would like to have as much information as myself on paper, you are more than welcome to have a copy each. I know it can be difficult on a new water, especially in a holiday situation when you come in blind. Not that this lake is hard or that it hasn't many obvious angling opportunities but I think it's always nice to know that fish have been caught from certain areas. Naturally I hope that you can come up with some spots of your own to add to the pool of information. These drawings simply bring you up to speed with the rest of us in terms of previous successes and are a handy guideline. You have to think of these things, you see."

Japp and Vim grinned at the last few words but the reason was lost on me. I would have ripped Alistair's arm off for a copy but decided to see if my senior fishing partner concurred.

"Nice one," said Rambo and took a couple of copies.

"Yeah. Cheers," I said

"Excellent," said Alistair. "We'll have a little chat about some of the best rigs a bit later, not that you need to be over elaborate or ultra sophisticated. Just for now perhaps it would be nice for you to at least be introduced to everyone. Now, who haven't you met? Clint? Have you met Clint?"

"Clint the cowboy?" Rambo said hardly disguising a smile.

"Yes," said Alistair. "Clint. The Cowboy. He is our main subject of ridicule apart from Paul, the Fatboys and that blessed dog of Ian's. Bob gets some stick for his ridiculous tee shirts and 'all right, chief's' and the less you know about those Dutch boys' father's business the better. Me? I guess I over analyse everything. Never

53

happy to just accept why it happens I've got to know the ins and outs of it. I see complications everywhere, I have to have theories for the why's and wherefore's. I work for my triumphs in carp fishing through logical thought application. I would love to be more spontaneous but I'm afraid that just isn't me. I just have to think of these things." He looked down at the floor in slight embarrassment. "I'm talking too much as usual, let's meet the others,"

So Rambo and I met Clint in Alistair's company. His real name was Clint believe it or not and he hated being called by it. Although he did idolise Mr Eastwood, as his father had done, he wanted to be called the Cowboy. He wanted to be the carp fisherman with no name. He so wanted to be the carp fisherman with no name that he had purposely bought custom built rods that you could have your name put on the butt. Then he had told the rod builder to put no name on them. Not 'no name' in nice joined up transfer writing under the lacquer, but no name. A blank space. A little area of non-inscribed butt.

The scope for ridicule was as Alistair had said. The Good, the Bad and the Mental. For a Few Brain Cells More. A Fistful of Bullshit. High Buffoon. The Magnificent Dickhead. The list seemed almost endless. The Cowboy wore cowboy boots, naturally, black jeans, a maroon shirt and a black leather waistcoat. As a role model on the clothes front the Virginian crawled from the depths of my foggy memory as a cowboy who wore similar attire. I could have been wrong but it was clear that the Cowboy tried desperately to live out his fantasy. Maybe he was a desperado. If only his name was Dan and he ate cow pies made by his Aunt Maggie and shaved with a blowtorch. That would be fine and Dandy.

Next to Alistairs' all thinking 500watt halogen light, Paul was 10watt nightlight – .that had been turned off. Alistair gave us a brief résumé of his life because Paul seemed unable or unwilling to tell it himself. He was as stupid as they come, superficially that was, Alistair had surmised. He had hypothesised that Paul did have it in him to be a useful human being but just couldn't relate to people. Paul was barely coherent in conversation but able to use a Sony PlayStation like a God. He was a games tester for the huge conglomerate and earnt more money than I ever had. He was fine in virtual reality, it was actual reality that was the problem. Given access to computer games at an early age it had been a button-bashing bedroom adolescence. Introverted, uninterested in the real world, Paul had stopped learning about anything that didn't get him to the next level and he wasn't talking spiritual enlightenment. In desperation and in guilt, his parents had given him his first Super Mario toy, his father threatened to chuck him out if he didn't get a job and an outside interest. He had got the job, perhaps the only one he could ever aspire to and chose carp fishing as a hobby because it gave him ample opportunity to play his games on the bank. He could also sit down a lot, Paul tended to get winded when asked to stand.

Unlike his games, the real world was much more dangerous. Game over was cyber death, but a sharp knife actually cut your skin and made you bleed and it hurt.

Perhaps years of playing ever more violent games brilliantly had conditioned Paul into thinking that violence never hurt anyone. Maybe he assumed that you just pressed the new game tag and you miraculously got pieced back together with full energy and nice set of shiny weapons. I made a mental note to get Rambo to tell him what war was really like. It wasn't the impression of the 'thickie Paul' that I had in mind, in fact it was rather sad in a way. Maybe lurking deep in that body there was a human capable of interaction but at the moment he was a danger to himself. His dad had driven him all the way to Lac Fumant. Paul was a genius at Formula One 99 on the PlayStation but he couldn't drive.

Lurking deep in the stomach of Luke there were at least twenty chicken drumsticks. There was a similar volume of food inside Greg. Both of them had a twenty stone habit to support. The pair of them were very fat and it seemed, very happy. They knew they were overweight and didn't appear to give a toss.

"I was really skinny when I was a kid, in fact I used to bulimic," confided Luke, "but I got sick of it."

The pair of them fell about laughing, their folds of flesh wobbling in synchronisation. They both had shaven heads that looked much too small in proportion for the tower of blubber that was beneath them and beads of sweat rolled down their ruddy faces.

"Luke the puke!" said Greg and they laughed even more. I could see that they were going to be a double act. I was loathe to join in their self-mocking piss take in case one of them sat on me and squashed me like a bug.

It was Greg who eventually asked me the question that I'd been dreading.

"So then, Matt. Where've you been fishing over the last couple of years?"

I shifted uncomfortably, not wanting to lie to my new bunch of friendly colleagues but then again not wanting to tell them the grizzly truth. I looked over to Rambo who just looked back. I was on my own on this one, it was my decision as to what I said.

"I haven't done much over the last couple of years, what with other commitments," I said feebly.

"What with all the kids?" asked Greg. "I noticed you had the people carrier in the car park. It was the only car I didn't recognise so I guessed it was yours."

"I haven't got any kids." What was it and that bloody car and kids. It was vehicle stereotyping. "It was more work problems than anything," I lied desperately. I didn't want to start regurgitating all the pus from the syndicate, not amongst this lot.

"What do you two do for a living, then?" said Luke.

I'm a reformed jailbird who's come into loads of money and my mate is an ex-army, ex-mercenary, arms supplier. "We're in construction and demolition, of sorts," I answered eventually.

Later Rambo would say to me, 'construction of a web of deceit and demolition of the truth.' Still, it worked and nobody continued that line of questioning. By now we had all moved into a crescent shaped huddle and opinions were flying thick and fast as at least three different conversations were going on. Japp was saying that he'd stalked a huge fish earlier in the year but had been unable to tempt it on a floater. He was convinced that given how other fish had grown over the three years he and his brother had fished the lake, the fish would be a fifty. Alistair was convinced that someone would catch half a dozen fish over thirty pounds of which at least two would be over forty and I told Rambo that I was getting anxious to get the fishing started.

It was as if Bob had heard my words. I turned to see him climbing onto the food table, which amazingly enough only had a few paltry scraps left and start clapping his hands together.

"All right, chiefs! If I can have some quality attention, please. Now, I think that you've all had a nice sort of chance to get to know our two new mates and chat about old times. But I can see that you want to move onto the fishing and get started. You all know the tradition. The people who have never fished here get the first pick of swims and the rest of you can sort it out amongst yourselves. I would advise Matt and Rambo to let Alistair chose for you. So, as soon as you've got it all worked out get down to that lake and start hauling them out. Good luck my sons!"

Everyone cheered and whistled.

"Well then, Alistair. What do you say?" said Rambo.

"I'm not on the spot, Rambo," Alistair replied with conviction. "I had surmised that this would happen and had given the question prior consideration. Do you want to fish in adjacent swims or are you not worried about that?"

"We'd like to be alongside each other I think. Wouldn't we, mate?" I said.

Rambo nodded to me.

"Ok. In that case, swims neuf et dix. I'll show you them when we walk down and point them out on the map and tell you a bit about them. They, in my considered opinion, are the best two swims to get started on and get some fish under you're belt. A move later on to other areas might be something you'd like to consider but for now that's where I think you should start."

All the others nodded and between themselves with only a little bargaining they sorted themselves out. The Cowboy was in the swim down from Rambo and Alistair in the one above me, the others dotted around the lake. Luke and Greg liked fishing alongside each other as did Japp and Vim. Ian liked fishing alongside the Hound of the Baskervilles so the three loners were Virtual Paul, as I had decided to call him, Alistair and the Cowboy. We all piled out of the room and into the hot, late afternoon sun and headed for the car park. As Rambo and I started to unload the mountain of gear I felt the ache to wet a line start to tug at me. It had been subdued slightly on seeing Rebecca close at hand and meeting the others but now it had returned. This was it. The holiday was about to really start.

CHAPTER 7

In two hours time I had my new home set about me in the most beautiful swim I had ever fished in. Swim neuf was to be my des-res for a duration unknown but a maximum of two weeks. Rambo had let me have first pick out of the two spots that Alistair had recommended and I chose the nine swim because it had a huge tree that I could put my bivvy under some ten yards back from the water's edge. I could see that the heat was going to be a big factor if the sun shone and I wanted the option of somewhere to get out of it. Most swims did have shade but not the expanse that I had and not in the exact location that you would have chose to bivvy up.

Prior to me putting my feet up on the old bedchair there had been the none too brief trauma of gear-lugging from 'A' to 'B.' Ten blokes shifting an amazing amount of kit from the car park to the lake had been quite a giggle. Rambo had, of course, carried a huge amount at his fast pace and no-one had been able to keep up with him. No-one except Spunker, that is. Ian had adapted a special rucksack for him to carry his own bivvy, water bowl, canned dog food and whatever else a dog needed to take fishing. The straps fitted underneath each of the dog's legs with an extra middle one to tighten around its girth, much like a horse's saddle. The rucksack had been divided down the middle so that it naturally balanced itself like a pair of pannier bags. Once tied on, the mutt was loaded to go, it was apt really, he was very nearly the size of a donkey and was now an honorary member of the pack-mule association.

The pair of them actually raced each other down to the lake, it was hilarious and it was on camcorder. There was Rambo striding off like a Terminator robot and the dog trotting along just behind with the two panniers bouncing from side to side. The dog's bandy rear legs showed off his ample set of bollocks to-ing and fro-ing in sync with the panniers. The camcorder shook with my laughter. This dominant male thing was going to run and run. Bizarrely as it might seem maybe Rambo had been right, maybe two-forty volts straight into his teeth and gums had done something very strange to Spunker's brain.

I took a video of everyone setting off and asked them to say a piece to camera, something simple and straightforward like their name and the swim they were fishing. Paul grunted something that could have been construed as his name and swim number or he might have been doing wild animal impressions. It was hard to say. The rest managed to say something intelligible and on the whole, for a group of carp anglers, I was impressed with everyone's ability to remember their own name without resorting to idiot boards.

In keeping with my documentary style I let the camera keep recording as I set off in mid-field with Alistair, Ian, Japp, Vim and the Cowboy. The Cowboy was even bandier than the dog and had perfected the John Wayne gait even when loaded down with tackle. Bringing up the rear of this motley crew were Paul, Luke and Greg. It was all too clear who the fittest people were and it was also abundantly clear who were the most likely heart attack victims. As I was going back up for my second load I met Rambo coming down with his, despite his swim being further on from mine. Rambo was closely followed by Spunker who just tried to keep up with Rambo despite still having the same stuff in his rucksack. Brains and brawn were not of equal measure in this hound and Spunker had taken no notice of Ian's shouts to heel and be unloaded.

I was pretty sure that Rambo was just testing the dog out otherwise he would have walked down with me. He was exerting a bit of pressure on the dog to see whether he was a worthy adversary in the battle for dominant male. Judging by the length of dangling tongue coming out of Spunker's huge pair of chops and Rambo's merely glowing brow it was one-nil to the human race at the moment. Rambo winked at me and said he'd see me in a bit. A little later I passed Luke and Greg taking time out at about half distance. Sweat ran from the pair of shaven-headed porkers and their huge tee shirts were wet through. The pair of them had shorts on and I could see that they were suffering from chaffing of the inside of the thighs, knees and calves. So tree-trunk were their walking appendages and so covered in excess fat that the whole of their legs rubbed together, virtually to their ankles. Luke was a light scarlet colour whereas Greg had graduated to mauve. Their heads looked like overblown party balloons (the small, cheap variety) and I was waiting for a capillary to go pop.

"I'm just going to fry an egg on his head in minute," joked Greg breathlessly.

"Yeah. But I'm going to eat it," wheezed Luke.

I gave them a smile and walked on. It was warm and I was feeling it a bit because I was walking faster than my normal speed, such was my desire to get sorted out and start fishing. We've all been there on that one. Eventually I came to Paul who was absolutely knackered. Whereas the Fatboys were of crimson hue Paul was deathly white. Colour had drained from his cheeks and he was at the stage of nausea. I had seen unfit, older men throw up at the first football training session of the season but I had never witnessed a young man get into the same state through walking. Admittedly he had a bit of weight on his back but come on, here was a lad of twenty-one. A lifetime of inactivity and sitting on his arse in front of a computer game had moulded Paul into both a physical and mental weakling. Rather nastily I felt little compassion for him and I decided I wasn't going to help him. The exercise would do him good, I told myself. Paul probably had fit thumbs but apart from that he was a mess.

Those exertions were now over and I looked around my swim and soaked in the atmosphere. By now even Paul should have managed to be all set up. I imagined all the other nine were feeling like myself, I was in the earthly equivalent of carp fishing heaven. Everything was in its place and I couldn't help but feel smug about my new tackle, especially my new alarms, bivvy, reels, bait boat . . . Oh all right I felt smug about every bit of it. Money may not be able to buy you love (a dubious supposition at the best of times, it could possibly buy you something that you'd be hard pressed to notice the difference) but it could buy you flash fishing tackle. Unequivocally and irrefutably.

I still hadn't cast out although all three rods were boilied-up because Alistair said that he was going to come down once he was set up and run Rambo and myself through the detailed intricacies of swims nine and ten. I was getting restless because I wasn't actually fishing, I would have put all my rods out straight away if it hadn't been for Alistair's offer. Fish were moving in several different areas and I was very fidgety. I told myself to calm down, another half an hour or so wouldn't make any difference after all the time I had waited. I was kidding myself as much as anything and had to occupy my time somehow. When in doubt make a cup of tea. I had just put the kettle on and was beginning to wonder where the bloody hell he had got to when Alistair turned up. I turned the stove off.

"Sorry I took so long," he said aware of how I was feeling. "I always feel that it is vitally important not to rush into things at the start of a long session. An extra hour taken getting everything perfect can save time in the long run. Get it done correctly once and once only, that's my maxim. We are here for two weeks after all. I know some of the others will have chucked out their three rods straight away without stopping to look and analyse or read the water. I tell them all the time but they just can't stop themselves. They can't step back and be objective about what they are doing, you see. To be fair some of them do quite well going with their hunches and gut feelings but I'm afraid that type of thing is not for me and I usually can out-fish all of them." He smiled. "Still, I see that you have waited. Now let me tell you what I can about this swim."

For the next half an hour Alistair gave me a detailed insight into my swim, referring to the map he had made at various points in the lecture. I use the word lecture not because he was talking down to me but in the sense of him being more knowledgeable than me and his great yearning to pass on that information to me. He was very detailed, perhaps too much so for me to take in and remember but I did my best to absorb what he was telling me. After the first five or so minutes Rambo came to join us and listened in silence as Alistair rattled on. Alistair had a look at my rigs and they met with his approval and he said that it was worthwhile fishing at least one pop-up out of the three. He told me what his baiting approach was going to be in terms of the amount of bait he was going to put in and his overall plan or 'big picture' as he called it for the fortnight. So lengthy was his explanation of everything that at one stage I thought I might have to get Rambo to render him unconscious with a bivvy mallet before I ran out of time and had to pack up and go home without actually fishing. Eventually he did finish and I thanked him. He was a smashing, genuine bloke but I could see why the others ripped the piss out of him for being so prolix.

Once my little teach-in had concluded Alistair went down with Rambo to his swim which was only about thirty yards from mine. Swims nine and ten were the closest adjacent swims on the lake. While they were gone I cast my three rods and put out my freebies. I heroically remembered to take the bail arm over every time I cast and to put the anti-reverse on each of the three baitrunners and to put the baitrunner on. I then remembered to turn on the alarms and my remote sounder box and give them all a tweak to see if they worked. I enthusiastically rubbed my hands together. Matt Williams - carp angler - was back and it felt good. Damn good.

I had used my fourth rod as a marker for the left hand rod, employing one of those large battery powered marker floats, for the obvious reason that this was the furthest cast of the lot and was the open water spot. I had clipped this rod up and made a mental note of the angle of the cast from my buzz bars to a large tree on the middle island that I hoped would still be visible against the skyline at night. The actual baited rod I had cast out and clipped up the distance as well so that I should be fairly accurate all round on that one. The margin rod would be no problem to re-cast at night and the middle rod was sided by the pads and I was casting level with them which I reckoned I could get close enough without resorting to clipping up. Also I wanted to be deliberately vague with casting distances and direction just as a variation. No doubt Alistair would have frowned at such a cavalier attitude but that was what I intended to do.

I was in one of the swims that didn't have easy casting to one of the three islands, apparently it was a good hundred and fifty yards to the island margin. The bankside margin to my right had several smallish trees and branches that hung over the lake by about four or five foot. A careful underarm lob had positioned the right hand rod directly under those branches. Alistair had told me that it was an excellent day-time spot because of the cover and also a good night-time bet as well. The carp in Lac Fumant evidently did a fair bit of nightly margin prowling. Out to the right in front of me were two large sets of pads with approximately fifty yards between them at a similar sort of distance out from the bank. The game plan, Alistair's game plan, was to fish the middle rod smack in middle of the two sets of pads during the night and then come in tight to either set during the day when I could sit on top of my rods. Fishing tight at night-time was a non-starter unless you were capable of light speed movement out of a sleeping bag and down the ten or so yards to hit the rods. My left hand rod could either fish the left hand set of pads during the day or go into the same area as the middle one at night. Alistair had said that the patrol route out of the left hand set of pads went away from me heading towards the middle island down past Rambo's swim. He therefore recommended a nice bed of baits about seventy yards out in open water for the left hand rod. A suck it and see evaluation as to the best place for the left hand rod i.e. pads or patrol route during the day was suggested. My three casts had been right margin, middle of the two sets of pads and open water patrol route but similar to a megalomaniac general my eyes looked further afield. To the distant island and invasion by bait boat in a few days time.

From my swim the view was wonderful and awe inspiring. I could look out over

60

the marvellous sets of pads to the densely wooded island, then, scanning up to the right, the island finished and I could see to the far bank. I could follow the curve of that bank as it turned back towards me almost until it straightened and became my margin some two hundred yards away to the right. The trees under which I had cast obscured my sight line to look back down into that corner. The Fatboys were the only anglers I could see on that far bank and their swim was the closest one to the path that lead back up to the cottage and car park. Perhaps they had picked that closest swim because they realised that they would be blown out from the tackle run. Virtual Paul, unable to represent himself with any force, being unable to converse with anything that didn't have a keyboard or control console, would have been made to struggle on a bit further but I wasn't sure where.

Alistair was to the right, hidden by the trees and Rambo close to the left. Looking out to the left the island stopped almost in line with my swim and I could look down and see the bank ease out into the lake slightly. This was pretty much the lake's centre and the bit that gave it the figure '8' shape. This was where Rambo was fishing. I could also see across the lake to the other side where there was a gap between my island and a smaller one which lay to Rambo's left. On that bank, Ian and Spunker were set up. Down to the left further still lay the bottom end of the lake, the end opposite to the path, where there was the third island. At the edge of that island, the edge which was pointing towards the middle of lake, was the Cowboy's swim. I could just see him from the water's edge looking over the top of Rambo's bivvy because the margin eased back in line with my bit of bank once past Rambo. If I gazed past the left hand end of the final island I could just see the very far curve of the bottom bank. The two bivvies there were Japp and Vim's, they were almost side by side as Luke and Greg's were. This meant that the only two anglers I couldn't spot were Alistair and Virtual Paul. I put all of that down on 8mm tape, videoing the whole view from my swim and zooming in on my fellow carp anglers giving a brief description of who was who just to tie in with their little bits to camera that they had done earlier.

An hour after I had cast out Alistair walked back up from Rambo's swim.

"Now to go and put all my theories to the test," he said laughing. "Incidentally," he started off again coming over to my bivvy, "I had to smile to myself when one of the others asked about you having children because of the type of your car. I knew that you certainly wouldn't take away your partner's main mode of transport if you had the number of children a car like that dictates that you should have. I expect you hired it didn't you?"

Yes, Sherlock. "Yes, that's right," I said.

Alistair smiled and tapped his nose. "You've got to think of these things, you see. Good luck."

"You too."

At last I could really relax now that I had been informed, to say the least, and was wetting a line. I re-lit the stove and sat back and admired the view. The sun was just starting to set and it was beginning to get murky but the temperature was still comfy enough for just a tee-shirt. I quickly ran the camcorder for a final ending scene to the first day and then put it back in its case. A feeling of great joy filled my soul. The setting, my companions and, not to put too fine a point on it, my bank balance were all A1. The unfortunate last few years of my life seemed eons ago, it was a new era, a re-birth into something much finer. A quick prick into the forearm with a stringer needle revealed it to be true. This was no dream, no fantasy, it was authenticity personified. Maybe I was living out many people's fantasy, that much was true but it was happening to me, Matt Williams. I shook my head with a touch of incredulity, not out of disbelief of my circumstances more of how it had all come about. Or, more pointedly, what it had all come out of. Just call me Mr Phoenix.

If I started hauling in carp then things would be complete. No. Maybe if I started hauling in carp and caught a fifty then things would be complete. No! Let's go for broke. Maybe if I started hauling in carp, caught a fifty and Rebecca started to come on to me then things would be complete. I smiled to myself at the very idea. The steam from the kettle was billowing out into the now still evening air. The sun had turned ruddy and the tea that I made from that boiling water tasted like nectar. I dug out a chocolate digestive from the cool box and sat on my bedchair drinking in the ambience and the tea. It was magical. A sudden beep from my middle rod nearly caused a heart attack and half a mugful of tea slopped to the edge but amazingly never went over. I walked down to the water's edge and studied the middle rod's tip. In the fading light I could just make out a slight nod but with no audible back up this time. Fish on the bed of freebies? Whatever, it was a good sign. Although not claiming to be any sort of expert in reading the carp fishing tea leaves I had always associated liners and beeps with more chance of a run than no knocks or nudges at all. I wondered if I dared quickly nip down to see Rambo. I had the trusty remote sounder box. As I decided that I did dare I mused that one day they'll make one that instantaneously transports you back to your rods when you have a take and they'll produce a cloaking device for all terminal tackle.

I soon reached Rambo's bivvy. He was inside it on his bedchair.

"All right, mate," I asked.

"Yeah, fine."

"I thought I'd just nip down to see you before it got dark. I've just had a knock on my middle rod, if you hear a scream for help that'll be me needing assistance with a monster carp."

"Not you screaming at Rebecca to get her clothes on and leave you alone, then?"

"I doubt it," I said frankly.

"The way your luck's going anything's possible. I'll tell you what, though. This is one hell of a fucking water. If we catch half what I think were going to catch it'll be a session never to forget."

"Most of my sessions seem unforgettable for one reason or another," I snorted. (See 'The Syndicate' (advertisement))

"Yeah. But this will be for the right reasons, not the wrong ones."

I nodded enthusiastically. "What do you think of the others?" I asked.

"Alistair's a windbag all right, but he knows his stuff and how many other blokes would give you all the info like he has? Not unless it's one almighty bum steer wind up, which I know it isn't, how many other places would two newcomers like us be given such a fair crack? Especially as they're all paying out good money for it as well. No, they all seem pretty sound blokes to me and I can usually suss people out, the bullshitters and such like. The young boy.."

"Virtual Paul?" I interjected.

"Yeah, I mean he's a pretty pathetic case but that's all, I'd like to have him for a bit of assault course training. I expect he'd be tasty at anything like flight simulator's and tank training simulators but he couldn't sprint ten yards if his life depended on it. The rest of the lads are going to turn out ok, I think that there's going to be some dumb behaviour, but nothing nasty or underhand. They'd all help you out if you needed them ... but we won't need them. These fish haven't tasted our all-conquering bait yet but when they do it'll be action all the way, boy." Rambo's voice abruptly turned cold from its previous up-tempo air. "The dog is the only thing around here that I'm not struck on. That animal needs a good lesson and I'm just the vicious bastard to give it to him."

My remote sounder box that was clipped to the top of my tracksuit bottoms emitted a double bleep. A quick look at the l.e.d.'s showed it was the middle rod again.

"I'd better get back. My first run may be imminent. Do you know it's nearly two years since I last had a take?"

"I bet a lot of those hard water boys would jump at a record like that."

"I'll catch you later, Rambo. Give me a shout if you need help and vice versa, ok? I think it's going to be hot again tomorrow. Have you got shorts with you?"

"Yep."

"What camouflage ones?" I asked.

Rambo gave me a 'do you really have to ask such a stupid question' look and I laughed and slapped his shoulder. It was like smacking cast iron.

"Good luck, mate." I said.

I walked back to my bivvy, it was almost dark by now and the night was perfect. As I looked over to the far bank a couple of the bivvies could still be made out because of a light inside them which made an eerie, soft, greenish glow which was pleasant to look at. Not a millennium dome but a bivvy dome. Once inside my bivvy I sat in total darkness for a while. Although I knew that I was very tired from the early start and the long drive I couldn't contemplate sleep. I just sat on my bedchair with the back up and the bottom out, arms folded and gazed through the doorway of my little home out into the night.

My mind wandered all over the place, it was a swirling tub of sub-conscious ideas and every now and then a specific notion would rise to the top and into my conscious. It would stay for a while before the undertow of my brain dragged it back down only for another idea to bob to the surface and take its place. Large carp, or rather the concept of large carp, must be unusually buoyant because that thought came to the top time and time again. The Rebecca idea had a lifejacket on but a slight trace of guilt sank her and Sophie always popped up directly after and then Sophie's mum and that cheque for two hundred and fifty grand. The more tired I got the more random and spectacularly stupid my thinking process became. I must have almost dozed off when a female voice called out.

"Hello? Matthew?" It was Rebecca.

"Oh. Hello, Rebecca. Sorry, I must have just nodded off for a moment."

"I've just come round to see if everyone has settled in ok. Everything fine?"

"Yeah. Great," I said earnestly but in retrospect perhaps a bit too simplistically.

"Good. Any action?"

"I've had a couple of touches on my middle rod," I said in all innocence, the double entendre being completely missed, on my part at least.

"Well . . . lucky old you," she said in a husky voice.

I laughed as much with embarrassment as anything else as I realised what I had said. Sadly my swirling tub of sub-conscious suddenly had the plug pulled out. Whereas just ten minutes earlier my mind was a seething mass of thought, now, when I needed it, all of it had drained from my head leaving it completely vacant. I had nothing and could think of nothing to say. Nothing bobbed to the top, there wasn't even anything to scrape off the bottom. The silence was excruciating.

"Anyway, I'll see you around tomorrow I expect. Who's next down from you?"

"Er . . . Rambo. Rambo's the next one down," I said, flustered.

And she was gone. What the hell was the matter with me? Had my two years of male company taken away all my social skills? If I ever had any in the first place that is. Apart from Sophie and her mum and my mum, Rebecca was probably the only external, for want of a better word, female that I had spoken to in all that time. She was the type of girl who, if I had met her at eighteen, I would have thought I stood no chance with because she would go for someone older. Somebody more sophisticated, more worldly, someone with a nice car while I was stuck on a moped. Now, being older and about the age that I would have thought was the right age when I was eighteen, I reckoned that she would think of me as an old git. An idiot who was passed it and out of touch with the young scene. I had to face it, I would never be the right age for her.

Perhaps the more important thing was why all this was bothering me at all. I had come here for the carping holiday of a lifetime and if I could get my carp fishing head on the chances were that I might get it. I had, at home, a woman who had stuck by me through thick and thin and without whom it was debatable if I would have ever survived my recent ordeal. It was because of my relationship with this woman that I was now fishing where I was and had the opportunity of a great life. It was her mother who had won the millions on the lottery, not mine. Yet despite all this I still wanted this girl, this girl who if she had been back in England could have still been at university, to have an interest in me. A sexual interest, let's be honest about what I was thinking about, I mustn't delude myself by kidding myself it was anything else. Perhaps I was still more mixed up about my time inside than I had imagined. I had recovered from it all, or assumed I had but then again maybe I hadn't.

Of course it could be more simple than that. It could be that being away on holiday and free from restraint my dick was exerting a substantial pull on my thought process. Anyway, I expected all the others were going through the same thing, lusting after her in their own way. I resolved to stop it and knock it all on the head. It was madness, there would be no more of it. As I tucked myself deep into my sleeping bag I resolved to throw all my energy, both mental and physical into catching carp and wipe her out of my head. That was it, it was settled.

My head nestled on the pillow and the sounder box nestled on top of my rucksack at the back of my spacious bivvy. Would it go off tonight? Would I get my first fish for nearly two years? I'd have to wait and see. Sleep eventually came and despite all my efforts and promises I had a dream about Rebecca taking her kit off for me because she was so impressed with the fifty pound carp I had just caught. Dream on . . . and I did.

CHAPTER 8

The sound burned itself deep into my head. I had been in a deep sleep but this was the wake up call that I had hoped for. The sounder box was pumping out the decibels at a jet-plane-at-take-off level.

We've all been there, the night-time take, sometimes you're just dozing, other times you may not be asleep at all but just lying in the dark brooding, but this was the most disorientating of circumstances. My fatigue had finally caught up with me and I was sparko until I was so abruptly awoken. I blundered out of the sleeping bag and crawled frantically out of the partially zipped up bivvy door. Staggering down to the rods I could see the middle Delkim l.e.d glowing brightly and the baitrunner was whirling happily away. I instinctively wound round once to take the baitrunner off before striking the rod. (How different from when I had first used the reels, yet despite all that time passing since my last run I still did it automatically. Clicking baitrunners off must be the equivalent of riding a bike, once you get the knack you never forget it).

The rod bent over and I felt the satisfying thump of resistance on the end as a good carp made its surge for freedom. The fish was heading to my left, no doubt making a bee-line for the large set of pads and I cranked the rod over in an attempt to halt the 2.30am Cyprinus carpio express.

It all came flooding back to me. The adrenaline rush, the pounding heart, the weak-at-the-knees feeling and then the questions. How big was it? Would it come off? And all the subtle sub-divisions of that question. Would everything hold, the hook, the line, my nerve? In those few seconds from hearing that buzzer go off to striking into my hidden quarry, I knew why I had a lifetime love affair with carp angling. The wait, although in this instance relatively modest, seemed to emphasise the action when it came. It was an all or nothing type of thing, one minute peace and serenity and a game of wait and see, the next, an all-out, no holds barred, struggle.

"Feel any good?" said a voice in the dark.

It was Rambo who had silently appeared at my side. Undoubtedly his technique had originally been learnt to accommodate the slitting of someone's throat but on this occasion it was just to impress me and get on the landing net handle before I was aware of his existence.

"Not bad, I think. It's hard to tell. I think I've managed to turn and pump it away from those left hand set of pads. It should all be ok from now."

I played the fish in, even if I say so myself, with a reasonable degree of competency considering I was rod rusty and it was night time. The fish fought long and hard but I felt in control all the time, whatever I may think about my time on the old syndicate water, the hours that I had put in had certainly made me a better angler.

Eventually, my first ever foreign carp was ready to land. She was just about discernible as she went onto her side due to the moonlight and Rambo waited for me to guide her over the spreader block and she was landed.

I made the decision to sack the fish until first light, a practise that was widely accepted according to the others. In splendid morning sun I could then ask Rambo to photograph me with the fish and use the camcorder to video me putting her back. What couldn't wait was the weighing. Between us with our torches a weight of 23-6 was settled on, a very nice start. The fish was a mirror and in perfect nick, taking the hook out by torchlight had revealed an undamaged curtain and no previous hooking scars. It was a pleasure to catch such a pristine fish and a pleasure to know that once again our magic boilie was going to do the business. Yes, I had committed the terrible sin of using carp fishing's most hackneyed and overused cliché but who cares. I felt great.

With the fish safely in the sack I went about putting on a fresh boilie while Rambo was giving me a good 'well done' back-slapping which was making it an impossible task.

"Excellent stuff, boy. First twenty on the first night . . ." He stopped and froze solid.

Now he was silent I could hear why he had stopped talking. "Shit! That's my buzzer!" he exclaimed.

And with that he turned and legged it down the bank at a prolific pace. I started to follow but quickly turned back after a few yards to return to my bivvy and pick up my sounder box and torch. Rushing out of the bivvy at full tilt I slipped and went flat on my face into the long, lush grass. I laughed whole-heartedly and picked myself up and pounded down to Rambo's swim giggling like a naughty rang-the-doorbell-and-ran-away schoolboy. When I got to his swim Rambo was into a fish on his left hand rod that had been placed in the margin.

"Feel any good?" I said a bit breathlessly, mimicking his first words to me when he had come out of hyper-space alongside my shoulder.

I caught the wide smile on his face. "Bigger than yours, boy. Bigger than yours."

The pair of us lapsed into silence although I was acutely aware of my rather noisy breathing caused by the short sprint. Rambo played in a fish that if anything was even more determined than mine to keep out of my Lac Fumant video. As Rambo battled the fish I considered a little pet theory of mine about how Rambo had heard his buzzer when I hadn't, at least not until he had brought it to my attention. The theory runs along the same lines of why you hear your name spoken in a conversation you're not involved with while in a crowded room. No other words normally can produce this result and it is accepted as happening because your brain is tuned to specific words that mean a lot to you, like your name, for instance. Another example is the response of a mother hearing the call of her child and being able to distinguish that cry from any other child's. If you are a hardened carp angler the dulcet warble of your bite alarm is the equivalent to that child's cry or the mentioning of your name. Many have compared the carper/buzzer bond to that of the mother and her infant but although the carp angler is sensitive to his particular buzzer brand he cannot distinguish it from other similar ones. The trouble starts and the fun begins when a group of you all have the same sounding whining infant, namely similar brand alarms. This accounts for the 'starburst angling groups' or STAGS as we carp fishing theologians call it. This is when a group of anglers are all standing in a little huddle on the bank, then a buzzer sounds and they all start running off in various directions, each thinking that it is they who have the run. Luckily my child was a Delkim whereas Rambo's little horror was a Fox. It's a crappy theory but it kept my mind off the worry of netting a fifty pounder in the dark that might be on the end of Rambo's hook.

The fifty pounder turned out to be an immaculate common of 27lbs dead which took a good fifteen minutes to subdue due to the invisible propulsion unit it had strapped to its back. Rambo was well happy and decided to sack the fish as I had done to get some nice early morning photos. We thought that maybe we would ask Alistair to video both of us putting the fish back ensemble, as we multi-catch, French anglers say. Rambo had safely put the common into the sack and was just tying the strings of the sack to a bankstick when the small box that was clipped to my jogging bottoms exploded into life.

"Shit! That's my buzzer!" I said. I pinned my ears back and sprinted back up to my swim.

"Go on, my son!" Rambo screamed as I powered out of my grass blocks.

I remember having an even wider grin on my face than when I had bolted the opposite way back down for Rambo's take. The words 'brilliant', 'this', 'fucking' and 'is' were wanging around my brainbox, but not in that order you understand. It was odd having the sounder unit on me, you get used to the noise getting louder as you get back to a run when you've been away but this time it was full decibels from start to finish. I'm sure the noise helped motivate me to shave off a few extra tenths.

It was the left hand rod that had been picked up, the one that was on Alistair's assumed patrol route and it was the rod that had been cast out the furthest of the three. As I hit into this fish it started kiting into the bank from where I had just run up. It felt like the fish was still a fair distance out from the bank so I decided to wind down as fast as I could and walk back down the bank and play the fish out from there. It was either that or probably end up pumping the fish back along the margin. Rambo ran past me as I was slowly coming back towards him, rod in hand, winding all the time to keep a tight line. He had sussed what I was up to and shouted that he'd get the landing net.

Returning to my side he asked, with tongue firmly planted in cheek. "Feel any good?"

I laughed. "That was just a bloody jammy call, you saying yours was bigger. There was no way that you could tell."

"Rubbish!" said Rambo with good humour. "I knew, boy. I knew."

I knew that I didn't know how big this fish was but I was fairly certain it wasn't going to top Rambo's common. True to expectation it turned out to be a plump mirror that was just over 14 but for the crack and the situation it had created it was worth its weight in gold. I decided to take a flash photo of this whippersnapper, or rather Rambo did and I put her straight back.

Once I had carefully done this I turned to Rambo. "Well, come on then. Your turn. Don't start ruining the roll by stopping."

Rambo shrugged his shoulders. "No way. It ain't going to happen . . ." He suddenly dipped a shoulder and half-turned his body as if to run. "Shit!" he cried. "That's my buzzer!"

He continued turning and sprinted a few yards before pulling up and saying very poshly. "Oh no. Sorry. My mistake."

I pulled my jaw off the deck. "You git! You really had me going then." I said chastising him but thinking it was funny.

The pair of us gabbled excitedly for a while before I finally set about getting my two rods back out and Rambo returned to swim ten to get his single one out. I re-cast the marker float first of all and then cast to it which I managed to get at the third attempt and the middle rod went next. This one was a bit hit and miss by design, having decided not to muck about clipping up. What with dawn only a few hours away, I went for a ten bait stringer with one of Pup's pop-ups. I was expecting to change at first light and cast again and put out a bed of baits as soon as I could fire them out accurately. The first attempt with the ten bait stringer went woefully short as I was suckered by the extra air resistance and so I had another go which was still a bit on the short side but passable. I could afford a couple of hours off target and who knows? It might throw up a new spot to consider. Once I was all set I went back to my bivvy and tried to snatch a few hours sleep before the dawn and, according to oracle-Alistair, the best feeding time at Lac Fumant.

My first dawn at Lac Fumant was a beautiful sight to behold. I had dozed off fitfully but there was too much adrenaline pumping around my arterial network for proper sleep and I had been wide awake to watch the night give way to the day. The lake looked even more amazing than it had done the day before and such was my fascination and desire to drink in the whole spectacle, I left the middle rod out much longer than I originally intended. It was like watching a slow motion unveiling of a wonderful piece of art as the light gradually leaked in and revealed the amazing image before me. I just sat and looked and marvelled. I know it sounds a bit crass to revel in the magic of nature and to contemplate the materialistic orgy that 250k in a joint bank account can give you, but I'm afraid that's where my meditation lead me. Either one of those facts would have given me great joy but the contemplation of how fate had dealt me both aces made my little heart sing. I know how pleased you are for me after all I've been through.

As a matter of course what you're now expecting is for me to tell you of the belting run that suddenly happened on the middle rod, which, by all rights, should have been pulled in long ago, yet wasn't, due to me being transfixed by the glory of nature. Not so. This is reality after all and not some novel where the unfeasible can be dreamt up merely to entertain and interest. In fact I had just decided to re-cast the middle rod when I saw the Fatboys pop out, or rather squeeze out, of their respective bivvies. I suppose it was their movement and the bright red and orange tee-shirts and turquoise surf-dude shorts that they were both sporting that caught my eye. I chuckled to myself as I considered Rambo, to my left, who spent his entire life apparently attempting to blend into the background and the two Day-Glo juggernauts on the lake's far bank who clearly weren't interested.

I reached for my binoculars and watched them set up their stove, a fine double burner tool, and proceed to fry at least half-a-pigs worth of bacon and loads of eggs with a frying pan that looked as big as a dustbin lid. Watching them move through the binoculars soon had me shaking with mirth. Neither of them was particularly agile due to their bulk and because their torso's were so huge their arms never hung down straight. Rather they curved outwards like massive bananas following the contours of their blubber and the friction of this meant they were virtually motionless. All movement was laboured and looked a real effort to make happen, which presumably it was. Their bare skin, on both their legs and arms, so at odds to their bright garments, was lily white. Only the faces and bald domes had colour and it was invariably of a reddish hue. The pair of them were sweating already.

Although perhaps slightly deficient in the mobility stakes the Fatboys could eat for England, no sweat. I'll phrase that again; plenty of sweat but with ease. With ease once it was all cooked and ready to eat and about three inches away from their mouths that is. I saw that they had pulled out their bedchairs to sit outside and eat rather than in their bivvies and noticed that they had the world's only pair of custom built, four-legged bedchairs. Extra-reinforced no doubt but with no go-fast stickers down the side.

I suppose it was cruel to laugh at them without them knowing. Fatist perhaps, or even roly-polyist. No-one in life is more derided than the fat person, they don't tend to become advertising role models, only as figures of fun, and show me a fat woman in a fashion magazine and I'll show you the alien bodies from Roswell. Mind you, you have to be very careful about voicing such observations, the way the law courts are judging stress, harassment and discrimination, calling someone a 'fat bastard' will probably set them up for a fifty grand payout. Mention the word 'black' and you could times it by ten, at least. I'd always been of the persuasion that I would be quite happy to be called anything anybody wanted for a tenner, sticks and stones may break my bones and all that. But the compensation culture is alive and well and growing, driven ever onwards by the greed of lawyers, political correctness and the something-for-nothing culture. Not like me, I got my money the hard way. Of course if you get your arm hacked off in an industrial mincing machine or maimed in a war you invariably get a lot less. That's life, no logic and upside down values.

The difference, as I saw it, was that the Fatboys seemed to relish their nickname.

They knew that they were a couple of lardies and didn't seem to care, they seemed happy with the way they were. They were comfortable with their size, mentally if not physically, surely nobody could lug that weight around comfortably. They were a shining beacon of self-worth to the vast majority of us none-perfect, ordinary, no modelling contract, humans. Or then again, perhaps it was a charade and it cut them to the quick every time a sizeist joke was cracked. I hoped not and I warmed to the pair of fat bastards.

You see it was this extra procrastination that willed away another half hour watching the Fatboys, rather than the simple procrastination of watching Lac Fumant greet the day, that got me the run on the middle rod. The run which I shouldn't have got, had I done what I said I would. It was a triumph of fate over planning, of sheer luck pissing all over design, method and strategy. Alistair wouldn't have got a pick-up from this fish, I said to myself as I scrambled, WWII fighter-pilot style, down to my rods. Large lunker loose at eleven o'clock . . . I stopped my line of thinking because I didn't understand my own banter.

As I struck into the fish that was heading for the left hand pads just as the first one had, I heard a voice.

"You in then, chief?"

It was Bob, same reversed baseball cap, same cut-down denim shorts, same plimsolls different tee-shirt.

Me catch heap big carp. Me make big bend in carbon kevlar rod. Me Big Chief Carphaulinrunninglead.

"Yeah. Feels a real good fish," I blurted to the man in the odd tee-shirt. And it did.

The fish was still piling off towards the pads despite me giving it plenty of side-strain and making the clutch slip, which I had pre-set as tight as I dared. I knew it was time to cup the spool with my hand and give it the make-or-break stick that was required. It was the type of situation that I would normally view with trepidation but deep inside me I just felt as if the hook wouldn't pull and I wouldn't get snapped up. I was an oddsbuster and things were not going to go wrong and true to form they didn't. I turned the fish and managed to pump in some line and after a short while I had the fish boiling about in front of me about ten yards out.

By now Rambo had come up from his swim and Alistair down from his. Rambo had picked up the landing net while Alistair and Bob stood a respectful distance back from proceedings, whispering sweet something's in each other's ear. With my little audience, and who knows, maybe a larger one if the opposite bank had woken up or finished eating, I felt the glow of the limelight bathe me. All my recent luck had given me an air of authority and confidence and I played that fish like I had played no other. I felt so cool, so sure, so up for it, it was unreal. I was at the peak of my game, I was Hendrix, Gates, Pele, Nicholas, Jordan, Cundiff??!!

I played the fish off the clutch, the anti-reverse still on, but if it went too far either side for my liking I feathered the spool just increasing resistance enough to pull it back. I moved my right hand off the butt and moved it down the rod towards the tip to shorten the leverage and give me more control. I held the rod up high to buffer the unseen beast that swam in short bursts this way and that beneath it. I was on top form. I knew it and felt it.

At last the fish began to tire and I got a good glimpse of a big mirror. A very big mirror.

"Thirty plus, boy," Rambo calmly whispered.

In days past the sight of such a fish would have made me anxious but not this time. My rod rustiness had gone and the whole pattern of my life had shifted from shit to shit hot. I bided my time, waited for the fish to be completely played out and then carefully eased the huge flank over Rambo's rock steady net. She was in. Rambo gathered the net together below the frame arms and pulled the net out of the water. A close observer may have thought the fish inside was a mere low double, such was his ease but the lump nestling in the bottom of the mesh, once its evident bulk was visible, told another story.

Carefully easing back the mesh, the great fish was shown in all her glory. From a hook hold deep in the bottom lip the bait and the tell-tale piece of tungsten putty three inches from it, told Rambo a little story.

"Pop-up?" he asked quietly.

"Pop-up," I confirmed.

He looked closer. "Pup's?" he queried, recognising that the bait was not one of ours.

"Pup's," I verified.

"Pup's, pop-ups?" He asked, as if wanting a final decisive authentication.

"Pup's, pop-ups." I said, giving it.

Rambo looked away in a slight daze as if he had seen something mystical. "Bugger me. Pop-up Pete's pop-ups producing a probable personal best."

His alliteration turned out to be perception personified.

I went through the whole weighing thing with great care. I zeroed-in the scales with the dampened weigh sling attached, took the sling off the scales and enveloped the big mirror in it. By now both Bob and Alistair had come in close to have a look at how far the handle on the scales was going to whiz round.

"You hold the scales, Rambo," I said. "You'll be able to control the weight much better and we won't get a lot of needle flicker from my puny muscles shaking."

Rambo obliged and picked up the Reuben's, the face looking away from his chest. Three quizzical faces peered at the dial, the thirty-six was without doubt and general consensus settled on the fairly insignificant eleven. 36-11. Inwardly I was giving it the clenched fist and was bubbling over but outwardly I was serene.

Alistair said that he didn't recognise the fish once it was out in all its glory for the photos, which was a nice little bonus. Not that I really gave a shit whether it had been caught before or not, I was just thrilled to have caught it full stop. I asked Alistair to video me holding the mirror while having the photos done and then I put her back.

Once she had swam away I told him, to camera. "There she goes, safely back into

Lac Fumant. A personal best 36-11 mirror and just down in here is the fish I sacked last night."

I pulled the sack out and a very frisky twenty got its mug on 8mm tape and photographed. Once I had put that back it was my turn to photo and video Rambo's common that he had been and got from his swim. I could see that this was impressing Bob no-end. Alistair was also quite taken with our evident angling skill.

"I must say, Matthew, you've got off to a cracking start."

"Cheers. I had a low double in the night which I put back as well, you know."

"Really. Did you have all the fish from areas that I had suggested?"

"Every one, mate. And the big one came on a pop-up." I told him.

Alistair nodded. "It's surprising how worthwhile it is keeping one rod on a pop-up, like I said before. It can quite often be the one that goes when things are slow or it seems to produce a better ratio of the bigger fish. Strangely, whenever I've tried to fish all three rods with pop-ups it never seems to be as successful as it should, the reverse in fact. I'm afraid I haven't managed to work out why that is but it just seems to be the case. This does irritate me slightly, the fact that I cannot fathom out why it happens, so I have to console myself with the knowledge that at least I have managed to ascertain that it does. Not wholly satisfactory but a fair compromise I suppose. What made you decide to fish with one at the outset? Just because I had mentioned it, or is it a tactic you use often? I find it amazing that guys actually go fishing without a hard and fast game plan or tactics. You have to think of these things, you see."

"Actually I didn't. I caught one from the centre of the two pads very early on, on a bottom bait and . . ."

It was from this point, for some reason, that I decided to not tell it like it was. Perhaps it was because I didn't want to offend Alistair's sensibilities after all the help he'd given us. Or maybe I didn't want to tell him that the main reason I had just upped my PB by nearly eight pounds was because I was too busy laughing at the Fatboys' Day-Glo breakfast, feeding of the five thousand. Too busy doing that rather than concentrating on my fishing and putting together a game plan that would have involved reeling in, re-casting and consequently missing the most important take of my carp fishing career. And to compound it all I'd stuck on one of Pup's baits. I don't even know why I'd done that. I made my explanation up as I went along.

". . . for some reason I just had a gut feeling to go pop-up and stringer. When dawn came it was just a case of calling the odds as to what to do. A case of to re-cast, or not to re-cast? That was the question and I decided to stick with what I had got and it paid off."

I was full of shit.

Alistair shook his head and laughed. "I'd have been up at first light and re-cast the bait I had put out in the dark, that would be for certain. I'd have wanted to be sure that I was exactly in the right spot with good free offerings rather than leaving a cast that I hadn't even seen hit the water. Percentage wise, I would be sure that that was the right thing to do, but as I've said before, I've never been a hunch-type angler. Too methodical. My strength, and perhaps at times, my weakness. I'll never change my ways now . . ."

"Have you had anything?" I said jumping in before Alistair went off on another one of his windy speeches.

"An eighteen. To a dawn cast bottom bait. It went about two hours after casting. Only just before I heard your buzzer actually. After I put it back I came down to see how you had got on. I thought that you had caught something in the night but couldn't be certain. Anyway, I'd better get back and get myself sorted out for the day." He glanced up at the sky. " It looks as if it will be nice, not too hot and some nice cloud cover. Might be able to get one out during the day and one this evening if I fish well."

"Yeah. Right . . . thanks for all your help. Its been nice. We do appreciate it." I said with genuine feeling.

"Oh, I doubt that you needed it that much. I recognise a good angler when I see one. The way you played that fish was lovely to watch. I hope you can get a better one, they're in here all right."

"Thanks . . . thanks a lot," I said, somewhat taken aback by Alistair's praise. What a nice bloke. A thoroughly, bloody nice bloke.

I watched Alistair walk back up to his swim and turned to Rambo and Bob who had been having a natter.

"Quality fish, chief," said Bob ebulliently.

I smiled at him and gave him a thumbs up. His tee-shirt had a small group of cartoon people all striding out in step, one behind the other with the words, 'Keep on trucking'. I had no idea what the hell it related to or what it was about and to be honest I wasn't that interested to ask.

Bob started talking. "Rebecca asked me to ask you and Rambo if you'd like a hot food service at any time. I was just telling him that rather than you getting or cooking your own food or coming up to the cottage she'll cook you up some quality grub and bring it to you in your bivvy. I did mention it to you when we spoke on the phone. She's got some special food bags that keep it hot and it's all wrapped up in foil inside the bag. She usually brings it around at dusk time. It'll cost you a few extra quid but it's all extra cash for her if you're interested. Chief, here, says he's up for it."

I bet he is, I thought and then crudely wondered what else she might do for extra cash. The idea of Rebecca coming around every day was a pleasant notion and apart from that it would be nice not to have to muck about with preparing food and losing fishing time. I'd really only need to go up to the cottage to shower as and when, or if I needed to get the camcorder batteries charged.

"That'd be great," I said.

"That's quality, chief," said Bob. "I'll get her to come round with the menu she does. If you need any day to day stuff like milk, bread, that kind of thing, I'll pick it up from the local shop and put it in my big fridge. You can get it from the cottage then whenever it suits you, I'll just put your name on it with a little label so that nobody else grabs it by mistake." Bob looked at his watch. "Look, I must go, chief. I want to see if the Cowboy is out ready to draw. It's quality that, real quality."

And with those rather puzzling words he wandered off down towards Rambo's swim.

"What the hell was all that about?" I said to Rambo.

"God knows. Still, we've got plenty of time to find out. What are you going to order to eat tonight?"

"Rebecca and chips." Rambo rolled his eyes and shook his head. It was a you-sad-bastard moment.

I stopped and thought. He was right. What the hell was wrong with me? Sophie was everything and more to me and yet here I was keeping on about this other girl. There must be some explanation. Was I going through the male menopause in my twenties? I didn't know but I had busted through the carp fishing twenties. I was a thirties man now, or at least a thirty man, I suppose, if you wanted to be pedantic. I was confident I could pluralise, if there was such a word, but even more mouth wateringly people do say that life begins at forty. Now there was a figure to conjure with.

Rambo went back to his swim and I made a cup of tea and sat down and chilled out for a while to let it all sink in. The holiday of a lifetime was living up to its name so far.

CHAPTER 9

That first Sunday progressed up to lunch-time at a leisurely pace. I had put out the middle-of-pads bait and after a little internal torment I went back to one of our bottom baits and a bed of freebies. I then pulled in the margin bait that was the only rod not to have had a take and put the pop-up on that one. I used one of Pup's rather than one of ours but still put about forty of our ordinary boilies around it. I cast it a little further down the margin for a bit of extra variation.

I did wonder whether I was getting a bit too confident for my own good because the clear tactic was to put the pop-up in the same spot as it had caught the thirty and move the margin bait tight into the pads and sit on my rods. In truth I felt a bit tired and didn't fancy the extra concentration involved, in any case I was doing all right. Was I going to underfish myself? I doubted it. The way my luck was going I just decided to go with whatever whim came into my tiny, vacuous little head and wait and see what happened. So far it had worked a treat. Alistair was impressed, Bob was impressed and Rambo? I suspect that he reckoned I was just a lucky sod.

The strict dictionary definition of lunch-time can either mean a midday meal or one in between breakfast and dinner, when dinner is taken at midday. This wasn't quite the case over the far bank, where the Fatboys seemed to be eating virtually all the time. I kept glancing up and they were eating, every single time. It didn't seem to matter when I looked during that first morning, or for how long, they were just eating. Eventually, somewhat intrigued by the whole situation, I trained the binoculars on them.

By chance, after I had been clocking them for about twenty seconds, all hell didn't break lose when Greg, who happened to be eating a baguette the size of a powerlifter's thigh, had a take. Now, if that had been me or you the grub would have been tossed aside without a second thought, but not our Greg. He stopped and wrapped the bloody thing up in clingfilm before carefully placing it on his bedchair and wobbling down to hit the run. Either he must have been fishing very open water or he was a lot sadder than I had marked him down to be. Greg managed to get the fish in ok and Luke did the honours with the net while I was praying that the pair of them didn't fall in, otherwise the lake level would have been up to my reel handles.

Now there was another thing wrong with me. Why did I keep cracking these silly jokes to myself about their size? I didn't have an answer. I just hoped the Fatboys didn't go tree climbing to spot fish because it'd be like a total eclipse and we'd all be plunged into darkness, or, even worse, if they fell in Lac Fumant the tidal wave would wash me back to Calais. It was no use, the more I tried to stop it, the more the jokes kept filling my stupid head.

The fish that Greg had caught looked a decent size but how big was impossible for me to guess. Virtual Paul made a shambling appearance during the weigh-in, so at least I knew that he had survived the tackle shifting walk.

I turned my eye elsewhere and suddenly remembered my promise to video an actual run as it happened. It could wait. Sitting in the shade of the tree on my bedchair, with a canvass of beauty painted in front of me and with a thirty-five plus under my belt, I was a human sponge soaking in atmosphere. I was laid back both physically and mentally, if it hadn't been for the rear of my bedchair I'd have been so far back I'd have been horizontal.

The day was sunny with bits of cloud cover as Alistair had predicted and the temperature was pleasantly hot without being too overbearing. I suppose I could have chased a suntan by moving down to sit on my rods with a bait fished in tight to the pads, but I was happy where I was. Forget the factor fifteen, better to stay cool in the shade.

Over the years I had experienced the feeling of desperation in trying to eke out a pick- up many times. Chasing jumping fish by casting to them, only to see a fish roll over the top of my original position that I had carefully baited up, was the classic. Then there was the endless chopping and changing for the sake of it with an increasing air of despondency. All those types of thing that lead to carp fishing frustration and ultimately to burn out, if the runs never came. That now all seemed to be well in the past. I sat in serene calmness absolutely sure that I was going to catch. I didn't feel the need to press too hard, it would all come to me in good time. If it didn't, then I could try a few things and up the tempo but I felt that it would all work out.

I suppose this was how I always wanted my carp fishing to be, on top of it mentally, doing things that were coming off and landing big fish. The Tom Watt Twenty Trophy had hardened me up but it had been a pressure cooker situation all the time. I couldn't see me ever wanting to be in that situation again.

Just after lunch-time, my lunch-time around one o'clock, not the never ending lunch-time on the far bank, the margin bait cracked off. It was a case of leaning out from the bank as far as possible with arms full stretch and apply as much side strain as possible. The margin area was nice and clear despite overhanging branches and although the fish stole an initial ten or so yards before I was onto it, I managed to pump it back up to myself without too much trouble. With the fish in front of me it was just a case of keeping it clear of the other lines, which I had back-leaded to right under the rod tips for just that reason, and let the fish tire itself out.

All-hearing Rambo came up to do the honours in an olive green tee-shirt and a rather fetching pair of camouflage shorts. While I was playing the fish out he told me that he'd had a twenty about an hour ago that picked up a re-cast bait before he had even had time to set the indicator and turn his buzzer on. Hence the reason why I hadn't heard it, or was it my buzzer theory proving itself? I suppose not, Rambo kept on hearing my one all right. Bob had been talking to the Cowboy for ages and he had come up from that swim and photographed it for him. Rambo said that he now knew what Bob had meant about watching the Cowboy get ready to draw.

"Come on, then," I said as I applied a bit of welly to turn the fish away from the middle rod.

"Land this fish first because it's going to break you up, boy. Believe me, it's going to break you up. And I'm not talking about popping Big Game line either. Forget about worrying to video a pukka take, you've got to get this bloke on tape. It sounds hilarious."

I was so titillated by what Rambo was going to tell me that I started to bully the fish a little so that I would find out faster. I really had no idea what it could be all about apart from the obvious connotations between a cowboy drawing his gun in a gunfight. What I couldn't see was how this related to fishing or why it was so funny. The fish was nowhere near ready to attempt landing it and still had its head down, showing no hint of giving up. I told myself to stop being such a dickhead, to calm down and let things take their course. I pushed the Cowboy to the back of my mind and set about landing the hard fighting fish that was giving a really good account of itself.

"It might be a good common," said Rambo. "The one I had fought harder than the mirror."

The words had hardly left his mouth when I saw my tubing break the surface, quickly followed by a broad back that was unmistakably the broad back of a good common.

"Know-it-all," I said to Rambo.

Once I knew it was a big common my stomach tightened just a little. I still felt in total control but even a twenty would be a personal best and this looked a lot better than that. There's something about big commons. It's all the scales isn't it? That and their relative scarceness, maybe.

Ten minutes later the line popped and I was reeling in slack. No, just kidding! Ten minutes later a very big common was safely in my landing net.

"Shit! That looks as if it might be a thirty," I said with a voice tinged with mild hysteria. I knew all about these things now that I had caught one.

Rambo nodded. "It's going to be very close, oh golden-bollocked one. You, my son, are on an unstoppable roll at the moment. I'll tell you what, if you stepped on a landmine . . ." Rambo's eyes looked deep into mine. "It'd blow your fucking leg off. Come on, let's weigh it!"

The pair of us set about the task with enthusiasm. Rambo seemed almost as excited as I was about the common, or on second thoughts, it may have been the second big success of a Pup pop-up. Maybe fate had dealt us up another edge that we never even knew we had.

"How many of those pop-ups have we got?" he asked as I checked the scales against a freshly dampened weigh sling.

"I think he said that there was a hundred. He kept banging on about his 'legendary' pop-ups but maybe they are as good as he said. After we've sorted the common out we'll divide them up and you can take half with you."

"I'll take fifty, boy. You've already used a couple, I don't want you ripping me off," Rambo said laughing. "Give me the sling and let me get this beauty dangling under the full pull of gravity."

I duly obliged and Rambo tucked the common safely in, threaded the sling's handles through the scales' hook and lifted up the Reubens yet again with the dial facing me.

"Magic thirty?" he asked.

"Yes!" I cried happily. "31 . . . 4. I think. You have a look."

We swapped over. Rambo peered at the needle.

"Might even be five or six, but call it four. It's no big deal. I don't suppose you'll lose any sleep over an ounce or two."

Rambo took some photos but had to put the spare battery into the camcorder as the other one was nearly flat to get a bit of footage of my latest contribution to the Lac Fumant video diary. The first ninety minute long tape finished as the common swam away.

I was chuffed. Two thirties and I hadn't even been fishing twenty four hours. One mirror and one common. My second bit of slightly lazy fishing had paid dividends. I had watched the Fatboys when a keener angler would have been out there sorting things out and had got the mirror because of it. Then, I had opted for the more leisurely approach, put the pop-up in the margin rather than in between pads, and sat back in the shade, going for the margin rather than for a tight cast to the pads. Because of that approach I had now caught the common. It was either brilliant angling or brilliant luck. They say that you make your own luck so I decided it would be brilliant angling when I told Alistair about it. If I'd have been writing an article about it I could have had a field day with references to hunches, watercraft, skill and suchlike. The truth was perhaps different but you couldn't argue with the results. They spoke for themselves.

After I had stopped producing adrenaline and had calmed down the more mundane side of the long stay angler's daily business came into being. I needed to use the toilets that were up at the cottage. Bob had thankfully decided not to desecrate Lac Fumant with chemical loos, we all peed in the surrounding area of the lake, but no-one dared, well you know what I mean.

I told Rambo and said I'd take up the camcorder battery and charger. "I'll pull in the other two rods and walk round the long way down past the Cowboy, Japp and Wim. You can give me all the spiel about what Bob told you on the Cowboy. Maybe I'll see him in action."

"I doubt it," said Rambo. "He won't be out to draw at this time of the day, I shouldn't think."

Silence.

"Cough it up, then," I said raising my voice and sounding a tad irritated.

"You don't want to know," teased Rambo.

"I bloody do. Stop mucking about. Tell me!"

I imagined my voice sounded a bit like a little boy who's pestering his elder brother for some big secret, only I wasn't tugging at Rambo's shorts. Not yet.

Rambo started to tell me what I wanted to hear. "After I caught my last twenty, Bob came up from the Cowboy's swim to take some pictures for me."

"Yeah, I remember you saying."

"Bob said that he was a bit gutted because the Cowboy wasn't coming out to draw and I, naturally enough, asked what the fuck he was talking about. Apparently what happens is, that when the Cowboy feels that he's in with a shout of a take, you know, liners, nodding tips, fish movement over his baits, all that kind of stuff. Well, he walks down to his rods, stands in between them, hands hanging by his side, fingers wriggling, ready to strike. Or, if you prefer to call it, and the Cowboy does, ready to draw. He just stands there like a gunslinger, eyes narrowed, waiting for the buzzer to call, 'draw.' Sometimes he even takes a cassette player down with him and plays Ennio Morricone spaghetti western scores. The one he likes the best is the one where the gang leader had the watch that played the chiming tune and he used to use it whenever he had a gunfight. When the watch finished the tune everyone went for their shooters. If he gets a run during that bit of tape it's a mind blower for him. Bob says it's all very melodramatic and if you see it, you'll piss yourself laughing. He wears all the gear, the hat, waistcoat, boots and he pulls on kidskin gloves as he goes down to the rods. The Cowboy is so wrapped up in this gunslinger fantasy that he can't see it for what it is. It's bizarre but it's brilliant."

"Bollocks!" I said, not believing a word of it.

"It's true. I'm telling you it's true."

I was stunned but still thinking. "How does he stand between his rods?"

"He doesn't use buzz bars, I've had a look. He's got individual banksticks that he places about a yard apart and he stands in between them. When he's on a three rod water like here, he puts the third rod as tight to the right hand one as possible. I'm just gutted he doesn't slip the rod butts into an elongated holster, but you can't have it all."

"What happens if he doesn't get a take? Does he just stay there or what?"

"Bob says that despite being a bit eccentric . . ."

"A bit!" I exclaimed.

"...the Cowboy is a very good angler. He won't just go and stand there any time, only when he's virtually certain to get a take. Now, that sounds a bit risky to me at the best of times, but that's what he does. If he gets a run any other time it's just like me and you going to hit it. It's only when he goes down to draw that he puts his reputation on the line. Once he's out there he will not come off draw status until he's hit a run. Bob says that he might do it about two times in a fortnight if you're really lucky and if things don't seem right, he won't do it at all. Now, run your mental condition tape over that one, then, boy."

I puffed out my cheeks. "I'll believe it when I see it. Getting that on video would be better than any take. Jesus, Rambo, I've got to witness that. You'll keep an eye on him won't you and come and get me?"

"When I see the paleface move, I'll send you a smoke-signal, chief," said Rambo trying to take off Bob.

After all this nonsense I wound my rods in, picked up the battery charger and battery and set off with Rambo after he'd grabbed his share of Pup's pop-ups. Leaving Rambo to try one on one of his rods I walked down to the Cowboy's bivvy and triumphantly noticed that Rambo could keep tabs on him easily from his swim. The Cowboy was inside his bivvy, or at least I presumed he was, I never saw him and I lacked the front to call in on him unannounced. He was clearly not right in the head or, on further reflection, an outrageous exhibitionist. I walked past and on to Japp and Wim who were sitting in the sun wearing just football shorts. Inside me I was begging that they'd ask me what I'd caught. If I'd have been blanking, I'd have been dreading it. Funny that. I wonder why?!

"Good fish this morning, Matt," said Wim.

"Which one?" I said smiling.

"The big mirror," said Wim. "Bob told us."

"I've just had a thirty common as well," I said, trying to hide my delight in case it came over as smugness.

"That is good, Matt," said Japp. " We have had a couple of fish each but nothing over the eighteen pounds. Rambo, he has had a nice fish as well. You two are doing fine."

"Thanks. I guess Alistair gave us good swims."

"Yes, but you have done very well." Wim stopped as if thinking about something and then he continued. "Your friend, Rambo. Is he from the army?"

I didn't want to go into Rambo's murky world of small arms dealing so I said that he was.

Wim continued. "He is a very powerful man. A very strong body and a very strong mind. Our father always needs people like that, for his business, you see. Perhaps we will have words with him later if he doesn't mind. Do you think that he will mind?"

"You can only ask. I'm sure he won't be offended." I said and thought that they'd better hit the deck quick if it did offend him.

I'd seen Rambo blow up before, under much different circumstances than now, of course. There was no snide Watt and motley crew to rattle his cage for a start. There was Spunker and all this 'dominant male' malarkey, but apart from the lifting episode and a bit of competitive yomping, it had yet to fully materialise. He was as benign as I'd ever seen him, the cold look of hate and violence had gone but it was still there just waiting for the wrong thing, or person, or dog, to resurrect it. I had no idea what the two brothers' dad did for a living, or what they might think that Rambo could do for them. I was about to ask when Japp had what turned out to be a big liner and the pair of them went to study the offending rod. I didn't like to hassle them so I said my goodbyes and carried on my little walk.

I walked slowly around the bottom end of the lake and started back up the other side. Once clear of the bottom island I could look to my side of the lake and see the Cowboy's swim. On another fifty or so yards and the middle island cut out the view of my side of the lake, a bit further still and I was up to Ian's swim, complete with two bivvies. One for him and one for the huge rottweiler.

Ian was in the process of making a cup of tea.

"All right, Matt? Fancy a cuppa? You can tell me all about this big mirror of yours. Over thirty-five wasn't it?"

"Yes. Yes and yes, mate," I said.

"Nice one." said Ian and motioned towards his bedchair. "Park your arse on the chair and I'll get another mug. He's not up yet," he nodded towards Spunker's bivvy. "Too much lager, last night."

I looked at Ian to see if I could detect any hint of jocularity but there appeared to be none.

"Are you serious?" I asked.

"Too right I am. He loves a drop of the stuff. The best bit is that he really can open a bottle of beer with his teeth. He just rips the cap off, holds the bottle in his teeth and throws his head back and down it goes. I suppose it's a bit of an indulgence to let him have it but nothing's too good for that dog. He saved my life you know. Here you are."

I took my tea and sipped it "Cheers. I remember you saying."

"So about this mirror, tell me all about it."

I gave Ian a blow by blow account of my Lac Fumant experiences so far and then laid the thirty common on him as well. Bob had clearly gone round and told everyone about the mirror but they had no way of knowing about the common. Ian was impressed. He'd had a couple of fish, both twenties and said that he was happy with the start that he'd made. He said that he'd have been orgasmic if he'd caught what I had and the use of that word edged me on to why on earth he had called his dog Spunker.

Ian told me. "He was a stray, actually, when I got him from the pound. He was a fully mature dog that had just been too expensive or too large for his former owner to look after and the bastard had just let him run free in the streets."

I imagined that a fully grown Spunker being allowed to run free on the streets was a bit like Godzilla on the block, trampling New York into the dust. Only a bit I must admit.

"When he was finally impounded and kept locked up it just happened to coincide with me wanting to get a dog. We were destined for each other. The thing was that no-one knew what to call him, he had no collar, he had no name . . ."

"Like the Cowboy?" I said butting in.

". . . hmmm, that's right, so anyway, I decided to have him and brought him home. A couple of nights later he was getting frisky with the settee. You know rubbing himself against the upholstered arm like you do . . ."

Nope, I thought, I couldn't remember ever doing that one even when I was fourteen, pulsing with hormones and the lingerie section in my mum's mail order catalogue was like a blue movie to me. I carried on listening in silence.

". . . and I told him to stop it. He didn't take any notice and kept on doing it only he was getting faster and faster. 'Come here', I shouted and the blighter had. Shot his bolt over the cushion and everything. Straight away I thought, Spunker by name and Spunker by nature. It was funny really, and that's basically how the name came about."

I felt my stomach heave. "Not so funny when you had to clear it up, though. I bet?" I said.

"Oh, I got the wife to clear it up. She was my wife then, she's left me now. Run off with a bloke who worked as a pooper-scooper driver for the council. I used to get Spunker to go down and shit all over the roads he had to clear up, the bastard. Running of with my missus. That dog's my wife now and my best mate. If it wasn't for him I'd be dead."

And possibly still happily married I thought. It was clear that Ian regarded Spunker as a soul mate and I hoped that this real or imagined (I wasn't sure) grudge match between the mutt and Rambo didn't offend him. He was after all, apart from the fact he was a bit mad, a nice bloke. I didn't want anyone to fall out with anyone, I'd been there and done that and the present situation was far more favourable.

"You didn't seem too worried about Spunker when Rambo lifted him up?" I said.

It was a leading question designed to sound out just how much Ian was likely to flip if Rambo decided to crush the hound. Despite the dog's size I felt sure that he would be fairly comfortably disposed of by a supercharged Rambo.

"Nah. Just a bit of fun. He's big enough to look after himself. When he starts biting the necks of other dogs in the park I just turn away and let him get on with it. He's old enough to deal with those things himself, he doesn't need me to fuss after him on that sort of deal."

There speaks the responsible dog owner, I thought sarcastically. I'd met a few of them but only a few, most of the others just didn't seem to care what their dog did. Ian was in the middle, he cared about the dog but because of his rather weird angle on the relationship, he would have probably turned a blind eye to Spunker eating a baby. Dogs could be a pain, whether passing crap out of one end, noise out of the other or dispensing bites needing tetanus jabs, they had plenty of scope for annoyance. At least Ian had a reason to love his dog, I suppose, even if it was a bit convoluted. I thanked him for the tea, said my goodbyes and carried on up to the cottage. Was he more touched than the Cowboy? Hard to say.

Virtual Paul was sitting outside his bivvy. He had his head immersed in a laptop computer, so much for getting away from his PlayStation and suchlike. I said hello and he moved his head and gave me a grunt and looked back to the screen. Just my luck to catch him in a chatty mood and hold me up for about three nanoseconds. He had some mouth, that kid.

The Fatboys were just getting ready for another fry up and they asked me to join them. I politely declined. If I went and stood near them I might be the straw that broke the camel's back and our combined weight might tilt the earth of its correct axis. There I was again, stupid fat jokes. They asked about the mirror and got told about it and the common as well. I had to keep reminding myself that it was new to them even if it was becoming repetitive to me. Mind you, having to keep on telling everyone about my carp fishing prowess wasn't that hard.

I walked up to the cottage feeling great. For the umpteenth time I had to mentally pinch myself to confirm that it was all happening. The cottage door was open but there seemed nobody about so I used the toilet, had a quick freshen up, put the battery on charge and headed back down to the lake. It was around three in the afternoon now and I could spend my time wandering back and getting my three baits out into position for the evening feed time. I suppose the two big fish so early on in the campaign had lifted any pressure off me. If I never caught anything any better, the holiday would still be a huge success but I had a feeling that I just might.

Let's face it, I was here to enjoy myself and although this was inextricably linked to catching carp, I didn't want that side of it to be the be all and end all of it. Yes, it was easy to say that now I had two thirties under my belt, realistically I knew that I wouldn't have been so easy going about it if I was still blanking. The other thing was that despite it being the holiday of a lifetime, with the money that I now had behind me I could do it all again. All my recent luck, both fishing and fiscal, had plopped me into the comfort zone.

I had been down the numbers road with the old syndicate. Sure I had taken great satisfaction in Rambo and I stuffing Watt, but this was better. Some of the guys at Lac Fumant seemed a bit odd but it was an oddness that didn't really affect anybody else or interfere with their fishing or enjoyment and besides they had all been so kind and helpful. There seemed no jealousy on their part of what I had caught, the opposite in fact, they all seemed genuinely pleased for me.

One thing was that they didn't know about my luck on the lottery which may have possibly pushed their goodwill a bit further than I would have liked. Money is the root of all evil, closely followed by lust and the capture of big carp. My fellow anglers had passed in flying colours on the third one but if I ended up screwing Rebecca and revealed my stash of money would they be so generous to me? There was little chance of either of those matters coming to fruition, so it seemed that I would be judged by carp success alone. Surely this was how carp fishing on a smallish water was meant to be? A beautiful lake, loads of big carp and a good set of lads to share it with and the chance of a laugh.

On the way back I passed the Fatboys and then came to Alistair's bivvy. He wasn't about and his rods were pulled in and little bit of me was slightly disappointed that I couldn't tell him about my common. He'd find out soon enough but I wanted to be the one who told him, just an ego thing, I guess. Once I got to my bivvy I couldn't see Rambo about either, so I set up the three rods with new baits, a Pup pop-up special went on the left hand rod this time. Middle rod between the two set of pads and right hand rod in the margin all as before. By four all was done and I was ready for the next adventure.

The adventure came in the exotic form of Rebecca, coming around to take my order for the evening meal. She was wearing a bikini top, skimpy shorts and looked stunning. She had a rich bronze tan that emphasised the perfection of her young, unblemished skin. With so little on I could see the contours of what was a voluptuous body very clearly. She was slim but had an ample bosom (Mills and Boon) or nice tits (everybody else) and her nipples were so visible through the sheer material of the top that I did know where to look. I followed the contour of the inside of her thighs and saw them curve in slightly at the top before her shorts cut into the flesh that was undoubtedly pulpy and svelte-like to the touch. I felt a bead of perspiration trickle down my brow. Would I lose the ability to speak coherently?

"Hi, Matt."

"Hi, Rebecca."

It was a good start. The monosyllabic opening had helped greatly and although the name was tricky I hadn't palomor-knotted my tongue in saying it.

"Dad said you'd like me to do Rambo and yourself food for tonight. Is that right?"

"Yeah, that's right," I said as casually as my intense concentration would allow. I was going great guns. I was sounding like an adult.

"I was going to do spaghetti bolognase. I'll do enough for the next evening as well if that's all right by you but I won't get it ready until about seven. I've been sunbathing this afternoon and I'm all hot and sticky and need to shower before cooking."

I knew the feeling with a slight difference. I was now hot and sticky but had already started cooking.

She looked me in the eye. "I'm trying to get an all-over tan," she pouted.

I begged my brain to think of something clever and sophisticated.

"I had a thirty pound common this morning . . ." I started, which admittedly wasn't a very promising opening. Come on brain! For fuck's sake, come on! ". . . But I'd have cheerfully traded that in to get a glimpse of you with no clothes on," I added cheekily. Relief and exultation. No need for a full lobotomy.

Holding my eye she smiled and raised her eyebrows coquetishly. "Really?" she said sensually. "And how long have you been waiting to catch a thirty pound common."

"Only all my life." I said.

"And you'd trade that just to see me with no clothes on?" she asked.

I was just about to say to fucking right I would (a white lie, I'd have to stop and weigh it up in the cold light of day) when I got a poxy take on the middle rod. Somehow the sexually charged ambience was somewhat decimated by a one hundred decibel alarm. Just my luck to get lucky and to get a run when I didn't want it.

"Sorry!" I said to her as I ran down to the rods.

"This had better be a big fish," I mumbled to myself as I hit the take.

As I played the fish I turned to see her walk off down the bank, to find Rambo presumably. The more I reflected on our conversation the better I felt. She had flirted with me. So she might flirt with all the others but now she was flirting with me, which was a result, unlike the fish, which turned out to be a measly twenty-two pound, picture perfect, linear mirror. I put it in the sack until either Rambo or Bob or Alistair or someone came around to wield the camera. I re-cast and waited for my meal and anything else that was coming my way.

CHAPTER 10

My Sunday evening turned out to be mildly disappointing, firstly Bob and not Rebecca had brought me my meal and I didn't have another take. Bob explained that she had unexpectedly had to go somewhere but it was her handiwork that I was eating. The meal was very tasty and had been piping hot due to the special thermal container it had come in. I took the meal from Bob and gave him a list of items, milk, bread and other similar things for him to pick up from the local shop on the Monday and I told him about the common. Bob seemed very pleased and gave me a nice smattering of 'Well done, chief's.'

Rambo had done the cinematic honours with the linear an hour earlier. He had been round chatting to Japp and Wim when I had come back from the cottage. He hadn't mentioned anything about the brothers asking him to do some work for their dad so I took it that they had bottled it. This was backed up by Rambo saying that they had talked a lot but only about the Dutch carp fishing scene, especially their canals, and Dutch football. Rambo also told me that the Cowboy had caught a fish but had just raced out of his bivvy much like the rest of us do. He hadn't been called out to draw and the only sign that there was something loose in his head was the rather boring fact that he was still wearing his cowboy boots when he ran down to hit the take. You'd have thought that the least he could have done was to have rode down to his rods shouting 'Yeahaa!' or other such cowboy vernacular, but it was not to be.

Rambo also said that while I was pouncing about catching thirties, watching the Fatboys, wandering around the lake, soaking up the atmosphere and thinking about and talking to Rebecca, he'd had his fishing head well and truly screwed on. He had spent a lot of time just watching the water, looking for fish and signs of fish. I admitted to him that I had been a bit lapse in this department, mainly due to the leg-up that Alistair had given me and my quick success. I told him how I felt about putting myself under pressure and fishing hard. Surprisingly he was sympathetic to how I felt and understood that the wounds of the old syndicate had not fully healed and consequently why I didn't really want to graft after every take. If I missed the odd opportunity due to my laid back attitude then that was just the way it was going to be. As Rambo pointed out, I was still out-fishing everyone else by some distance, so he reckoned I should just carry on as I was until the wheels fell off or I emptied the lake.

The point that he was trying to make was that he had spotted an area that was nearly half-way house between our swims that had shown a lot of signs of fish action. Tomorrow he was going to climb up the tree that was giving me my shade and run the binoculars over it to see if it was worth baiting it up. The area was a good one hundred and twenty yards out and lay about thirty yards to the left hand edge of the island in front of me. I knew that I couldn't cast that far or no where's near it, but Rambo had his 3lb test curves with him and he said that was well within his range. I could well believe it as well, what with his long levers and supremely strong upper body. I had the bait boat to get my hookbait out there if I wanted and to put out freebies, Rambo said he could use a stick to bait at that sort of distance provided there wasn't a head wind. Even he had to be restricted by the laws of physics sometimes. Rambo said he'd keep an eye on things, make further investigations and depending on how things shaped up on the current areas we were fishing, we could decide whether to make a play for it or not.

After I had eaten, had a cuppa and frittered away the time churning over things in my mind I suddenly felt very tired. I tucked myself into the bag and must have fell soundly asleep almost straight away. That night, that undisturbed night as it turned out, I dreamt of Sophie and when I awoke at six on the Monday morning it was to a feeling of guilt. There I was leering and lusting after this young girl and yet I had this awesome woman who had supported me through all my ordeals in my life already. She, who loved me, who was very attractive in many ways and who, if the truth was known and it was something that I had never denied, I had written it in 'The Syndicate' notes many times, had saved me from myself. Maybe the money and the big fish had started to turn my head, perhaps I was believing my own publicity.

In short I was being a bit of a dick about this Rebecca thing. Now, whether I was actually interested in giving her a bit of dick was something I hadn't really sorted out in my mind. Superficially, yeah. Wanted her to flirt with me and vice versa, yeah. Wanted to look and leer at her, yeah. Wanted to do all sorts of naughty things to her, yeah. But only yeah, in a brain in the groin type of way. Not a yeah, I've considered all the possible repercussions of my actions and the associated guilt. I mean what if Rebecca was so obsessed with me she found out where I lived and arrived on my doorstep to confront Sophie about the whole torrid affair? I'd lose Sophie, my money, my house, the lot and for what? A few nights of amazing passion with a girl who had the body of a goddess.

Of course you do only live once and some opportunities come along just once. To miss out on one such opportunity can deprive you of a unique experience. And how would Sophie ever find out? I was a red blooded male after all. What man would turn her down if given the opportunity? Why, I'd be duty bound to have sex with her on behalf of mankind. I'd be a laughing stock if I refused.

I was full of shit. That was the top and bottom of it. For one thing I was doing an Alistair over a situation that didn't exist. I'd only said a few words to the girl and it wasn't as if she'd even been bothered enough to bring me my dinner. But those few words were pretty suggestive . . . and off I went again, on another circle within a circle. I suddenly made a mystical and lucid connection. I would just treat the whole thing with the same laid back manner that I was treating the fishing. That was the answer, none of this ridiculous soul-searching and picking through my thoughts of events, both real and imagined, with a flea comb. It was dumb. There would be no more of it.

Having absolutely, positively and irrefutably decided that that was that, I immediately speculated on how things would go when I next saw her and what she would be wearing. It was hopeless. I knew what Alistair meant when he said he could not carp fish on a hunch, that it just wasn't his way. I knew exactly what he meant and how trapped he was by his own personality and approaches.

I wanted to know why I was going through all this. Was it my time inside? A young man on holiday thing? An early male menopause? Pure lust? Something else? Whatever it was it needed even more navel gazing to try and get an answer. It was unlikely I'd be able to come to a conclusion even allowing for the huge amount of pondering time a carp fishing holiday can give you. I told myself to snap out of it. It was pathetic. A few words of banter with a young girl, regardless of how attractive, and it was doing my head in. Go and re-cast those rods, I told myself, and I did.

For some reason that Monday was a slow day and it had followed a poor night, when I eventually found out that nobody had so much as a beep. The fish were just not feeding and that was it. Even I, who had not exactly been studying the form, noticed a distinct lack of fish movement compared to the previous days'. Rambo came up at about eleven and declared it to be a bit of a struggle. At half past Alistair came down for a chat and an hour later the Cowboy, Japp and Vim turned up. The Dutch boys had come up to see Rambo and not finding him in his swim and his rods pulled in decided to see if he was with me. Which he was. The Cowboy had just come along for the ride.

No sooner had they all arrived when Bob bowled up with my goodies from the local shop.

"Morning, chiefs!" he called out to us all.

"I ain't no fucking Indian," said the Cowboy with no hint of irony and we all fell about laughing. It sort of set the tone.

Alistair was very interested to hear about my common and even more interested in my strategic plan that had been nothing of the sort.

"You mean to say that you actually changed the spot from where you had caught the mirror on the pop-up and put that particular bait into the margin?" I nodded. "When all logic would have told you to re-cast to the same place with the same set-up."

I nodded again. I could tell the agonies that this was putting him through.

"Why?" he asked.

I could tell it was getting to him because he was speaking in short bursts, which was very un-Alistair.

"To be honest it just seemed like a good idea at the time." I saw him almost wince. "I guess it was just a hunch."

How cruel. I had turned the blade but it was the dagger of truth, or as near as damn it. I had stretched the facts a little when I had related my tactics concerning the mirror I had caught but not this time. Of course it hadn't been a hunch, I had just got lucky. Again.

"Alistair. When do you think the fish will start to feed again?" asked Japp.

Alistair's face brightened. At last, something that he could relate to. "You know as well as I, Japp, you've fished here as much, that these 'dead days' do happen every now and then. Usually, because there are so many fish in the lake and because we are here in the warm months, activity is nearly always there to see. At most times, especially during the known feeding times, that goes without saying, there are fish feeding somewhere. The fish do seem an active strain. I guess that we've all fished other waters where the carp just don't seem to move or feed as much as elsewhere and it just happens that at Lac Fumant they do. Perhaps it is the competition amongst themselves? It doesn't seem to be weather related, these barren days have happened in varying conditions. To be honest it is one area which I feel that I can safely tuck under the mat. I don't have to know the reason why the fish are so active, although I would like to know obviously, all knowledge is useful, I just need to know how to use that to my advantage in terms of catching them. All I can say is that at least the 'dead days' happen fairly infrequently, which is good news for all of us. However, in answer to your question, past experience has shown me, and I expect that you have noticed this as well, that on days like this the next feeding spell can be a good one. I think that this evening is a good time to catch possibly two or three fish. I have fished really hard during days like this, not just static fishing but walking round and stalking and have rarely had success. In actuality I cannot remember a single time that I've had a fish, to be honest. That is why I'm here in Matthew's swim with three rods wound in. I am as certain as I can be that a pick up now is a very remote concept, although I am aware of the maxim, 'never say never'."

"So in short. Tonight," said the Cowboy flicking the rim of his hat so that it sat back on his head. "Man, you could talk for England. Don't ask him anything else, my ears can't take it. In any case I've got to go home a week on Saturday and that doesn't leave much time for him jawing and the fishing."

"Mind you, chief, the way this lad is fishing," said Bob nodding at me. "He might catch one this afternoon. Alistair tells me that you're a quality angler, son. Where have you been doing it over the last few years?"

Despite the praise it was not a question I wanted to hear. "You know, here and there. Mainly in a syndicate but I've come out of it now. I don't fish any of the well known circuit waters," I said, being conservative with the truth.

Bob seemed satisfied. "Why do you think that you're doing so well?"

I shrugged my shoulders in a display of humility. "Alistair chose the swim remember. I suppose it's fair to say that our bait is a good one although the pop-up that has caught my two big ones was a bit of an unknown quantity. Until now that is. I suppose everything I've done has just come off."

"It's funny why one bait works a bit better than another on one water. Then again it might not produce such good results somewhere different," said the Cowboy.

"Yes, but it's not as straight forward as that . . ." started Alistair.

"I never expected it to be with you around!" said the Cowboy in an irritable voice but there was the hint of a smile on his face. "You're worse than all that shit that gets written in those poxy carp fishing magazines. They must sit there at their computer or whatever it is they're using and think. Shit. Two thousand words to bang out this month on the same topic that I've written about for the last six years. What shall I dream up this time? I know, I'll write something about bait that no-one can prove or disprove that covers such a vague set of ideas and theories that it's no bloody good to anybody when they've read it. This is due to, amongst other things, it bearing no resemblance to the type of fishing you're doing, the time you've got available and the fact you can't fill the lake with Mr Sponsor's boilies."

"No, I think you're being a bit unfair there," said Alistair but the Cowboy was not to be denied. He had both guns blazing.

"And what about all those fucking rigs you read about? All nicely drawn out in black ink diagrams, everything perfect and in its place. It's bollocks. Smack it out eighty yards in a cross wind, it sinks down through ten foot of water onto a bottom of leaves, twigs, bits of weed and Christ knows what..."

"Shopping trolleys, bike frames, old cars, Mafia victims," I said warming to the Cowboys cynicism.

"And then what would it look like? How would that two foot, PVA'd concertina, confidence rig be sitting then? Like a pile of old bootlaces, that's how. Forgetting pop-ups, prove to me how a bottom fished rig has actually caught a carp because of its design rather than simply converting a chance that another type of rig would have as well. It's all about a fish picking up a good bait because it was in the right place at the right time. Show me that it's anything different and I'll show you the Colt revolver I've got tattooed on my knob."

"Shoot it from the hip, pistol prick," I said getting carried away.

The Cowboy was undeterred. He had shot the sheriff with his gun and was now mowing down loads of deputies with a Gatling gun. "I'll tell you what. All these blokes who write for these magazines know nothing. They only catch because they spend all their bloody lives on the bank. The wrong place must be the right place eventually, if you're there long enough. They fish the best waters, can load it with bait regardless of cost and if they're doing an article they shut the water so they get the best swims."

"Some of it is a bit too much. But generally we like to read people's opinions and what they think. Imagine trying to learn about carp fishing just on your own without being able to put together lots of people's knowledge and experiences. You would be dead of old age before you ever got around to inventing a hair rig or boilies," said Wim looking at Japp who nodded. "Some of them are good anglers, you have to admit that."

"Human knowledge is invariably pushed forward by pioneers who work alone and then share findings. Maybe more so in the past, today large institutions, whether

91

commercial or scientific, push the boundaries forward. Carp fishing is no different. Shared knowledge benefits all except perhaps the first one to have it. Imagine being able to fish the hair rig today and nobody else knew about it. They soon would, as happened originally I believe. Getting take after take soon makes you someone worth watching. Actually that's the reason we're all sitting in your swim, Matthew. We're spying on you," Alistair said, chuckling away to himself.

"We've had a bit of that in our time haven't we, mate?" I said to Rambo who nodded.

For some reason my attention turned to Bob and another one of his funny old tee-shirts. This one had a large, naked, pink body pointing a finger upwards and to the right a smaller, pink, naked body. Above this the slogan 'Sod off' was printed. I had to ask.

"Bob? Where and what the hell are all your tee-shirts about?"

"Time warp, classic seventies quality, chief," he said. I should have guessed I'd get an answer that made no sense.

The thing that happened next made no sense either. It killed all conversation stone dead and everyone turned in mute disbelief to look at the offending object. It was as if an alien craft had just swooped down and landed. It was unbelievable, unexpected, unforeseen, unlooked-for and above all else, 'unexplainable', which is spelt inexplicable, inexplicably.

My left hand rod was away. Away as in getting a take. It was run-bound. It was a pick-up with the accompanying Delkim concerto. Fortissimo. In what key, I have no idea.

I looked to Rambo who stared back at me in bewilderment. Alistair gawped at the Cowboy who was transfixed by the moment while I turned to Japp for help, but his eyes were glazed. I then went to Wim, but he was grappling with the ridiculous notion of what was happening and he could not aid me. I saw Alistair implore Japp to supply an answer with pleading eyes. Japp gave the merest hint of a shrug and turned in silent desperation to his brother who agonised for a second before he beseeched Rambo to help. Rambo could only turn in angst to me, the person on whom the deed had been laid, to try, with all his might, to will me into some semblance of comprehension.

"You going to hit that run, or what then, chief?" said Bob and the spell was broken.

I clambered off my bedchair and sped to my rods, wound one turn to click the baitrunner off and strike. The rod, as one is duty-bound to point out at this juncture, lurched over into an alarming curve. Some seventy yards away an unseen force shifted into third gear and started taking line from a tight clutch. It felt big. Real big. My first thoughts were to get a record of this while it happened and I must admit I went a bit psychotic.

"The camcorder! The camcorder!" I screamed.

"Where is it?" said Alistair.

"The rucksack! The rucksack!" I hollered.

Alistair rummaged in the rucksack and found it. "Which button..?"

"Give it to Rambo! Give it to Rambo! You do the net! You do the net!" I told him, my voice teetering on the edge of hysteria.

Rambo had the camcorder and started to video me playing the fish, Alistair took hold of the landing net while the others formed a viewing party behind Rambo. As Rambo started to film he commenced a pseudo-documentary voice-over.

"Welcome to Lac Fumant. It is Monday afternoon and the supposed Lac Fumant carp fishing fraternity experts have declared that it is a dead day. However, carp angling's hottest new sensation, Matt Williams has proved them wrong and is playing a huge carp as we speak. Matt has become so successful that he is becoming a victim of his own ascendancy. Wherever he fishes a pathetic group of hangers-on, groupies and rival carp experts shadow his every move . . ." Out the corner of my eye I saw Rambo pan back to the others who were starting to giggle and then back onto me. ". . . As we watch the expert ply his trade let's have a quick word with some of these people who have come all this way just to watch this boy. The Cowboy, here. Now you've been on the trail of this lad for some while. What do you think of him?"

The Cowboy cleared his throat and started. "Look. Imagine me throwing a dime into the sky and me shooting that dime with a six gun and hitting that dime six times out of six. But every time I hit that dime, the next time the bullet would hit it on the other side so it would get dented, straightened out, dented, straightened out, dented and then straightened out. When I had finished the coin would be perfect apart from two marks, one on one side, one on the other. Well, this lad, he's even better than that."

"Alistair. Something short. Please," said Rambo in false agony.

"Well, he's pretty tremendous in terms of his casting and bait application and rigs and bait and playing of fish in general," said Alistair.

"Japp?" Rambo again.

"Holland should have won the World Cup in 1974 and 1978."

"Wim. A word please."

"I am not an angler. I am just trying to get off with the women that are not quite pretty enough to make it into the sleeping bag with Matt."

"I think that says it all. Now we'll just watch the master at work and be humbled by his skill." There was a gap before Rambo turned away from the camera so that it sounded as if his last comment shouldn't be picked up. "God I hope he doesn't let the fucking thing come off this time. We've only got two more carp left in the tank, you know. We should have got Jim Gibbinson, this bloke's a tosser!"

It was high comedy, or at least those present thought that it was, but the humour gradually drained away as it became clear I was into a big fish. Once again as had happened before, the fish moved off down towards Rambo's swim and I followed it. By pumping and winding I kept the fish on a tight line and edged myself down the bank to cut down the distance between me and my underwater adversary. The pressure that I was exerting was making the fish kite into the margin but this was the rod that had been seventy yards out and even now after much heave-hoeing the carp was still fifty yards out from the edge. It was fortunate that Rambo's rods were pulled in because the fish was down level to where he would have cast to and there was no-way I could stop it. I suppose if he had been there I would have cupped the spool and gone for it but it was something I didn't have to resort to. The fish just kept pulling and taking the odd bit of line from the clutch. This was some feat seeing as I had a fair bit of line in the water and the stretch on it must have been considerable.

After about five minutes I had managed to shuffle my way down to Rambo's swim. Alistair had shuffled down with the net, Rambo had shuffled down with the camcorder and the Cowboy and his posse had just shuffled down. Then I felt the angle of the carp's run alter, it swung in and started to swim back towards me. Now as you all know, a fish swimming back towards you is an unnerving experience, you frantically wind like mad, convinced that the loss of a tight line is going to cost you with a hook pull. I was no different and wound like I'd never wound before. I managed to keep in contact and then started to feel the familiar pull as the carp drew level with me and started to ease the clutch out again and take me back up the bank from where I'd came. As I shuffled up the bank so did all the others. The comedy was back again but we were oblivious to it. Only the Fatboys on the far bank, if they could take their eyes off their food, would have grinned at this slow motion, partly synchronised, carp angler herd.

I was about ten yards from being back to square one when I managed to stop the fish and then turn it. It went back the other way but I turned it again, the runs were marginally less powerful and at last I could stand still and play the fish out. To be honest I had forgot about the entourage and only became reminded when Alistair edged to the side of me and squatted down, landing net beside him.

I still felt supremely confident that I was going to land the fish despite the rather odd pattern of the fight so far. I was in the 'now zone' as professional sports psychologists call it. Unflustered and unfazed by what had already occurred and not fazed by the prospect of catching this monster or pondering how big it might be. I simply played the fish and took action as and when it needed it. A little man with a crowbar did try to lever open the doors of the 'now zone' and shout 'D'you think it's a forty?' but I resisted him. With a mental arc welding kit that buzzed a quick butt weld up the centre of the two doors I foiled him completely and shut him, and any worrying thoughts, out of my head.

It must have been a good half hour before I got to the stage of the beast boring around five or six yards out. The others had moved in closer now, all of them as keen as myself to see what was on the end of my line. They murmured amongst themselves but in soft whispers, they clearly didn't want to do anything that might put me off my stroke. The fact that I knew that they were pulling for me actually increased the pressure a bit. I didn't want to let them down, I wanted to be as good as they thought I was. I felt I was, without being big-headed, simply because of my unshakeable belief in my own good fortune of late.

I could tell that Alistair kept wanting to say something by the way he kept sucking in a gulp of air as you do when about to ask a heavy question. Nothing materialised from his mouth because he was desperately trying to stop himself from being himself, i.e. talking all the time, in case it disrupted me. Eventually he could hold it no more and asked me if this was another pop-up fish and I couldn't remember! I had swapped the pop-up around a fair bit to get the other fish and for the life of me I couldn't remember whether this was the rod or not. Saying that I didn't know was hardly conducive to me maintaining my mystical angling abilities so I kept my gob firmly shut. Alistair took this as a bit of a rebuff and apologised for interrupting me.

I felt the line ping over the carp's fins a few times, which can be disconcerting, especially for people like the Cowboy who get emotionally upset about reading such clichés in carp magazine articles, but it happened and was duly noted. A collective 'Ohh' went up from the gallery when the fish first broke surface. It was a common and a very big one at that. The size of it gave me a little extra slug of adrenaline and the heart beat responded accordingly. (This happens when the adrenal gland's inner section, the medulla, secretes epinephrine and norepinephrine which constricts the blood supply to the belly and skin so that more is available to the heart, lungs and voluntary muscles. The classic stress reaction to 'fight or flight.' Not many people know that).

A few more short runs and it was nearly time. Alistair was the picture of determination and concentration, I knew that he wouldn't let me down and that he was out to prove his worth. The common's head came up, Alistair had the net in place by now and was holding it submerged and perfectly still. I walked back a couple of places and drew the fish over the net, Alistair lifted it up. As Virtual Paul may have said if he could talk in other's company, it was game over.

A small ripple of applause broke out from the crowd. I smiled gregariously and bowed. I held my hand out to Alistair like a lead actor does to his lesser co-star and started to clap like some 'luvvie' in a West End play. Alistair nodded and smiled and getting my drift, blew kisses to the crowd who were now clearly an audience. Generously I called in the camera man and Rambo came in stage left to shouts of 'more' and 'get'em off' from the cruder members of the audience. The common got stage fright and just lay in the net. It looked every a bit a forty. It had been caught on one of our red boilies after all, which was nice, I didn't want all my success put down to Pup's pop-ups alone. I was getting to be a right tart.

"Thirty-nine pounds, thirteen ounces," said Alistair carefully regarding the scales that Rambo held. The needle was flickering about a bit but there was no way it touched the forty mark. It looked a good call. I nodded in agreement.

"Am I unlucky, or what?" I said with false seriousness.

"OR WHAT!" called the others. And they were absolutely right.

CHAPTER 11

After the common had been photographed from every conceivable angle, and some that weren't, the lads quickly evaporated away to their swims. No doubt spurred on by the site of my magnificent fish and soothsayer Alistair's prediction of a hot time coming up. I didn't have the heart to mention how wrong he'd been about the chance of a pick-up during a dead day. I suppose that he had covered himself with his 'never say never' maxim and it just showed how odd a sport carp angling can be. No matter how certain you are about an idea there will always, and the word is 'always', be a time, even if it is only the once, when that idea will be disproved. If it coincides with a situation like that which happened to me, your status can become legendary, to a small group of people, that is. The ten of us at Lac Fumant would go to their respective death beds remembering the day a certain Matt Williams caught a near forty on a dead day.

After they had gone I pulled in the other two rods, took some fresh clothes and ablutionary bits and bobs and went up to the cottage for a long, hot shower. I felt as if it was the right thing to do, I know others would have been fishing hard on a wave of euphoria but I had plenty of time and the hot evening spell was due in the evening. It was hard to believe that we'd been at the lake fishing for two days only. Not in the way that the time had passed because it had gone quickly, like it always does when a session is going well. It was just the quality of fish that I had pulled out in such a short space of time. I'd had fish that you would have been hard pushed to have caught in a lifetime's hard effort in England and I'd done it in two days. This was the lure of continental carping, that was clear. Would scratching around for a few doubles on a club water in the UK ever be the same? It was doubtful. Above all else, what had happened to me was amazing, everything was amazing, the whole thing. Even the hot shower felt amazing as it cleansed my sticky body. A towel down, fresh clothes and it was back to the fray, refreshed and now ready for more action. It was great.

Back in my bivvy with all my rods sorted out evening soon came along. Bob was the waiter for my evening meal with Rebecca once again detained elsewhere. About four of us had opted for the evening meal, the rest were all happy to cook their own food that they ordered from Bob or had brought with them. Bob was chuffed about how well I was doing, he said that it meant a lot to him when things were going great guns. He said that he found himself feeling personally responsible if people struggled and had lots of fishless days. Rather arrogantly I told him that he couldn't be held for other anglers' ineptitude. The carp were in the lake, as advertised, and that was all he had to worry about. All I had to worry about was me getting a little bit too big for my boots simply because of three big fish and a wedge in the bank. I duly noted my self-inflicted slap on the wrist and in retrospect regretted saying it.

That night was run city, Alistair's call had been spot on. They were having it big style. The lake had its fishing head on and there was a plethora of plenteous, profuse, pulsating, pandemonium producing pick-ups. It was a tremendously terrific, titillating, tempestuous, tantalising tumultuous, turbulent, triple-topping, typhoon twisting, tongue tingling, totally tranquillity trampling, take-time. The breeze had dropped to nothing and the clear night air seemed exceptionally conducive to the transmission of sound. It was the night of the talking buzzers and with thirty of them situated around the lake, all audible from any swim, their limited, staccato, vocabulary told a tale of carp angling heaven.

There was no luxury of a net-hand, cameraman or crowd that night as there had been for my previous fish just a few hours ago. It was every man for himself and if you wanted a night-time photo because you had run out of sacks you walked to your nearest fellow angler and if they weren't playing a fish they might help you out. Provided you were quick. Sometimes you put the smaller one back unphotographed, to gain sack space for a better fish. It was carp fishing's version of gazumping. You had a good offer of size in the sack but you hadn't signed up with an official snapshot and when a better offer came, the sackholder just had to take it. It was a sackholders' market, there were none for rent and the offers from better fish just kept on coming in.

I performed the sack shuffle a couple of times and I had two sacks. Sack one went from 19 to 22 to 29 and sack two from 18 to 24 to 31. I self-photographed the twenty and the thirty but had to rush the first one of them when the middle rod rattled off in mid cheesy smile.

It had all started when Ian, I think, had a take at about 8 pm and gradually increased in tempo to a peak at 11 pm when I'm sure that every angler on the lake had at least three pick-ups in the following hour. That's thirty takes in sixty minutes. I got a huge rush, a buzz from the buzzers if you like, just listening to them as I sat outside on my chair. I started off just mentally noting the runs to begin with but as it became clear what a hum-dinger of a night it was going to be my excitement and enthusiasm, fuelled by my own takes, became ever more pronounced. When it was going absolutely, completely fucking bonkers, for want of a better phrase, I was reduced to hysterical laughter.

Dedededededede! Down from me, probably Rambo. Couple of minutes later. Dododododododo! (Different tone). Up from me, Alistair. Dedededede! Much quieter, from the far side, Ian or Virtual. Dadadadadadaddadadadadadadadadada! Quieter again but longer to hit the take, one of the Fatboys on a gut-wobbling, waddle to their rods. DEDEDEDEDEDE! Well loud. Shit! That's one of mine. Dededededededededededdedededededededededededede! Rambo again but the poor bastard's still playing the other one. Dadadadadadadadadadada! Overlaid with dedededededededede! Down from me but not as loud, Japp and Wim with simultaneous takes. Dad-dad-daddaddad! (a take to the tune of 'The Good the Bad

97

and the Ugly,' only joking but a buzzer that plays a song, it's got to happen soon). The Cowboy's buzzer. Was he up to draw. More than likely but I'd never see it with my eyes tonight, they were needed elsewhere. Dadadadadadadadadada! Very quiet, Ian or Virtual again and so it went on.

Just when I thought it would slow or be a longer time until another take I'd hear one or a couple in quick succession. It was brilliant listening to them all and trying to imagine who's rod it was and picture in my mind's eye what they were doing. I imagined the Cowboy drawing for all his worth, sometimes both guns at once, the Fatboys sweating with the effort of maintaining a vigil on their rods, of Virtual pressing the baitrunner on his reel to make it wind in automatically and trying to put new batteries into his rods. There was Ian getting Spunker to use the camera to take photos of his better carp but the dumb mutt kept trying to eat it. Alistair, hopelessly trying to fill in meticulous take log-books with infinite detail and just not coping because he'd get another take and then another and get further and further behind. And my old mate Rambo, camouflaged up, monstrous grin, two on at once, re-casting the third with his teeth, hence the monstrous grin, having a whale of a time and blessing the day he'd asked me to come in on bait with him, a few years ago. It was a magic image, backed by a magical sound track.

After midnight it did slow down at a similar tempo to how it had originally speeded up but the dawn feeding spell was as strong as normal. I later found out that from 8 pm that Monday evening until 8 am on the Tuesday morning over a hundred carp came out. Six thirties, to Rambo, Alistair (two), Japp, the Cowboy and myself and eighty-three twenties and everyone had at least six of those, even Virtual. Any repeat captures? Who cares. It was magnificent and I doubt whether I shall witness anything like it again. Even if I did it would never blow me away in the same manner as it had that very first time.

It had not been a night for sleeping.

The mid-morning after the night before revealed ten carp anglers laid waste by an excess of action. We were hung-over on takes and even though Ian had the hair of the dog that hadn't bitten him all over his sleeping bag, it never helped. We were all a bit run down, we had run out of energy, we'd been run over, run dry and run off our feet during an arduous run-in. And if you think that's a lot of runs you should have been there. Our combined lust for carp had been temporarily sated and by eleven everyone was chilling out and chatting about the phenomenon that they had been lucky enough to live through.

Even Japp and Wim, who had been on the water the most in terms of trips and over the longest period of time, had never witnessed the lake fish like that. Even more impressively this included the times when it was a virgin water in terms of angling pressure. Everyone had an anecdote to tell about how they had been mugged by a take when they were either playing a fish, weighing one, photographing one, having a piddle, drinking a cup of tea, picking their nose or just climbing into the bag with their shoes off, all that type of thing. There was even an unconfirmed rumour that Virtual had been on the receiving end of a three at once special. This had left him so bemused and stupefied that he went and hid in his bivvy until the fish weeded themselves. Once the stereo plus one racket had subsided he felt unpressured enough to try and pull the carp out one at a time. It was an unlikely story but with him who could tell? Life was just too real for that boy to get his head around it. Building civilisations from scratch and guiding the ample form of Lara Croft were child's play but actuality unmasked Virtual as just that. A child.

I spent much of my time from midday onwards in Rambo's swim, rods still out, chatting to him. Later on the Cowboy and eventually Alistair, Japp and Wim came along to talk about the previous night. Rambo's thirty, a 32-9, had been a stunning linear mirror that had come at around 4 am. In the morning I had done the honours with the camera and had just managed to get a nice bit of video taped before the battery had issued its warning of impending flatness. It was a smashing fish and one of a sixteen carp haul taken in the time slot I mentioned earlier. I think I'm right in saying that nobody topped that.

Rambo and I swapped our tales of mayhem about the night, each of us trying to relate the excitement that we had felt. We didn't need to try too hard because we both knew exactly how the other had felt, we'd lived through it. We had shared a unique experience together although we had been thirty yards apart.

While Rambo rustled up a little hot something on his stove I asked him a question that didn't need asking.

"Glad we came?"

"No," he said brusquely. "It's been a total waste of time and energy. You've completely ruined my whole perception of carp angling. How am I going to put up with blanks and single figure fish now? And as for winter."

I shrugged knowing exactly what he meant. Many a true word said in jest. "Maybe we can start up a carp fishery like this in England?" I said and a little bee buzzed in my head. Now there was an idea to be toyed with.

Rambo seemed to go with the idea. "Why not? We could import the fish and the weather."

"I was thinking more of a fully enclosed water, with a roof, kept at a constant 23C air and water temperature. I'd have it permanently overcast with a wind machine blowing south-westerly and introduce rain via a sprinkler system as required. The water would be oxygenated, naturally, to enhance growth and stimulate feeding of an already strong head of carp."

"Naturally. Large carp?" asked Rambo.

"By the skip load. Only the finest foreign imports carefully hand selected. All with a boilie eating habit."

It was a case of high spirits leading to an awful lot gibberish being spouted between the pair of us. I suppose it would have been impossible not to feel emotionally lifted, after a carp catching spree like we had just had, how could it be otherwise? When the Cowboy came along to join us it was clear that he had a bucket-full of experiences from the night's action that he simply had to unload. It was the only possible subject of conversation.

"Christ! What a frenzy that was then. How many did you end up with?" He asked.

"Sixteen," said Rambo.

"Twelve," I said.

"I ended up with ten. The best bit was when I was just going to have a piss and I had a take on my middle rod. The thing fought like hell and took me over twenty minutes to land. I got it in, weighed it, a 26 something and sacked it. Then I decided to get the rod back out even though I was really wanting to go. So, anyway, I do that and just about get my cock out to have a whiz and the bloody left hand one goes off, so I tuck it back in and hit that rod. That one fights like hell as well and by the time that's in the landing net I think that I'm about to wet myself any minute. I put the rod straight down, the net and fish on the unhooking mat and what happens?"

"You do piss yourself," said Rambo.

"No! The other rod rattles off. Now not am I only busting for a whiz but I've got no net and a carp on the bank that's going to be in a sad old state if I can't land the other one quickly. In the end I went for scatter, sack and strike. Actually that's not true, I turned the buzzer volume down on the run first. I mean it would be so embarrassing to leave it going for all you lot to hear. It wouldn't be classed as quick drawing would it, a buzzer sounding off for three or four minutes?"

"It might do for the 'Over ninety all-arthritic gunfighter's championship, first qualifying round' but not for a young gun." I said.

Rambo and I went through our individual tales of glory which we had told each other earlier. To be honest it was all pretty much the same kind of thing and just a variation on a theme but it was fun to recollect it. From the outset I had the Cowboy down as a complete nutter but I was getting to like him more each time I met him. He was very belligerent in his attitude towards the commercial side of carping and was of the considered opinion that it was mostly all bollocks, as he had mentioned earlier. Get him off on that topic and he was great fun to listen to. True he had this gunfighter and cowboy thing that was a bit odd but if that was his bag, then so be it. As long as it didn't interfere with me and he didn't go round shooting me in the back every morning and I didn't have to say . . . 'It's no good, Jake, I . . . gasp . . . ain't goin' make it,' I didn't mind. Actually, it was rather entertaining and I still wanted to see him go down to draw. Later on that day he told me that he was a plumber by trade, so maybe he really was a cowboy after all.

When Alistair joined us he had a wide, wide smile. Not only because of what he'd caught but because of what everyone else had as well. He couldn't resist the obvious statement but the three of us didn't begrudge him his moment of glory.

"Hey! What did I tell you? What a night's carp angling that was. I've never been subjected to anything like that before. I had two on at once, twice and both times the pair of them had thirties. Amazing. I had a thirty, five minutes after I had cast out on the rod that I had just caught a twenty-seven and then the other one went, and that was a thirty as well. Thirteen fish in one night and not one under eighteen, the biggest thirty-five. I was caught between trying to get some decent photos or just getting a bait back in the water as quick as I could. It was so manic that a half hour lost on a rod might have cost you a couple of fish and one of them might have been a forty." Alistair's conversation was turning back to its favourite theme, that of picking the bones out of happenstance. "To be honest I am amazed that not one forty came out. I don't know how many there are in here but there must be a fair few, at least twenty I reckon and that doesn't include the fifties that are a real possibility. You see, if the fish that we have previously caught and then caught again, if their weight gain is a yardstick, then some of thirties from several years back must be getting on that way. And yet no big fish were caught. Extraordinary. I mean it's all relative, not calling mid thirties 'big fish' is an oddity in itself but you see what I mean. You must always be thinking of these things and my line of thought is that I find it very curious that no monsters were caught."

We all laughed at his last line. Poor old Alistair, he'd just had the best carping night of his life and yet he was worried because he couldn't work out why the forties hadn't appeared.

"Perhaps it's just a statistical anomaly," I said trying to provide an answer. "Ok so we don't know the exact numbers but at a guess I would think that around a hundred carp were caught last night. How many fish are there in here? How many of them are forties? What were the odds of one forty coming out in a hundred carp? What are the chances? We might have one fish each in the next day and a couple could come out. I've always thought that it's all down to luck, not unless you can stalk an individual fish. The more fish you catch the more likely you are to get a big one, that's a cert, the rest of the time it's just probability and chance."

I felt that I was a bit of an expert on the subject of luck seeing as how well I was riding it. I was a top jockey, a mahout, a pilot and a driver all rolled into one man stuck on a flying dose of fortuity. But I guess that could have been luck as well. My head started to ache at the prospect of getting to the centre of all the relevant machinations that were the onion-like layers of probability so I gave it up as a bad job. It was happening, I was doing all right, thank you very much. End of story. Me no Alistair, me land on feet smelling of roses. Me Tarzan, Rebecca, Jane.

"I'm not so sure about that," said Alistair. "But you'd have thought that one would have come out. Just one. Wouldn't you?"

Before either Rambo or myself started to beat the living daylights out of Alistair the Cowboy decided to tell his story to Alistair, which Rambo and I had already heard. Once he'd finished filling Alistair in on the details, I relayed my twelve hour saga and Rambo told his. When Japp and Wim decided to drop by for a cup of tea, they each told their tale of carp angling paradise and then Alistair told his, the Cowboy his, I told mine and Rambo told his. Of course by then I could have told Rambo's story myself, or the others for that matter seeing as I was now hearing Rambo's for the fourth time and the others for the third. It was just a good job that

Japp and Wim came around together or we would have all had to do it another time.

It wasn't that it was boring, far from it, but the temptation to jazz up an unlikely story even more was becoming tempting. As it were, with no added embellishments our anecdotes were hard enough to believe had you not sat through it. If we had been telling our stories to anglers at home we would have been labelled as liars. Bullshitters to a man. Yet at Lac Fumant it had been, for that one night, run of the mill. And that's the last run joke, I promise.

Eventually everyone got it out of their system, they had quelled the need that all anglers have to tell of their own success. Perhaps that has been the one great achievement during the commercialisation of carp angling, that of freedom of information. Imagine what it must have been like in the 60's, 70's and early 80's catching a big carp and then keeping quiet about it. Even murderers have been caught telling some bloke in the pub how they managed to bump someone off and got away with it, and then suddenly they haven't. It's deep in the human psyche to want to tell. I mean if you have done something pretty cool or clever or risqué it hardly seems worth it if nobody knows about it. At least the carp angler of today doesn't have to worry about that one, not like in days of old. Quite the reverse. In fact, according to the Cowboy, it's so far in reverse that rather than not tell you about something that happened, carp angling writers will tell you about something that didn't happen. If you get his drift, bait used, fish caught, fish caught from where, all that type of stuff.

The conversation had turned to other matters until the Fatboys came around and started it off all over again. I would have like to have said that a night of constant action, with no time to eat, (or was I misjudging their ingenuity?) had shaved off a few pounds. I'd have like to but I'd have been lying, they were as fat as ever. The pair of them had ended up with nine fish each, only Greg had a badly dented bum from slipping on a banana skin on his way down to hit fish number seven.

"Is this a real banana skin or a metaphorical one?" asked Alistair suddenly snapping out of his forties conundrum.

"Oh, it was a real one all right. Old lard arse gave me a bruised arse because he's a litter lout," said Greg pointing to Luke. "He'd eaten a whole bunch of them and had just chucked them all over the swim. When muggins here goes to hit a run, I step on one and it's silent-movie time for me with a big up and over."

"If you came down as hard as that," said the Cowboy, "I'm sure we'd have all heard it."

"All felt it, more like," said Alistair. "That would be at least a number two on the Richter scale, you coming down from a couple of feet."

"Yeah," said the Cowboy. " Don't ever fall off a ladder, it'd be like that film 'Deep Impact.'"

"All right, all right, you pair of spindles. Just remember if we ever go down with a ship in cold seas, I'll be the last to die. But I'll tell you, you wouldn't want an arse as bruised as mine," said Greg rubbing the offending cheek gingerly.

"I wouldn't want an arse like yours, full stop," said the Cowboy grinning.

"I didn't chuck them all over the swim," said Luke indignantly playing catch-up with the conversation. "I just happened to be eating one every time I got a take and I just finished it off mega-quick and dropped the skin in my rush to hit the take."

"All I know is that it looked like a herd of monkeys had been eating in our swim. But they hadn't. It had just been you," said Greg stabbing a finger at his fishing partner.

"A herd of monkeys?" said Alistair looking worried. "That doesn't sound right. What's the collective noun for monkeys?"

"Bananas give you energy. All those tennis players eat them and it was so furious last night I needed to keep up my stamina," said Luke, keeping his defence going.

"All bananas give you," said Greg clearly speaking from first hand or rather first buttock experience, "are a bruised arse. He couldn't have been drinking a cup of tea when he got a run, like everyone else. Oh no, he's got to be eating a banana," whined Greg.

"It is your destiny, Luke. Feel the dark side of the banana. Never underestimate the dark side of eating lots of bananas," I said, more daft bleeder than Darth Vader.

"We have got a video that includes bananas," said Japp.

The others all laughed. It was an in-joke which Rambo and I weren't party to but my train of thought went – Dutch Brothers – Amsterdam – Red Light District – Porn Videos and terminated at Fruit Fetish Central.

"It's a 'wank' of monkeys," said Rambo smiling. Had he read my mind? Was telepathy amongst his attributes or did I have a depraved mind.

"It's a 'troop,' isn't it? Hold on, that doesn't sound right either," said Alistair shaking his head.

It was at that moment that the first truly nasty deed of the holiday occurred. Spunker came haring round into view, his enormous jowls bouncing up and down like spittle-laced pannier bags, and purposefully, one might even say malevolently, cocked his leg up Rambo's rear buzzer bar and peed on it. Once this had been done to his satisfaction, he ran off.

"Now there's an act of war if ever I saw one," said Alistair.

Rambo said nothing but I had seen the look on his face before. It was the look of evil, with a touch of malice and a big slug of 'revenge required' thought process. I wouldn't have wanted to be in Spunker's paws.

The conversation had lost its thread until Ian and Virtual Paul could be seen walking up from the Cowboy's swim.

"Ah," said the Cowboy. "Here comes the man whose life was saved by a dog and computer game boy. Look, he's got that bloody laptop with him that he plays his games on. Honestly, it's like a kid with rag doll."

"Actually it's more like a kid with a computer game, these days," said Alistair sagely.

"I call him Virtual Paul," I told everyone.

"As in virtual reality?" asked Alistair. I nodded. "I like that and may start calling him it."

"What about last night, then?" asked Ian as they arrived within earshot and his question was received by a chorus of groans. "I had nine fish. Can you believe it?"

There were various shouts of 'That all.' 'Pathetic' and 'Useless.' We all had elephants and we all had boxes to put them in. Everyone had been there, done it and got the tee-shirt. Except Bob, his tee-shirts were something totally different.

"We can believe it." Said Japp.

"Yeah and we also believe it to be the lowest total yet," said Greg. "What about Paul, though? How many did you catch then, son?"

Virtual's cheeks reddened or maybe that was just from the effort of walking, it was hard to say.

"Wound in after four. Playing chess with some bloke in South Africa. My arms ached," he mumbled.

We all looked at each other in amusement.

"The voice of the young, has spoken," said Wim.

"Paul?" said Alistair, slightly sarcastically. "What's the collective noun for monkeys? You see, Greg had a load of them in his swim last night and we'd like to know the proper terminology." Rambo snorted indignantly. It was not high on his wish list. "We'll I would, anyway," Alistair admitted.

"Find out," mumbled Paul and he sat down on the ground and opened up his laptop and started tapping away.

We all looked at each other in amusement again.

After a couple of minutes he asked Alistair how to spell 'collective noun', which he did. A minute later he had found something and started to speak in his indistinctive way

". . . Congress of baboons . . . Shrewdness of apes . . . Oh, tribe of monkeys," said Virtual looking up from the screen.

"Says who?" asked Alistair.

"AltaVista search engine found a website with 'collectivenouns dot html.' Laptop's got a mobile, connected to the Net," muttered Virtual.

We all looked at each other in amusement for the third time. What the hell was he on about?

"Son," said the Cowboy, "you've got fingertips like beavers' tails. Now it's either genetic or you're pressing too many buttons. Why don't you just chuck that thing in the water?"

"No!" said Virtual and cuddled the laptop tight to his chest.

"I wonder if Altawhatever can tell us why nobody caught a forty," said Alistair getting us back into carping mode and his own worry mode.

It was unlikely Mr AltaVista could shed much light on that one but I was sure that it was just one of those things and I was convinced that it would happen soon. The law of averages would even things up, it might go as far as uneven things up and let a couple of fifties come out. Now there was a mouth-watering prospect. As little pockets of conversation fired to and fro about me I seemed to become immersed in my own little world for a while. To catch the first ever fifty out of Lac Fumant, that would be something. I'd leave Alistair to his collective nouns and other obsessions, Virtual to his inter-continental chess, Greg to his black and blue bum, Luke to his fruit, Rambo to his revenge and concentrate on fifties, or if pushed to compromise, forties. I would have to try and fish a little bit harder, if I could force myself, to try and make it happen.

CHAPTER 12

Just before I tucked myself into my sleeping bag that Tuesday night I made the resolution in my head. It was time to put my foot down a little harder on the old accelerator pedal and go for the really big fish. This made little sense as I had earlier admitted that unless you could stalk an individual fish, it was a matter of chance as to the size. The more you caught, the better your chance was, that much was evident but Alistair's musings on the lack of a forty pound fish, out of a haul of one hundred and fifty plus carp so far, had set me thinking. Perhaps he had hit on something? I came to a theory that possibly the bigger fish, that by all accounts were definitely in Lac Fumant, might come out from different spots from those that were usually fished.

I realised that this had all the hallmarks of desperate reasoning, but what if the fact that people kept fishing to the same spots and doing very well, by accepted standards, was one of the reasons why the bigger fish weren't getting caught? If the lake had been more difficult and takes had been very hard to come by this would have pushed people to be more adventurous and try a different approach. However, seduced by good catches of still very good sized fish, they just kept on hammering the more accessible spots and looked no further because they had no real reason to do so. Another possibility could be that the lake hadn't been subjected to lots of different anglers. This group that Rambo and I were a part of were the first to have anglers outside the original clique who had heard about it on the grapevine and from friends. Rambo and I were the only outsiders, the first to visit the lake from seeing it via an advertisement. My suggestion was that the others in the group had become slightly blinkered in their approach because of their insular nature.

An individual's observations can sometimes end up set in stone. 'That's the way it is' says everyone as the observation is passed down the grapevine and becomes a widely held opinion, yet its roots might lay in just one occurrence. A little of that may have happened at Lac Fumant. It takes a lot of self-belief to fish against the accepted norm, blanking while fishing conventionally is a lot easier to take than blanking while fishing differently. But my mind was made up, as was Rambo's, we were the ones who would give it a crack. We had proved our abilities to fish on the back of Alistair's game plan but now it was time to try and push back the frontiers of carp catching knowledge at Lac Fumant. It sounded very grandiose, when put like that and so it would be, if it came off.

I was convincing myself that Lac Fumant needed fresh ideas from outsiders and we were the kiddies to do it! Or not, as the case may be. There were a lot of ifs and buts but (there's another one) I was keen to give it a go. The area out in front of us at one hundred and twenty yards where Rambo had spotted the activity was going to come under attack and I also intended to have a go at the island margin with the bait boat. Rambo hadn't got around to climbing the tree that shaded my bivvy like he said he would a couple of days ago. The dead day, my near forty and the run frenzy and all the discussions after had seen to that. I had discussed my theory with Rambo after everyone else had drifted off from his swim and just the two of us remained. He was up for it as much as I was. If we tried with just one rod each to begin with we could hedge our bets a little and see what transpired. We had nothing to lose as such and Rambo said that I had the golden touch at the moment and it would more than likely work a treat. I felt confident as well, I always intended to have a crack at the island with the boat but Alistair's thoughts had made me bring the action forward by several days. When I asked myself why, it was because I had been doing all right where I was and this sort of backed up my half-arsed theory.

The afternoon with the others had come and gone. It had been a laugh to have them all around and the piss-taking had been good. I felt as if I knew them better now and we arranged to all meet up on Saturday night only over on the other bank in Ian's swim. It was certainly a lot different from my last session on the syndicate water where I would hardly have talked to another angler other than Rambo, let alone swap banter and jokes with them.

Bob had been the last person that I had spoke to before it was time to get some shut eye. He apologised profusely about there being no evening meal and explained that Rebecca had been away to visit a sick friend but would be back tomorrow. I told him it was no problem and had heated up some beans and sausages from a tin after he had gone. Before he left I gave him my food order, milk, bread that kind of stuff and gave him the spare video battery to charge up.

I pulled the bag up over my shoulder and snuggled down. Tomorrow was another day but it was the first day of the new strategy implementation and I would get to see, or should I say gawp at, Rebecca. That night I felt a fresh tingle of expectation. Would my theory pay off? How few square inches of material would Rebecca have covering her glorious body? I still couldn't resolve my inner turmoil over my lusting for Rebecca but there was no denying it was there. There was also, rather strangely, a desire to catch the lake's first fifty. Having taken an easy going attitude to the fishing side of things I now felt that little familiar gnawing in my gut. It was hunger, only a mild spasm at the moment, but hunger it was. The hunger to succeed and catch one of those monster fish. It was nowhere near being the ravenous beast that it had been when we were trying to defeat Watt in the TWTT but a little bit of it was back. And only a few hours earlier I hadn't been aware that it was there at all. Perhaps my recovery was nearly complete and I was nearly back to the same carp angler I had been during the old syndicate days?

Whether I'd be any the better for it was debatable, if anything it might make things worse. I loved my laid back attitude and it had served me well. Sometimes trying too hard can be counter productive but I'd just have to wait and see how things materialised.

That night I had two twenties and it hardly registered as anything special. Too much of a good thing? Undoubtedly. Somebody, well something, and that something was Lac Fumant, had shoved my carping goalposts ten pounds to the right. Doubles now registered as singles, twenties as doubles, thirties as twenties and forties as thirties, even if I hadn't quite managed to catch one of those. It was sad in a way. Although some amongst us endeavour to make us regard weight as an inconsequence when carping, they are ploughing a very lone furrow. They are ploughing that very lone furrow with a rusty plough and a knackered, three-legged ox with asthma and a skin condition that needs an application of cream every half an hour. The have to plough uphill, into the wind and driving rain and the harness is so rotten that it keeps on breaking. That furrow is so lone that there isn't a living creature within a hundred thousand light years, because they're on another planet. You see the point?

Try telling your average carper that a five pound common is the same as a twenty pound mirror and expect abuse. Keep on about it and then you can expect violence followed by a short stay in the corridor of a national health hospital, being ignored by over-burdened staff, before you end up being murdered by an injection of rat poison administered by a bogus doctor, who is an ex-psychiatric patient, who has just been released into the community. It isn't worth it. It isn't true. Big is best and bigger is even better. Like cocks and tits? I guess so, unless it's you who is saddled with the unenviable task of lugging around freakish appendages and wondering where you can put it all so that people will stop staring.

At around seven in the morning Rambo came up to my swim with his marker rod and one of those marker floats that have batteries and we set about getting the float out to the area we had discussed. We carefully loaded the float and its attachment of line and weight into one of the boat's side panels and shut the lid down onto the main line. I took the float out on the boat while Rambo held the rod and let the line go from the open bail arm reel. Once it was in the area that he felt he had seen the activity I lifted up the side cover with the radio control unit and Rambo gently pulled the float off the boat.

He had previously set the depth of the float to match that of the bottom elsewhere. Lac Fumant's bottom appeared to be fairly uniform with hardly any variation once you got away from the margins where it did shallow slightly. As Rambo tightened up, the float moved over in the water more than he expected before pulling on the lead. There was only one explanation, the water in that area was shallower. Rambo quickly set up another rod with a marker as he didn't want to lose the spot we already had, set that one a couple of feet shallower and I towed it out to various different spots around the original float. It was a result, there was a small plateau around ten yards in diameter that was over two foot shallower than elsewhere and the original float was almost bang in the middle.

Now you could call that a stroke of fortune but this was Rambo's doing and had no connection to myself (if I was a greyhound I'd be racing under the name Lucky Boy). It was he who had diligently noticed the movement of fish in this area, no mean feat seeing as how easy it was to be side-tracked into just watching the areas where all your action was coming from. How many carp anglers would have bothered to have investigated other areas when the were doing so well else where? Not many and this was the crux of my theory and why no one had found the plateau before. If they had, Alistair would have put it on his map or told us about it. It still had to produce fish, of course, but both of us felt proud to have found it. If it fished well we would pass on the knowledge and would have given a bit back, rather than just taking, like we had so far. Maybe it would be named Rambo's Plateau and if my idea came off it would be a case of Matt's Margin.

Once in position Rambo put an elastic band around the spool of the reel and pushed a spare bivvy peg into the bank and made a mental note of a feature on the far bank, a tree I believe. His satellite guidance system was complete. He had distance from bank to his spot and a sight line from his peg to feature. He could bait up, pull in the marker and be happy he could accurately get back out there in exactly the same area.

Rambo then went and got one of his long distance rods, a thirteen foot, 3 oz test curve beasty with a butt ring big enough for a ferret to crawl through. The rod was kitted with a brand new Shimano Big Pit baitrunner loaded with about six miles of eight pound line. There was a tapered forty-five pound shock leader, 4 oz pendant lead, and a short mono hooklength with a single boilie on a size two hook to complete the set-up.

Before casting Rambo staked out a tiny little mat of canvass material and placed the lead and boilie upon it, he then took a wide stance at right angles to the bank, so positioned that the mat was now behind him and to his left shoulder. He compressed the rod a bit by pulling tight to the lead and then powered the whole lot into orbit. The lead fell some five yards past the marker. It was awesome. I had never seen anybody cast like that, his technique and upper body strength were superb and it all looked under control. I guessed he still had quite a few more yards in the tank if he needed it.

Rambo pulled back from the spot trying to feel the bottom to make sure he wasn't casting into one of the few dense weedbeds that the lake had. It was clear. He peppered a few more casts around the general area and it all seemed fine.

"Ok, boy. Are you going to get that toy of yours on the move and bait up for me."

"Aye aye, Cap'n. I'll splice the microprocessor and run up the jet pumps. Shiver me high density plastic. Yo-ho-ho and a bucket of boilies," I said, giving it my best salty sea-dog impression.

Rambo gave me a 'sad bastard' look and helped me fill the boat with boilies.

Now I don't really want to go into the whole ethical and moral dilemma that constitutes the bait boat argument. I know that it's a tricky subject prone to making people froth at the mouth like a rabid animal and transporting them into blind fury and rambling rhetoric. If you ain't got four hundred and fifty odd notes to blow on one then discussion is futile, you'll only be accused of the politics of envy. If you have then it's best left to individual choice. Is it cheating? Is it angling? Is it scientific development taking away the very essence of our beloved sport? All the questions are pretty subjective. To some people using a fixed spool reel and a carbon fibre rod are sacrilege, let alone buzzers, bivvies, boilies, hair rigs and all manners of modern day tackle.

I guess it's still angling but in some ways it isn't. In the US they call it bank fishing as opposed to boat fishing, they are two distinct types of fishing. So is any boat acceptable for carp fishing? Rowing baits out, playing fish from boats, getting fish out of weed from boats, in some ways these things are even more intrusive than a little battery boat. I suppose the size of the water determines acceptability to some degree and what is tolerable on foreign waters may not be the case back at home. Lac Fumant was very borderline on the grounds of its size but it was in France and I felt that because we wouldn't be interfering with any of the others it was ok to use my new toy. Bob had never specifically said that there was a boat ban but then again I don't think that I had ever directly asked him, which was an oversight on part, I suppose.

All I know is that without the boat we couldn't have baited up so meticulously and put out a lovely even carpet of boilies exactly where we wanted them. Sure, we had an advantage over the others, provided my theory worked and we actually caught something from those distant areas. Life is rarely fair and the fact that I happened to have run into some money meant I had the means to fish more accurately at distance than I could ever hope to achieve using conventional equipment. To use football managers' speak, at the end of the day you do what you feel happy with. I suppose if everyone had a little bait boat zooming about it would be a bit naff. Then we'd have to wait for some smart company like Mr Nash or Mr Fox to come up with an anti-bait boat submarine and we could all play Battle of Midway until the batteries went flat or everyone was sunk. See that spot twenty yards out from the weedbed? Big bait boat snag. They reckon there's about a dozen down there, good holding area for carp. All the boats went down with a full cargo. Don't laugh, it's bound to happen sometime.

Not having the tackle or the ability to cast like my mucker I had to tow my terminal tackle into place out by the island. The other side of the island was much closer to the bank and was regularly fished. I was sure that both Ian and Virtual had at least one bait each up against it but from my side it was a long way, a good thirty yards plus further than where Rambo's feature was. Luckily my margin area was weed free as well and I put a trail of bait along a ten yard section and fished bang in the middle of it. My greatest concern was that I was going straight out between my two sets of pads and might have serious problems should a fish get into the back of them. I did have enough room to get down the bank either side and go for a big lot of side-strain and go either outside the pads or for a straight pull through the middle. A pick up at night could be very interesting but I had set myself on giving it a go. If I started getting runs and losing fish then I would have to evaluate things but I felt that I could play fish in safely, if I had a bit of luck.

The middle of the afternoon saw Rambo and I a few hours into our new campaign and then rumour came round via Alistair that Virtual had only been and gone and done it. He'd cracked it. He'd actually won. It was checkmate against his chess playing, South African based, Nethead.

"I'm thrilled for him," I said to Alistair with a hint of sarcasm but inwardly I was somewhat relieved. I'd wondered what he was going to say and for one mad minute I thought it was going to be that Virtual had pulled out a fifty and left all of us looking like a troop of monkeys, or whatever it was.

Alistair was thinking about monkeys as well. "I know it's a bit sad but you have to admire the technology that allows you to play a game of chess from a remote lake which has no electricity and no telephone line against someone you've never met, thousands of miles away. Even that thing about the collective noun for monkeys impressed me. Amazing, all that information just sitting there waiting to be looked at. I expect that nearly the whole sum of human knowledge is on the internet."

"I bet it doesn't tell you how to catch a fifty out of Lac Fumant," I countered.

Alistair laughed. "No. I don't expect that it does. Paul says that there is a load of stuff about carp fishing, though, and that it's increasing all the time. Apparently the biggest thing on the internet is pornography. Japp and Wim's father have a porn website."

"What?!"

"Of course, you don't know, do you? Their father is in the, shall we say, adult entertainment business. They're quite a big concern, I believe."

"But they said that they wanted Rambo to do some work for their dad. Jesus Christ! They didn't say what kind of work but I can guess," I blurted.

"Yes. They're always keen to get hold of the right type of .. er, model. I know that they have half-heartedly asked Rebecca a few times, when Bob's not nearby I hasten to add, but she's told them to get lost."

My brain nearly fused at the images that briefly formed in my head at that snippet of info until I suddenly remembered something else.

"I'm sure that Ian said something about that when we had the introduction party. I'm convinced that he said that they were always asking about that dog of his working for their dad as well."

Alistair looked embarrassed. "More than likely. I'm afraid that they do cater for a wide range of taste, some of which, I must admit, I find rather disgusting."

"What I find disgusting is that the bastards haven't asked me. Oh yeah. Ask Rebecca. Ask Rambo. Ask Spunker, for God's sake, but not me, Spunker by nature and Spunker by name. It's an insult, don't they think I'm up for it or do they think that I can't get it up? What are they trying to tell me?" I said jokingly. Many a true word said in jest.

"If it makes you feel any better they've never asked me, the Fatboys or Paul, either."

I gave Alistair a dead pan look. "Not really. If anything it makes me feel a darn sight worse. What about the Cowboy?"

"They've asked him. They said they wanted him to be in a Wild West one that they were making at the time. It was called 'Cum fight at the OK Corral.'"

I burst out laughing. "What did he say?" I asked, intrigued.

"He said that he was too busy with his plumbing job to get the time off."

"I can understand that completely," I said with mock sincerity. "Why waste your time jetting off to have loads of perverted sex with porn starlets when you can be stuck under a bath, scuffing skin off with a pair of stilsons. It stands to reason. It was the only possible decision he could come to."

"I think it was more to do with the fact that the whole film concept would be parodying and belittling the subject that the Cowboy holds most dear, namely the Wild West."

"Now you've put it like that it makes even more sense. I don't think."

Alistair changed the subject. "That was your bait boat I saw earlier on I presume?"

I nodded. "Yeah. Me and Rambo had a chat and decided to try different areas that haven't seen so much pressure just to see if they might produce. To be honest it's not to catch more, as such, we're more than happy with what we've caught, it's to try and see if we can sort the bigger fish out. I suppose most bloke's going abroad are after the fish of a lifetime rather than just bagging up loads of twenties, you seem to get immune to twenties very quickly. I know it's a terrible thing to say but now I'm into my fishing I just had the desire to try and get a forty plus out and, dream time, a fifty if possible. I was very easy going in my attitude to begin with but the thought of a fish that big has made me want to try for it a bit harder."

Alistair gave me an understanding smile. "There's a big difference between a high thirty and a forty isn't there? I feel as if it's wrong to admit to such a thing but it would be a case of me simply lying to myself. Of denial almost. There are these mountains to climb in all walks of life, they are milestones and if you are not careful, they can become millstones and weigh you down with frustration if you can't achieve them. Most of the time they are just a number to either get under or over. Imagine if Roger Bannister had broken the world mile in four minutes and one tenth of a second rather than the three, fifty-nine point whatever it was? His whole life would have changed, no immortality, just another temporary world record holder. Us type of anglers are comparable to an athlete today trying to go sub four, only we're trying to go forty plus. Others have done it many times and by great margins but it is a very strong personal goal. Other events or sports have different criteria but it all boils down to making a magic number, a number that is universally accepted by people in the same field as having a strong significance in terms of achievement. Now whether your line of attack will bring the results you desire is another matter. I have tried fishing at range, not with a boat mind you, I wouldn't use one, not that I'm being judgmental, each to their own and all that, but long range didn't work out for me. I analysed all my results and decided that the best plan lay in the numbers approach. In other words I was playing the probability game that states that the more fish I catch, the more chance I have of landing a monster. It's very hard to stalk individual fish here because of the colour of the lake, as you've no doubt noticed if a fish rolls close in it has only to go down a few inches and you lose it very quickly. Therefore I have disregarded that approach as a short cut and tend to fish static most of the time with bottom baits. It's very successful but you have little control over what size of fish picks up your hookbait. I have seen no evidence in my results, or that of others, too conclude that certain areas produce the better fish. On some waters, maybe, but not, as yet, on Lac Fumant. The other thing about fishing at distance is that it is more difficult. Your boat will help eradicate some of the problems but if you have to fish a lighter main line and get a big fish in from a long way out the chances of losing it are greater. Without a boat it is much harder to get free offerings as you would like them, as well, so you have to think of all these things and make a decision because they do make a difference. Unfortunately that epitomises my whole attitude to carping, it is my strength and also my weakness. You have shown me how you have caught fish by juggling baits and areas, albeit ones that I showed you, in a manner that I would never have done. I would have fished to my plan and not caught the fish that you have. By the end of the fortnight it'll be interesting to see if things have evened up, but you have the edge for the moment and I have to say that I have been very impressed with what you have done. I shall be very keen to see how you do, I can tell you. I can't recall a bait boat ever being used before or the island being fished to from your swim which makes it doubly compelling. I'm glad to be in the next swim up and get a first hand look at your ideas. I hope it works out for you, if it does, it'll be food for thought for all of us."

"Thanks," I said. "I wouldn't have done so well without your help that's for sure. It might be that I've provided a bit of variation on your groundwork and it's worked out all right. The area that Rambo is fishing at distance could be a winner. I'm not going to say why just yet but if it turns up trumps we'll fill you in on all the detail. Personally I think it's going to be a hot spot but I don't want to get too cocky and put a jinx on it."

Alistair nodded and eventually said his goodbyes. As it turned out the only jinx I was running was the one that kept stopping Rebecca bringing my grub around. Bob played waiter again and told me that she'd phoned to say that there had been a problem on the railway and she wouldn't be back until late at night. I'd have to wait a bit longer to see her again.

Soon after Bob had left me Rambo had his first take from the plateau, a lively common that went just under twenty and took him nearly an hour to get in on his eight pound main line. I heard his buzzer and went down to start videoing the fight in a slightly fading light but the camouflaged-one couldn't land the fish within the hours of camcording daylight. I tried to do an amusing voice-over but the whole thing went on for so long that I just ran out of things to say. When eventually I did manage to net the culprit and Rambo turned his nose up at the size of it, it was clear that something was going to give. Rambo was not one to debate a subject or to give something another chance. He would make his mind up there and then and would ride out the consequences whatever they might be.

"Fuck that for a game of soldiers," said Rambo with heart. "That was hard graft, I didn't feel as if I was in control at all, the bloody thing just ran me all over the place. If I decide to use my other rods with 15lb line can you give me a tow out with that boat of yours? I won't get out no where near far enough with main line as thick as that even if I re-spooled the long distant rods. I can't see much point persisting because I think that if I do hook one of the real big ones it'll just take me where it wants and end up snagging me, probably back in the Loire, and I'll end up losing it."

Naturally I said it would be no problem. Rambo said he'd sort it out in the morning and fish one of his original spots for the night because he couldn't be bothered to do all the marking out at night. Secretly I was pleased because I just wanted to slump in my chair for a few hours before sleeping and try and remind myself of the beauty of my surroundings. Like the size and number of fish I'd had, the lakes appeal was being taken for granted and that was wrong.

I went back to my swim and then remembered that I had forgotten to tell Rambo about Japp and Wim's family business and what line of work he might get asked to do. I turned to go and tell him but the island rod gave a short staccato run which I quickly hit. Fishing so far out against an island was never going to give me a belting run and I felt resistance as I struck. I gained line by pumping and winding for about five minutes and then the hook pulled. I couldn't believe it. My first blip of misfortune in ages.

Trying to take it philosophically I decided to fish that rod in the margin for the night, thinking much as Rambo had. How ironic, I thought, if that rod turned out to produce a forty that night. The idea turned out to be hypothetical, it never happened. I had two fish, one on each of the other rods, both twenties again, but my mind focused on the one that got away. Had it been a big one? A forty? A fifty even? It would have been just my luck for it to have been a monster on the one time I had a hook pull. I was partially joking when I thought that but the doubt still nagged at me a little. No, I had to be positive and write that one off, after all it was only a scrapper twenty, if that. Wasn't it?

CHAPTER 13

As agreed, on the Thursday morning, just as it was light enough to see, I played at being a tug-master and dragged firstly the marker float and then the terminal tackle of my carping buddy out to the plateau. Rambo was on Pup's pop-ups for the first time and despite his lack of enthusiasm to set the plateau swim up in the dark he was chomping at the bit on this morning. No long distance rods required, no shock leaders and skinny main line, just good 2 lb T.C carbons and well filled Shimano 8010's with 15lb line. Once he was sorted out hookbait-wise I started to bait up the plateau with the boat. Now we were doing it this way it felt even more of a cheat than when Rambo was casting out and I was only doing the baiting. Modern technology moves on and those in a slow car get flattened, let alone the ones who stand still. Ethics and morality (standing in the bus queue waiting) can sometimes get crushed into oblivion, but what the heck, it's called progress.

During all this bait boat malarkey I casually dropped into the conversation the nature of the employment, as perceived by myself, that was likely to occur should Rambo ever take up the offer to do work for Mr Japp and Wim, Snr.

"They want you to be a porn star," I said to Rambo after telling him that it was all about adult entertainment.

"I can think of worse ways to make a living. Come to think of it nearly every way I can think of is worse than screwing beautiful women for money," said Rambo, unfazed as usual.

"It's not as simple as that is it?" I said as I unceremoniously dumped another hundred or so boilies into a watery grave with just a flick of my thumb. Boilies overboard!

Rambo shrugged. "That's about the size of it, as I see it."

"Please," I said holding out an upturned palm. "Don't mention size. I'm an ordinary mortal, boringly medium. I don't need your size rammed in my face."

"Don't think I'd ever want to, either," said Rambo, revolted.

I continued on my previous theme. "I mean, superficially it sounds great, but what about everyone watching while you're at it? Telling you to get your leg back out the way so they can zoom in on your dick and end up closer to it than what you are. I could imagine it all just draining away."

"All what draining away?" asked Rambo.

"The blood. I think the technical name for it, is 'wood'. Can't get 'wood' means floppy-doppy time and with four cameras, two sound engineers, a director and make-up all watching, it's easy to imagine why."

"I'll have to just wait and see what they come up with but I'm a single bloke, no ties, you never know. I might have a go," said Rambo giving me a pair of raised eyebrows and a cheeky smile. He'd have to pull some different faces to that if he wanted to make it as a male porn star.

I said nothing. Imagine watching a porn video with someone in it who you knew well? What if they had a really spotty arse? Watching that go up and down could really do your head in. You wouldn't know what to say to them. Or maybe you would. It struck me as being funny that Japp and Wim were living out a national stereotype. Think Holland or Amsterdam and ask people to say what they associate with those places and sex and drugs would be high on the list. Definitely above canal carping but below tulips, total football and bicycles? I guess it would depend on what your bag was. Someone once said to me that they were in Baghdad when I was in my dad's bag, but they were just having me on.

Back in my swim I put my island rod out and baited that area with the boat. I'd been a full cheat from the offset. I wondered where my sense of unease came from concerning the boat and decided it was Alistair's dismissal of them. Of course my unease wasn't strong enough to stop me using the boat and effectively wasting four hundred odd quid but I could see any success may be written off as 'he only caught them because of the boat.' I'd have to live with it, I mean you could say the same about catching at night with buzzers or to its extreme a bolt rig. I bet myself that if things did go well there'd be a few of the boys saving up for a boat of their own.

I too, was on the 'legendary' Pup pop-up and was back in exactly the same spot that the take had come from last night. My other two rods I kept to the successful spots on our bottom bait. It was quite a paraphernalia doing the island rod and Rambo's plateau rod, made worse, I expect, because it wasn't something that I did quickly and naturally simply because it was still a new ball game, or rather boat game, to me. Once I had finally finished I got out the solar panel charger, faced it up to the direction of the rising sun and topped up the bait boat's battery. I then moved my chair into the pleasantly warm beam of sunlight and gave my own batteries a top up. It was a very pleasant situation to be in and the first cup of tea of the morning made it even better.

I felt confident that my game plan would work out but I was unsure how fast the action would be. It was all great stuff nevertheless and I vigorously rubbed my hands together and smiled. I was really up for catching an eff carp, tee's would no longer please. (Forty and fifty pound carp required. Twenties and thirties not big enough. Come on keep up).

As I sat there, hands clamped behind my head, I sucked in the fresh morning air and tried to make myself realise how marvellous it all was. The thing I needed to really make me realise how marvellous it all was, was either a twenty-four hour blank or a forty. On the one hand it would teach me not to be blasé about all the fish I'd caught that were now not big enough and on the other the obtaining of such a personal goal would ensure instant ecstasy. I wanted that forty! Hell! I wanted that fifty come to that! I had a place of destiny on Pup's wall, just by the light switch, that needed fulfilling. My minds eye pictured me telling him I'd caught a fifty on one of his pop-ups and him filling up with tears of delight, grasping my hand and kissing it and saying 'oh thank you, oh thank you.' I decided it would be better to concentrate on catching the effing fifty than waste time mulling over that sort of rubbish.

For a while I sat in silence meditating on the fact that I was dying to see Rebecca again after such a long absence. I'd been blanking with her for about eighty-odd hours. I suppose it did at least prove my earlier point about taking things for granted and the need for something to be confiscated before you appreciate how nice it was to have it in the first place. Not that I'd had her, in the carnal sense, but she had at least talked to me with a hint of sexual innuendo and that was good enough for starters.

I knew I was starting to ramble and getting a bit too deep into Alistair country to feel safe. A couple of hours of serenity was what I needed, a time for idle speculation not analytical navel-gazing. It was not what I got at all. Ten minutes later, with my first cuppa barely drained, Rambo had a take off the plateau so it was down there to help him net the fish, weigh it, photograph it and do a quick video because it went just over thirty.

Rambo, resplendent in camouflage shorts and no top, showing off an incredibly muscled torso, complete with intricate tattoo-work, was much happier using the heavier line. He'd bossed the fish, even from such a long way out and felt that with the 15lb main line and the amount of water at his disposal he could land the biggest that Lac Fumant could offer. I went and got the boat, took it off charge, towed out the marker float to its pre-destined rubber band stop, took the terminal tackle out to the marker float and while Rambo pulled in the marker I baited up again. Then I took the boat back and re-connected it to the charger. Now for a sit down.

I'd just sat down when Alistair came round and said that he'd caught a corker of a leather that went just over the thirty mark and could I come and photograph it for him. He hoped that I didn't mind asking because the Fatboys had gone into town with Bob to help him carry their food and drink back. Usually he asked one of them, the idea being that as they were fishing as a pair one could help him and the other could guard the six other rods. I said yes to shut him up before he told me the history of the world. True, it had been a sit down, but not of the duration I had intended.

As we walked back to his swim Alistair told me that he was sure that the Fatboys had it in mind to bring back plenty of lager for the Saturday get-together in Ian's swim. It suddenly dawned on me that I hadn't touched an alcoholic drink for over two years. You see they don't serve wine or chilled beer in the Her Majesty's home for the rather naughty and I had no reason to drink any when I got out, simply because I had no deep desire to do so. The day the numbers came up or when the cheque had been cashed I only drank tea, there had been no champagne or anything like that. I made a mental note to steer clear of the stuff, one mouthful and I could see me shooting my mouth off about all sorts of things that I didn't want the others to know.

Having duly obliged Alistair, I came back, sat down and got straight back up because of the call from Rambo. Another fish off the plateau, this one a nice 24 plus common. Once that fish was sorted and back in the water it was time to re-position and re-bait. It seemed obvious he was going to be into fish all the time so I got him to be helmsman under my guidance and let him get used to using the boat for himself. When he'd finished I told him to keep the boat in his swim and fetched him the solar charger and all the other odds and sods. I wasn't going to get my bit of peace so decided it was time for me to set up the camcorder in his swim with a new tape and see if I could get a take on film. So much for my serenity, this was more like work. Of course one loves one's work in the film industry.

With only tapes of 90 minutes duration and a battery life of even less getting a take on a home video isn't all that easy. Deciding when to start filming must be similar to the decision the Cowboy has to make when he comes out to draw. Quite frankly I was starting to think that I might never see him do it, the lake had fished pretty well so far and yet Rambo assured me that he hadn't been out. Still, I wasn't the Cowboy and now seemed a very good time for me to set up the video in Rambo's swim, shout 'action' and watch his indicators power off.

To divert off for a second, my only omission on the tackle front and it was something that was so glaringly obvious that I can't believe I missed it, was a set of indicators specific for long range. I had my hangers, the type that you could add extra weight to, which were fine up to a point, but I didn't have the ones that could be put under tension like Rambo did. I mean I knew that I might fish at range on the odd occasion, that was why I got the boat but I just didn't get anything suitable indicator-wise. I wished that I'd got something a bit more responsive than just heavy hangers. With over a hundred and fifty yards of line in the water I was now aware of the shortcomings of trusting a small weight to register a take, especially on back drops and especially at night.

I told Rambo about my concerns and he gave me one of his swingers as he'd bought a boxed set of three which was nice, although I wasn't about to admit it.

"Not a yellow one," I whinged, mucking about. "I want the pretty blue one, to match my buzzer l.e.d that's blue on that rod."

Rambo laughed. "Look, Mr Speilberg, you'd better hurry up with that camera because it's been over an hour since my last take and I'm due another. These carp won't wait for anyone, not even a Hollywood big shit, sorry, shot like you."

"Bloody prima-donna, know-nothing actors. There'll be a directors cut all right, from here to here." I said laughing and run a finger across my throat.

I went and got camera one, set it up on a bankstick, called for silence on set and was about to cry 'action' when it came to my right hand rod fished in the margins. I legged it up to the swim and played in another twenty common which Bob, who was on his daily round, offered to net for me. All through the fight he kept encouraging me with calls of 'Go on my, son' and 'Go on, chief' and 'Quality' when I pulled it over the net and he worked the handle.

I went through the usual actions afterwards with Bob photographing and checking the weight for me while saying 'chief' and 'quality' nearly every other word. He said those words like some people say the word 'fuck'. They were just randomly peppered throughout a sentence without adding any significant meaning. It was his oratory habit and yet it was rather curiously addictive and I found myself starting to mimic his speech pattern.

"Thanks for that, chief. Quality," I said by way of gratitude.

"That's all right, chief. By the way, Rebecca said that she was going to do a quality pizza tonight. That all right, chief?"

"Quality," I said unselfconsciously.

"Good. I'll catch you later."

Bob went off down to Rambo and I re-cast the margin bait and put out some free offerings and then followed in the chief's footsteps. As I got halfway down to Rambo's bivvy I heard his buzzer go off and broke into a jog. Rambo was well into playing the fish by the time I reached him.

"Too late, boy. You ought to stop fishing yourself then you might get some descent video footage," said Rambo.

"There'll be another," I said wearily and picked up the landing net and waited for him to pump back a hundred yards of line. It was the plateau rod again. On Saturday we'd have to tell the others of our discovery of this underwater feeding table, well Rambo's discovery, I was just lending the hardware to fully exploit it.

This latest plateau offering was another twenty and well up to the usual immaculate condition that we had come to expect from the fish of Lac Fumant. All their mouths were immaculate, there were no parrot shaped lips where years of pressure and being caught had caused hard, scar tissue and side of the mouth erosion. It was a pleasure to see such lovely fish, all scale perfect and all perfectly to scale. There were no gross over-weight, gut-dangling monstrosities either, just fish of classic proportions. It was a wonderful place but my feeling of hunger for a real leviathan was still with me.

As I watched Rambo set up the plateau rod again with him at the controls of the bait boat I suddenly became conscious of time. Today was Thursday and this evening saw the completion of five full days fishing and when that happened it meant that there were eight more to go. It left me plenty of time to catch the fish that I wanted but the first five days seemed to have gone very quickly. Paradoxically I found it hard to think back to my time at home and what it had been like before the fishing here had started. That seemed ages ago, so I was stuck with this muddled picture in my mind of my time here going fast and yet having felt as if I'd been here for longer than I really had. It was strange but not unfamiliar, I'd experienced a similar set of feelings to this before when I'd been session fishing. A case of dèja vu? I was in the right country.

I set up the video camera and turned it on after zooming in tight to Rambo's indicators, it was easy enough to get all three in focus and sat and chatted to him.

The carp on the plateau decided to play it coy and battery number one gave up the ghost. I quickly put in the spare and soon after had to change the tape and then eventually that battery run out. Nearly three hours of continuous filming and not a sniff. Ten minutes after I had put it all away the margin rod set off on a blazing run. I couldn't believe it, they were taking the piss.

I vowed that we'd get them tomorrow with the batteries re-charged and the two tapes re-wound. I did think of marketing the tapes, ninety minutes of static indicators might well prove to be a big hit. At least all carp anglers could relate to it and on the first viewing who would know whether they were going to go off or not? The suspense would be gripping, although admittedly, ultimately a complete anti-climax. Perhaps those two tapes really captured the essence of carp fishing? All keen and enthusiastic, a long protracted wait in hope and the final kick in the bollocks, the blank. Yes, most could see themselves in that one rather than videos of endless huge fish being pulled out left right and centre from exotic waters. Initially I thought there would be some therapeutic value to them. You could put the tape on during the winter months and sit indoors in complete comfort, glancing up from time to time to look at the motionless indicators, and end up with a result not dissimilar to what you might have achieved if you'd actually bothered to go. Minus all the hardship, cold and effort of course. It had potential but perhaps not much.

That afternoon I had a couple of fish from the two rods in the original spots but nothing from the long distance island rod. I wasn't overly concerned, if this rod lived up to my theory it wouldn't be an all-action scenario but when I did catch the fish should be bigger. Everyone else seemed to be picking up fish here and there and generally doing fairly well. If anyone had hit the jackpot I'm sure that word would have come around straight away but it seemed that my fish, the 39-13 common, was still the biggest and I was confident that I had caught as well as the others, not that anyone seemed to be counting, which in a way was rather nice.

By early evening I was getting more excited by the prospects of Rebecca showing up than anything else. How did I start talking to her again? I could hardly begin on the same footing as our last conversation, not after all the time that had elapsed. I'd have to go with the flow and hope that my brain was sufficiently in gear to cope with it. Out of the blue I became acutely aware of how grubby I felt. Personal appearance is one of the last things on your mind when fishing a session but when a lovely young girl is shortly to bring your evening meal around it becomes a bit more important. It was too late now to do anything much about it but I washed my face over with some of my drinking water and slicked my hair back. My fingers still had the vague aroma of our boilie flavouring and I thanked heaven for small mercies that the bait boat didn't run on diesel.

It was dark by now and I sat on my bedchair and childishly imagined Rebecca bringing the pizza on a Honda moped with an oversized white topbox that made the skinny machine look ludicrously top heavy. Not so childishly I imagined her in skin tight leathers with a top unzipped to show a touch of cleavage or a split skirt revealing an expanse of bronzed, supple thigh. She kept pulling up and saying – 'Do you want a ride' but not before she'd licked her top lip with the tip of her tongue. It was pleasant imagery and I was so engrossed in my own sordid schoolboy version of reality that when the real thing actually turned up, I was taken completely unawares.

"Hi, Matthew. Pizza delivery girl!"

I snapped my head so quickly to the right to look at her that I felt it crack. She had walked away from the margins and had come in round the back of my bivvy and I had not heard her at all. For once she didn't have on shorts but a really tight pair of peddle-pushers and a tee-shirt with a plunging v-neck. Frantically I ran an underwear check. Down from the full pouting lips to the cleavage and out a bit, no sign of a bra there. Air a bit cooler tonight, nipples prominent. She knew that I was looking. What a fantastically powerful, manipulative tool her body was. Just the slightest hint that she might let you begin to get anywhere near it would make men crawl through solid rock or give away their most intimate rig details and bait recipes. Down from the boobs to the button on the trousers and follow the line of the zip to the crotch. More pouting lips but at ninety degrees to the first pair and pushed apart by the closeness of the white material that made up the peddle-pushers. I knew that I was looking too long but couldn't tear my eyes away.

"Do you like my trousers? She asked in an innocence voice that shocked me with its worldliness. "I bought them today. What about the fit around my bum?"

She turned around to show me her perfect butt which she ever so slightly pushed out towards me to make it look even better. Unsure of how long I had to look I hastily searched for a knicker line across each buttock. There was none. She was either wearing thong panties or none at all. This thought coincided with my mouth drying out quicker than a sixteen ounce mix in a furnace.

"They fit great," I croaked. The words 'toy' and 'putty' clanged in my head.

"Budge up," she said and tapped my legs.

I swung them round so that we both had room to sit across the bedchair and she eased her gorgeous body down onto it. I could only guess at the strain her tight clothing was taking and into what crevices it was working as she bent her body into a sitting position. My left thigh touched her right thigh and an electric sensation ran through my body. Was it similar to the jolt that Spunker had received when he had performed his cable chewing trick? I understood in an instant why new couples can't keep their hands off each other in public and why two years later they never walk hand in hand. It's the buzz of something new, something unfamiliar, something exciting and in this instance something very, very exciting. Mind you if Rebecca was your partner I couldn't see you getting out of bed for at least four years, let alone not bothering to hold her hand in under two.

"Those alarm things of yours aren't going to go off this time are they?" Rebecca asked casually.

They better fucking not. "I don't expect so."

Rebecca took the pizza out of its insulated case. "Shall we share the pizza? It's an extra big one I made for us?"

'For us?' "Yeah. Why not, that'll be nice," I said trying to sound at ease but my heart was thumping.

We sat and started to eat the pizza and I watched in fascination as her mouth opened to show those perfect, square, white teeth which bit through the pointed end of a pizza slice. How could anyone make eating pizza such an erotic spectacle? She licked the sticky fingers of her pizza holding hand one by one. A bead of sweat formed on my brow, our thighs were now in contact all the time and I could feel a bulging in the crotch of my jogging bottoms. Get a grip! I screamed to myself, now was not the time for Mr Tentpole, I was only eating a pizza for God's sake.

"Was it horrible in prison?" she suddenly asked, shooting me a sideways glance.

"What?" I said utterly taken aback, Mr Tentpole, gone in an instant "How . . . ?"

"Your friend Rambo told me. I was asking him about you. I said that there was something a little shy about you, that you seemed a bit intimidated by me and I couldn't understand why. I had to really keep on about before he told me, he kept asking me why I wanted to know and then I had to tell him it was because I thought you were kind of hunky, in a funny sort of way, and only after that did he tell me. He made me promise not to tell anyone else."

My first thought was that he hadn't even told me! I was shaken. There was an awful lot for me to digest in her last little speech. Presumably Rambo had decided to cover my social ineptitude by throwing the prison thing into the open but only when it became clear that there might be some mileage in it for me when she said that she thought I was hunky. And what a revelation that was! Hunky in what sense? Did Rambo think that saying I was an ex-convict would make me more appealing? Why? What? How? Let's face it I was confused. Why hadn't he given me a warning? Why hadn't he told me about her asking about me?

"It wasn't very nice," I said at last. "In fact I don't think I could have survived it without the help of two people." It was no good, I couldn't lie about something like this.

"Who was that?" she asked.

"Rambo and Sophie, my girlfriend."

"Are you still together?" Rebecca said quietly.

My mind tumbled through the sea of emotions that had been my private swimming pool over the last three years. "Yes, we are. It was touch and go at one stage, which was my fault, but she never gave up on me and waited for me."

"She sounds a lovely person."

I nodded. "She is."

Rebecca had stopped eating and looked down at the floor. "I've just been to see a friend of mine who's very ill. It really brings it home to you how precious good health is and how we all must live our lives to the full when you see somebody as unwell as that. You've got to live for the moment, life is too short to worry about whether to do something or not. If you want it you've got to go for it." She looked up and turned her stare to me. "Do you see what I mean? Sometimes you have to do things for yourself, just yourself, because if you don't do it, you might end up never doing it and you've only got one chance. Just one chance, that's all. And if no-one knows about the things you do, it can't hurt them. Do you see what I mean. Matt?"

I sort of did but wondered if I was seeing the right thing. I wanted to ask if she would write it down on a bit of paper exactly what she was going on about, but one life only or not, I wasn't going to ask to do it for fear of making myself a fool.

With me floundering in a whirlpool of perplexity and no answer forthcoming Rebecca stood up and brushed crumbs off her lap. "I've got to be off now. Dad needs some help up at the cottage. I expect I'll see you at the get-together on Saturday, I'm afraid I won't be around tomorrow, all right?"

I said goodbye. Was that a major come-on or what? One minute I saw it as a definite, another as a not sure at all. Perhaps she talked and ate with all the blokes like that. As I watched her flawless arse disappear into the gloom I knew that wasn't a plausible idea. If she sat and ate pizza with all the guys she wouldn't have a figure like that, she'd look more like the Fatboys.

I sat in the dark and mused. My fantasy had taken a step towards reality, clear Alistair-like analysis must dictate it was so, but I wasn't Alistair and had I mis-read the signs? It was worrying, even more worrying was if I was right, what was I going to do about it? Perhaps I had already blown it by mentioning Sophie, guilt had made me do that and I was only sitting eating pizza with her. Doing the business with Rebecca and doing the dirty on Sophie was not an easy option after all that we had been through. My previous lusting had stopped well into Virtual's territory but like him actual reality and all its consequences were much harder to deal with. I still felt the need to catch a forty/fifty before I went home and to have Rebecca put into the equation meant I needed to do some serious thinking. My holiday of a lifetime was throwing up a few tasty questions and none were easy to answer.

CHAPTER 14

The plateau just didn't fish at night. No explanation other than the bare statement of the fact. Six fish off of it during the day, the first day that Rambo, ex-army, ex-mercenary, gun runner and now self styled dating agency matchmaker had fished it and not a snifter at night. In a way it was a good job because if it had fished during the night like it had fished during the day the poor sod would have got about as much sleep as yours truly. Mr Washing-Machinemind. A sad, mixed-up, confused, flummoxed, higgledy-piggledy, all at sea, sixes and sevens fully paid up member of the club for the terminally befuddled. And I only had two takes that night. You guessed, two twenties, again.

"You look a bit wrecked," said Rambo when he came up for morning tea. "It can't be from carp pressure, I only heard your buzzer go off once."

"Twice," I corrected him.

Rambo gave his head a quick upward jerk. "Any good? Can't have been or you'd have been down pestering me."

"A couple of low twenties which is good but for Lac Fumant it's nothing special, I suppose."

"What you been doing all night, then? You look as if you've had about two hours kip, maximum."

"Two hours," I said tragically, "would have been a lie-in. I had a lot on my mind last night . . ."

"I'm glad you never said 'in your mind' or I'd have had you up on a trade descriptions rap," said Rambo, laughing.

I smiled weakly. "It's all your fault."

"My fault!" said Rambo looking shocked and innocent.

"Let me boil up the kettle and I'll tell you all about it," and with that I did.

I told Rambo about my conversation with Rebecca word for word and when I'd finished I asked him why he had told her about my visit to prison and why he hadn't told me about her interest in me. I had racked my brain over these two questions all night, along with all the other questions and now I was about to learn the truth. All night thinking, I was Alistair personified! How I pitied him. What torment.

"The reason I didn't tell you was that I forgot all about it. She hasn't been around for a while and it was such a time ago, what with me having the old carping head on, it just slipped my mind. When she first kept on about you so much I thought if I told her you'd been inside it might put her off and give me a shout. I mean you've got Sophie and I'm just a single bloke . . ."

"Yeah, yeah, yeah, I know. So you thought you might give her a try along with being a porn star," I said, slightly surprised by Rambo's candour and his scheming against me.

"Maybe at the same time," Rambo added.

I'd been well off the scent trying to suss out that one. There I was thinking that Rambo was trying to give me a leg-up to get a leg-over when in truth he was trying to blow me out of any blow-job.

I handed him his mug of tea in silence and I could see that he knew that he had slightly hurt me.

"I did forget, honest. I wasn't trying to stitch you up. I mean, I know you fancy her, everybody does. If you had the chance you wouldn't do anything about it would you? You love Sophie too much and you could kiss goodbye to an easy life once you'd split and the money was gone."

I gave a sigh of resignation. "Yeah. You're right. Don't worry about it. It's me being dumb, that's all." I said the words but didn't know whether to believe them or not.

Having a fling with Rebecca in France was not me splitting up with Sophie in England. Cake and eat it? What the eye can't see, the heart can't grieve over? I was getting my knickers in a right old twist. What was I here for? Carp fishing. What did I want to catch? A forty, nay, a fifty. I told myself to buck up and fucking well get on with it and to stop acting like an adolescent jailbird, unused to the attentions of new female acquaintances, who was away from the missus on holiday for the first time. Which was more or less what I was.

It was Friday morning and the Saturday get together was thirty-six hours away and I decided to fling myself into them by fishing hard. Despite feeling knackered and still in a quandary about Rebecca I decided to really go for it until Saturday afternoon when I would reel in and go up to the cottage to have a shower in readiness for seeing her again. I left Rambo to the bait boat and plateau and moved two of my rods tight into the pads either side of me, the island rod that had been out all night I decided to leave rather than re-cast. If I had re-cast that rod I would have put out more bait and disturbed the swim a bit. I was sure my original lot of bait would still be there so it seemed pointless putting out a load more. It was a small gamble not to check to see if the boilie was still on the hair but seeing as the terminal tackle had been delivered first class by boat there was no real likelihood of a tangle. I decided to chance it.

Sitting out by my rods in the intermittent sun, fishing tight to a snag, was far more demanding than lazing in the shade of my tree, cast to open water. Two quick takes, one on each rod that resulted in a nineteen and a twenty-three mirror kept me going through the morning but by midday the strain was starting to take its toll. Although the weather had been monotonous in its similarity all the time we had been at the lake, overcast with sunny spells, it was still fairly hot. I hadn't been worried by it at all and my idea to bivvy up under the tree had been a good one. Now exposed and sitting still with no cover I was beginning to feel uncomfortable. I went and got my old 50" Nubrolli and set it up to give me some shade and that, coupled with the waft of wind that sometimes managed to find its way around the umbrella, made life much more comfortable.

Now that Rambo knew I was fishing on my rods he came up to my swim with a procession of fish for me to photograph for him. The plateau was still giving him a take in less than two hours and with the other two rods chipping in he was pulling out a lot of carp. The videoing of just one of these takes was on hold because I couldn't be so carefree about wandering down to his swim and because Bob hadn't returned with the two camcorder batteries. Rambo could have set the video up just to capture the indicator roaring off on his own but the idea was to have that and then video the whole fight and landing of a fish as a nice neat parcel. It would have to wait until next week, we had plenty of time.

Friday afternoon drifted by, not one person came to see me apart from Rambo. It appeared that everyone was sitting tight and trying to use the hours as best they could and not fritter them away by pulling in and going on social calls. All the others might have been catching, which would have made walkabouts less likely, but I hadn't heard much in the way of buzzers, which was odd. On the night of the run frenzy I had heard everyone's buzzer from all around the lake yet during the day the sound never carried so well. Despite this I frequently heard Ian's and the Fatboys' alarms if I was sitting quietly, although not today. By late afternoon I finally twigged why, the wind that had started off gently finding its way around my umbrella was starting to push it about a little. The wind was coming off of my margin and pushing across to the bank to where Ian, Spunker and Virtual were. This wasn't the prevailing wind direction, normally it came from the opposite way and that was why I could hear the far bank buzzers and it also accounted for why I couldn't hear them today.

Being a reader of carp literature and being hopelessly conditioned to the irrefutable belief in the high significance of wind direction, I felt a little excited about the prospects of the long distance, island margin rod. I could picture the text in my head:- 'Throughout the day the wind had increased in strength and was now pushing into the island margin that I had been previously baiting. This was a new wind and what made it even more exciting was that it was a warm wind. Previous experience told me that I had a hookbait in the best position possible and crucially, through meticulous interpretation of recent weather reports and my own meteorological observations, I was in position before the carp. My trap had been set and was in place. There would be no disturbances, no baiting over the top of fish, it would all be there ready and waiting. In many aspects of carping you need to be one step ahead, none more so than in the location, or in this case, the pre-location of where carp are going to move to next. The rig I was using, one invented by myself, called the 'Tarantula'™ (Pat. Pending) consists of a dummy hair which has two sliding mini-rings that are bi-laterally connected to the main hair . . .' By which time the Cowboy would have shot the article into a million little bits and the author as well, if he'd been available.

Nevertheless, I was a convert, or a brainwashed member of a weird sect, and felt a little more hopeful for a take on a rod, on what had been up to now, a bit of a disappointment. Ten seconds later, Rambo's high tension indicator performed a karate chop that would have taken a leg off if you had been unfortunate enough to have it underneath the plunging metal. A back drop, registered big-style, from a carp picking up a bait some hundred and fifty yards in front of me.

Sitting right next to the rods I struck immediately, pulling the rod away to my right to clear the brolly that had been set up on tilt at a shallow ten degree angle, convex surface to the left of the three rod set up. I nearly fell off the chair as I struck into nothing. Profanities flowed from my lips as I vigorously started winding down to try and pull in the slack and make proper contact with a fish that was clearly heading straight for me at high speed. I imagined the fish with a nuclear payload on its head trying to make up the yardage to the bank and blow me to kingdom-come for my audacity in hooking it. At last I felt some sort of resistance and, by now I was standing, I struck hard again directly over my shoulder. The rod made it just past the upright before it lurched over into an amazing arc and the fish instinctively veered away from the pressure.

My mental game plan was up for the acid test, the real thing, and as the fished pulled away to my left I walked up the bank to my right, applying sidestrain and pumping and trying to gain line as quick as I dared. It was hard to feel how good the fish was because despite the fact that it was pulling off to my left it was still coming towards me, albeit on an angle. If I could squeeze it past the edge of the pads I was home and dry, the 'if' had been a 'no problem' in my mental game plan but I wasn't feeling so cock-sure now.

I walked further down to the right to try and drag the fish off its intended course and to get a better angle of pull to get it away from the pads. Once I had reached the tree where I had been putting the margin bait, there was nowhere left to go, apart from more frantic pumping. With so much line in the water and the sun shining in from that direction it was hard to tell, or to see, where the line was entering the water. Wherever it was the fish was another five, ten, maybe even fifteen yards further over. I leaned the rod out and heaved, frantically wound down and pumped again.

It crossed my mind that Rambo had been spot on about how hard he had found it when he had cast out his long distance rod with the 8lb main line and had to play in a lively common. There was no way that I could have given this fish the stick I had done so far without snapping up and I thanked which ever deity was listening for my 15lb Big Game Line. After more pumping and winding, everything suddenly went solid and a quick look to the edge of the pads showed the line heading right to the most extreme tip. Leaning ever harder into the rod, surely at the point of breaking even the 15lb line, I felt a movement and then it was as before. I'd done it, I had managed to ease the fish out of a couple of the extreme edge pads. Now this was done I started walking back up the other way, making sure to keep everything tight until I was back by my other rods and the fish was just twenty yards out.

Both my other rods were back leaded right under the tips so I was confident that should this fish go through one of the other lines, it wouldn't, if you see what I mean. As long as the fish wasn't dead tight to the bottom and no underwater feature or snag had lifted the back leaded line off the lake's bed the fish should swim safely over the top and not cause any hassle. This was exactly what happened and soon I had the unseen beasty boring around under my rod tip. Rambo made a timely appearance.

"Long distance rod?" he asked and I nodded.

"Playing it in has panned out as hoped, now to see if the fish size theory is up to anything," I said gravely.

Deep inside me I felt that this was a hell of a lump. Unlike before when I had played out the previous big fish in front of an audience, my mind filled up with the images of the size of the fish I was playing. I saw the scale's needle fly round past the forty mark. I saw the photo of a deep fish being cradled by myself right by the light switch on Pup's wall. I saw Rebecca gasp in shock and gaze in awe at the huge fish that I had tamed. Switching from images in my mind's eye to the eyes in my head I saw the bomb break through the water and a few seconds later I saw a scraper twenty common break the surface. As its tail thrashed the water, it shattered the surface and with it, it shattered my illusion.

"Theory as yet unproved, boy" said Rambo as he netted the common.

I went through the motions of weighing and photographing the common, 20-12 for the record and put it straight back. I was left with a strange feeling, that of disappointment, which I hadn't experienced at all, in carp fishing terms, apart from the single hook pull which was hardly tragic, so far on this holiday. Quite the reverse actually. My seemingly endless run of good fortune, hunches coming off and things just generally conspiring to work out for me had ended. I had been convinced that my plan to sort out the really big fish from an unfished area was a good one and my first gut reaction to the take was that this fish was going to be one of them. I wandered down to Rambo's swim to get the bait boat to re-set the long distance rod and in the time it took to do that I came to my senses and saw things more positively.

Since when was a twenty pound common a major set-back? The wind was still pushing the right way and perhaps this fish might be a taster for things to come. I might be lucky but to pull out a forty, second take from a swim, would be stretching even my apparent ability to bend statistical normality. It would be a bit like winning the lottery and I had only managed that by the back door route of knowing someone well enough to give me some of the proceeds.

I took the bait boat back to Rambo and settled in under the umbrella with a clenched jaw. It was game on for the long slog to Saturday afternoon, no quarter asked or none given. Tight to the pads with two rods, persevere with the long distant rod on the other one.

The evening feeding spell gave me a flurry of runs to the two tight fished baits, one of which turned out to be my fourth thirty of the week. This fish was the most beautiful fully scaled mirror I had ever seen and that included photos in magazines. As I was playing it Bob arrived on his daily walk round and had with him the batteries for the camcorder. Just to prove I was capable of walking and chewing gum I talked him through putting the batteries in while playing the fish, something he wasn't familiar with, and got him to capture me playing the fish. As it happened it couldn't have worked out better because Rambo was into yet another plateau carp and couldn't give me a hand. I had to net the fish myself but it made me look an even better hero, especially when the radiant beauty of the fish was revealed when I peeled the layers of netting away under the very nose of the camcorder.

As soon as I saw the fish it reminded me of Rebecca, it was that stunning. Everything was in perfect proportion and the multitude of large scales, all linked down that big, slab-like flank were something special to behold. I ran down to Rambo to get him to come and feast his eyes on her, only to be stunned by the fish that he had just caught. Off the plateau, where he had been banging out run after run of mid-twenty fish, my camouflaged-clad buddy had just caught the biggest carp of his life. An 'eff' fish in more ways than one.

"Fucking hell," I said, well impressed as I stared at the monster.

A pang of jealousy nipped my stomach. Despite my efforts to feel only happiness for my friend I have to admit I couldn't stop it happening. My thoughts came out aloud

"Look at the size of that, it makes my thirty look tiny. Come on, how big?"

Rambo said nothing but simply covered the great fish in his weigh sling, hooked the scales through the chords and lifted the whole lot up for me to see.

"You say," he said.

"Forty-six . . . ten. You bastard! On one of Pup's?"

"Yep!"

"Off the plateau?"

"Yep!"

"You bastard! You jammy bastard! Just your luck to spot an unknown underwater feature by diligent observation and to have a mate with a new bait boat to enable you to fully exploit it." I said.

Rambo laughed and held up both of his hands in a gesture of defence. "I know, I know. I'll give you an assist on this one."

"Too bloody right you will. Come on, bring it up to my swim, if you can lift it that is, Bob's there and he can do a very special bit of videoing. There won't be many braces more impressive than this."

Bob was ecstatic. This was quality, quality. The photo of the pair of us with our respective fish would be his main advertising photo, he declared. After all it had the lot, a gorgeous fish, a fucking great big one and two highly photogenic, personable carpers. (We managed, through clever camera angles, to mask out the more threatening and abusive tattoos on Rambo's muscle-stuffed skin).

I would have cheerfully traded places with Rambo but kept that little secret deep inside my bitter, ungrateful soul. Rambo had reached the 'eff' carp milestone before me and at this moment in time he held something that I could only hope to aspire to.

He stood atop the mountain, while I slipped and slid and scrambled for grip around camp four. I was a mere sherpa, by definition of him awarding me an assist, on his haul to the forty pound summit. He could come down any time, go well below me, return to base camp forever, sure in the knowledge that he had been to the top and had made it before me. In truth I suspect we both knew that at a fishery as brilliant as Lac Fumant either of us were just a take away from myself redressing the balance, or him climbing to the peak of an even higher mountain and catching a fifty. Obviously if he did I would have to murder him in his sleep, what with him being a close friend and all that.

The two fish, the pretty one and the big one (how they so resembled their conquerors! Only joking!) were carefully placed into the coloured waters of Lac Fumant and both swam away strongly. Rambo and I high-fived it and slapped each other on the back, threw a few pulled-up-short jabs into each others faces and went back to our respective tasks. Me, to catch what he'd already caught and him, well knowing Rambo he wouldn't wallow in self-congratulation and take his foot off the gas he'd be after that elusive, first for the lake, fifty. Banging out the fish had worked for him, as I'd said before and Alistair as well, the more you catch the more likelihood there is in catching a big one. Although concurring with this theory, I had set one third of my stall out differently and decided I would risk with the continuation of it, but not at night.

While I had enough light left to cast accurately, I moved the island rod into the margins as before and took the two tight fished baits and fished one in between the pads and the other out to the open water spot. Nothing remarkable happened overnight, I had a couple of twenties and Rambo left the plateau rod out to not so much as a liner. Very strange. At the crack of dawn on Saturday I was back in my daytime spots, under the brolly rather than under the tree, staring at three rod tips less than four yards away. I'd give it until five in the afternoon and then go up and shower. I think the sight of Rambo's forty had galvanised me into trying even harder. I wanted one and knew that whatever I caught in terms of numbers, nothing would compensate me for not catching an 'eff' carp. Disregarding the rights or wrongs of that, it was the way I felt and that was that. Mind you, I didn't begrudge losing a few hours to make myself clean and see all the others, especially as you-know-who would be there.

I felt as if I fished well that day as I converted five chances out of five from the tight to pads baits. No mean feat over the eleven or so hours that I sat next to those rods, attached by an unseen umbilical chord consisting of hope, determination and a grim enthusiasm that the next one would be the one that really counted. As it transpired they weren't, the biggest was a 26-12 and the island rod just didn't produce a take. The wind that had been so favourable the other day, favourable in terms of what I read into it rather than genuine conclusive proof that it was favourable, had all but died away. The wind just flitted about in a capricious manner, not able to make up its mind whether to bother to blow, or from what direction. The weather was cloudy with sunny spells like it had been all week and although the lake fished as well as ever, Rambo had his usual glut of fish from the plateau plus runs from his other rods, the island was a washout. It remained to be seen if the swim would fish well in any conditions, Alistair had thought not, but I was determined to keep having a go. It wasn't as if I was struggling with the other rods and I was getting ample action from them to put up with a blank on the third one.

At bang on five I wound in and went up to the cottage. I had a quick chat with Alistair which I managed by not letting him get a thousand words in edgeways. I told him about my thirty and Rambo's forty and the fact that we had discovered a very important feature to go onto his map. I told him it was this feature that had produced loads of runs and the big one itself. I could tell that he was keen to know all about it but I said that all would be revealed later at the get together.

Greg and Luke were their usual cheerful selves and told me to get my drinking head on for the upcoming event. There was no chance of that, but I didn't intimate the fact and quickly made my excuses to get on and get cleaned up. Once in the shower with the hot water flowing over my body, I began to contemplate two subjects. That of me catching a carp to match the size of Rambo's lunker and how to play it with Rebecca. Once again for about the hundredth time I wondered what she had really meant that night she had parked her perfect arse on my bedchair and said what she had said. The recollection of how she ate the slice of pizza and then sucked the greasy juices off her fingers, in an act of blatant fellatio parody, sent shivers down my spine, despite the hot water that was running down it.

Of course I'd blown it by mentioning Sophie, or had I? I didn't know black from white, whether my arsehole was punched or bored, or shit from dirty pudding. Once I'd got past the intricacies of all that, there was still the subject of what I proposed to do about it, should she really turn out to fancy me. Still, it would be a nice problem to worry about.

CHAPTER 15

"So where exactly did you catch this forty from?" asked Alistair. I looked around at the semi-circle of eight carp anglers and one mammoth-sized mutt standing in front of me. They were subtly lit by the temporary lighting that Ian had put up around his and Spunker's bivvies. Japp and Wim, side by side as ever. The Fatboys, already on their third can of lager and starting to bead up with sweat quite nicely. Virtual, sporting a corker of a shiner having managed to poke himself in his own eye with a spare rod rest. Ian with his bodyguard, chaperone and honorary member of the human race, (by Ian's decree) Spunker. The Cowboy, immaculately turned out a la 'Virginian' complete with stetson but minus horse, although he was so bandy it was unlikely he'd notice. Finally, there was the asker of the question, Alistair. The nicest carp angler I'd ever met? In someways he was, deep, intellectual, analytical and apparently not a hurtful or resentful bone in his body, aware of his own strengths and all too aware of his weaknesses. He was so right, there just had to be something wrong with him. They all waited for an answer from my carping comrade who was at my side, except possibly Spunker, who looked more inclined to leap up and have a go at ripping Rambo's throat out. For this special get together my old mortgage paying pal had ditched the camouflaged trousers and was wearing a nice pair of chinos. No. I'm lying, don't panic, he had them on and a camouflaged tee shirt as well.

Rambo described in great detail, the exact bearing of the spot that the forty had been taken and then dropped the killer line about the underwater plateau feature that we had found. There were murmurings of approval, especially when Rambo told them what it fished like during the day and how many takes he'd had. Much to my surprise Rambo gave me half of the credit, but it had been his initial observation of a few rolling fish that had made us look in the first place. Without that it would never have been found.

Rambo was now onto the mechanics of fishing the area. "Without Matt's boat it would be pretty hard to fish it properly. You need a strong main line and the distance is too great to get there with the 15lb line I use. I cast it with 8lb line but trying to control a hooked fish in a water with a few major snags like this one has got is well dodgy."

"You can cast a hundred and twenty yards?" said Greg clearly impressed.

"I saw him do it," said the Cowboy. "Right off the deck and it went sailing way out there. If he'd have cracked off it would have killed one of you lot over the other side. You'd have been eating lead, you low-life, scum suckers!"

"I had some once," said Luke with a big grin. "Very filling but not much taste. Pass me another can will you, Greg."

Greg obliged and sarcastically poked a finger into Luke's midriff that disappeared up to its wrist. "Don't go getting a beer gut, old matey."

Luke wobbled his spare tyre, (for a tractor) and calmly replied with great control and dignity.

"This has got little to do with beer, old son, but much to do with food that is high in cholesterol, high in fat, high in sugar and most importantly food that is piled high!"

We all chuckled except for Spunker who was eyeing Rambo up in a similar vain to how I imagined Luke eyed his pile of food.

"I think congratulations are due on two counts," said Alistair. "Once for the capture of a remarkable fish and secondly for pushing forward our collective knowledge of Lac Fumant. I'm sure your swim will be even more sought after following this little revelation. The distance it is at will no doubt deter those who think bait boats cannot be justified under any circumstances but others will undoubtedly follow in your footsteps. We thank you for giving us the opportunity to have the choice in future visits. Well done!"

The others gave a few cheers and the group splintered into smaller sections to talk about their fishing so far and other things that interested them. My main topic for the night had yet to arrive and I felt unable to concentrate on chatting to the others because I was forever looking at my watch and peering up from Ian's swim to see if I could see her or Bob arrive. Not for the first time I felt like a teenager when dealing with situations revolving around Rebecca, only this time I was in a pub waiting for a date to turn up. Luke thrust another can of lager in my hand and told me to get it down my neck. I took little sips but lots of them, with nothing else to do with my hands, raising the can was all that was open to me. Simply holding a drink and not drinking it is a very hard thing to do, even if you are mindful of drinking too much. Even though I knew it would take very little to get me drunk, due to my recent abstinence, I was on my second can and already feeling the effects of the first one.

"Are you enjoying your first trip to Lac Fumant?"

It was Japp, dressed in an orange Dutch international football shirt. Wim had one on as well and both the Fatboys were pursuing their beach-dude, neon frenzy, tee-shirt and shorts attack. My shirt, the best one I had with me, was bright red and Ian and Alistair were both in white. Virtual was in black as was the Cowboy's leather waistcoat but the shirt underneath was purple. If there was a sniper lurking in the bushes he'd have plenty to aim at and I'm not just talking about the Fatboys. Rambo as ever had covered his back and in the right coloured stuff .

"Yeah. It's been really great," I said truthfully. "Good fishing, good company and good weather. All I need to do is catch a forty and it'll be perfect."

"All right, chiefs?" shouted a voice. It was Bob and it was Rebecca.

"Nothing else you would like to do?" asked Japp pointedly, as we both gazed upon the young vision of feminine loveliness that had just slinked into our all male group.

I gave him a broad smile. She looked stunning tonight dressed in a short skirt and a vest top. She had her hair up and wore make-up for the first time that I had seen. It made her look older, more sophisticated and even more unobtainable. Why on earth would a woman like that look at a carp angler like me? It defied all logic, perhaps I'd imagined the whole incident on the bedchair with the pizza, or maybe she was just mucking me about. That was it, the others said that she liked flirting, it was all a wind up. I took a large slug of lager.

Bob and Rebecca were talking to Ian and Spunker. Even the dog seemed mesmerised by her and its great big, lolling tongue hung out to one side and drooled. That dog looked how I felt, how we all felt, I suspected. A few minutes later while I was small talking with Japp, Rambo appeared at my side.

"That's just evened things up a bit," he said smiling. My frowned expression formed the question. Rambo jerked a thumb over his shoulder. "I've just been and pissed all over that dog's bed in its bivvy. I've been bottling it up for ages, if a job's worth doing and all that. You see nobody cock's a leg up my buzz bars and gets away with it."

An escalation in atrocities. I took another slug of lager and looked at the Cowboy. Give me another two fingers of your finest whisky, bar tender. I was starting to lose it.

Rambo and I were clearly high on Bob's pecking order because it was to us that he and his daughter from heaven next came over and chatted.

"How's my two new boys, then, chiefs? Quality photo the other day. Real quality. Don't forget to send me a few prints of the one with the two of you with those fish. It'll go in the advertising campaign, that one. Quality!"

"We won't," said Rambo. "But if you want to really pull in the punters you ought to get a picture of Rebecca into the ad somewhere. Have her down as the lake's official cook and publicity agent, or something like that. Us carp anglers like a beautiful lady to look at."

Rebecca smiled while I struggled for something to say as usual. My gut reaction was for Rambo to lay off my girl, which was as laughable as me being able to do anything about it, even if she was my girl, which she wasn't. I was definitely losing it. I took a slug of whiskey . . . er . . . lager.

"How big is it, I mean was it?" said Rebecca in a voice of innocence yet giving Rambo one hell of an up and down look.

"Forty-six pounds plus," said Rambo apparently missing the innuendo.

"Was yours smaller, Matthew?" she said to me in voice that was a bit ah-diddums.

"Yeah, but mine was much prettier to look at. In fact it was so pretty it reminded me of you," I said.

At last my brain had kicked in but it wasn't me talking as such. It was Dutch courage and had nothing to do with the valiant Japp and Wim but everything to do with the lager supplied by Eating United, aka the Fatboys.

Talk of the devil. "'Ere, Rebecca," said Greg suddenly thrusting his huge, lime green, clothed body with canary yellow shorts and sweating head just inches away from hers. "Wanna lager?"

"Thanks, Greg," said Rebecca taking a can with one hand and touching his ham-like forearm with the other.

"S'all right," said Greg and he lumbered off to Luke and Ian who were talking baiting up tactics.

"Got a can for the dog?" asked Ian as he walked towards them.

As Greg wandered off Alistair appeared on Bob's shoulder and whispered something to him and the pair of them walked away while Japp had started talking to Rambo and gestured him to go and see Wim. Miraculously all distractions and personnel had been spirited away and I was left alone with Rebecca. My luck was back to its best.

"Just me and you, then?" said Rebecca.

"Just me and you," I replied, slipping into my mysterious superhero character, Echoman.

We started chatting and the combination of being able to talk to her one to one and not have to contend with vying for her attention with the others relaxed me. We made small talk and I found out that the small tattoo on her stomach was Japanese for friend. Would I become one? Or would it be something more than that? It was heady stuff and there was the drink as well. I took another sip of lager. I was starting to lose it even more and feeling a touch light-headed.

She was soon straight to the point. "Have you thought about what I said the other evening?"

Only every thirty seconds. "Yeah, but I'm not sure what you really meant," I said being equally as forthright and hoping that she would tell me.

"I'll show you."

And with that she took my hand and walked me by, and then round the back, of Spunker's bivvy. A whiff of urine seemed to go up my nose as we made our way past its opening. She stopped once we were out of sight and put her hands around the back of my neck and kissed me. You know, tongues and all that. I kissed her back and held her lightly around her waist.

"That's what I meant. That's what you can have," she said as we finally came up for air.

She took a step back and took hold of my right wrist and guided my hand onto her right breast. She then moved my hand up and down over her breast with her own. I could feel the hard point of her nipple.

"And there's an awful lot more of me to have," she said huskily. "But not tonight."

She kissed me again, gave me a little wave and walked back to the others. My poor old dick didn't know if it was coming or going, but I knew it wasn't going to be coming. Not tonight. I quickly went back to the rest. Nobody seemed to have notice us go and I stood in splendid isolation unsure what to do until Rambo quickly latched onto me. He had a peculiar look on his face, one that I had never seen before.

I tried to figure out what it was. It was consternation, not fear, I never expected to see that on his face whatever the circumstances, but it was something akin to worry. I wanted to blurt out what had happened to me but he beat me to the punch.

"Guess what just happened?" he said, in a voice that had traces of being slightly unnerved. Him being unnerved really unnerved me.

"What? What happened?" I asked, starting to panic.

"Well, you know that you told me about Japp and Wim's dad being in the porn video game and that they were going to ask me to be in them?"

"Yeah." I said wondering he was going to say.

"Well, they've just asked me. They don't want me to be with the girls! They want me to be in a gay porn movie! I don't look gay! Do I?" There was a hint of desperation in the last two words.

I hardly felt in a position to form an opinion on Rambo's perceived sexuality, what with my testosterone levels having been upped and then unceremoniously downed by the most attractive girl I had ever clapped eyes on. I took a huge slug of lager that finished the can. I was starting to get a headache.

I shrugged my shoulders and blurted, "I suppose it's possible that because you look so butch and hard, people might think that you're gay."

It was the wrong thing to say. "What kind of a fucking comment is that?" exploded Rambo. "I pride myself on how tough I am, so how can that make me look like a fucking poof? I've been to war, boy. Killed people. Dealt with some of the most unspeakable scum you could imagine and had loads of women. And if that makes me look like a shirt-lifter . . ."

"Another can of lager, mate?" It was Luke this time in an all brilliant blue number, totally oblivious to the ranting tirade that he was interrupting. "I saw you finish that one off. Let me take it."

"Cheers, Luke," I said absent mindedly swapping an empty can for a full one. The Fatboys were the hosts with the most.

". . . Then I don't know fuck all about it," said Rambo rather limply, the wind somewhat taken from his sails. I knew that feeling very well. My head was beginning to really throb.

"Maybe there was some mistake," I said, trying to see where Rebecca was.

At that moment Japp and Wim came alongside. The pair of them looked extremely harassed.

"Rambo, my friend," said Japp. "There seems to be some kind of misunderstanding."

"Too fucking right there has been." said Rambo getting all fired up again.

Wim held up an upturned hand. "You must excuse our English, Rambo. I think we have said something the wrong way round or have not said it quite correctly and the meaning has been altered . . ."

Wim's voice faded out of my conscience as I scanned the people in front of me seeking out Rebecca. All I saw was Spunker bite into a fresh can of lager with a pair of massive incisors and then lift it up in his gargantuan chops and drink it. I could see his throat bobbing up and down as he downed the can in one go while Ian and the Fatboys clapped and egged him on with calls of 'Spunker! Spunker! Spunker!'

My head felt like exploding. I downed half of the new can that Greg had given me to ease my pulsing temple. It was a big mistake and it made matters worse. The world started to slowly spin, I began to see double but realised that the two images of orange were Japp and Wim. The other colours, the purples, the whites, the yellows, the greens, the blues and the blacks began to swim and merge into an aurora borealis of leisure clothing. I began to feel slightly nauseous.

"Matt?" said Alistair. "I was just wondering if you would like to have a chat with me and the Cowboy about penning some articles about this trip. We feel that between the three of us we could come up with some very useful instructional pieces that would be of great interest to the carping community as a whole. Now as you know the Cowboy . . ."

I held out a shaking hand. "Not now, Alistair. I don't feel to good."

"Hmm. You do look a bit pale," said Alistair sounding concerned. "Sit down on this bedchair."

I slumped down and held my banging head in my hands. Lager commercials never mentioned anything about this. Alistair went off to talk to someone and came back with Japp.

Japp offered me a small white tablet. "Take this Matthew, it's a tablet to stop sickness. It will make you feel better."

His words sounded soothing and I swallowed the tablet immediately. By now Alistair and Japp had been joined by Rambo and Wim, they all stood around me muttering platitudes.

"What did you give to him?" asked Wim.

"The anti-sickness tablets you keep for your headaches that were in your jacket," said Japp.

"I think that I'm going to go back to my bivvy and hit the sack," I said. "Sorry to be a party pooper but I feel a bit rough and need to lie down. I'll see you all tomorrow."

"Do you want me to walk round with you," said Rambo.

"No thanks. I'll be all right," I said groggily.

I got up and started to walk off round the lake back to my little house where I could be all on my own and lie quietly.

My group all said their goodbyes as I shuffled off, the others, Luke, Greg, Ian and Virtual never noticed me go, Bob and Rebecca seemed to have disappeared. I walked slowly and deliberately, sucking in the fresh, cool night air. The nausea seemed to have passed although my head was still pounding but by the time I had made it around to the Fatboys' swim, I felt a little better. Actually my head seemed to have cleared remarkably well considering how I had felt a few minutes earlier and I put it down to the tablet that Japp had given me, which seemed to have done the trick.

When I reached Alistair's swim my head had not so much been cleared of muzziness but seemingly my whole perception appeared to have been upgraded. I was acutely aware of everything, the sky, the trees, the grass, the stars, the clouds, the air, my body, my heartbeat, my breathing, everything. It was as if I had suddenly been given the ability to see what I had never seen before, to hear what I had never heard before and to feel my relationship with all other things, sentient or otherwise. It was weird.

With every passing footstep this new sense of heightened awareness and appreciation increased. My perception seemed to be at its very limit but then the next stride would make it even more discerning and the next more so and the next more so again. In its earlier stages it had been quite an odd experience but things had gone so far that I was now beginning to become embroiled in my newly found abilities.

I felt the individual blades of grass fold and get crushed under each of my thudding footsteps and then rebound, but not sufficiently to hide the impression of my footfalls. As my diaphragm rose, decreasing the air pressure within my body, the greater external atmospheric load pushed the mass of swirling individual molecules down the spiralling void that was my windpipe. I counted each individual one of them as they went past my epiglottis and ended up in my lungs only to be passed into my bloodstream via very thin-walled capillary vessels. I felt the blood giving up its carbon dioxide and that new set of molecules being forced back up my windpipe, past my epiglottis for another quick tot-up and out into the night air. The trees and plants would take this gas and convert it into oxygen during the sunlight hours but they knew that I knew that.

I looked at the stars and knew which ones held life on their surface and which ones were barren and bleak, like a gravel pit in winter. I saw clouds float in front of the stars, I knew their composition and recognised their shape. There was one like the pretty mirror I had caught earlier and with it, a vapour trail from an aeroplane. I knew which type of plane, how many people were on board and that the captain was screwing the pretty, blond air hostess. It looked just like a helicopter rig as it cast its way across the sky and ended tangled, so much for that theory, on the moon as it moved through the sign of Libra.

The moon. A disk or a globe? How odd that it should rotate at the precise speed to keep one side of it hidden from us as it orbited earth. I knew the reason why. I could see round to the dark side and I knew what it was made of. I also knew that it was actually a 3,476,000,000 mm boilie, not a satellite, consisting of rock and dust. It was a great, big bottom bait which was made entirely from all the discarded boilie mixes that were thrown away after failing to catch on their first outing. It wouldn't be fair to tell you which mix made the biggest sea, it certainly wouldn't be tranquillity for the bait company involved.

As I neared my swim, all the trees turned into anglers with their branches now a mass of rods pointing in all directions. It took the term 'all round angler' to the extreme as it was 360 degree rod coverage with the water only to the front of them. I walked serenely past the margin tree anglers that were to the right of my swim, knowing they would all blank, and came to my bivvy. I stared out into the lake and watched the big boilie's reflection ripple and distort on its surface.

Underneath that surface I could see all the carp in the lake. I knew all their sizes, knew if they had ever been caught, knew everything there was to know about them and there amongst them swam the titan, who had never been caught. At over fifty-five pounds it was truly awesome. I connected to its psyche and looked into the dull brain that was the monster's mind. It was a watery mind of base instincts; To eat, to survive and to procreate were its goals. It had only a microscopic conception of what lay above the surface but a complete understanding of its own world below. It had full knowledge of sunlight, of dark, of hot and cold, of pressure, of wind, of the changing seasons, of weather, of other fish, of other aquatic forms both sentient and plant-like and of the lake, its own personal universe. Most of the carp's knowledge was instinct, inborn but a small bit was knowledge that had been acquired over its life. It was enlightenment that had been learnt over a period of just eighteen years.

There was no guile present in this brain as I read through it. No real intelligence, no understanding, no thought process, as such, but a deep, inbuilt self-protection mechanism. This mechanism set the reaction to a set of circumstances dictated, not by the application of logic, but by how good it would be in order to eat, to survive and to procreate. The base instincts again. Rain made the desire to eat a little stronger because of the way it improved the water's quality, which in turn made the carp more active in the same way that warm water did. Cold water, on the other hand, made the monster slow and lethargic and uninterested in food. It was aware that small round balls were food, very good food, not of the carp's universe, but from somewhere else. A conflict within the base instincts and the self-protection mechanism existed concerning the eating of these balls of food, so far self-protection had been the stronger urge on nearly every occasion, apart from a few. Natural food gathered by the island when the wind was right but experience told the carp not to hurry, there was time enough and food enough for all in its rich universe. It felt happy feeding freely when it was by the island under those conditions because it felt safe. I smiled to myself, I had found his weakness during this mind-meld and I carefully watched him swim away and let his mind unravel from mine. I had him sussed, he would fall to my rods soon. I just knew.

I turned away from the lake and looked at my three rods, their hooks and boilies attached to butt rings, waiting like silent cannons for me to fire them into action. I eyed them with complete knowing, when, to my utter astonishment, they slowly started to melt and drip thick, treacle-like globules of grey carbon onto the ground. The material was so viscous that the blobs never managed to break away from their starting points but merely stretched the grey discharge into thinning chords until they made the ground, where it started to pool. The three rods oozed onto the ground and then so did the buzzers, the indicators and the buzz bars, soon all that was left was a quicksilver puddle. Suddenly, I didn't know what was happening, I had no clue as to what was the cause. A wave of terror started to form in my guts.

With fearful fascination I knelt down beside the puddle and slowly extended an arm to touch it. I put in a finger, then a hand, and then the whole of my forearm into the quicksilver puddle. I felt no sensation but when I lifted up my arm it had gone, cut clean away at the point of deepest immersion. I recoiled in horror and ran screaming into my bivvy and turned on my fluorescent tube torchlight, with the hand that I didn't have. I sat shivering in the glow of the light and turned my wide eyes onto the huge bag of air dried boilies that I still had left.

As I looked, the bag started to move and writhe, slowly at first, then becoming more and more violent. It looked as if Mike Tyson was trying to punch his way out as the sides of the sack bulged as an unseen force pummelled away with an ever increasing, brutal intensity. At last the sack could take no more and the boilies exploded out, peppering me in a red, stinking hailstorm, yet rather than hit me, they went straight through me. My torso was littered with holes, my one and a half arms were riddled with holes and my legs were like pieces of Swiss cheese. Still the boilies flooded out and those that had previously escaped seemed under no jurisdiction as far as gravity was concerned. These ones swarmed in my bivvy like a host of angry bees. I held up my arms in self-defence as thousands of boilies whizzed around and through my body. There was no physical pain but the mental anguish of seeing my body gradually being eroded away was staggering. I was a hole-ridden Matt Williams, which became a Matt Williams lattice-work fence, which became a Matt Williams net, which became a single strand of Matt Williams. My life hung by a thread. My life was a thread, because that was all that was left of my body.

My viewpoint changed. Now I was riding on the back of a boilie as it flew like a crazed bluebottle about my bivvy. I circled the light several times in a wide, looping orbit and then straightened out and headed for the thread. Like a frightened pillion passenger on a motorbike I desperately pulled to one side, not to upright a leaning bike, but to destabilize a boilie destined to cut me in two. It had no effect, desperately I tried again, but I had no physical form, no weight, however tiny, to deflect the speeding bullet. I was out of my skinny body riding on the very thing that would finally cut me to the quick. My strand came closer and closer until I was inches away, at least from that close up perspective it looked as if I was putting on weight. I wasn't quite the 'on heroin' supergaunt, supermodel of three yards back. Snick! 'The Golden Shot.' Bernie's bolt on target. Bang! Clint Eastwood's rifle bullet parting rope in spaghetti westerns. Cut! 25lb shock leader on a gravel bar dotted with zebra mussels. The boilie parted myself and the two limp threads fell onto my bedchair. Blackness. Void. Emptiness.

I awoke to a fuzzy green light. I sat up. I was all there, even if I wasn't all there. Limbs, body, head present and if not correct, then maybe correcting. I let out a mild groan. The green lighting changed subtly and a head poked into my bivvy. It was Japp.

"Thank God, Matthew. Are you fine?"

"A bit groggy. Jesus! I had a strange dream. I've had one bad dream earlier this year but it wasn't as odd as that one. I can remember coming back from the Saturday night get together and then going out of my head."

"A good choice of words, Matthew," said Japp hanging his head in shame. "Do you remember I gave you a tablet to stop your sickness?"

I nodded. Japp continued. "I had them mixed up. What I gave you was one of Wim's recreational tablets, an LSD tablet. You just had a bad trip."

"Blimey!" I said in shock. "I've never done drugs before. Mind you, I did a Spock-type mind-melding thing with a fifty-five pound mirror while under the influence."

Japp seemed unimpressed. "LSD is a very powerful, hallucinogenic drug. People have died from using it, convinced that they can fly and have jumped off tall buildings. As soon as I realised what had happened I came and sat with you. By then you had fallen asleep."

I gave him a wry smile, I was perking up and feeling better. "Still, no harm done. I'm going to prove there is a fifty-five out there and go and catch it. What time is it?"

"It's nine in the morning. Monday morning."

I blinked as the implication of what he had said sank in. A real thirty-six hour blank if ever there was one.

CHAPTER 16

By Monday afternoon I was back into the carping groove having related my drug trip to all the others, who, having heard of my regaining consciousness, had come round to see how I was during the morning and over lunch. By all accounts the combination of alcohol and the drug had knocked me out after I had experienced the trip and the lads had taken it in turn to keep a constant vigil over me during the lost day and a bit. Wim said that it wasn't a common occurrence to slip into a coma but it had been known. Between them they had managed to get me to sip a little water to keep me hydrated, even though I was comatose, and as long as I had managed this there was no real cause for alarm. Apparently! This particular drug had never been known to cause fatalities and was non-addictive. Not that there was any likelihood of me trying to cadge a few tabs off of Wim. Getting shot to pieces once, even though it was twice, in a manner of speaking, was enough for me. The taking of mind-altering substances was going to be purely a one-off, as far as I was concerned.

Alistair seemed especially interested in the bit where I had joined minds with the fifty-five. He was fascinated and kept asking me over and over again to reiterate on small points of detail or to clarify various images that I had described far to vaguely for his ever-probing personality. In the end I suggested that he took one of the tablets himself and had a go at it to see what he could come up with. I was convinced that he thought that there was some carp fishing wisdom in it somewhere, and to be honest, I was totally convinced of the existence of the fifty.

Wim, on the other hand, had been highly sceptical and pointed out that all the heightened perception and depth of insight were just tricks of the chemical lysergic acid diethylamide. The Cowboy, who was sceptical to the point of ridicule, said that it explained all the carp magazine articles. According to him, all the authors were on the bloody stuff. Even Virtual, on the point of being chatty with his new found usage of whole sentences, seemed interested. Perhaps it was because it was a different type of virtual reality to the one he operated in, namely, chemical induced mind games rather than cyber space, that caused his attentiveness. Greg said his new association with the real world was because he had dropped his laptop in the drink three days ago and couldn't get online. What with having no link to his beloved games he was being forced into taking part in reality and it was gradually sucking him out of his shell.

Rambo just ripped the piss out of me mercilessly about the mind-meld thing. He thought it hilarious that I could even begin to be serious about considering the fish existed. I think nearly all the others thought the same as well but were too polite to say so.

Rambo had also sorted out the mistake with the Dutch boys over what type of smutty video they might like him to appear in. I cannot remember the exact phrase that caused the ambiguity but they were the best of buddies again now that it had been sorted, although I sensed that Rambo was cooling to the idea. What was not cooling, quite the opposite as it happens, was this Rambo v Spunker dominant male thing. What with Rambo having marked himself right at the very epicentre of Spunker territory, i.e. having pissed in the dog's bivvy, the tension and loathing had mounted.

On my day of the big sleep Spunker had run a daylight raid deep into Rambo country and ripped up a weigh sling like a child tearing a tissue. Rambo had not seen this act of criminal vengeance and the perpetrator had slunk away, no doubt laughing like Mutley, 'shackle-razzle-futzal-craz,' while Rambo was left to do the 'Drat! Double drat!! And triple Drat!!!' It was all out war now and it was going to end in tears for somebody. I had a shrewd idea for who.

The wind was blowing into my face as I sat by the side of my bivvy under the shade of my tree. It was coming from Ian's side and it was not the direction that I considered to be a good one for fishing the far distant margin by the island. I had therefore put out my three baits as I had on the first day at Lac Fumant. The reason for not fishing the two other rods tight to the pads was my physical condition. I didn't feel ill but a day without food and the trauma of subjecting my brain to unfamiliar chemicals and my stomach to more lager than it was used to made me feel a little delicate. It felt good to be back fishing and despite the fact that I'd lost a day I was convinced my meeting of minds with a massive mirror might make a monumental mobilisation to the momentum of the mad mission to catch it. Despite what Wim and the others might say.

The other uppermost thought was whether Rebecca's placing of my hand on one of her erogenous zones was part of the acid trip, or had happened before. I didn't dare ask for confirmation; 'Here Bob, did your daughter really thrust my hand on her tit or was I under the influence?' I knew it really had happened but the more I thought about it and her amazing offer the more unlikely it seemed.

I shook my head to clear my thoughts and summed up what I wanted to achieve on this carping caper of a holiday. In no particular order it was; Catch an 'eff' carp. Watch the Cowboy draw or even better, video it. Video a take from start to release of the culprit. Be around when the shit hit the fan with Rambo and Spunker. Resolve my course of action with Rebecca.

It was unlikely I would manage all five and the last one I had serious doubts about when I thought it through from the head. How could I cheat on Sophie after all that she had done for me? From the experience of the Saturday night I knew that in the heat of the action my brain would be robbed of a descent blood supply by you know what. Under such circumstances, I wondered if I would ever be able to make a sound judgement, it was more likely that I would just get swept along with the moment. If somehow I managed to think straight and I didn't take that moment would I live to regret it? Alistair! Alistair! Alistair! I was asking myself the same old questions and getting the same know-nothing answers.

A ripping run on my margin rod dragged me from my self-absorption and navel gazing. Despite not getting down to the rod as quick as I'd done before I struck into yet another Lac Fumant carp which fought so hard I tired before it did. Heroically, with knocking knees (not nerves, just weak legs) I managed to win the day and netted another lovely looking common but the effort had done me in. I got Rambo to photograph the fish but he had to keep chastising me to hold the fish up because I felt so tired and weak.

"Hold the bloody thing up, boy! You keep letting the flank tilt down, its only a bloody twenty, not that fifty-five you've got on the brain."

"I've got no energy. I'm wasted," I pleaded.

"No energy! You've just slept for nearly thirty hours. How can you be tired after sleeping for that long?" he said with no sympathy.

I didn't know the answer but suspected that my body had burnt itself out during my period of heightened awareness and a lack of food had exasperated the problem. Once the common was back in the lake I wound in the two other rods and headed up to the cottage to have a long, hot shower. Bob was outside the front door in a tee shirt that had a picture of an old man, in an old fashioned bathing suit, complete with bathing hat, snorkel and flippers. His flippered feet were on a springboard but his hands were inside a woolly hand warmer. The legend 'muff diver' was written behind him. I thought of Rebecca.

"All right then, chief? Got over your little escapade now?" I nodded. "Quality. We came and saw you. We thought you were either Rip Van Winkle or the Sleeping Beauty. Rebecca did give you a peck on the cheek but you didn't wake up."

I gave him a wry smile. "Can I get something to eat up here tonight?"

"No probs, chief. Rebecca's not about tonight but I can rustle you something up. What d'you want?"

I chose something plain, had my long hot shower, considered the whereabouts of Rebecca and sat down to dinner with Bob who joined me in eating up what he had prepared. I told him about my drug trip, because he asked, but recalling it for the umpteenth time made the regurgitation of the run frenzy tales seem insignificant. I wanted to ask him all about Rebecca but decided to leave it. I wasn't too sure how he would react to such inquisitions, fathers can be very protective about their daughters.

He thought my story was all rather hilarious too, and kept laughing at each revelation. The bit about the boilies making me more and more hole-ridden made him laugh the most. The 'more holey (sic) than thou jokes' came thick and fast. He said it reminded him of the fairground and compressed air guns that you loaded with a tube of lead pellets in the hope of shooting out a star to win twenty quid. I'd never witnessed them but like his tee shirts, Bob was a seventies man at heart. The only thing that didn't make him spit his dinner out with laughter was the detail of the mind-meld with the mirror. Especially the bit about the food collecting alongside the island margin when the wind was right.

"If you believe in it, chief," he said in all earnestness, "you may well be fishing that swim very soon. This quality weather we've had is going to break. The forecast is for gale force winds and frequent periods of rain, some very heavy with the odd thunder storm. The wind direction is from your side of the lake into the island. It's not the normal wind direction but they reckon it might last as long as the rest of your stay, chief."

I felt the hairs on the back of my neck start to prickle and my skin became covered in goose-bumps. The feeling of luck and fate which I had felt so strongly at the start of the holiday came back to me. It had subsided a little during the last few days, what with one thing and another, but now it was back with a vengeance. Was this the hand of fate again? Was my destiny to catch this fish of my dreams in the swim where I had imagined (or had it been real) its very own mind had told me it would be under certain conditions? And were those conditions about to start happening? Had the whole thing with the tablet been fate's elaborate way of telling me to stick with the mainly unsuccessful long range island rod? Or was it all bollocks? No. I had come too far on my run of luck for me to turn on it now. The lost day might be a small price to pay for the information I had gleaned from my LSD inspired dream. There and then I made up my mind. I had seen the way to the 'eff' carp and I would give it my best shot. If the others all mocked, then so be it. Alistair wouldn't.

"When's this weather going to start then, chief?" I asked Bob.

"The forecast is for the front to reach us early tomorrow morning, chief."

"Quality," I said winking at him. "Quality."

When I left Bob it was getting dark, the walk down to the lake through all the trees brought back memories of my Saturday night jaunt around the lake. Thankfully the trees stayed as trees and didn't morph into carpers. I felt much better now, having a meal inside me and my strength was slowly returning. I decided not to fish that night, I would set the alarm for first light and wake up refreshed and raring to go. I reckoned that a good night's sleep would be more advantageous to my big picture plan than my usual trick of pulling out two twenties during the hours of darkness. I would ask Rambo not to come up and ask me for any help during the night. Maybe he could ask the Cowboy instead.

It was with this thought in my mind that I decided to walk the long way round the lake to my swim. By going this way I could square it with the Cowboy under the pretence of me still feeling a bit rough, which was true, and then tell Rambo afterwards. I felt that with nine or ten hours kip under my belt, and I was sure that I would sleep every last minute of them, I would be as right as rain. Especially if the rains had come and that wind with it.

The smell of bacon wafted up my nose as I neared the Fatboys' swim. The two of them were having a massive fry-up. Now there was a shock, I don't think.

"All right, lads?" I asked them genially.

It was a superfluous question, the two of them were fishing, cooking and eating at the same time. They were happy as pigs in shit as opposed to, as unhappy as an ex-pig in a frying pan. I felt genuine warmth for the pair of them, as I did for all the lads on the water. They had all taken their turn to play Florence Nightingale to a druggy carper and sacrificed some fishing time to do so. If my ordeal had happened in the old syndicate days there would have been a queue at my bivvy door to smother me, not with kindness, but with a pillow.

"Yeah, fine. You better now?" asked Greg.

"I still feel a bit shot but I'm on the mend. Thanks for helping look after me, I know it must have been a real fag."

"I'm just glad you didn't die," said Luke laughing. "It would have caused no end of hassle deciding who was going to move into your swim! I suppose I shouldn't tell you this but while we were taking turns sitting with you we fished your rods. I mean it wasn't as if you were using them and it was bloody boring just sitting there."

"Nobody told me that," I said nonplussed. "Who fished my rods?"

Luke answered without embarrassment. "We all did. The Cowboy and Rambo had a twenty each and Alistair had a nineteen. We also made a video of a chapter of your Lac Fumant holiday that you could never do. The sipping of the water scenes were very moving."

"Who's idea was all this?" I said with slight indignity but also with humour. The cheeky bastards.

"You won't get us like that, mate," said Greg. "We all make one step forward on that one. It was meant to be a surprise when you looked at the video but my big-mouthed, big, fat mate here has blown it."

I shook my head and laughed. "Maybe it's as well, I might have recorded over the top of it if I didn't know that it was there. I think'll go and have a little shufty at it. I'll see you later."

The Fatboys said au revoir and put their full attention into eating. Watching them get stuck into their food was like watching two kids eating a chocolate cake, each one knowing that the quicker he ate, the more he got. It was the dictionary definition of 'voracious' as told in mime (no time for talking) by two twenty stone carp anglers, two four-legged bedchairs and an over-worked cooking stove.

I carried on down to Virtual who was sitting outside his bivvy. His eye was still black as far as I could tell in the fading light but now his wrist was all bandaged up.

"What you been up to, then?" I asked him.

"I burnt my wrist on the stove when I knocked it over and the boiling water went on my ankle. Look at all these blisters." He rolled up a trouser leg to reveal a painfully skinny, milk-white leg with scald marks.

"Have you been moon bathing again?" I asked jocularly.

"Do you know," he said sounding hurt and I was sure it wasn't because of his eye or leg, "I was the only one who they wouldn't let look after you."

"With your track record, son, I'm not surprised," I said sounding like the voice of experience.

"I can't help being clumsy with some things, yet I'm brilliant on a keyboard," said Virtual.

"Throw a boilie into the water," I told him.

"What?"

"Pick up a boilie and throw it into the water as far as you can," I said explaining to him again.

Virtual shrugged but did what I told him. It was the most pathetic throw I had ever seen. Imagine an unathletic girl throwing a ball with her left hand (if she was right handed) and you have it. (Please don't accuse me of sexism, it's simply a fact that very few women can throw. Call it chucking challenged, but not after a few drinks.)

"You see," I said. "No co-ordination. A simple thing like throwing and you can't do it. Too many hours on the Gameboy or PlayStation aren't good for you, you should be outside doing real things with real implements. Get fishing more and leave all your computer toys behind you. Since you managed to fumble your laptop into the drink your conversation has improved no end. At the start of the week all you could do was grunt."

"Alistair said that as well." Virtual gave a long pause. "Do you think that Rebecca's got a better figure than Lara Croft?"

I looked Virtual in the eye and said dead-pan. "It's not about looks. It's personality that counts and however much you try with Lara, she just comes across as being a bit two-dimensional, which is better than being one dimensional, but not as good as three."

"I'm going to write a computer carp fishing game," said Virtual going off at a tangent and either missing or ignoring my little joke. "You'll be able to chose your bait, tackle, venues and how hard or easy the venue is. There'll be different ways of catching the carp with different rigs under different conditions and at different times of the year. You'll get belting runs, back drops, bleeps, liners, hook pulls, fish landed, getting snagged, getting snapped up, different playing of fish techniques, the lot. It'll be mega. I'll put in every detail that there is and make it really technical. I might even introduce different jobs that the players can have which allow you to either skive off or not be able to get away, not unless you can get promotion, and then you can skive off more, or give them families with kids or a nagging wife, or even a wife that wants to come fishing. Yeah! That'd be cool. And sometimes your gear might get nicked or you could get done for not having a rod licence or fall out with other anglers and have to fight them to get in the best swims. Real cool. A beat'em up carp fishing game."

Bloody hell, I thought. Couldn't get a word out of him a week ago, now he won't stop. Apart from that he was coming out with some of the absurd things I'd lived through while carping.

"When do you think that people will play this game, then." I asked

"Oh, I don't know. When they've got plenty of time on their hands and nothing much to do." Virtual's mind made the sudden connection. "Christ! When their carp fishing, of course. Mega cool!"

My brow frowned at the idea of a lake full of carp anglers sitting on bedchairs playing a computer carp fishing game and controlling a little cyber carp angler who was waiting for a run, while they waited for that run, while they waited for a run.

"Give me a ring when you make your first million," I said. In about two years I thought. "I'll catch you later and remember . . . hooks are sharp and pointy."

I decided to avoid Ian and Spunker, well it was Spunker I wasn't too happy about meeting to be honest and it seemed as if they were both inside their bivvies. I took a rounded detour so as to not disturb them and walked all the way to the bottom of the lake to where Japp and Wim were fishing. The pair of them were both zipped up tight inside their little green homes so once again I gave them a wide berth. The pair of them had been so apologetic after the tablet mix-up that it had almost got to the point of me feeling embarrassed about it. As much as I tried to play the whole thing down, they made it up to some terrible thing that they had done.

They were descent blokes from a very wealthy, respectable home and the liberal Dutch society which had shaped them clearly never had the same taboos as the UK. Recreational drugs and easy access to porn were just a part of life, if you wanted it you went and got it, if you didn't then you never bothered. It was a lot more sensible than the way we got all hot under the collar when a pair of boobs were shown on telly or someone owned up to puffing the odd spliff. Still, it would have been unlikely for me to have an LSD tab given to me, or my mate getting all upset because he was being, or thought he was being, asked to appear in a gay porn video on an English day ticket water. In the end I wasn't too sure which philosophical viewpoint came out on top and decided to opt for another, that of apathetic nihilism. I didn't care because it was all a load of crap.

"Howdy pardner," said the Cowboy.

For all his cowboy fascination it was unusual for him to use any supposed ranch-hand vernacular. Maybe he was being ironic.

"All right, Cowboy," I said.

"Had any word from that big mirror lately?"

I knew he was taking the piss, the Cowboy was one of the world's cynics. When he wasn't slagging off carp fishing magazine writers, the claims of carp bait manufacturers and generally anything written about carp at all, he was slagging off everything else. The criminal system, the welfare system, the political system, the lot. He moaned about the way criminals got treated better than victims and how juvenile delinquents were sent on expensive beanos to foreign climes, while law abiding kids got nothing. He moaned about how those who had always worked hard and saved got penalised in old age by having to pay for nursing home cover, while those who sponged off the state and contributed nothing for their whole life, had it paid for them. He moaned about the rising culture of victimhood, how people exploited ridiculous race and sex discrimination laws to line their pockets and how very keen the legal-aid financed lawyers were to help them. He moaned about political correctness and vociferous minorities trying to undemocratically impose their narrow-minded ideals on the rest of us who just want a quiet life. He moaned about collusion in big business to make us pay more for goods that we were being conned into wanting by unscrupulous advertisers. And he was unimpressed with stories of anglers locking intellects with unknown carp and finding out where to catch them, under what conditions, and how big they were.

"Nah," I said playing it safe.

"You really think that your going to catch that fish don't you, you mad bastard?"

This was coming from someone who wore cowboy boots and a leather waistcoat while fishing and Quick Draw McGraw'd his rods. Allegedly.

"Stranger things have happened," I said non- committedly.

"Try naming one," he countered.

Rebecca wanting to have it off with me, I thought instantly. I shrugged my shoulders and changed tack.

"Would you do me a favour tonight. Is it all right if I say to Rambo that you'll help land any fish he catches tonight if he needs it? I'm not going to fish tonight, I still feel a bit shitty, and I want to try and get a good night's sleep in."

"So that you're fresh to try and catch that mirror tomorrow," he said.

"Something like that."

"You tell him I'll be only too pleased. You get your head down, pal."

"Bob reckons there's a big change in the weather coming," I informed the Cowboy. "Big winds and rain."

The Cowboy's face lit up. "This place always fishes after a long dry stretch on the first rain. I'm not saying it'll be a run frenzy night but it'll be really good for a couple of days. I might even call myself out for a draw if things look right."

I said nothing but hoped that I could witness it first hand. I said good night to the Cowboy and then went and explained it all to Rambo. I could tell that he thought that I was a bit of a wimp for not fishing but I had my ideas and I was going to stick to them. Rambo gave me the bait boat and the control panel as he wasn't going to fish the plateau at night as on previous occasions.

Back in my bivvy I wound the tape back that was in the video and watched what the others had recorded on the viewing screen of the camcorder. Alistair had his face into the camera and started off in a serious voice.

"Good morning, I am Brendan Humphrey and today on Sportscene we take a look at one of the world's most dangerous and demanding sports. One that requires total, physical conditioning and a lifetime of commitment. It is a sport where an ability to make the most difficult of decisions, under the most arduous of circumstances, is not merely essential, but prerequisite. Amazing mental stamina, prodigious work rate and gifted insight would only serve to make one ordinary in this sport of the titans. I am, of course, referring to the fascinating sport of carp fishing."

Alistair walked towards my bivvy and introduced the viewer to the Cowboy. "I have with me today, Wayne Kerr, one of the leading exponents of the carp fishing world. Now, Wayne. Why do it? Why take the hideous risk?"

"Well, you see, Brendan. It's there, the fish are there and, you know, you feel, like, you need to have them, right, and that's what really drives you on. You forget about your own safety, like, and just go for it."

"And the hours?"

"Frightening. Absolutely frightening. I once fished a swim for twenty-six consecutive months, you know, and the only time I left my rods apart from, calls of nature, like, was for two hours, to get married."

"Incredible. And the buzz?"

"You know, it's like being in a helicopter on the front of a rocket, you know, you're so high, you're alive, you're there, you're up for it, and then you're down, so down, like, so low, and then, you know, you get one, you're up, so up, so fucking up, but you never fuck up, you know, because you're there, you're carping, like, it's brilliant."

"Quite. And the boy that we've come to see to day? A genius? One for the future?" said Alistair.

"Definitely. Like, he's awesome, he's like a caged animal, you know, he's hyper, he never rests, like, his mind is a seething mass of . . . I can't read that, mate . . ."

". . . Seething mass of carping questions, queries, quandaries and conundrums," said an unattached voice off camera. It was Luke.

". . . A seething mass, of what he just said, you know," said the Cowboy.

"Shall we meet him, then," said Alistair and the pair of them piled into my bivvy followed by the camera.

I was like a stiff on a mortuary slab and the sight of my inert body briefly gave me the shivers. While the Cowboy and Alistair looked on, Ian came in and gave me a sip of water by cradling my head and holding a glass to my lifeless lips. Amazingly, by some inner reflex action, I did take some of the water.

"He's a bit jumpy at the moment, you know, what with the camera and all that," said the Cowboy.

Alistair continued in a voice of reverence. "I can see what you mean about him. His intensity and tenatiousness are overpowering. You get the feeling that you are in the presence of someone who is destined to become a legend, one who will go down in the annals of carping history as one of the true greats. Are we witnessing the growth of a carping genius?"

"Well, like, yeah. If he ever gets off that fucking bedchair, you know?"

They all started laughing and went outside where Rambo was playing in a carp on one of my rods.

"Wake up, boy! I'm wearing your gear out fast!" he cried in delight.

The camera turned itself around onto the face of the person using it and to my shock it was Virtual. "This has been a Lac Fumant Gang . . . minus one . . . production."

The tape faded to an ending and I put the camera down, still chuckling to myself.

150

The saucy whelps, ripping the piss out of me like that, but it was funny, so I'd let them off. I went outside to make a brew before going to sleep. The night was fairly still and the stars shone out from behind the sporadic clouds. The tea tasted great.

It had been a very slow couple of days for me on the carp catching front, what with my period of oblivion and my half-hearted efforts today and my non-existent effort coming up tonight. The Cowboy hadn't been out to draw, Rebecca hadn't been around since Saturday and the Rambo v Spunker heavyweight fight hadn't raised its ugly head. Again I looked at the sky, it looked as it had looked all the time I'd been here. There was no hint of the weather to come, if indeed it was. I speculated, on the myriad of different fronts I was thinking about, that perhaps tonight was the lull before the storm.

CHAPTER 17

The alarm sounded, not a buzzer alarm but a digital clock one, and I awoke from a night of complete rest. I tried to focus in the gloom of my bivvy but for some reason it seemed more murky than usual. I turned on my light and then checked the time. It was as it should have been, namely 6.30am, the usual hour that I had been setting my clock in order to give me time to get my faculties about me, have a quick brew and a bite to eat, before re-positioning my baits, if required, in adequate light. I pulled myself out of my toasty sleeping bag and undone the zip to the bivvy door and poked my head outside. This morning, seeing as I never had a bait out, breakfast would wait until all three rods were in position.

'Woke up, it was a Tuesday morning and the first thing that I saw' . . . were dark clouds. Very dark clouds. In fact the clouds were so dark that it had made the morning much darker than usual and therefore more difficult to spot the dark clouds. It was a vicious circle of darkness, compounded by the failings of the human eye under poor lighting conditions, and also the chameleon-like ability of dark clouds to melt into a dark background.

A bright thought came into my head. I strained to check the direction of the clouds across the sky. I walked out from under my shade-providing tree thinking that its prime objective, as regards to sun screening, might now be superfluous. I stood in a more open area and felt for wind and scanned the sky for movement. I gave a downward, clenched-fist, punch on an angled arm and a little cry of 'yes!' to myself. The wind, although only slight, and the clouds, whose movements were hardly perceptible, were pushing over my head and into the island. The weathermen, and as a result Bob, had got it right.

The prophecy was coming to bare I thought and then told myself to hang on a minute, it wasn't even raining yet. But it looked like it would. As I glanced down the lake I saw, or imagined that I saw, the briefest glimpse of a shadowy figure. The figure was gone in an instant, moving away from me down towards the Cowboy, having been in Rambo's swim. The creature, if that's what it was, looked to be moving on all fours. It happened so quickly and was so unclear that I wasn't really certain that I had spotted anything at all but my gut reaction was that it had been Spunker. I waited for a cry from Rambo having discovered some mischievous wrong-doing. None transpired and my attention moved onto more important matters, such as getting some baits in the water.

The air felt very warm and humid as I unhooked one of my terminal rigs from the butt of one of my rods and let out some line off the baitrunner. I crouched down into a squat and put one of the red bottom baits onto the hair, picked up the rod, clicked off the baitrunner with a quick wind and underarmed the bait into the margin swim down by the trees and put on a back lead. Fifty free offerings plopped in soon after and then the process was repeated for the open water rod. This took me three casts to get the exact position after I had put the marker rod and battery float out. I catapulted the free offerings out and was instantly reminded that the wind was going the way I thought it was. Even though it was barely a breeze, the boilies went out much easier than when I had last fished this spot, then the wind had been in its usual direction into my face.

Finally, I put on one of Pup's pop-ups onto the last rod, pulled off a few yards of line and sat it on the middle lane of my buzz bars with an open bale arm. I had left the bait boat at the side of my bivvy so I took it down to the water's edge with the control panel, which I had got from inside. After carefully putting the hooklength and rig into one of its sides, I shipped it out to the far margin and dumped it overboard. I wound down tight and set the tensioned indicator. On with the buzzer, a quick tweak of the line to check all was well, as I had with the previous two rods, and then it was time to put out some bait with the boat. I decided to put out only forty or so free offerings, but in a trickle along the line that I thought a fish might patrol around that margin. I did this with four trips of only ten boilies and spread them along a ten-yard stretch either way from the hookbait.

To be perfectly frank I wasn't too sure why, the old adage of it seeming like a good idea at the time about sums it up. I suppose the mental picture of my fifty-five cruising around the margin and picking up the odd bait appealed to my sensibilities. In any case I wasn't expecting him yet, my mind reading of him had said later, rather than sooner, and the wind had to blow more and the rains had to fall before he would show.

I put the kettle on, once I was all set, and brought my chair out from the bivvy. I parked my bum on it and watched the steam start to appear from the kettle's spout. I was mildly surprised that Rambo hadn't been up to see me and get the bait boat for his daylight plateau assault. Maybe he was having a lie-in, or maybe the ghostly figure had been Spunker and Rambo was at this moment lying on his bedchair with his throat ripped out.

So strong was the image of my mucker's downfall, however ludicrous it might seem, I felt a fervid urge to go and check on him to make sure he was ok. I clipped my remote sounder box to my jogging bottoms and jumped off the bedchair and walked briskly down to his bivvy. When I was no more than ten yards away from Rambo's bivvy his left hand rod fairly hammered off. At least a hundred decibel's worth of alarm banshee strongly hinted at the take and I could just about pick out the slightly different tone of Rambo's sounder box from within the bivvy. It was odds-on he'd have got the message.

If he wasn't out and at the rods in ten seconds I was prepared to bet money that his throat had been ripped apart. Even then, Rambo would have considered it a pretty lame excuse not to have got to them. I started counting: One, two, I heard a muffled expletive from inside the bivvy. Three, four, sounds of a large body pulling off a sleeping bag and getting off a bedchair. Five, the sound of the zip on the bivvy door being undone. Six, large, muscular, camouflage-clad human with enormous, tattooed biceps powers out of the bivvy like a missile from a silo. Seven, said large, muscular, camouflage-clad human with enormous, tattooed biceps steps straight into a mountainous pile of dog shit. I note a lack of footwear and now different coloured socks. Eight, extremely angry, large, muscular, camouflage-clad human with enormous, tattooed biceps hops on the non-shit encrusted leg down to his rod and hits the take as I say nine. In my mind it's mission accomplished – reputation preserved.

As I stood and watched Rambo attempt to play a powerful carp on one leg, I realised that he was in a world of his own and hadn't noticed me standing nearby. I'd never considered the difficulties that you might encounter having to play a carp while standing on one leg, but I could tell by the way that someone as strong as Rambo was struggling, that the mechanics of it were tricky. He was doing a little one-legged pogo bounce to keep his balance and counteract the leverage of the rod and the force being applied to it by the fish. If I'd had a spare hula-hoop, I'd have asked him to gyrate it around the other leg just for the crack. (One to my skull if I'd dared). Being dispassionate about it I could see one reason for his inability to cope, I was sure that he wasn't quite as focused as he should have been on purely playing the fish. I guess this was understandable, having one of your feet completely smothered in evil-smelling, dog shit and knowing full-well which mutt had delivered the disgusting dollop of doggy-do, could easily distract anyone. It was a faecal fact.

I grimaced as Rambo had to dab a crap-covered toe to earth for a second when applying an extra bit of side-strain. The sock was undoubtedly starting to soak up the hideous coating and his discomfort was clearly increasing as the reality seeped in, so to speak, and the hopping leg began to tire. Another thing was that there was the smell to consider. The whole situation must have been really getting up his nose.

I watched, still unseen, and started to wonder at the intelligence of an animal that had so worked out its victim's stride pattern, that it could place a pile of excrement in the exact spot where he would tread in it. Or had the dog just got lucky, or Rambo unlucky, depending on how you looked at it? One dog's meat is another man's poison. Whatever, it was still a remarkable piece of planning and a gifted piece of application. Rambo had been right all along, the bolt of juice through Spunker's lager-can piercing jaws had done something very strange to him. Something very strange indeed.

"Need any help, mate," I asked, announcing my supposed appearance on the scene.

Now, whether it was the surprise of my voice, or the moving of his head coinciding with a lunge from the fish, or a tiring leg that caused Rambo to lose his balance, I shall never know. All I do know is that as he turned his head to look at me he lost his uniped stability and the carp, literally, pulled him in. Rambo plunged into Lac Fumant sideways on but like the trooper he was, he never let go of his rod. From the far side of the lake I could just make out a dog howling in triumph.

'It was only your sock that was dirty.' 'Feeling a bit hot were you.' 'Fuck me, that's some fish you've got on there.' 'You'll never be able to water-ski behind a carp, mate.' 'You've just spooked your margin rod doing that, pal.' And finally, 'They say Jim Gibbinson (or submit your most respected carp angler) can stand on that stuff . . . (and if you particularly hate the afore-mentioned carp angler) . . . or at least the prick thinks he can,' were all things I never said to Rambo as he came up for air and carried on playing the fish.

"Are you all right?" I asked with no real anxiety. Rambo was made of stern stuff.

Rambo theatrically spat a mini fountain of lake water from his mouth.

"Come on in. The water's lovely." He gave me a huge grin and then told me matter-of-factly. " Do you know what that dog did to me?"

I nodded. "I saw it all. I was coming down to see you when you had the take and came piling out of the bivvy into the pile."

"The dog is as good as dead. Mark my words, boy, as good as dead, which doesn't mean I'm going to kill it, it'll be far worse than that," stated Rambo, with a delicious curl to his top lip. The grin had gone by now.

I didn't doubt it for one minute. Rambo stood and played the fish in about four foot of water and then to my surprise he actually waded out a bit further so that he was some six foot from the lake's edge. From this position he got the carp back to underneath his rod tip and then played it out in a complete circle about his body. At times the carp was closer to the bank than Rambo was. By now the Cowboy, who had probably heard the splash, was sidling up alongside me and watching the whole show with unconcealed amusement.

"Interesting method you've got there, Rambo. Care to expand on it," he enquired.

"It messes with their minds," said Rambo casually, "when you pull them away from the bank and back out into the lake."

And as he said those words the fish decided that it couldn't cope with the bizarre situation and promptly threw in the towel, that Rambo would soon need, and put its head up. A large, partially scaled back came to the surface and Rambo simply waded towards the carp, turned to face the same way as the fish, while keeping it on a tight line with his rod-holding, left arm and scooped it up with the other. With what looked like thirty pounds plus of carp under his armpit, Rambo stomped out of the water and up on to the bank.

"Actually, this is Nigel, my pet carp, and I was just taking him for his morning walk," he said.

It was unlike Rambo to be as overtly funny as this and I put it down to over-compensation of a seething inner core of Spunker-hating bile and loathing. Perhaps he also wanted to draw attention away from the fact that he'd been well and truly done. It was the first time I'd ever seen anyone, or rather anydog, no, despite cries of anthropomorphism, let's stick to anyone, get the better of him. That dog was one weird animal and not an adversary to be sniffed at. Especially when he was laying down shitty landmines that were similar in size and shape, if not consistency and composition, to a Mr Whippy ice cream cornet pulled by a summer recess, sports science student, who had fallen asleep on the handle for about twenty seconds. No flake, either.

While Rambo weighed the fish I went up and got the camera and camcorder. A few minutes later another chapter in the photographic story and docu-session video of the fortnight at Lac Fumant were recorded for posterity. Also included was a touching, brief bit of footage of Rambo easing the remains of the offending pile of stood-on dogshit into a plastic bag. The Cowboy put the fish back into the lake and Rambo popped into his bivvy to get some dry clothing on. The mirror was another thirty but the untold story of Rambo's sodden clothes was one that I would have dearly loved to have had on 8mm tape. I told him as such, once the Cowboy had ridden out of town and back to his swim.

"If you come down to my bivvy tomorrow at around three in the morning," Rambo had told me, "I'll give you a bit of action that will make the mockery that Spunker has made out of me this morning seem small beer, boy. Small beer."

Rambo had that glint in his eye. The one he had kept for looking and talking about Watt in the old syndicate days.

"We're not going to be able to see much in the dark are we? Can't you do whatever you're going to do in the daylight?" I complained.

Rambo grabbed me by the scruff of the sweatshirt. "I'm going on a night time raid, boy. And you are coming along to get a piece of the action on tape, if you want, that is. You are just there to record the event, not to have any input into it and certainly not to help. This is me and him, man versus dog. All right?"

He put me back onto the ground. "What are you going to do?" I asked.

"You wait and see," he said mysteriously and then not so mysteriously. "I'll be up to borrow the bait boat a bit later."

As the morning wore on the clouds started to move over a bit faster but it actually became less dark. It now looked less like rain at dinner time than it had first thing. I had caught my smallest fish from Lac Fumant about an hour earlier, a fifteen from the margin, yet the morning feeding spell had been largely unproductive. Alistair had come along as I was having a bite to eat and he too had been struggling to get takes. He asked me how I was feeling and again broached the subject of writing some articles with him and the Cowboy at some stage, to which I answered in the affirmative. I told him about the predicted weather and he said much the same as the Cowboy had. Any amount of rain after the longish dry spell we had encountered should make the lake fish well.

He asked me at length, yet again, about the mind-meld with the mirror and whether I really did feel as if my sticking to a mainly unsuccessful tactic (fishing to the long range island margin) would pay dividends in the end. He also asked if I would have stuck with that mainly unsuccessful tactic if I hadn't experienced the mind-meld. Alistair was asking questions that I didn't know the answers to and I was eternally thankful to the 26-9 mirror that had the kindness to pick up my open water bait before I could fully expose my ignorance to him. Television might be a conversation killer but so is a belting run and it gives you a great excuse to sprint away from the person you're talking to.

With Alistair gone I felt as if I could relax again and paradoxically start settling down to the prospect of getting nervous, by contemplating what Rambo was going to get up to in the night. The thing that made it even more worrying was whether it had been such a good idea to suggest that I go along and try and video it. Not that I could actually remember suggesting it. If I had, Rambo must have sublimely planted the thought and if he wanted me to go that much I'd have to in any case. That's what friends are for, imposing on each other. He had said no more about the night raid when he had collected the bait boat and he hadn't been up to see me since. The novelty of photographing and videoing every fish had worn off so it was possible that he'd had a few off the plateau, I'd have been a bit surprised if he hadn't, but it was likely that the fish were nothing of real note. Probably only twenties! Usually I would see or hear him having action but with Alistair around I might have easily missed it all.

Now that Alistair was out of my face with his never-ending question show, I also had time to consider more fully my fishing strategy. I was pretty sure the island rod would come up trumps and I admit that the mind-meld reinforced the idea and had given me confidence to stick it out. A pragmatist would have been rolling on the floor with laughter but I had duped logic and chance before on Lac Fumant and the mind-meld seemed to be an extension of that. On other matters I decided I would concentrate on getting a take on video tomorrow. The rain that was due should speed things up and I had only to set the camcorder up under a brolly to protect it. I mentally rubbed my hands together with glee, this new weather front and the general opinion of it making the lake fish well might even drag the Cowboy out to draw. Now if I could get that and a take on video you could forget all about such piffling trivialities as UFO's, Nessie, Lord Lucan and the Abominable Snowman.

On a wider scale my earlier feelings of being on a free-wheeling roll of luck had slightly subsided as had my elation about the 250k in the bank. The length of the fishing session had detached me from such everyday things as finance. I think angling distracts you from most everyday things and is a fundamental reason why so many of us do it but there were no shortage of replacement subjects to consider. Familiarity had stopped me thinking of the beauty that was Lac Fumant and loads of good carp had made me blasé about twenty pound fish. It was ironic really, considering how life or death they had been in the old syndicate session. No, my main emotional involvement was Rebecca and her amazing offer on the Saturday get together. To most blokes I suppose it wouldn't have been a subject of any ambiguity or soul-searching and certainly not something to get Alistair-like over. It would have been, to put it crudely, a get in there and shag it situation, but for me, the prospect of doing the dirty on Sophie, because of all that we'd been through, was bordering appalling and appealing at the same time. How could I ever face her again if I betrayed her? How could I even contemplate unfaithfulness after she had stood by me while my syndicate madness had raged and my prison sentence passed? Rebecca was some looker, though, and I was willing to bet a fair lump of the dosh that sat in my bank that she was a sexual wild cat. A woman who knew no bounds, except perhaps in bondage, as regards to erotic dalliance and every new perversion, and a few old ones as well, was something to plunge into with illimitable energy, enthusiasm and abandonment. Ho-hum! Dilemma.

That afternoon through to early evening saw the wind pick up a little more, yet despite a fully overcast sky not one drop of rain fell, although it had become a few shades greyer on the emulsion colour chart from earlier. From 'Morning Mist' to 'Frigate Grey' if referring to Brolac's 'Nautical Landscapes' catalogue, which includes the infamous 'Belgrano Blood Red' and the psychedelic, multi-fleck 'Force 10 Throw-up.'

Bob had his usual walk around the lake and told me that the bad weather was absolutely, one hundred percent, definitely on its way, yet Rebecca wasn't. Her friend had taken another turn for the worse and she had left to visit her in some hurry. This had left Bob in the lurch for supplying any dinners and he apologised for the inconvenience. I wasn't too worried, I had some tins of stuff which I could heat up with my typical aplomb and told him it was no big deal. I could be a chef, chief. I gave him the bait boat battery to charge up and the camcorder battery from the unit itself. I asked him to have them ready for me for early Wednesday morning and he said that he would leave them in the porch, ready for a first light pick up. I re-fitted the unused spare one into the viewcam. I didn't want it to run out tonight.

The evening feeding spell was unremarkable. I had a couple of takes to the margin and open water rods, both of which were twenty pound commons. It sounds incredibly arrogant but I considered that these fish were simply marking time for me until an 'eff' carp came along. At the start of the vacation they made the blood pump but now they had lost a bit of their impact. I was so conditioned to thinking that my 'eff' carp would come to the long range rod it never really crossed my mind that one of those two takes could be a monster. This was dangerously flawed thinking, and it had to be asked if my drug trip had given me brain damage or carp fishing tunnel-thinking. Then again, I bet 75% of carpers would be classed as having brain rot if that was the definition and we were all honest with ourselves.

Before the light went completely I wound in the long range rod to check on Pup's pop-up. It was still popping up like a good'un but I put on a new one and decided to fish it in between the two sets of pads for the period until I would be off to video Rambo's revenge. At nine Rambo came up to see me. He'd had six fish off the plateau but not one was a twenty. Everyone had been like-peas-in-a-pod nineteen mirrors which were not the same fish, he had said, before I could tease him with the suggestion. It was a rather odd coincidence, I suppose, but these things happen, I was testament to the vagaries of chance. Rambo told me to be at his bivvy at 3 am prompt if I wanted to get the action on tape. I told him the viewcam was Sharp by name and would be sharp by nature.

I went to bed early that night and it turned out to be a wise decision because at midnight I had a take on the pop-up rod and it took me forty-five minutes before the culprit, a fully scaled 28-6 was safely in the sack. The fish had run me up and down the margin once I'd got it close in and had picked up the open water line despite it being back leaded. This lead to a right old romp in the dark and a hideous tangle, which luckily didn't cost me a fish, but did take two rods out of action for the rest of the night. With only two hours or so to go before I was due to report to Sergeant Rambo at bivvy HQ, I had neither the desire or the willpower to untangle everything at that moment. I left the one remaining rod out until 2.45am when my alarm woke me up and I wound it in and steeled myself for the coming adventure.

I was to be a war correspondent, an in-the-field, video operator. My sole purpose was to capture on tape, with no slant, no bias, as it happened, the deeds of the night. I was to be impartial, unbiased, non-discriminating. I was only there to record. Let history and the people decide who was right or wrong, let them make up their own minds and let me supply them with images to make their judgement. More to the point there was going to be a rumble and I wasn't directly involved but had a grandstand seat. I wonder how many press correspondents had thought that and ended up with a stray bullet in the head?

Rambo was ready and waiting in camouflage clothing, his face blacked out. He had taken black facial paint on a carp fishing holiday like other blokes might take shaving foam or soap. I wasn't really that shocked but it did make me crease my forehead a bit and wonder what on earth he had supposed he might need it for. Surely he never imagined going on a night time raid to duff up a dog when he was packing it. Soap, toothbrush, shower gel, comb, black facial paint, hmm that'll come in handy if there happens to be a rottweiler that needs sorting in the dark. Who knows?

Rambo gave me a large torch on a shoulder strap and one with a tiny pencil beam.

"When I give the word you can turn the big one on, but not before. The little one you just point at the ground so you can see enough not to fall over. No talking whatsoever and keep five yards behind me. Ok?"

"Right. What are you going to do exactly?" I asked.

Rambo put a finger to his lips and moved off. My stomach started to crawl as I followed him, it was the prebaiting raid all over again. I started to record, I knew that no images would come out but it gave a good impression of what it was like walking about in the pitch black with a minuscule light shining just ahead of your toes. We set off in a direction away from the lake and took a route around the back of everyone's bivvies, going as far as forty yards behind them. I had never walked out this far but Rambo seemed to have an idea of the route. He must have checked it out at some stage earlier on in the day because he was sure-footed and knew exactly where to go.

Eventually after some fifteen minutes or so we must have got to a point where we were about forty yards behind Ian and Spunker's bivvies because Rambo slowed and took much greater care. We had stopped circumnavigating the lake and were now heading back towards the water's edge. I felt the tingle in my guts as caterpillars turned to butterflies and all of them took flight.

As we edged closer a light suddenly appeared in a bivvy that was just ten yards in front of us. Rambo turned to me, turned off his torch and I quickly followed his lead. We stood still. I heard a zip being undone and then footfalls, then I heard another zip and a spray of water hitting the ground. It was Ian, getting up for a piss. The water stopped, a quick zip, more footsteps and finally the sound of the bivvy door zip finished proceedings.

"Turn the video off," said Rambo in whisper. "We'll have to wait for him to fall back to sleep, I'll check his breathing pattern when I think it's safe. You stay put from now on until I give the word. "

We waited a good twenty minutes, which was great fun, before Rambo went right up to Ian's bivvy, presumably to listen for regular breathing and then crept on to the enemy's fortress. I was some ten yards back and VT was rolling. This was Rambo's sphere of excellence, the thing that he was good at and the thing that he knew best. Not one sound, not a snapped twig or a rustle of clothing, not a clumsy footfall or a tickley cough came from the big man as he seemed to float across the ground towards the bivvy opening. The pencil beam of his torch gave tantalising glimpses of his silent motion until suddenly it went out.

I knew that Spunker's bivvy was a Sundridge one man Millennium Dome or rather a one dog Millennium Dome. Clearly a dog had no need for the door to be zipped up so Rambo's stealth was understandable and the light going out could mean only one thing. Rambo must be standing right by the entrance. My heart was thumping and then I heard a dull, sickening thud. Almost immediately the pencil beam came back on and Rambo was outside the bivvy pulling the pegs from the ground. Once he'd done this he lifted a corner of the bivvy up and gathered up the material hand over hand until he had made the bivvy into a large, green sack. He heaved this onto his shoulder and carried it over to me.

"Torch!" he whispered.

I turned on the big torch and tried to direct it onto the sack and wield the camcorder at the same time. Rambo was now back on the move, getting out of the area as quick as he could, looking like an eco-version of Father Christmas or, if you like, an unleaded Santa, as opposed to a four star one. I followed him and could plainly see a large lump lying in the bottom of the sack as it got bounced and buffeted by Rambo who was by now, virtually jogging. We kept going until we came to a large tree that was situated before Japp and Wim's swim. Rambo dropped the bag, none to gently I might add, and pulled out a thick rope from somewhere and tossed it over a sturdy branch that was about twenty foot up.

My first thoughts were that he was he going to lynch the mutt. Was I the sole witness to a kangaroo-court style hanging? The rope flopped over the would be gibbet arm first time. To my relief Rambo then tied one end around the huge neck of material he had formed out of the bivvy, as opposed to tying it around Spunker's neck directly. Once this was done he pulled the sack up into the air via the branch pulley until it was as high as it could go. Then, while taking the strain, he threw the rope over the branch again and pulled it down quickly. The rope was now around the branch twice.

"Hold this," he said to me, giving me the loose end. "One hand is all you'll need, now it's wrapped around the branch the friction on the rope will make it easy to hold."

I took the rope one-handed and to my surprise I could hold it easily, which was good, seeing as I was right underneath the rottweiler + bivvy bundle. While I stood gawping at the huge package above my head Rambo shinned up the tree, took hold of the rope and tied it off around the branch and slid back down the tree's trunk.

"What the hell have you done to him?" I asked.

"Oh, it was just a quick jab to the jowl to put him out, he'd have made too much noise otherwise. How he gets down from this situation is up to him. If he chews his way out it'll bring the bastard back down to earth in more than one way." Rambo gave me a wide smile, his teeth looking much whiter than normal set against his blacked skin. "Well, if you've got all the footage you want, I'm going to go to bed. A good night's work, I think, don't you?"

I nodded. "I'll see you tomorrow." Rambo gave me a thumbs up and left me alone.

I shone the torch onto the oversized party bag that was swinging in the wind. Not many pleasant knick-knacks in there only a very large, very unconscious, soon to be very pissed off, very angry, rottweiler and a couple of broken fibre-glass poles, I shouldn't wonder. The tree's branch started to creak a little every time the bag swung and I started to smile.

Only Rambo, the inimitable Rambo, could conjure up a revenge raid like I had witnessed. No-one else would have had the skills or the power, he was truly awesome when provoked into aggression. Gazing up at the parcel with the big torch was like looking up at the jolly green giant's scrotum, dangling between unseen massive thighs. I laughed and the tree started to creak and groan even more. I looked more carefully, expecting it to be Spunker having come round and starting to thrash about, but it wasn't, he was still out cold. It was the wind that was making the package move, it was beginning to really pick up and becoming stronger by the minute. The predicted weather front must be arriving at last.

"Goodnight spunky, Spunker," I said to the swaying package.

After giving a little salute to the dangling dog, I too, made my way back to my base camp. By the time I had returned to my bivvy it was starting to rain.

CHAPTER 18

Wednesday morning came and although I felt tired I had a host of things to do, the first of which, having had a look outside, was to put on the waterproofs. The wind was now blowing nicely over my bivvy and into the island and the rain was continuous, if light. I was dying to know whether Spunker had been the dog who fell to earth since we had left him but there was no way that I could see his hanging tree from my bivvy. To be honest I wasn't too clear in my mind where it was, so I'd have to wait until I saw Rambo to find out and get the latest news. I was sure that he would have been out for a shufty to see what had happened to him.

My second job, having put the waterproofs on, was to nip up to the cottage to get the bait boat and camcorder batteries. This was a bit of a pain, but with no sun for the solar charger and the camcorder battery having been used last night, I needed them both. The brisk walk up to the cottage made me a bit sticky in waterproofs but the batteries were in the porch as requested. Fortunately Bob was up and about so I gave him the spare camcorder battery to charge and asked him to have it back as soon as possible. He had a few things to do as well but said he would put it on charge straight away and bring it back down in a couple of hours. Quality, chief!

The next task, once I was back at the lake, was to sort out the tangled rods and get them out into position. Luckily enough there were no knots in either main line but I took the precaution of changing all three hooklengths. I stuck to fishing the one pop-up on the long range rod and using my bottom baits on the other two. Margin, open water, long range to island margin, were the spots I intended to fish and that was the order that I put them out. Once this was done I lifted the lovely fully scaled mirror out to check that she was ok and put here back, still in the sack. Rambo could snap her for me later because, like most fully scaled mirrors, she was a beautiful fish.

The fish in the sack made me think of the dog in the sack and having clipped my remote sounder onto my jogging bottoms underneath the waterproof trousers, I went down to see Rambo. It seemed really odd having to contend with a little bit of rough weather after the previous dry spell, having to worry about keeping things dry and wearing waterproofs felt most peculiar. Even wearing long trousers, as opposed to shorts, felt a bit strange but I told myself it was a very small price to pay for the upcoming carp catching bonanza. I poked my head around the opening of Rambo's bivvy to find him sitting on his bedchair. He must have brought a gallon tub of make-up remover with him because his face was as clean as a whistle, but, if you'll pardon the pun on a subject that fascinated me, he had a bit of a hang-dog expression upon it.

"All right then, mate?" I said in a bright tone.

The reason for Rambo's deflated countenance soon became apparent.

"The bastard's down. And the fucking bivvy. And I've seen him walking about over the other side of the lake without so much as a sodding limp," said Rambo rather disconsolately.

I took in the information as best I could. "How did he manage that, then?" I asked.

"You tell me!" said Rambo totally nonplussed. "I was up at first light and he was down by then, bivvy and all."

"Maybe Ian got him down?" I said thinking aloud.

"He's still asleep and I doubt whether he'd have got him down in the dark. I doubt whether any of you lot could even climb the tree, let alone carry or lower the best part of 200lb of dog plus bivvy down from the tree. No way I . . ." Rambo had spotted something that had cut him short. He raised an arm and outstretched finger. "Look! Look!" he cried.

Rambo's voice was up an octave and he was pointing over to the other side of the lake. Clearly visible through the light rain was Spunker, dragging his bivvy back to its original position. Rambo had the binoculars on the dog in an instant.

"Look at him! No injuries and even the bivvy doesn't look torn. I'll tell you what, that dog is some weird animal. This war isn't over yet by a long way, not by a long way."

Rambo let the binoculars rest and shook his head incredulously and then dismissed the problem from his mind and snapped his carping head on. "Oh well, plateau time. Where's your bait boat then, boy?"

A slightly muffled remote sounder box chose that instant to belt out its familiar tune.

"Shit!" I cried, as I tend to do under such circumstances.

Then with false calm and a pseudo upper class accent that I think Rambo had done before, I said. "It's in my swim. Must dash old chap, got a frightfully large carp tugging on the old terminal tackle. What?"

I legged it back to my bivvy as quick as I could, my feet wheel spinning in the wet, long, grass and hit the margin rod. The rod leapt over and the fish made off on a vigorously powerful run taking line from the clutch which screeched its shrill protest. The wind blowing across the taut line made an eerie singing sound as I furiously applied side-strain to the underwater, nuclear sub that had picked up my hookbait. At last I managed to turn the fish as a small earthquake opened up a bottomless chasm in the ground, which I managed to straddle, while still keeping a tight line. I pumped the fish back up the margin as if my life depended on it. Molten lava started to explode from the now gargantuan fissure between my legs, thankfully my 'Brand name' waterproofs were of illustrious quality and the liquid rock simply oozed off them, without leaving so much as a stain. The water was now boiling around in front of me, although it was hard to tell if this was the fish or the lava superheating the water of the lake. The line pinged over the carp's dorsal fin and then over several more as a pod of dolphins swam through my line. At last I got the carp's head up and pulled the fish over the spreader block of the net and she was mine. I lifted her up and sank back onto the hot, volcanic bankside, emotionally and physically spent, but inordinately jubilant.

Yes, it was every carp playing cliché that you'd ever read or that I'd ever written. There was no adjective too extravagant or too exorbitant to be used, nor any idea too far-fetched to supposedly increase one's admiration for the author. But it was all true, ask the Cowboy. He likes all that type of prose.

"Any good?" said Rambo.

"Low twenty, I suppose. Nothing special," I said matter-of-factly.

"Photograph?" asked Rambo.

"Nah. I've a better one in the sack . . . on second thoughts do them together, that'll be a little more interesting."

Was I really that nonchalant or was I getting an inflated ego and just pretending to be?

By the time Bob came down with the other battery I'd had two more fish. Every time I went down to set up the camcorder on Rambo's plateau rod to try and get a take on video, I'd get a run and have to go back. While I was away sorting myself out Rambo would get one, conspiracy theorists would say that the carp were doing it on purpose and perhaps they would be right. I had reckoned that getting a take on video might be a bit tricky but I hadn't considered that catching too many fish would be one of the reasons why. It's a funny old world, innit?

In between all this I had noticed that Ian and the Fatboys were getting action as well. I had no reason to doubt that the others, who I couldn't see, were pulling them out as well. Spunker's bivvy was now set up again and the mutt looked to be having a doze inside, oblivious to all the buzzer action around him, bless his slobbering mandibles. The rain was working its magic all right but I still hadn't had a run on the long range rod.

I'd toyed with the notion of reeling in for a couple of hours to video Rambo and had decided against it. I had missed too many fishing hours of late and for the first time there was the consideration that the days were slipping by. If I was going to catch the fish of my dreams, drug-induced or not, I had better utilise my time wisely from now on. I suddenly thought that maybe Rambo would be prepared to come up to my swim and video me, after all, he'd caught his 'eff' carp. It seemed a sound idea so I nipped down to ask him how he felt about it. When I got down to his swim he was standing on the other side of his bivvy looking down the lake, as soon as he heard me he spun round and motioned me towards him with a rapid hand movement. I promptly thought that he'd spotted Spunker sneaking up on a revenge raid of the revenge raid. I was wrong, it was much more exciting than that.

I ran to his side. "What is it?"

Rambo was highly animated. "It's the Cowboy, he's had three fish so far this morning. I've just got a gut instinct that he's going to come out and draw. Them's a-carp are calling him out, boy."

I froze. Like the man who spots a naked girl in a window, I was torn between two stools. I wanted to get it on film but was not keen on having to go and get the camera in case I missed anything. Besides, she might be gone when I got back.

"Well! Go on then!" said Rambo.

"What?" I pleaded.

Rambo rolled his eyes. "Get the fucking camcorder!" I stood my ground. "Now!" he barked.

I ran to get it and got back moving faster than I did for any take. "Here it is," I said out of breath, "but we don't want him to see us filming him, he might bottle out."

For some reason Rambo was struck with the notion that the situation needed an influx of silly humour.

"To the bivvymobile, Robin. I'll open the window enough to use the Batcorder," he said.

I was all for it. "Holy, tangled, terminal tackle, Batman," I said and crammed myself into Rambo's bivvy. "Derna-nana-nana-nana, Fatboys!" I said, like you do.

Rambo adjusted the window and we piled in and the pair of us peered through the gap in the window and started to giggle like a couple of stupid schoolboys with their noses to the sweet shop window. Our expectation was almost as big as our hope.

"Come on, my son," said Rambo under his breath, "get out there and do the business."

We watched, we waited and then we watched a bit more.

"Come on. Come on," I said with rising frustration.

There was nothing we could do but bide our time. The pair of us fell silent and stared at the Cowboy's bivvy for what seemed an age.

I was expecting one of us to get a run any minute and blow the whole gaff, and that included the Cowboy. What a thing to do when you're carping, to hope not to get a run. Outrageous. I bet there were poor, deprived carpers all over the third world who would have given anything for a take and there I was, sitting in a safe European bivvy, quite happy to pass one up, all for the sake of viewing a spectacle.

My knees were beginning to ache when it happened, yet when it did, my complete absorption in the event meant that all pain left my body. Majestically the Cowboy came out from his bivvy in a stoop and then stood upright, legs astride. I started filming and zoomed in on him from top to toe. Stetson, small cigar in mouth, large poncho around his shoulders, jeans and cowboy boots. His hands hung limply by his side as he looked up disdainfully at the sky and then peered out into the lake. One hand moved slowly up to the cigar and held it, by thumb and finger, for one last drag through pursed lips. He sucked in smoke with squinting eyes, exhaled a cloud and then tucked the cheroot into the corner of his mouth. With an absurdly deliberate movement, a pair of tan, kid-skin gloves were pulled from a belt and meticulously placed on each hand. Fingers wriggled into each glove as they were pulled on. To complete the act, each individual digit was rammed into the glove by punching a finger web into the thumb and index finger web of the opposite hand.

"Is this guy for real?" I asked, as much to myself as to Rambo.

The Cowboy seemed a great guy normally but watching his preposterous posing and preening, plus the pure self-indulgence of it, was a bit disarming.

"Shut up!" said Rambo. "And keep on filming. And don't wobble that video, either. This is something I'm going to want to watch again and again."

With the gloves now fitted to his satisfaction the Cowboy locked two thumbs over his belt and walked to his rods.

"He's a bandy, git," I whispered, watching his John Wayne-style gait. "I wonder if he's always been like that, or whether he had to perfect it by walking over hundreds of pigs in a narrow alley."

"Hundreds of fat pigs," said Rambo.

"Or crawling Fatboys!" I said spluttering with laughter.

The liquid crystal display on the viewcam lost all horizontal hold as the image of the strutting Cowboy pogoed in sync with my heaving body.

"You're just being stupid now," said Rambo chastising me with false earnestness. "Not even the girls in Japp and Wim Senior's films could get their legs that far apart."

We regained our composure and reigned in our hilarity to fall silent again as the Cowboy came to his 'guns'. He was in between his rods, standing level with the reels, one rod to his left hand, two rods to his right. He surveyed the lake one more time, slowly panning from left to right and then unhooked his thumbs and let his arms hang down. His arms stretched for the ground, his fingers spread-eagled and then the digits played a synchronised scroll three times. The fingers stopped and hung limp, the Cowboy eased his whole body up onto the balls of his toes and then sank it back down. He eased the poncho back from his arms, four deep breaths and then, finally, he was ready to draw. The Cowboy cut a fine figure as he stood motionless in the drizzle. He was ready, but how long would he have to wait before that well known desperado, the Carpio Kid would make his move?

My head swam with Ennio Morricone scores and visions of Clint Eastwood, Lee Van-Cleef and Eli Wallach in the grave yard with that all important stone in the middle of them. On the stone was the name of the grave where the money box was buried. Clint had left the stone blank because the money box was buried in the grave of an unknown person. Clint had no name. The grave had no name. The stone had no name on it, just like the Cowboy had no name on the butts of the rods that he was standing next to. It was clear who the Cowboy wanted to be. If the Cowboy was Clint then Rambo was Van-Cleef and I was Tuco and it was a kind of three way draw to see whose buzzer went off first. In the film I'd rooted for Clint and in this instance I was rooting for the Cowboy.

Although I kept filming the Cowboy, the different celluloid vision and sound filled my senses and stopped my eyes from seeing him. Pictures of twitching gunmen, their authentic faces and steely eyes, from a time of legends and deeds, took the place of the Cowboy and Lac Fumant. With those brilliant images combining with an even better, incredibly atmospheric film score, I was completely enraptured.

As in the film, the music reached a deafening, climatic crescendo.

"Jesus!" cried Rambo. "Hark at that rain."

Snapped from my memories' cinematic recollection, I was back with reality and it was fairly chucking it down. The thrashing rain created a wall of sound (my head had turned it into Ennio's music to counteract it) as the large droplets pummelled the bivvy's outer skin remorselessly. The Cowboy, despite being less than thirty yards away, was virtually obscured by the lashing rain. Heroically he stood his ground as the elements tried to drown him under the most torrential deluge I had ever witnessed. It was Monsoon City. It was Bucketsville. It was Teemming Town. It was, above all else, I could tell by the way he tried to ease his body away from sticking underpants, running out the Cowboy's arse.

Undeniably soaked to the crotch there was worse to come. The once proud, stiff brim of his hat soon became waterlogged and lost the will to curve away from Mother Earth's gravitational pull and collapsed in sodden surrender. Rather than being a fine stetson it looked more like a twenties' flapper's cloche. As well as this, the rain had soaked the heavily made poncho and the bright colours of it were starting to merge as the different dyes began to run and mingle. It was now an amazing, technicolour poncho that looked as if it had been designed by twenty chimps with access to a paint store, or, by some overpaid, marginally gifted, modern artist/fashion culprit. The victim was all too obvious. The coloured water drip-fed down the legs of his jeans, which, by virtue of being tucked into his boots, had filled to overflowing. If he'd have jumped in Lac Fumant there and then it would have probably dried him off.

From looking a reasonably cool gunhand, if somewhat pretentious, the Cowboy now looked like a big drip. His cigar, all ardour and fire long extinguished by the rain, was all limp and floppy. Its pathetic, wilting, droop to earth seemed an apt visual phallic metaphor for the Cowboy's disposition and even though the rain had now eased back to the earlier drizzle, the damage was done. His tan gloves looked a much less pleasing brown, now that they were soaked, and his hat looked as if it had been pulled down on top of his head by an irate Russian shot-putter, female of course. Rambo, being Rambo, was killing himself laughing. Despite the fact that I could appreciate how uncomfortable the Cowboy must be feeling and how he must have been cursing his luck to come out to draw a few minutes before the mother of all cloudbursts, I was cracking up as well.

The pair of us cackled and guffawed at the wretched figure but the best was yet to come. Suddenly, and right out of the slate grey, as is usual, the Carpio Kid made his entrance and the outside of the two rods to the Cowboy's right wanged off. Sergio and Ennio had long gone and with them all trace of glamour. All that was left was Clint the Cowboy, Clint the wet plumber from Cornwall dressed up as Mr Eastwood, but nonetheless, still the Cowboy, ace carp angler. The Cowboy drew the right hand rod in a blur of wet clothing and sodden footwear and struck hard, but an error had been made.

Whether it was the discomfort, or whether it was the cold, or whether it was water on the brain that caused the mistake, we shall never know, but the Cowboy committed a carping faux pas. The equivalent of a real cowboy forgetting to pull the trigger, is the carp angler who never winds once to click in the baitrunner. Even though I'd done it instinctively the first time after two years and had thought that it was like riding a bike, in terms of never losing the knack, for that one instance, the Cowboy had forgot or had lost the knack.

The Cowboy struck hard into a loose-set baitrunner that simply whirred in mockery as the force of his powerful strike met nothing and the momentum of his own efforts, with nothing to offset them, caused him to fall backwards. With no grip from leather soled boots on a saturated ground, the Cowboy was gunned down and crashed backwards onto the bank. The Cowboy had bit the grass.

Cruelly our laughter increased, in fact it was directly proportional to the misfortune befalling the Cowboy and boy was he falling. Like two hyenas we rushed out from the bivvy and down to where the fallen carcass lay, hoping to find more bones of laughter and large meaty chunks of mirth for us to pick over. When we reached him he was lying flat on his back and not moving, his rod poking vertically up into the air like a puny mast from a scuppered ship. It was then and only then, long after the initial hit, that the Cowboy finally remembered to wind. His Shimano gave a solemn 'clunk' as the baitrunner came off and he continued reeling in from his prone position, the circular movement of his left wrist, the only sign of life.

A trace of various coloured dyes had seeped out onto the grass around the Cowboy's body marking his perimeter. I imagined it to be something like the white chalk line the police draw around corpses, only in rainbow paint. Eventually the Cowboy's in-line bomb pulled into the margin and snagged him, he gave the rod a jerk and the weight popped out of the edge and landed on his chest. He hadn't quite been filled full of lead but good enough. The Carpio Kid was long out of town, riding into the sunset.

"What happened?" I said to the fallen carper, as if I didn't already know.

As I spoke I couldn't help but notice that the Cowboy's legs were like two inward facing bananas even when he was flat on his back

"The bastard got me," groaned the Cowboy.

"You look a bit damp," said Rambo gleefully as he leaned over the horizontal carper.

"Damp?" said the Cowboy, moving only his eyeballs to look at Rambo. "I'm fucking waterlogged. If I was a football pitch, I'd be deemed unplayable. I haven't been so wet since that 28mm stopcock came off in my hand and I flooded two basement flats."

"Your poncho looks a bit Jackson Pollock," I ventured.

The Cowboy jammed his chin into his chest in an attempt to look at the multicoloured mess that clothed him.

"Who was he then?"

The moment had passed so I didn't bother to tell him. The Cowboy lay motionless for a few more seconds before deciding it was time to do something about his predicament. The first thing he did was to pull off his boots, empty them and chuck both of them over his shoulder.

"Shan't be needing them again," he said and proceeded to take off his hat, poncho, waistcoat, shirt, jeans and finally gloves. He dumped them all on top of the boots. "Or them," he added.

In just his underpants and socks the Cowboy went back to his bivvy and disappeared inside. I looked questioningly at Rambo who looked back at me. The word 'intrigued' formed in big letters above our heads. We ran to the Cowboy's bivvy.

"Here, Cowboy. What do you mean you won't be needing all the clobber?" I called.

The voice from inside answered. "Clint. My name is Clint. The Cowboy is dead. He was shot down. Not in a blaze of glory, but in a downpour."

"What are you on about?" I said.

The Cowboy's head poked out through his bivvy flap. "I'm on about a man so fixated with the Wild West that he named his only son after a bloke called Eastwood. I'm talking about a childhood filled with guns and Indians and outlaws and gunfights and cattle rustlin' . . . the whole cowboy thing and a little boy sharing his father's infatuation. I'm talking about a boy growing up into a man and still getting pleasure from all those things. Then, when I started carping, I came up with my own little game, to gunfight the carp, to beat them to the draw. I kept it special, I only did it when I knew the chances were very good but I told myself the first time I lost it would be like the real thing. Death. The death of a cowboy. Thirty-nine gunfights down the road and I've just lost my first draw. It's over. I'm plain old Clint from now on . . ." The Cowboy's head bowed a little and his voice became a touch melancholic. ". . . Besides, it was a bit much I suppose, all the show and the gear, I guess I'm glad it's finished in a way but I couldn't have stopped it. It was a part of my life, there was only one way for it to end, and I did all that I could to try and make sure it didn't. I made a mistake, that's all. A basic mistake."

And with that he went back into his bivvy. Rambo and I had witnessed the death of a legend and had laughed at it. I looked at the forlorn pile of sodden clothes. They looked what they were, a pile of useless garments. Without a body to shape them they were empty husks, they had no soul and no means of animation. I was going to miss the Cowboy.

"There's a moral to all this," I said to Rambo as we made our way back up to his swim.

"Yeah," said Rambo. "and what might that be?"

"Buggered if I know," I said truthfully, "but I bet there is one."

"Hmm," said Rambo. "You're probably right."

"Or a proverb, maybe. 'A dog in the bivvy is worth two kicks in the bush,'" I said.

169

"No. 'The only good dog, is a dead dog,'" replied Rambo with feeling.

"I think we've seen enough of death for this morning, don't you?" I asked. "What with the Cowboy R.I.P."

"Ok," said Rambo easily. "I'll murder Spunker this afternoon."

I nodded my concurrence. "All right, then." I said laughing.

For some reason I became reflective and spoke my thoughts aloud. "You know this session is like chalk and cheese compared to the old syndicate one. All that bile and bitterness just doesn't exist here, apart from you and the mutt that is, but that doesn't count. This holiday has been brilliant and killed off all my doubts about fishing again, you know."

"That's good," said Rambo approvingly.

"Yep, the old hassles have gone. Do you know I haven't a clue how many twenties I've caught since we've been here. It's 'The Syndicate R.I.P.' all right."

The only thing that got murdered in the afternoon, fear not canine lovers, were the carp, well, slaughtered rather than murdered and not in the literal sense. The action was pretty hectic, not quite so manic as the frenzy night, I doubt whether anything could be as mental as that, but it was a take every three or so hours on each rod. Except one that is. My long range rod refused to budge despite the fact that the wind was becoming ever stronger and was in the right direction. Rambo was canning fish on all three rods, the plateau one still outstripping the others, but my triple was firing on two cylinders.

Nagging doubts came to me again and any idea of getting the camera out to video a take got side-tracked. I was still photographing and videoing fish on the bank for both Rambo and Alistair. Even the Cowboy, sorry, even Clint came up and asked me to do a quick clip of a fantastic upper thirty that he had caught. The viewcam recorded him for posterity in wellies and waterproofs, less than fifteen minutes back on the same tape was his former self. One day I'd tell him and let him watch it. Maybe he'd laugh at it or maybe he wouldn't.

By evening the drizzle was rain with the odd heavier shower coming along now and again but there was nothing as heavy as the downpour that had drenched the Cowboy. The squalls never lasted long because the wind was really starting to whip the weather over us pretty quick. Despite not having a take on the long range rod I had managed to convince myself that all would end up as I hoped.

News came up from Rambo's swim via Virtual, of all people, who was on a lap of the lake for some reason, that he'd had another huge carp. I rushed down to his swim, the rain stinging the left hand side of my cheek as I ran, to see him cradling another monster 'eff' carp. Rambo had hooked and landed a massive 43-7 common on his least productive rod. When he told me I knew what he was inferring, although he didn't come right out and say it as such. By telling me that this second 'eff' carp of his had fallen to his less likely, but still sensibly placed rod, he was hinting that I should move the dud long range rod. With that rod fished in the middle of the two sets of pads, where I had caught well before, my catch rate would definitely be upped and who knows what bonus fish might come along?

My faith was rocked but through either stupidity, determination or my belief in fate and my druggy dream I fought temptation and knew I would stick it out until I had to leave. Another couple of days was all I had left and a small sense of unease filled me. Only a few hours earlier I had scoffed at my previous desire to catch twenties, yet here I was gagging for a forty despite all I had caught and all the fun I'd had. It was different in a way because I was not up against how many someone else had caught, it was just a personal goal, yet I have to admit I was jealous of Rambo. One forty was bad enough but two, that was a killer, especially as I needed one so bad. I was pleased for him, he was my fishing buddy after all, but deep inside I wanted it to be me and not him who had caught the second forty. It was a most human emotion for sure, one that many of us who fish with a mate must have surely experienced, but it was not a pretty one, or one that I was proud of.

"Well done, mate," I said to him sincerely.

"Thanks. I hope the next one's yours," he said, with equal honesty.

I walked back to my rods hoping his hopes would come true. Something in Rambo's eyes had told me that he was willing me with all his might to get the fish I wanted. There was no doubt he wanted me to catch one as much as I did. Would I have been as magnanimous if the boot was on the other foot? Too right I would, magnanimity comes easy with two forties under your belt.

CHAPTER 19

B efore I turned in on the Wednesday night I re-baited a pop-up on the long range rod and put it back in the same spot it had came from. I had made my mind up not to put out any more bait, it seemed a bit mad to be piling it in without having any action. I could only see it decreasing the chance of a take rather than increasing it. The other two rods were set in open water and the margin as they had been for some days now. I cooked, or rather heated up, a tin of muck for dinner and hoped that Rebecca would be back tomorrow as Bob had said, one to get some decent grub and two, to get what was coming to me, if I could sort out my head enough to want to take it. I was too tired to start thinking it through for the umpteenth time and got myself to bed very early. What with the hectic day's angling, the demise of the Cowboy and the previous night's exertions concerning Spunker, I was totally shattered. Despite sleeping in uncomfortable waterproofs because of the now persistent rain, I feel asleep almost straight away.

I was wrenched from my peaceful slumber at one in the morning by the remote sounder box's familiar cry and a quick glance at the little black box sent my spirits soaring. The blue l.e.d was glowing, the one that was connected to the blue l.e.d buzzer, not physically of course, there was no hard wiring on my state-of-the-art buzzer system, and it meant a take on the middle rod. I scrambled out of the bivvy into a rainy, windy night and ran to my rods. The buzzer was no longer sounding and Rambo's tensionable swinger showed that a classic backdrop indication had occurred. I thought of the Cowboy as I clicked in the baitrunner and I wound down until I met resistance and started to pump and wind as quick as I could. Playing in a fish from this far out with pads in front of me in the dark was a nightmare. I had no real conception of where the fish was and I was very mindful of how I had only just managed to clear the left hand set of pads on my one other take from the island. And that had been in daylight.

I tried to feel from what angle the carp was pulling and walked up the bank to ease her away from the pads she was nearest. Amazingly all went without a hitch, the fish gave less problems than the daylight one had and after about ten minutes I had the carp netted. A quick peak with the torch revealed a twenty mirror which I weighed (22-2) and then released. I didn't feel as if the bait boat and long range position was a viable proposition to set-up at night so I banged out a new pop-up with a six bait stringer into the area between the two sets of pads and went back to bed.

Lying awake in the bag listening to the wind buffeting the bivvy and driving the rain against its skin, sometimes a little louder when the wind gusted, I wondered if this latest fish was a turning point. Would the long range rod now start to produce a few takes for me? Would my mind-meld, monster mirror eventually show? I was happy to think that I had turned the corner and the weather conditions had at last caused a few fish to move into an area they clearly didn't frequent very often.

I knew that I would have to be up at first light to set the rod and put some more bait out. After all, time was starting to run out, from first light tomorrow I had forty-eight hours to go, give or take a little depending on when we packed up on the Saturday. The holiday had been superb but an 'eff' carp was the icing on the cake that would make it all perfect. I fell asleep dreaming of a huge cake loaded with icing, in which, much to my delight, Rebecca was hiding. She leapt out from beneath the hinged, top-layer-of-sponge lid dressed only in thong panties and a push-up bra. Luckily for me, in terms of possible embarrassment, the call of the buzzer interrupted my dream which halted any chance of it becoming like the weather outside.

My instinctive look at the sounder box revealed it was the middle rod again. My immediate thought was that the long range swim really had turned around until I remembered that I had re-cast the rod somewhere different a few hours earlier. Don't roll your eyes, you'd have been as addled as I was if you'd just been dragged screaming and kicking from the dream I was having. The fish was another twenty and that run concluded the action for the night. Two twenties in a night! Again! Most peculiar.

At first light, with it still tipping it down, I sent the bait boat out with its cargo and baited up with about a fifty freebies along the line of the island margin as I had before, spreading them little and often. It was a slight increase in the amount of bait that I had put in before without, I felt, over doing it and compromising my chances. I left the other two rods alone seeing as they had been untouched all night. I was all done and having a brew when Rambo wandered up, in camouflaged waterproofs.

"All right, mate?" he asked. "Anything last night?"

"The usual," I said smiling.

"Two twenties?"

"Yeah. Amazing isn't it. I've had two twenties and I mean just two twenties, nothing else, for the last six or seven nights. Solid, if unspectacular, I suppose. No forties though, not like some jam-strangling gits I could mention."

"Luck of the draw, boy. Still, you have persisted in carrying on with your self-inflicted handicap, which isn't going to help," said Rambo, who was no Star-Trek fan, nor was he in the 'Mind-meld a Mirror' appreciation society for that matter.

"One of the twenties came on the long range rod," I said defensively. "Besides the drug-dream said that it would take time."

"Of which you haven't got loads of unfortunately," Rambo pointed out.

It was something I had to concede. "I know, I know. You wait and see. I'll prove you wrong."

Rambo gave me a playful punch on the upper arm that would later leave a bruise. "I hope you do, boy. I hope you do."

"Seen anything of the mutt, then?" I enquired, changing the conversations tack.

"Not round this side but I could see him over by Ian with the binoculars. I spent a little of what time I had between takes checking him out. The funny thing was that every time I clocked him through the glasses he was staring at me. It was as if he was trying to eyeball me out, you know, stare me down or something. Like that was going to frighten me. I reckon he'll be round soon for the big showdown, he knows I won't waste time going to him, if he wants to settle things he'll have to do it on my doorstep, in my territory. And when he comes, I'll be ready for him and I'll crush him like a bug."

There was no hint of irony or make believe on Rambo's face, just that cold hard look that had been his everyday mask when we were fishing the old syndicate session. I was tempted to conclude that Rambo had gone a bit barmy but he had been right about the dog's behaviour so far and who was I, the man who claimed to have touched the mind of an unknown carp, to start calling someone barmy. A little coin ran down the slot from the top of my head, went ker-ching, and gave me twenty pence-worth of idea. A bare knuckle/bare paw fist fight between Rambo and Spunker on video would be well worth having. I'd have to keep an eye out for that contest because if it happened, my attempted video diary of the Lac Fumant holiday would have a woeful hole in it without it.

Rambo soon disappeared after commandeering the bait boat with the promise that if I hadn't got round to getting a take on video, he would come and sit in my swim on the final day and be cameraman in-waiting. A bit unkindly, I saw that as an admission to him having caught two forties and he could therefore afford to waive a final day's fishing because it was 'mission accomplished'.

At nine, the margin rod went off, a 19-6 common, and ten minutes later the open water rod gave me a very nice 28-2 mirror. The last fish was netted by the Cowboy, who wasn't the cowboy at all any more, he was Clint.

"Cheers, Clint," I said, having to remind myself not to slip up as he lifted the mirror onto the unhooking mat.

Clint didn't look like the Cowboy any more. He looked like any other carp angler in his waterproofs and wellies as he was safely back in amongst the uniformity crowd. Apart from that, while it might have been a trick of the baggy cut of his waterproof trousers, he actually looked less bandy than before. Perhaps not being in his alter ego character had changed his body posture, or maybe it was simply that his old cowboy boots were a bit tight on his bunions.

"How you doing, then?" I asked of him as I unhooked the mirror.

"Oh, I'm all right. It might hit me after this fortnight is over when I go to fish my local waters and have to tell everyone and their dog about what happened. That'll be a right pain."

I was tempted to tell him that he needn't explain he could just flog them the video, provided I ran him off a hundred copies or so, but I bit my tongue. It was a rather graceless way to watch him die, especially with the painfully uncomfortable laughing and giggling soundtrack from the unauthorised, pirate video-makers.

Once Clint had snapped the mirror for me he carried on up to the cottage to have a shower. There he would wash the final remnants of poncho dye from his skin and with it his last physical, lingering connection to the Cowboy. How sad, how poignant, but at the time, how funny. Of course, once he had walked past Alistair, the Fatboys, who had rushed and told Virtual and Ian who had passed on the message to Japp and Wim, I had a succession of gentlemen callers, as the old pro's used to say, eager for knowledge of the event, rather than sexual favours. Thank God! But like the old tart I was, I gave it to them blow by blow, only giving the whole affair an air of dignity it never had by saying I was convinced the Cowboy had suffered from a weapons malfunction when the baitrunner had refused to come off. A bullet stuck in the breech, or something like that. I reasoned that they would never know, not unless Shimano ever found out and took me to court for slander and I was forced under oath to tell the whole truth and nothing but.

To a man they all left shaking their heads at the tragic loss of the Cowboy. I was sceptical as to how deep they were really cut and thought it more likely they were gutted at not seeing it happen and consequently, never seeing it happen again. Rather melodramatically Alistair said that it was a bitter blow to carp fishing's individuality of character. Personally speaking I reckoned that had keeled over and died many years ago and the age of the flock-of-sheep carp angler was currently with us. All boilie bashing on fixed leads with identical tackle, slavishly following the latest fashion and fad. Not so, you say? Show me a carp angler still using monkey climbers and an overwrap brolly bivvy and I'll show you someone who's sneered at. If he's not using three identical rods with colour coded hangers or swingers or danglers to light emitting diodes then he's a Noddy. We're all reading the same stuff from the same people who keep on plugging the new gear. By the way, I'm not affected by advertising, I bought all that gear out of my own choice. Yeah right, I'm in the flock as well.

Bob came down to lap the lake at dinner time and stopped in my swim, like I knew he did in everyone's, for a chat. He was all wrapped up against the rain, a saving grace in some respects, there was no crazy tee-shirt visible for once. He told me firstly that Rebecca was on her way home, she had telephoned to say so and secondly that the weather was due to start easing up and the sun come out some time tomorrow afternoon. At least I'd had the good news first but a fair old chunk of time had been carved off my remaining 'eff carp' time scale. I couldn't see the swim producing the goods if the wind dropped off so I reckoned I'd just have to catch my mirror before tomorrow afternoon. No sweat? Well, I still had a strong inner confidence that it would work out for me like it had all along so far. I had this feeling that everything was leading up to a final climax and I'm not talking about Rebecca! Whether my luck finally failed me and all this turned out to be self-delusion, only time would tell. I was clinging to my hopes and aspirations for the moment.

By the middle of the afternoon some deep rumbles of thunder started to make themselves heard and the already overcast and dark sky turned inky black. The thunder got progressively louder and sudden flashes of light illuminated the sky behind me in the direction away from the lake. It was only a matter of time before the storm would be directly overhead judging by the way the wind was now howling into the island. It crossed my mind that for this brief period I wouldn't have been upset to be fishing split cane rods or even glass fibre come to that. The prospect of getting a run on carbon fibre rods and 20,000volts-worth of sky-juice homing in on your rod tip was shocking, to say the least. In retrospect even the Cowboy might change his mind about his luck in consideration as to the weather he had to draw in.

I decided to pop down to Rambo's swim to say something terribly British about what awful weather we were having, in case he hadn't realised. The thunder boomed even louder as I trudged down to his swim and the cricket match would have been long stopped for bad light, let alone the rain. It had become really quite dark, almost eerily so and the spasmodic flashes of lightening that brightly illuminated Lac Fumant made it even more unearthly. In between a crack of thunder I thought I heard a dog howl and the hairs on the back of my neck involuntarily stood on end. KEEERAAKKK!! OOOOOWWWWLLL!! It happened again. Most odd.

Rambo was perusing the far bank with his binoculars when I reached his bivvy.

"Look at that," he said harshly, thrusting the binoculars at me as I approached.

"At what," I said as I panned the glasses up and down the far bank, "hold on, I see what you mean."

There on the far bank, just about visible in the murky light and then splendidly lit by lightening flashes, was Spunker. His huge chops opened and a split second later I heard his stomach-curdling wail. Light does travel faster than sound. It was every stereotypical horror film you had ever witnessed, the howling beast, the dark set, the lashing rain, the thunder, the lightening flashes, the hideously mutilated human-organ eating landing net. I shivered a bit but only because of the cool wind, you understand.

"He doesn't like the thunder and lightning, does he?" I said.

"It's me he doesn't like and he's coming to get me," said Rambo and he stood up and exposed himself to the driving rain. The rain soaked Rambo's hair quickly and water ran down his face as he turned directly into the wind to talk to me. "You'd better go back to your bivvy, boy, this could turn ugly."

Great. I wasn't watching a horror film, I was in it.

"Are you serious," I said as a deafening crack reverberated directly over head. A massive flash of sheet lightening incandescently floodlit the lake.

"Look!" said Rambo, emphatically pointing across the wind-whipped surface of Lac Fumant.

I searched the far bank for the rottweiler but he was gone. The next howl came more to the left and the next one was even further round. The bastard was pounding his way around the lake and there were no prizes for guessing where he was headed.

"I'll go now," I said quickly and shot off to my swim as soon as Rambo grunted his agreement.

I ran to my bivvy, stuttering and falling, half expecting to get mown down by a dog with a serious grievance. If Spunker could Houdini his way out of a suspended bivvy six or seven yards up, he probably knew that I had been an associate in the act of putting him there. As outlandish as it may seem, stumbling amongst the blackness, pouring rain and frenetic thunder and lightening, I feared for my life. The thunder was now so loud and so frequent that the noise was disorientating, the cold rain slapped my face and the associated lightening was more like a strobe. This was a storm to make the Cowboys drenching seem mild, yet in fairness to Clint the rain was not quite as heavy, it was all the sky-juice and noise that was intimidating. I reached the sanctity of my bivvy but despite part of me wanting to crawl under my bedchair the most persuasive bit of me wanted to watch. I had the feeling it was Ali v Frazier time.

I went outside again, having picked up the viewcam and crouched in the lee of my bivvy. The lightening flashes made the droplets of rain sparkle as they reflected the light and their cruelly slanting route to earth, as driven by the wind, was clinically exposed. However, this did mean that I was virtually dry all tucked up against my bivvy door flap. I put the viewcam into video mode and the liquid crystal display came to life and showed me a miniaturised vision of what I would be filming, once I pressed the record button. I waited, staring intently into the gloom at Rambo's bivvy where the dogslayer, or dog-slayed, was sitting.

I heard a louder howl and then another and then the Hound of the Baskervilles came into sight, loping around the back of Rambo's bivvy and straight onto mine. I started recording and nearly shit myself as nature's strobe gave me a brilliant view of 200lbs worth of salivating death, with a leg in each corner, come galloping towards me until he suddenly, thankfully, applied the anchors. His ears and jowls walloped forward on their own momentum but the rest of him halted, large lumps of frothing slobber that were less permanently attached fell to the ground. The great dog lifted his head and looked about himself and reassessed his position. He had overshot the runway, or lost his bearings, or something like that and during his stillness I could almost see his brain ticking over. Quickly he realised his mistake and turned his attention on the bivvy behind him rather than in front of him. Never was the site of an intermittently lit dog's arse so gratifying.

Now sure of where his deadly foe was to be found Spunker hammered into Rambo's bivvy giving it the old demonic howling routine as he did so. The bivvy erupted into life and started to bulge and wobble all over, on a smaller scale it was like two ferrets in a green football sock. A massive thunder clap was instantly followed by a series of lightening flashes that flickered with bright intensity and somehow backlit the whole bivvy. The jet black silhouettes of a powerful man and a huge dog involved in a vicious, titanic struggle were shown in truncated, cheap cartoon action. Flash – Rambo's shadow grabbing dog by throat – Flash – dog's shadow now on top of Rambo – Flash – dog thrown to other side of bivvy – Flash – dog powerdives into Rambo – Flash – Rambo bulges out the back of bivvy – Flash

– Rambo leaps across onto dog's back – Flash – dog comes flying out of bivvy door – Flash – nanosecond turn around – Flash – dog in full stride going back from where he came.

Spunker hammered into Rambo's bivvy giving it the old demonic howling routine as he did so. The bivvy erupted into life and we were into round two. It would never go the distance. The bivvy exploded into action as another eardrum-bursting clap of thunder played a hundred decibel plus synchronised soundtrack. Now, instead of bulging out all over, the bivvy now looked as if it had a wall of death motor bike rider circumnavigating the inside skin as a colossal, moving lump flowed around it. The lump reached the door for a third time and then, abruptly, the pair of them emerged out the bivvy flap, entangled together, seemingly as inseparable as Siamese twins, all rolled up like an enormous, deranged, organic bowling ball.

By now Rambo was howling more than Spunker as the pair of them careered up and down the bank, each having the other in a vice-like grip. Twice they veered right up to the lake's edge, only to roll back the other way, but on the third time they teetered on the very brink, edged back a fraction, then edged forward a bit, wobbled, and fell in. Spunker had now caused Rambo to get a dunking in Lac Fumant twice. Smoking? Fuming, more like. The water was thrashed into foam as the two fought tigerishly for air and supremacy, air supremacy you'd call it, I suppose. I casually noted that the lake's oxygen levels would be up even higher and that surely something would have to give soon. It did, the two fell apart as if prised by an unseen, all-powerful crowbar and as they did Rambo hit Spunker full on the jaw with a left uppercut that had 'head release mechanism' written all over it. The dog's energy levels were instantly downsized from nuclear power plant to unwrapped 1.5volt AA Durcell in kitchen draw. Lightening flashed and froze Spunker in mid-air, jaw up, head back at an alarming angle, legs hanging limp. Rambo was captured in perfect follow-through, his left fist way above his head and the rest of his sinew and muscle strained body chasing it.

The light receded, the moment was gone and Spunker splashed back into the lake like a heavily cast marker float. The bomb eye was too small and it, like the dog, never came to the surface. Rambo stuck both his arms into the lake and fished the inert hound up to the top, he grabbed him by the collar and dragged him across the lake's surface and up onto the bank and beached him. I ran over to them in the pouring rain, still recording.

The dog was flat on his back à la Cowboy, his great big tongue slumped out the corner of his cavernous gob.

"Mouth to mouth resuscitation?" I asked.

"Be my guest," said Rambo, holding out the palm of his lethal left hand. It was over, it wasn't a fist any more.

I cringed. "Well, maybe not. He'll just have to die, I guess."

Rambo shook his head. "He'll be all right. He's a strong one, I'll give him that. At one stage I thought I might have to start really trying," said Rambo, giving me a grin and a wink.

Spunker gave a watery cough and rolled over and tried to stand up but his legs were like jelly. His brain must have still been severely scrambled and he staggered about like a drunk, with little or no co-ordination, in tiny, erratic circles. The thunder clapped again but it was from the other side of the lake, the storm had passed over while Spunker had passed out.

I went over to Rambo and held up his right hand by the wrist, high above his head. "Ladies and Gentlemen. The winner . . . and still . . . the undisputed dominant male...RAAMBOOO!"

By now Spunker's head was nearly clear. He turned and looked at Rambo, stuck his stumpy, little tail between his legs and sloped off back to his bivvy to lick his wounds and, I expect, his bollocks, if other dogs are anything to go by. He had been defeated and now he knew his place. He had arrived full of fury and confidence but had left dejected with a grudging acceptance that it was Rambo who was top dog.

I left Rambo to change out of his wet things and went back to my bivvy. The rain was still falling steadily but the storm was getting quieter, disappearing over Will's mothers. The wind was still as strong, or at least I perceived it to be, but in my heart I was sure that it would start to abate until it died at the time Bob's weathermen had predicted.

For the first time I felt a sense of urgency tinged with a trace of desperation. Time was running out for my dream to materialise. I put the viewcam into the bivvy and went down to my rods and gave the middle, long range one a pep talk that bordered on a bollocking. It was the first time I had sensed any frustration since starting to carp fish again after coming out of the stone jug. It brought back many a memory of times gone past when I had done a similar thing, when I was blanking or trying to beat Watt and his cronies. It wasn't how I wanted my fishing to be, but my desire to top off the perfect holiday with an 'eff' carp was pretty keen. To say the least.

I spent the afternoon hitting takes on all three rods, my pep talk must have worked, and looking at the death of the Cowboy and Spunker's demise on the tiny liquid crystal display of the viewcam. The takes were all low twenties but I took heart in the one on the long range rod. Fish were obviously against the island now, I had to hope that there was a monster there as well. The tapes of the two major incidents were brilliant and had me falling about with laughter, it was all so spontaneous and real, what with our snide comments coming out as well. I simply couldn't stop myself having a look at them even if the downside was that I had flattened both batteries by the end of it. The 'take' video would have to happen on our last full day, if it was to happen at all. I would give the batteries to Rebecca when she came round and ask if she'd bring them down early or something like that.

Rebecca. Rebecca! Rebecca? Or even Rebecca!!!?? I was still no nearer a solution to my course of action with her, what with all my internal, conflicting emotions. I desperately pushed it to the back of my mind and hoped that I would cross the bridge when I came to it. It was clear that I had no chance of sorting something out in my head now and sticking to it in the future.

Rebecca came to see me early evening, all wrapped up against the rain, with no expanse of silky, svelte-like skin to gaze upon in lust and admiration. There was no area of flesh in view to wonder what it felt like to touch, to feel and to caress. We made chit-chat to begin with, I asked her if she would run the camcorder battery errand for me and she said that she would. She started to tell me why she hadn't been around Lac Fumant all that much recently and touched on the subject of her sick friend. She was going to be ok but at one stage it had been a bit naughty, apparently she had contracted a virulent strain of flu that had lead to pneumonia. Luckily her youth and strength had won the day and she was expected to make a full recovery. Rebecca was both relieved and philosophical.

"Life is so precious," she said looking me in the eye, "and illness makes you realise how tenuous our time is on earth. Live life to the full, we must, to not do so would be a betrayal of our one chance that we have."

It was pretty bog-standard stuff but I felt that the underlying message was to convince me that I should just go for it with her. As I looked at her gorgeous face I wondered how many times in her life she'd had to pull this one. She must have to fight blokes off with a baseball bat usually. Then again, how many traumatised carp anglers had she met? Stupidly, I realised that this was the daughter of a carp lake owner and thought . . . Bloody hundreds! But how many had been to prison? Yeah, I know, very funny.

Somehow one thing lead to another and we ended up kissing and snogging each other and I got to grab some of that delightful flesh that was tucked away under the waterproofs. We came up for air after one long, passionate kiss and she held me back with her arms.

"Tomorrow is your last day," she said breathlessly. "Come and see me tomorrow night, what I've got for you will beat anything swimming in Lac Fumant."

I mentally weighed up the situation, 'eff' carp or an 'eff?' Of course there was no guarantee of an 'eff' carp but the other 'eff' looked a dead cert. If I could go through with it. Who was I kidding? I'd made a pretty good start at it, but hold on, this was just pre-foreplay. A kiss and a cuddle. What about going further? I thought of Sophie. Damn this morality/guilt chip on my motherboard.

"Ok," I said gently.

"I'd better go now," she said and kissed me once more.

"Ok," I said. "Don't forget the batteries, will you? Can you leave them in the porch as soon as they're charged. I'll pick them up sometime tonight."

She nodded but for some reason I noted a touch of annoyance. I had one of those eureka! moments, if I pissed her off, my problem would be resolved and there would be no more mental torture. No offer from the lady meant no decision to agonise over. Situation sorted. All worry and responsibility taken completely from my hands. A few more clumsy lines like the last one and I'd be home and dry.

"You're the most attractive, sexy woman I've ever met," I said.

She smiled, all hint of animosity gone. What the fuck was I playing at?

CHAPTER 20

First light Friday morning, our last full day, I was up and ready for the big push. In the night I'd had . . . three twenties! Fooled you! The bonus fish came to a now active middle rod, which I hadn't bothered to re-set in the dark after the take. It was my first task of the day and one that I did with ruthless efficiency, my familiarity with the bait boat now well established. The weather was still overcast and raining and the wind was still pushing in the right direction. It had, however, dropped off slightly, there was no mistaking it or no denying it, but I did dismiss it. Everything would work out as I'd imagined unless Wim had got a duff lot of LSD, a cache of LLSD – lying lysergic acid diethylamide and then I'd end up disappointed.

Next on the agenda was the morning cuppa which, as ever, tasted great. I felt as if this was going to be a big, big day. I was up for it, as I had been for the camcorder batteries at four in the morning, or at least up for 'them.' I didn't want to waste a vital half hour out of the day, especially during the morning feeding spell, going to get them at first light. I felt full of confidence, I had no doubts, no doubt because I had been buoyed-up by the attentions of Rebecca, despite all the gut-wrenching it caused. Being pursued by a cracking looking girl never did anyone's ego any harm. It might end up ruining certain aspects of their life after the event, sure, but I hadn't got that far. Yet.

Rambo came up and shared a mug of tea with me and told me that he wasn't going to fish the plateau, he wasn't even going to fish three rods because he was going to get this blessed take on video for me. He said he'd leave just one rod out, he couldn't bring himself to not fish at all, and sit up in my swim with me ready to do the business, if I could do the business. Once that business was done, there was the business about doing the business with Rebecca and the business about an 'eff' carp. Still, first things first. You have to work through the list on busy days.

While we were setting up the camcorder on a bankstick under the shelter of my spare umbrella I told Rambo about an idea, some might say fantasy, I'd had.

"Wouldn't it be ironic if after all this time the one take we get on video happens to be my mind-meld mirror?"

Rambo gave it some thought. "I don't think 'ironic' would be the word or words, 'fucking unlikely' maybe, or 'bum-hole lucky.' Something along those lines, boy."

"Yeah. I suppose so," I said, yet I was not convinced that I couldn't pull it off.

My feelgood factor must have been attached to my bio-rhythm-high and between themselves, what with egging each other on, they were playing tricks on my rationality. Perhaps that's what confidence is? I certainly felt even more sure of myself that morning than I had a few days earlier, which was patently absurd because I had less time to achieve my dreams.

"What d'you reckon on that, then?" said Rambo having tweaked the viewcam's position.

I turned on the display screen and saw three indicators in view waiting for me to cue them in from my director's bedchair with a sharp call of 'action!'

"Perfect," I said. "When one of them goes you can lift the video up along with the inner stud of the bankstick, get me hitting the take and then just unscrew the camera adopter and bankstick right out the way. That way it'll be obvious we haven't fiddled the original run by just pulling the line through the buzzer and editing to the playing of a pukka take. All we've got to do now is decide when to turn it on."

"The sixty-four thousand dollar question," said Rambo. "Every second that you don't turn it on is saved battery and tape, yet it might rattle off the very second after you didn't turn it on. Dilemma!"

"Don't talk to me about dilemmas. I'm riddled with them," I said, seemingly swatting an imaginary fly with my right hand.

Rambo gave me a frowned look but didn't pursue that particular subject.

"Well!?" he said eventually.

"Well, what?" I said.

"Well, when are we going to turn the bloody thing on?" he said nodding at the camcorder.

"Oh . . . Right . . . Yes . . ." I waffled, momentarily paralysed with the weight of decision and then, remembering all my previous confidence and self-belief, I shrugged off the shackles of hesitancy and said. "Now. Turn the bloody thing on, now!"

Rambo ceremoniously held out an index finger in front of him and went over to the viewcam. "Lac Fumant. Last full day of holiday. Getting a take on video. Take one . . . we hope . . . and . . . Action!"

Rambo theatrically pressed the viewcam's record button. Nothing happened, of course, except that the viewcam's vital tape and battery resources started to diminish.

"Very good," I said. "And now in time honoured carp fishing tradition we just sit back and wait but not for too long, I hope. The tape is only ninety minutes worth and that's got to include playing and landing the monster from the deep."

Rambo nodded appreciatively. "It's a pity the camcorder hasn't got one of those LP buttons like on your video recorder, that'd double the tape length. Then you could play it back on the correct speed and it'd be in slow motion."

I thought about this for a while and tried to get my head around the apparent anomalies of time-lapse photography.

Eventually I said. "Wouldn't it be speeded up if you done that? You know, like the old black and white silent movies or the Benny Hill chases. When you film slower and play it back normal, it becomes quicker. I'm sure that's right."

As usual Rambo was empirical in his answer. "Whatever. All I know is that if the poxy indicators don't move we might as well have Leonardo Da Vinci or

Michelangelo painting them as a camcorder videoing them . . . at any speed."

"They'll move," I said. And I believed it.

I sat back in my bedchair and idly followed Rambo's theme and started thinking of the Mona Indicators, the Sistine Buzzers and the magnificent statue of David – Carp angler with his kit off, or 'tackle out' as it is termed by the carp-art cognoscente.

The rain continued to pitter-patter down as I sat in the extended opening of my bivvy, my eyes firmly glued to the items that were being so closely recorded. Mucho macho Rambo sat unsheltered in waterproofs directly adjacent to the video umbrella. Fifteen minutes passed and nothing happened. Half an hour elapsed and nothing happened. This soon ran into half a football match's worth and then in a mere instant the half-time interval was over and players were out for the second half. Time and the tape were flying, now over an hour gone and still no goals.

I was up off the bedchair, or maybe it was the dugout, pacing up and down the touchline in a puffy, three-quarter coat with my team's name and a major sportswear company's logo plastered all over it, frantically gesticulating at my three players. I was bollocking the buzzers for more effort and chastising the indicators for lack of movement, lack of ball skills, an over-severe haircut and an over-inflated ego and bank balance. Midway through the second half I had to make a substitution but I couldn't pull in one of the players, my hopes rested with them. Sure I organised them, picked them and set the tactics, but they were the ones who won or lost for me. It was I who paid the price for their ineptitude but I also took the glory for their triumphs. At this point in time my fate was in their hands, I was reduced to sorting out the match video. I rushed around to the viewcam.

"What you doing?" inquired Rambo.

"There's no way we'll shoe-horn a take in, plus the landing and a bit of carp-on-the-bank footage on this tape now. I'm going to wind the tape back with this battery, put in a new one and re-start from the beginning and just hope we don't get a run while I change over."

"Two things, boy," said Rambo.

I was crouched under the video-brolly fiddling with the control buttons. I had the feeling that a bit of pee-taking was coming my way and I wasn't wrong.

"One. Don't you want to keep the video of the sleeping indicators? I'd have thought that could have been a big seller with the right advertising. And two, you've got no chance of doing that without the run happening. It's every piss you've ever gone to take, every cup of coffee, every brew of tea, every visit to the next swim when that well known angling phenomenon, 'the bite at the wrong time' occurs. It's a temptation of fate, you see. You've only got to remember the run frenzy, everyone had it happen to them."

By now I'd stopped the video recording and was rewinding the tape back. Time to parry the thrust of Rambo's sarcasm with the blade of reason.

"Firstly," I said with a voice of unconcerned authority, "I doubt whether the motionless indicator video will be quite the best seller you envisage. I'd already thought about this earlier on in the holiday. You see, every bastard's seen it, been there, done it, got the tee-shirt, apart from Bob, he stopped buying them in 1980 and doesn't need the video. Secondly, that old chestnut about getting the one run during the five minute cuppa, stroke piss, stroke chat thing in a twenty-four hour session is the number one carping myth. I've tried pouring out a cup of tea to get a take and it's never worked. The run frenzy was just a one-off, you couldn't call that everyday carping."

"It doesn't if you do it on purpose, you moron," argued Rambo, ignoring the run frenzy reference. "Only if it's a genuine beverage requirement situation will the fates conspire against you. If you're doing it on purpose to try and buy a take it would be helping you out and that's not the game plan at all."

"And that is carping myth number two," I smugly retorted, the words turning to ashes in my mouth as my right hand rod's buzzer sounded.

I froze as the hanger indicator, fished on a nine inch drop, zoomed to the top, stopped and then inched backed down to its original position. A liner.

"Lucky boy," chortled Rambo.

The tape had finally wound back. Damn and confound its cursed slothfulness. I changed the battery over with a complete lack of dexterity due to the pressure, not doing my chances of getting onto the Ferrari F1 pit team any favours, and we were finally, safely, back to square one. Well, square two, really, one battery down and an hour and a half of the feeding spell kissed goodbye. We did have the liner, so that could mean fish in the swim, which was a good omen. I slumped back in my bedchair and breathed easier. For all my apparent scorn at Rambo's leg pulling I did believe in Sod's Law and was very aware of the chance I'd taken in running back the tape and swapping batteries. Not that I had any option, it had to be done. I suppose it had been a case of seeing whether Sod's Law had more clout than Lady Luck, who had been perched on my shoulder for some time now. I had successfully managed the last operation so perhaps not. Maybe Mr Sod would try and get me later.

"That one'll rattle off in a minute," said Rambo. "And then you'll probably drop it or it'll be a low double common," he added mischievously.

Was he turning psychic? No, I knew it was more sarcasm than anything because I'd talked about the video take possibly being my as-yet-to-be-proved-to-exist mirror. I simply smiled and refused to rise to the bait.

"You crafty old trout!" said Rambo with amazing insight once again.

Rambo's predictive powers reached new heights when ten minutes later the right hand rod did go and it really was the time for action. I waited for Rambo to pick up the viewcam and lift the inner bankstick and then I hit the run as he panned out from the tight focus on the three indicators. Rambo filmed me from almost directly behind so that his body sheltered the lens of the camcorder from the rain, as he effectively became a human windbreak. All went well, Mr Sod was clearly detained elsewhere, giving people flat tyres when they were all dressed up to go to a wedding and making credit cards jump from wallets shortly before completing the fortnightly supermarket shop. After a struggle of no more than ten minutes I had landed a nice mirror, a very nice mirror, in fact, but not a mind-meld mirror.

Although elated at having achieved one of the ambitions of the holiday it was a bitter/sweet experience and I have to admit to being marginally disappointed. Rambo later pointed out that it had been a margin fished bait and I should have expected it. He was getting to be quite the comedian. Nevertheless, the fish went over thirty so I could hardly moan about that, a look down the stats, if I'd bothered to have kept them as religiously as I should, would have shown it to be a nice long shot to get one take on tape and it turn out to be a thirty.

Rambo had kept the tape churning over while I unhooked the fish, weighed it, held it up for some trophy videoing and returned to its home. It was a lovely bit of history to have down on tape for posterity and for it to have all worked out so clean. I was dead chuffed that another objective had been reached but the most arduous one was still left for me to achieve. The conversion of a drug induced, cross species mind-meld vision into a fifty plus, hulking great mirror on the bank with my hook and boilie unequivocally attached to its bottom lip.

Once the thirty was done and dusted Rambo went back to his swim to make the most of the last day and to get his two other rods out. Incredibly within fifteen minutes of him getting back the one rod that he'd left out had another Lac Fumant twenty try and snaffle his boilie. I shook my head in wonder and for the first time I had to ask myself the question about how much luck I had used up, and more to the point, how much I had left.

I had no more action that morning and nothing happened until mid afternoon when Alistair came down to see how I was doing. By then the rain had almost stopped and the wind virtually abated, although its direction was still wafting into the island. Mr Lifeunderanelectronmicroscope started asking me questions about my faith and my belief. Nothing to do with God you understand, that would be much too freaky, but all to do with my druggy dream and whether I was serious about believing that it would happen. I told him to come back tomorrow and I'd let him know, which was a lie. Bob had said that the weather would change that afternoon and I was convinced that I had foreseen the big mirror off the island only with the wind as it was. As far as I was concerned once the wind turned the other way the game was over. Alistair could come back this afternoon rather than tomorrow.

Unusually Alistair didn't stay long, possibly he sensed my rising unease. I was a man holding up a placard inscribed, not that the end of the world was nigh, but that the fifty was nigh. Where did those people go when the world kept on turning? Where did they hide their embarrassment when the wheels didn't come off? There was always tomorrow, or the next planet conjuncture, or the next significant date, or whatever and I, too, could use the first but I would look no less silly. Perhaps I should have kept the mind-meld thing all to myself? If it came off, though, no-one would have ever believed the mind-meld story after the event. My neck and reputation had been firmly placed on the line, by myself.

By late afternoon the rain had stopped, the wind was non existent and I was beginning to think that my chances were that way as well. They were flagging, becalmed on a high sea of expectation. I had set sail earlier in the day convinced of reaching the new world, but what is a sailor without wind?

"Don't worry about it, chief. It might never happen."

It was Bob, who had snuck up on me and spotted my doleful looks.

"That's just the trouble, Bob. That's just the trouble," I said not bothering to explain myself.

"Quality. Look, I can't hang around I've got to go and see the Cowboy who isn't any more. I've also got to give you this, chief, I'll catch you later. Bye."

Bob gave me a small white envelope with my name on it. As soon as he was gone I opened it and saw that it was from Rebecca as I had guessed. Inside there was a small note, it read: 'Dear Matt, Meet you tonight at eight. Come up to the cottage a bit earlier for a shower and I'll be waiting in my bedroom. It's up the stairs, third door on the right. Rebecca. This message will self-destruct in ten seconds.' It didn't say that last piece of course but I laughed at the idea until I thought that it could be me that might self-destruct in ten seconds, if we did it twice. The note really jolted me back into the whole torrid thought process of will I, won't I, would I, should I and all its implications.

I expect a lot of you would think I was totally barmy to even think of not having her but maybe others of you will understand how indebted I felt to Sophie. What a shit of a thing it would be to do to someone who had held my head above water for so long. I just didn't know what to do, I was racked with indecision.

Sitting on my bedchair I felt dual anxiety at the two themes that were dominating my entire existence, namely catching a fifty and having sex with Rebecca. One I had thought I could do, but it was now looking less and less likely. The other, I would never have dreamed of attaining but now, provided I could shift my arse up to the cottage and locate her bedroom by eight pm, I could. Weird.

The possibilities were myriad. There was the remote chance that I could ignore Rebecca and the extra time on the bank would enable me to catch the fifty. Realistically, I had to admit, even though it galled me, missing the deadline and fishing on I was more likely to end up with the big zero. Middle ground was just to go up at half seven, forgo catching the fifty, or at least giving it my best shot, and have amazing sex with an amazing looking girl. The mad one was to somehow catch the fifty and go up there in time to have her, or, madder still, or not depending on your moral viewpoint, was to catch the fifty and go up there, get all moralistic, deny base urges, declare my undying love for Sophie and be faithful.

I looked at my watch, it was just turned five and I had no idea what to do. I mulled it all over one more time. It was hopeless, I could have sat there inside a timewarp for eternity and not come up with a course of action. There was only one thing for it, I would let fate decide. I would relinquish all responsibility of choice, if I really, truly believed in my drug dream then I must go with it. All that had happened to me from the time that I had left prison seemed to have been manipulated by exterior forces, interacting with decisions by myself, that had led to success after success. A run of luck, a very unlikely run of luck, but a run of luck that had re-shaped my life. Only the very first chunk of it, the big one of Sophie's mum winning the lottery had been totally free from my interference. The rest of it had been. Finding Lac Fumant and therefore Rebecca, timing it to coincide with the others and their direct influence, like Alistair picking our swim, Jap and Wim being here and them making the mistake to give me the LSD, that just happened to be in his rucksack alongside the proper tablets, that I only needed because Greg and Luke had bought loads of lager and I'd drunk too much of it and had begun to feel rough and needed the tablet in the first place – the list of happenstance was endless. All the hundreds of chances there must have been to make it happen for them to be here at the same time as me and Rambo. The choices I'd made to catch the fish, the pop-ups, getting them from Pete in the first place, all the little nudges and nicks that had conspired to make this holiday so fantastic were mind boggling. Even getting the Cowboy on video, seeing the Rambo v Spunker fist fight and the thirty take on video were amazing bits of luck. If just one tiny link of the chain hadn't occurred then the whole lot could have been lost, it was so uncanny as to be scary. All this could not be denied. The decision on not making a decision was made. I would fish on until I either caught the fifty or packed up to go home. Rebecca would or would not, depending on how fate decided, have to wait.

An hour passed, I heated up some spaghetti in a can and ate it. Thinking through the lines of the chain had given me fresh hope. Was the fifty to be my destiny, or had I reached the end of the chain when I had the thirty put on 8mm tape? I would know soon enough. The weather had finally cleared and the clouds were gone, there were no markers in the sky to check the wind. I wetted a finger and held it up, neither side felt colder, the evening was dead still. Yet even at this eleventh hour, I had time enough.

Six o'clock became seven and in my mind's eye I imagined Rebecca in the shower, the hot water falling onto her hair and her hands pushing it back from her forehead and over and down to the nape of her neck. I could picture the tiny rivulets of hot water running down all over her body, over her breasts, down her curvaceous sides, running around her toned buttocks, flat stomach and dripping off the end of the pubic hairs between her legs. So! She wasn't a true blond! It was agony, so I focused on reality and three silent buzzers which were somewhat less appealing. A sight of her towelling her unblemished, silky skin flitted back into my head and a perfect limb was suddenly guided into a delicate pair of panties, pointing toes first. Next she was drying her hair and as she flicked it into the hot dryer's blast, her boobs wobbled magnificently, her nipples pert and hard. I slapped my own face. This was crazy. Come on middle rod! A Freudian thought?

The night was starting to come and light was fading but the images in my head were getting brighter. Rebecca, now in a short skirt, crop top but no bra, was putting on a deep red lip gloss and then, amazingly, was eating a banana. She delicately peeled back the skin, exposing it and then went down on it and swallowed the whole thing in one bite. Come on middle rod! She rolled and cavorted on the bed swinging a pair of handcuffs in the air and laughing. Maybe if I got a take on the middle rod I'd go even if it wasn't the fifty. She ran her hands all over her body, rubbing herself between the legs, simultaneously arching her back off of the bed and making low moaning noises. My mouth was dry and my heart was pounding. Come on middle rod, for fuck's sake! I followed the vision up from her crotch to her breasts and saw that her face wasn't Rebecca's face . . . but Sophie's! I recoiled in horror, a wave of deep guilt running through my very soul. She smiled at me and beckoned me to her with a wicked look of lust and a curling finger and then, inexplicably she was gone. I'd lost her. She'd found out about my wandering, depraved lust and I'd lost her. I refocused on the buzzers and looked at my watch. Ten past seven.

Seven thirty. The light was almost gone and I need a drink. I put the kettle on and distractedly listened to it boil and watched the swirls of steam escape from the spout like I had done so many times on the holiday. I popped a tea bag into my disgustingly brown-stained mug, poured the water in and bullied the tea bag with an equally unhygienic teaspoon. I fished the bag out on the teaspoon and squeezed it out between a thumb and forefinger while still over the mug. I slung the tea bag into an old crisp packet and then added some milk powder to the black tea. I stirred it, tapped the mug with the teaspoon and chucked that onto the ground sheet of the bivvy. It would be too hot to drink straight away so I just sat holding the handle of the cup, with its base resting on my right leg. Eventually I took a wary sip. Well hot but just drinkable. Perfect. I took another and nearly drowned myself in scalding tea as the sounder box screamed de de de de de de de de de de in slow staccato time! The tea went all over my leg, the whole cupful virtually, but I was oblivious. The slow drop back meant middle rod. Goosebumps covered my body and my skin crept. Was this it?

I ran down to the middle rod to see Rambo's swinger down to the deck and the line slack from the rod tip. I wound down and struck hard and made contact. Had our minds met before I asked? No answer was forthcoming but I was convinced. The fish was still heading back towards me and I gladly wound in tandem with her as she came in yards and yards and yards. She was soon back level with the pads and still coming. None of the other fish had done this and consequently I had no idea of the size of her by the tug she gave me. It's always difficult to judge at the best of times, not pulling hard the opposite way made it even harder to do so.

"RAMBO! RAMBO!" I screamed at the top of my voice. "Quick! Up here, mate!"

Almost immediately I could hear my bosom buddy pummelling up the bank towards me.

"What's up? What's the matter?" he asked in genuine concern.

"Wind the other two rods in, mate. This is it, it's the big one," I said in deadly seriousness.

"You sure?" he asked as he snatched the left hand rod up and reeled in furiously.

"Maybe," I said.

Rambo despatched the left rod to the back of the bivvy and ran round, whipped up the margin rod and whisked that out of the equation as well. I hadn't bothered to do this any other time but my gut feeling was that this was my one chance and I must capitalise on it.

Rambo had the net in his grasp and watched from the side as at last the fish turned parallel to the bank and laid down some rubber with a mighty run that stripped line off my tight-set-for-15lb-Big-Game-Line clutch.

Rambo let out a low whistle. "Power boat time! You might be right or it's another one of those cranky commons."

I was in a world of my own, totally wrapped up in landing the fish. "Shit! It'll be up in Alistair's swim in a minute if it carries on like this," I said.

"I'll go check he's on back leads," said Rambo. "Don't land it before I come back!"

"Cheers," I said, only half hearing what Rambo had said.

Rambo ran off into the night and came back with Alistair in a couple of minutes. The fish was still way up the lake and I didn't have a clue where, only to say it was to my right. I had walked down as far as the trees in the margin swim, where the right hand rod was usually fished and was battling on from there.

"I've pulled all my three rods in, Matthew, so you've no worries there, all right?" said Alistair.

"Cheers, mate," I said not taking my eyes off of the rod tip.

The fish had stopped taking line and it was my turn to lay, not rubber, but line back onto my spool. I pumped and wound down, pumped and wound down, pumped and wound down. It took an age but eventually the rod tip stopped looking round the corner and started to look down, then it started looking the other way and line was pulled off the clutch yet again. I had always played fish off the clutch leaving the anti-reverse on and it proved a useful tool because the fish was now heading right down tight into my left hand margin. I gripped the rod above the handle with my right hand and grabbed the butt with my left and held the rod way out into the lake, far further than I ever could while trying to grip a reel handle, to counteract the direction of the run. The rod made a virtual semi-circle but I stopped the run and pumped back up so that the fish was directly in front of me where it seemed happy to bore around in circles. I felt in control but couldn't budge the fish any higher up in the water. Rambo was back alongside me with the net and I could hear Clint's voice talking softly to Alistair. He'd clearly heard the commotion and his curiosity had been piqued and he'd come up to see what was going on.

The light had nearly faded but I could still make out the boils in the water as the unseen fish forced large amounts of water about with its fins. I tucked the butt of the rod into my stomach, kept the tip well up and stood and waited for the fish to tire. After what seemed an age I managed to get a couple of turns on the reel and then a couple more and a few more after that. Gradually I gained more and more line and at last my rig tube broke the surface. Tantalisingly I watched it snake through the water like a shark's fin and then inch up higher and higher until the bomb was visible. The water suddenly exploded and a glimpse of a massive flank was visible for a fleeting moment. The massive flank of a mirror.

Rambo was now kneeling beside me with the net. He had a very serious expression on his face because he had seen the size of the fish, it looked enormous and I knew that he was determined not to foul up. It was role reversal from the time I had netted the winning twenty for him in the old syndicate days. I remembered how keenly I had felt the pressure being on the net and knew that he would never forgive himself, and it was unlikely I ever would, if he fouled up the netting manoeuvre.

The fish was showing itself more and more yet I wasn't seeing more and more because of the fading daylight. I was tempted to force for an earlier netting but I kept my calm and waited until she was ready. At last she rolled on her side, head up and I guided her over the rock solid net that Rambo held. A gentle lift by my man and she was safe. I let out two lungs full of air. Rambo gathered the net's mesh into one handful and lifted her clear of the water.

"Fucking hell, that's heavy!" Rambo exclaimed.

My mouth dried, if Rambo said it was effing heavy, it was effing heavy. We walked over to my unhooking mat and Rambo gently let her down, I put down my rod and cleared the folds of the net away to reveal the carp. She was massive, absolutely huge. She was clearly the biggest fish of the fortnight by some distance. My hook and boilie, one of Pup's pop-ups, were emphatically embedded in her bottom lip.

"My God," said Alistair in low tones of reverence, "you've only done it, Matthew. What a fish. It has to be a fifty let alone a forty. What did you say the weight of it was in your vision?"

"Fifty-five," I said, somewhat shell-shocked.

I gazed down at the fish. The size of it! Rambo had gone and got my torch, my weigh sling and my Reuben sixty pound scales. I shone the beam over the carp's enormous bulk. I'd got it all wrong before, I had started off from near the end of the chain talking about the coincidences after coming out of prison. My whole life, from the very moment of my conception, had been a chain of events and incidents that had lead, directly or indirectly, to the catching of this fish. I was at my fishing pinnacle for the moment. Yet, who knew what chain lay stretching out in front of me? Who knew whether this event that was happening now would turn out to be another small link leading to even more fantastic carping adventures? It was a sweet, sweet moment. The euphoria that I felt was amazing. I'd done it! Despite all the odds, I'd done it as I'd foreseen that I would. In a way it was a little freaky but in another it was the high to match all high's.

With the scales zeroed in, the leviathan in the sling, it was the moment of truth. Rambo was the lifter, who else? And Alistair called the shots. He shone the torch beam onto the large dial face of the scales and a ghostly half-light reflected back into his face as he stared intently, from no more than a foot, to get an accurate sighting.

"Fifty . . . five . . . twelve. Might be fourteen. Does it matter? Incredible! Utterly incredible! If I wasn't here to have witnessed it I would never have believed it. Life can be stranger than fiction."

"I'm here witnessing it and I still can't fucking believe it!" said Rambo. "What can I say, boy? What can I say? You've fucking done it! You have actually, fucking done it! Fantastic! You lucky, lucky fucker! Fucking hell! I can't fucking believe it!"

In truth, now that it was sinking in a little, nor could I. Alistair turned from the scales and addressed the three of us, all of who, to some degree or another were in a state of shock. No prizes for guessing who was in deepest.

"But now it's time for a decision. Do we sack her until the morning, so that Matthew can get the photos he deserves and the rest of the lads can see her? I'd love all of us to be able to share in Matthew's achievement and take some photos of this very special fish. If I can be so bold as to say this: Why don't we sack her and take turns to check that she is all right every hour or so on a rota system? That way we'll minimise any potential problem. What do you say?"

"Well, that would be great by me," I said gratefully.

"I'm up for it," said Clint.

"Me to," said Rambo.

"Excellent," said Alistair. "The margins here are pretty deep and what with all the rain we've had there's plenty of oxygen. I don't think there will be any problem at all."

So there it was, the deed was done and my mind-meld mirror was carefully put in a sack and placed in the margins. She went down straight away, she'd be fine and in the morning we'd all have a proper look at her.

"Right then," said Rambo. "It's half eight now, I'll check her at half nine. Clint can do the honours at half ten, Alistair half eleven and you can do the midnight hour plus thirty, Matt. All right?"

Everyone agreed and then a arrow whizzed into my head. Eight thirty! I was meant to met Rebecca at eight! Shit! And shit times infinity!

"Er, excuse me lads. Brilliant. Thanks for all your help. Fantastic. But I must go up to the cottage. Gotta use that toilet . . . it's all the excitement! Cheers." I was gone and three slightly bemused carp anglers were left in my wake.

I ran up the path to the cottage but my time in prison and two weeks sitting on my arse carping had taken the aerobic efficiency of my heart and lungs down to an all time low. In the end I settled for a brisk walk with a jog here and there. This was one scenario I hadn't considered, catching the fifty and it making me late. As I sweated and gasped my way up to the cottage my mind was a whirr with thoughts of the fish I had just caught and the possibilities of what may be before me. If she was still there was I going to go through with it? Would she still want to? I hadn't even showered yet. There was no time for that, I'd have to go straight to her room and take it from there. I realised that fate had sent me to her room but it had far from resolved what would take place there.

At last I came to the cottage, the door was open and I went inside. I walked up the stairs and came to the room that was the third on the right. The door was shut and the carpet pile was tight to the underside of the door, I could see no chink of light under it or around the sides. I stopped and listened but could only hear my rasping breath and my heart, both still loud from my recent exertion. I stood for a minute and breathed deeply and slowly. What way did the chain go now? What was to be my destiny with Rebecca? I pulled down the door handle and went in.

*   *   *

"Cheese! Say cheese! Not you, you plonker, the carp. We're not interested in you," said Luke.

The others all laughed. Clint, Alistair, Paul, Japp, Wim, Ian, Greg, Rambo, Bob, Rebecca and even Spunker had a look on his face that, if you were prone to hyperbole and anthropomorphism, could be construed as being a sort of a grin. I held the magnificent mirror in my two hands as carefully as a father holds his new-born son while the others clicked away with their cameras and Rambo took the final piece of Lac Fumant video. Alistair was also taking snaps with my SLR, the best of which would take pride of place below a certain bait maker's light switch.

What a feeling it was to hold such a marvellous fish in such beautiful surroundings on such a perfect morning. I was the luckiest man alive on many levels. These people, my paparazzi of the moment, shared in my fortune with no hint of animosity but with collective pleasure. They were my friends and I hoped that I would fish with them many times again, especially Rambo, but that really went without saying. I followed down the line of them as I posed with my fish until my eyes met Rebecca's. She gave me a little smile and raised her eyebrows. She was my one qualm in the whole delightful Lac Fumant experience. Holding that great fish and looking into her brown eyes, I wondered if I'd ever live to regret the events that had unfolded the previous night in her bedroom.